THE STING OF LOVE

The Sting of Love

A Novel

Janet Graber

Minneapolis

ISBN 13: 978-1-63489-355-8

Library of Congress Catalog Number: 2020909426
Printed in the United States of America
First Printing: 2020

24 23 22 21 20   5   4   3   2   1

Cover design by Luke Bird
Interior design by Patrick Maloney

Wise Ink Creative Publishing
807 Broadway St NE
Suite 46
Minneapolis, MN, 55413

To order, visit www.itascabooks.com or call 1-800-901-3480.
Reseller discounts available.

www.janetgraber.com

For Katherine,
with profound thanks and love always.

AUSTRIA

YUGOSLAVIA

Pontebba Tarvisio Kranjska Gora

Telmezzo Fella Soča Radovljica

Bovec (Plezzo) Kranj

Gemona ITALY YUGOSLAVIA

Tarcento Ljubljana

ITALY

Cividale Zone A Spilimbergo

Udine Logatec

Codroipe Gorizia

Palmanova Ajdovščina (Aidussina) Isonzo

Opatje Selo (Opacchiasella) Zone B

Cervignano Monfalcone Komen (Comeno) Postojna (Postumia)

Latisana Duino Sežana (Sesana)

GOLFO DI TRIESTE Trieste Zone B

Capodistria

FREE TERRITORY OF TRIESTE Buzet (Pinguente) Matulji (Mattuglie)

GOLFO DI VENEZIA Mirna (Quieto) Motovun (Montona) Rijeka (Fiume)

Poreč (Parenzo) Pazin (Pisino)

Rovinj (Rovigno) Labin (Albona)

TRIESTE

—··—··— 1937 International Boundary

▬▬▬▬ Post World War II Boundary

▬▬▬▬ Morgan Line

▬▬▬▬ Interzonal Boundary as agreed Oct. 5, 1954

0   5   10   20
MILES

0   5   10   20
KILOMETERS

Vodnjan (Dignano)

Zone A O. CRES (ISOLA CHERSO)

Pula (Pola)

Cres (Cherso)

10719 6-47 (Revised 10-54)

Every moment in your life, every event, is a story in itself.

Vida Jurman, Slovene Partisan
Born 1923 –

AUGUST 1994

Chapter One

I CAN'T RID MYSELF OF AN UNEASY SENSE that my dearest daddy is keeping something from me; a sense that all is not right in his world. He has been uncharacteristically contrary and peevish for the past few days—snapping at his cleaning lady, the most obliging person one could wish to meet, and at the last minute declining to attend a matinee with us at the Royal Shakespeare Theatre in Stratford. I've promised myself to get to the bottom of what is bothering him before my daughters and I return to the States.

Usually, I would be basking in the sheer pleasure of this English summer evening. The restaurant buzzes with comfortable conversation; a gentle tinkle of crystal; the muted clamor of china plates. Windows open onto the terrace, offering a view of distant hills awash in twilight shadow. Louisa and Annabel are with me to celebrate my father's seventy-seventh birthday, and our satisfying meal is drawing to a close. The roast lamb, locally sourced, was pink and juicy, the wine a smooth, full-bodied Barolo.

Adding to my disquiet, there is a sudden gush of angry words between my supposedly grown girls. They've bickered all day, a common occurrence, but now it's exploding into a knockdown, drag-out confrontation.

"Don't you feel the least bit guilty?" Louisa shrills into her sister's face.

Unfortunately, this startles their grandpa, making him jump.

Coffee spills from his cup, and a small brown smudge stains the tablecloth.

"You're not normal," Lou goes on. "Normal people feel guilt when they deliberately do something wrong."

"Go to hell," Annie replies.

"What do *you* think, Grandpa?" Lou leans over the table, seeking an ally. "Aren't I right?"

"Guilt is a complicated question," Daddy mutters, tugging on the cuff of his blazer. Always a sign of distress. Both girls stare at him. "But you are right. Most of us feel guilty once in a while."

"See, Grandpa agrees with me," says Lou with a satisfied smirk.

"It's none of your fucking business!"

Annabel's ripe language stuns the table next to us into a distressed silence. Heads turn. Brows furrow. Lips purse. *Oh, Annie, why do you always have to be so crude?*

"Enough! Shut up, both of you." I thrust the bill and a bundle of pound notes into Lou's lap. "Deal with this. I'm going to walk your grandpa home."

In future, my children can cross the Atlantic alone to visit their grandpa. They're adults, after all. But I worry they won't bother. Too easy to forget all the wonderful childhood holidays with their English grandparents.

Daddy and I link arms and head along the street toward his flat. Through the sleeve of his blazer, I can feel his body stretched taut as piano wire. Whatever else is bothering him, Lou and Annie between them certainly seem to have hit a nerve. I wonder vaguely what set off Lou's alarming sense of moral indignation today?

Pondering the predicament of guilt in its various guises—shame, remorse, regret, sin—Michael comes unbidden to my mind, as he so often does. But I'm positive I was never wracked with guilt during our time together. Perhaps Annie inherited the "guiltless" gene from me, *innocens erit.*

We reach Cross Keys Court, where my father has lived comfortably in a roomy garden flat since my mother's death five years ago. Quite suddenly, he pulls me back to reality. "There's something I *must* discuss with you, Georgina."

"I thought as much," I whisper, kissing his cheek. "You haven't been your usual genial self all week. What's got into you?"

"I heard something recently. To do with the war." A bead of sweat pools on his forehead.

"The war?" I'm bewildered. He's hardly ever spoken about those awful years. Of course, Mum invariably interrupted him: "*Stop picking away at it. Everyone had a terrible war. Nobody wants to be reminded.*" But I tread lightly, not wanting to discourage him in any way from continuing on.

"Tell me more?"

But we are interrupted by my daughters, clomping up the path in their Doc Martens boots. Annabel's henna-dyed frizz of hair, girdling her head in a massive cloud, looks even more ghastly in the porch light. She elbows her sister aside. Louisa, slightly shorter but perfectly proportioned, deftly thrusts out her foot. They arrive, side by side, sulking now, ignoring each other. They really do exhaust me at times.

"Speak to you later, darling." Daddy turns the key in the lock and ushers us into the building.

As soon as my badly behaved offspring head to bed, I pour generous glasses of port for Daddy and myself. We settle around the fireplace. "I'm sorry the girls upset you this evening. I can't wait for them to properly grow up. They can be so obnoxious."

He dismisses my comments with a wave of his hand. "Do you remember, Georgie Girl, after the war, when I got a short leave at the end of 1945? A whole year before I actually returned to England for good. I've often wondered."

"Of course I remember. How could I not? It was the very first time I set eyes on you."

I'd been so thrilled to have a daddy in the house at last. My friends and I were growing up, uncertain what the role of a husband-daddy was supposed to be, since all able-bodied men had been away for so long, fighting all the bad people. He stares bleakly into the artificial coals of the electric fire.

"I dreaded it."

"You didn't want to come home?" An involuntary shiver snatches claw-like at my shoulders, and I reach to the floor for a cardigan Lou had discarded earlier.

For a moment or two, Daddy tugs nervously at his cuff again. "No, I didn't," he finally mumbles. "Been away such a long time . . ."

My mind spirals back to our first meeting, printed indelibly on my memory. I was in the backyard, playing with my pet rabbit. The gate leading from the lane behind our house creaked open. A man I'd never seen before stood there, staring at me. Why wasn't I afraid? Why hadn't I run into the kitchen? Because I'd instantly recognized him from a black-and-white studio portrait hanging above our mantelpiece. My daddy. In his uniform. He'd dropped the filthy bag on the ground with a loud thud. Sank to his knees. Smiled. Whispered my name. Opened wide his arms. Calmly, I'd put my bunny into his hutch. Latched the door tight. Then catapulted myself into my daddy's life. But I was only four years old. Am I remembering things as they were, or as I want them to be?

"Getting home in one piece was what we all tried to stay alive for." Daddy gulps a mouthful of port. "But when the time came, I found myself numb with fear . . ."

"Why? What were you afraid of?"

Daddy rubs his chin. "Being a disappointment, I suppose. Or being disappointed. Falling short somehow."

When I had begun to struggle with my own marriage, I'd grown more curious about how my parents managed to reconnect after being a continent apart for all the long years of the Second World War. I ache for a cigarette. A deep drag of nicotine into my lungs.

But if I go outside right now, he'll know damned well what I'm doing. After Daddy was forced to give up his beloved ciggies after the heart attack, I promised him I'd quit. Which I almost have, just not completely.

"You've been fidgety since I got home. Not yourself at all. I knew you had something on your mind. What is it you've heard? Is it what you want to talk about?"

"In a roundabout way." Daddy pauses. Glances up as if the answer's somehow prowling around on the ceiling. Then he gazes directly at me with his familiar, robin's-egg-blue eyes. Draws a deep breath. "Will you take me to Trieste?"

"Northern Italy? Where you ended up in 1945?"

He nods weakly.

Does he really mean this? My father has never indicated any desire to return to the place where he'd served during the Allied Occupation. In fact, after he was demobilized at the end of 1946, he'd refused to set foot in Europe again. So, what has he just heard? What's changed? Why now? And why Trieste?

"Are you really up to traveling? Being so far away from home?"

"If you'll help me." But his face has paled to a milky white. He looks all in. I seriously wonder if such a trip won't be too much for him, so soon after his heart attack.

I get up to pour myself another drink, stalling a bit for time. My fall schedule looms—school visits to prepare for, a literary conference in Seattle I've already promised to chair—but I suppose there's no reason I couldn't make some time after that. "I have meetings with Penny scheduled in London for October to talk about writing a sequel to my latest book," I say. "Perhaps we could think about going when I get done—"

"I need to go as soon as possible."

Summer dusk is fully settled in now. Before I sit down again, I draw the curtains across the French windows and turn on a table lamp. I'm completely unprepared for the unshed tears I see welling in my father's eyes as the light catches them. Putting an arm around his shoulders, I ask, "Is it really so important to you, Daddy?"

"Yes, Georgie Girl."

Truth be told, it's beginning to dawn on me that he's offering on a platter the perfect opportunity to delay my return to the States a bit longer. Paul, my husband, won't be best pleased, but just like my father years ago, I don't really want to go home either. Not right now. Not to a stale, monotonous marriage. To the annual Wharton Labor Day Holiday Extravaganza, rearing its predictable and boring head. Here's a perfect excuse to avoid my tedious extended family, and their even more tedious obligations, for a couple more weeks.

"I'll work things out tomorrow, I promise."

When I reach for my father's hand, I feel that old, comfortable twitch on the invisible thread that has connected us, comforted us, reassured us both, since that long-ago day when we set eyes on each other for the very first time.

Chapter Two

I'M WOKEN IN THE WEE HOURS BY MY FATHER, shouting in his sleep. He's howling the same desperate words he has for years: "Stop!" "Please!" "Stop!" When I was a child, I assumed this behavior was perfectly normal. Mum blamed his night terrors on a cockamamie story about how he'd fallen down a cliff while playing with his brother, Charlie. I'd accepted this as one of any number of facts you learn at a tender age. *A* is for apple; tigers have stripes; cliffs equal nightmares.

In those days, he would frequently burst into my bedroom, grab me out of bed, and carry me down the stairs in his arms. Then we would sit at the kitchen table. Daddy made Horlicks for me. Poured whiskey for himself. Smoked cigarettes. Only once did I ask why. Was he saving me from someone? Something? Who or what was it? He had clenched his fists so tight the knuckles swelled big as marbles. I knew he would never hurt me, but I didn't ask again. Besides, I treasured those times together, and was too young to question why my mother wasn't included in these night watches.

It wasn't until I was an adult, living in the United States during the Vietnam War, that *PTSD* became part of the vernacular, and I understood my father's nightmares were connected to an event or events from his long years of war.

I'm just about to roll over and go back to sleep when there is a loud thud on the other side of the wall. What is Daddy doing? Eventualities flit through my mind: falling, needing medicine, forgetting how to use the telephone—just about anything is worrisome, really.

I unravel myself from the sheets, drag fingers through my hair, and knock on his door. He doesn't respond, but I go in anyway, a reversal of those long-ago nights when he came barging to my rescue. All the lamps are switched on. A stack of much-thumbed Penguin Classics are toppled in a heap, his desk a mess of papers. The wastebasket is overturned, balled-up correspondence strewn over the floor. And my father in his dressing gown, what's left of his hair thoroughly tousled, stands forlornly in the midst of it all.

"Are you all right?" I ask, stepping over the mess. He ignores me, eases painfully onto his knees, and starts rummaging through the bottom of his wardrobe.

"What are you doing? It's two o'clock in the morning."

"Got it," he mumbles, pulling out a small, battered suitcase. Good grief, is he wanting to pack for Trieste already? I haven't even had time to let Paul and the girls know our plans, never mind buy the tickets.

Daddy sits down heavily on the bed, the case on his knees.

"What have you stashed away in here?" I ask, settling next to him.

He clicks open the rusted clasp. I'm confronted first by his swagger stick, which so hypnotized me when I was a child. Its gruesome monkey head is weighted with ball bearings, apparently designed specifically to maim with a single stroke. "Had it made in Cairo," Daddy reminds me, placing the fearsome object carefully on the candlewick bedspread.

Otherwise, there doesn't appear to be much inside. Just a few bits and bobs. There's a tinted photograph of himself with his brother Charlie, dressed like little Dutch boys for some long-forgotten reason. Charlie died at the beginning of the war, drowned during the evacuation of Dunkirk. Next to the pair of them is an old studio photograph, the kind that was color tinted, giving it an unnatural look.

"Is this your father?"

He nods wearily. "I was only fifteen when he died. Suffered horribly. Stomach cancer. Was in bed for months. I sat with him every day after school."

"You looked very like him when you were a young man." The same patrician features, suggesting a Roman nobleman, and of course the keen blue eyes, which I, unfortunately, did not inherit.

Then I study a dog-eared black-and-white snap of the grandmother I never knew. She too died, just three years after her husband. Although she is sitting on a park bench, it's clear she is almost six feet tall, slender and elegant. In my imagination, I loosen her fair hair from its tight bun and dress her in linen slacks and a casual shirt—it's as if I'm peering into a mirror.

There are several official papers in the heap. Birth certificate. Marriage certificate. A Soldier's Service and Pay Book. Officer's Release Book. Under them lie his medals: the MBE, 1939–45 Star, Africa Star, Italy Star, Defense Medal, and Victory Medal.

I retrieve a signed letter from King George VI, proclaiming Captain James Alexander Drummond to be a Member of the British Empire, which makes my tummy do a little flip. It was so long ago, when there was still an Empire to be a member of. "I'm very proud of you."

"Nonsense," he replies with a sad little smile. "Just lucky to be alive."

Yes, you were, Daddy. So many of my friends' fathers never returned. The notion that I could have been one of them can still leave me feeling all hollowed out.

"Here it is." Daddy warily plucks a frayed buff envelope from the bottom of the suitcase. One corner is singed, presumably by a cigarette. He edges the flap open with his thumb. Pulls out a grubby piece of red felt, cut in the shape of a star, along with a faded brown photograph of a little boy sitting proudly on an old-fashioned sledge. There is lots of snow, and the boy's bundled up against the cold. In the background there is a weathered well-pump which looks to be distinctly foreign.

"Who is that?" I ask, staring at the picture.

Daddy shifts slightly. The movement is subtle, but I notice. And it hurts. He obviously doesn't want to tell me. When was the photo taken? Where? Why has it been stashed away in the dark, in a tattered envelope, in a ratty old case? It seems fairly obvious to me he hasn't opened this grab bag of memories for years. Have Lou and Annie inadvertently reminded him of this ancient photograph? Is it somehow connected to what he has learned recently in regard to the war?

"Aren't you going to tell me?"

Ignoring me, Daddy slips the snapshot back inside its envelope.

But he continues to hold the red star in the palm of his hand, as if it's a holy relic.

"If I'm going to take you back to Trieste, I think you should explain," I say with a sniff.

He still doesn't respond. Just gazes at the dingy piece of felt, presumably lost in a fog of remembrance. But of what? What is he not telling me?

Chapter Three

DESPITE THE ODD AND DISTURBING EVENTS of last night, or perhaps because of them, I'm quite decided I will make arrangements to take my father to Italy as soon as possible. He's sleeping in late this morning, so before Annabel and Louisa can begin verbally bashing each other again, I broach the subject over breakfast.

"I've decided to stay on a bit longer with your grandpa this year. Probably another couple of weeks or so."

"Because you're fed up with us?" asks Annie, chewing loudly on a spoonful of granola.

"Not entirely."

"Or maybe you planned this all along so you could avoid Grandma's Labor Day bash!"

"Annabel, for goodness's sake—"

"Dad will be mad."

Of course he will. But the regular annual get-together at the Wind Lake Resort is more than I can tolerate these days. Twenty-odd Whartons competing like mad for dominance in boating, swimming, tennis, golf, and if it rains, dominoes! Even the under-tens' sandcastle-building events have been known to turn nasty!

"Sorry," I respond with a sigh. "It turns out Grandpa has something he needs help with."

"You promised Dad you'd go to Wind Lake this year," complains Louisa. "And we're supposed to be flying home together."

"Oh, for crying out loud. It's not important. You're not kids anymore. I'll run you up to Heathrow. It's about time you were getting back anyway, Lou. You need to figure out your next steps. Job-hunting? Graduate school? And you, Annie, need to explain things to your father, now you've dropped out of college."

"You already knew!" Lou's cheeks flame beet red.

Oh, dear girl, so this was the genesis of your "guilt" tirade. Was it really so important you had to spoil our evening? "Of course I knew."

"Hah! I bet you didn't know she impersonated Grandma when she called to withdraw. Told the dean's office she'd come down with bubonic plague! And wasn't expected to live!"

Oh, dear God—that, I confess, I didn't know. But the plague? It's hard not to laugh.

"Somehow, it's always all right when Annie behaves like a jerk. If I'd dropped out of school, you would have had a fit." Lou's astonishing, arched eyebrows disappear indignantly under her bouffant fringe.

She's probably right. But despite Annie's childish behavior, I'm pretty sure she's made the right move. Her talents clearly lie elsewhere. If anything at all interested her a year ago, it was the College of Visual Arts in St. Paul. But my mother-in-law, Ellen Wharton, deemed that to be a waste of time. Instead, while I was overseas on a book tour, she donated a place for her granddaughter at her alma mater, St. Olaf College. Husband Paul, in my absence, raised no objections. And that was that. Mission accomplished.

Annabel is scooping up the last of her cereal. "Maybe, Mom, instead of changing our tickets, Lou and I can go up to London for the last few days." The spoon clinks irritatingly around her bowl. "We could do some shopping. Sightseeing. Have fun."

I open my mouth to say *You don't deserve treats, you have no money, nowhere to stay,* but I stop myself. I'm not going to object. After all, I'm constantly wittering on about how reliable and self-sufficient I was at their age. This is an opportunity for them to show a bit of gumption.

"Why not? Good idea. I'm sure you can stay with Penny. She won't mind. But one of you call your dad and see if he'll advance you some extra cash. I'm not forking out any more money."

This is one of many bones of contention between Paul and myself. He's far too quick to spoil them both, whereas I firmly believe they should be learning to stand on their own two feet. Paul says it's my British intransigence, to which I like to reply, *"And where would my country have been in 1940 without it?"* When I'm in a really foul mood, I like to add insult to injury and point out, *"All we got from your lot till the end of 1941 was dried eggs and Spam."*

"Thanks, Mom." Annie, clearly thrilled with the turn of events, leaps out of her chair and heads for the wall phone in the hallway.

"Not yet, Annabel. It's the middle of the night back home. That is not the way to extract moolah from your father."

"Oops. Forgot."

"What an idiot," mutters Louisa, slashing the head off a boiled egg with vengeance.

"What you *can* do is start getting your bags packed," I add. "I'll give Penny a quick ring, and assuming she's on board with the idea, we'll be on our way to London by mid-morning."

WHEN EVERYTHING IS ARRANGED with Penny, my editor as well as a dear friend, I load the car. We are outside in the parking area, abutting the walled garden of Cross Keys Court. It's a hot day, and I wish Daddy's car had air-conditioning. It will be a sticky two-and-a-half-hour ride into London and back again.

"It was lovely to see you, Gramps. I'm sorry I cussed in front of you last night," says Annabel. "It wasn't the time or place to let rip with my foul mouth." But she grins her cheeky grin all the same.

Daddy clasps her shoulders and gives her a little shake, setting the frightful frizz of red hair awhirl. "Never mind, pet. Just be true to yourself. Find what it is that will make you happy. Take your time. You have your whole life ahead of you."

Annie looks a bit astonished at this unsolicited advice. Her grandpa doesn't usually intrude much in their personal lives. He holds her in a tight hug. "Goodbye, dear girl."

"Thank you for having us to stay again, Grandpa," says Louisa. "I'm sorry too if I upset you last night, going on about—"

"That's all right, love," my father interrupts. "You got me thinking about things." He pauses, momentarily losing his train of thought. "With college behind you, there's lots for you to think about too. Decisions to make. Just be sure that whatever you choose will bring you real satisfaction."

"I'll try, Grandpa."

Dear, earnest Lou. I'm not sure she really understands what he's getting at. Her grandpa hugs her hard. "Goodbye, dear girl."

The roads are relatively quiet, and before too long we are rattling our way through Oxford, heading for London. Daddy's advice is good. I just worry that when my girls get home, Paul's mother will start meddling. She'll be livid Annie is refusing to return to St. Olaf. Probably take it as a personal insult. I'm the only member of our family who accepts that Annabel will continue to strew pebbles in her path for a long time to come. It's simply part of her impulsive nature to trip herself up at every opportunity. It doesn't help that Louisa excels academically and seems perfectly content to walk the straight and narrow.

For once, the pair are chatting nicely to each other in the back seat—making a list of things they want to do, what they want to see, including a couple of West End shows. I laugh to myself. Their dad had better wire them a bunch of cash. But I know he will.

"You're going to have Penny's flat to yourselves," I mention as we approach the outskirts of the city. "She's up in Scotland for a meeting."

"That's cool." Carefree Annie.

"Are you sure she doesn't mind?" Cautious Lou.

"Not a bit. And it's a perfect opportunity for you both to take care of yourselves. Don't forget—"

"Yeah, yeah, we know, Mom," says Annabel. "You were only twenty when you lived by yourself in London. We've heard it all before."

"So, I'm not going to give you any lectures about being sensible. Or acting your age. It's up to you."

"What about getting to the airport?" frets Lou.

"Penny will be home by then. She'll phone you at the flat to tell you exactly when, but it will be in plenty of time to run you out to Heathrow."

When I drive up Ormonde Terrace and park outside the gracious 1930s building, Penny's neighbor is waiting at the top of her basement steps with the key. Once inside, Lou makes us all a pot of coffee. I stand at the picture window overlooking Primrose Hill, dotted with lovers, prams, toddlers, and dogs on leashes. By odd coincidence, I lived in the same block of flats before I moved to America. When Penny and I made that connection years later, our future collaboration as editor/author was a done deal. The view is making me homesick, which I know is silly—I've lived in the States for almost twenty-seven years now. But it's the Englishness of it all, I suppose. Smaller. Greener. Cozier. Recently, for one reason or another, I've been beset with more than my usual bouts of nostalgia.

"The London Zoo is at the bottom of the road," I remark. "I used to feed the wallabies my leftover toast every morning, while I waited for the bus."

"That's neat," says Annie.

"I'm sorry I've been a bit distracted. But I've a lot to think about at the moment. And as I said earlier, Grandpa needs my help with some problem or other that has cropped up."

"So, tell me, Mom, are you and Dad getting a divorce?" asks Annabel.

This is somewhat out of the blue, although she is usually the more perceptive of my two girls. I sit down abruptly on the piano stool.

"Of course they aren't," yelps Lou. "How could you ask her such a thing?"

There is much that children can't begin to understand about the lives of their parents, I suppose, getting to know them as they do at variously different times in their adult lives. Nevertheless, the question hits too close to home. Once upon a time, when they were little girls, I *had* decided to divorce Paul. It was a long time ago, and fate had intervened before there was any opportunity for me to act on my decision. No words about it had ever been spoken between Paul and me.

"Well, Mom?" Annie persists.

I've such an urge to slap the piano keys and make enough noise to block out the questions. More especially, the memories of that time in my life.

"What on earth makes you ask me that?"

"You don't seem to be home much anymore. Dad's complaining about it. A lot. *And* Grandma. She keeps pointing out that Dad's always there for us, steady as a rock, but you're like a phantom. Forever traveling. No sense of responsibility."

"Grandma should mind her own damned business!"

Ellen, Matriarch of the Tribe Wharton, who had desperately wanted Paul to marry a nice Midwestern girl. Connie was quite literally the girl next door. And he almost had. Till she dumped him for a guy who was later killed in the Vietnam War.

"Well, Mom?" Annie is like a dog with a bone.

"Your dad and I have never discussed separating."

Technically this is true. But I know I'm fudging. In my head, the idea of a different kind of life lurks, never far away. No matter where I am. No matter where I go.

Lou sits down hard on the sofa, tears streaming down her cheeks. I take her in my arms. Brush her hair off her forehead to better look into her remarkable eyes, dark, toasty brown.

"But what does that mean?" she gulps. "It sounds like you'd rather be on your own? That's what Grandma says, anyway."

"She really does need to keep her opinions to herself."

"Anyway, divorce is wrong, just wrong," Lou moans on. "What would poor Dad do? He would be so helpless."

She's right, of course, but that's surely not a valid reason for me to stay with him forever.

"Well, I think you deserve to be happy like everybody else, Mom." This from Annabel. She suddenly sounds so sensible. I hug her too.

Daddy told the girls to seek out what will make them happy. I should heed his advice too. Take the extra time away in Italy to reevaluate the rest of my life. What do *I* really want? What will make *me* truly happy? And how do I achieve that goal, whatever it might be?

Annie clears the coffee pot, cups, and saucers and wanders into the kitchen to wash up.

Lou is still marooned on the sofa, mascara streaking her cheeks, clothing bedraggled. I pull her to her feet and walk her to the guest room, where I've stayed frequently. We sit side by side on one of the twin beds.

"Sweetheart, you are all grown up now. A college graduate with career decisions to consider. You're about to go out into the world and forge a life of your own. Don't dwell so much on everyone else."

"But I'm not like you, Mom. I don't know what I want to do."

"For starters, stop bickering with Annabel all the time. Surprise her. Unpack. Hang up your clothes for a change. Because right now, you are in a glorious, cosmopolitan city. Make the most of it. And enjoy each other for a change."

While both the girls are occupied, I draw them a map of how to get to the shops. Over Primrose Hill to Chalk Farm, or left across Abbey Road of Beatles fame, to St. John's Wood High Street. I even mark my old local, The Star, where I spent many a happy evening drinking cheap shandies and flirting with the out-of-work-actors who frequented the place. All so long ago.

I SOAK IN THE view of Primrose Hill once more before I leave. The trees are laden with dense green foliage, and the footpaths meander in all directions, offering a potpourri of choice.

How would my life have unfolded if I hadn't been lured by the glitzy glamor of Los Angeles? Hadn't been introduced to Paul by a friend of a friend during a Memorial Day weekend in San Diego? Hadn't assumed (incorrectly, as it turned out) that the rest of America would be exactly like Southern California? Hadn't believed my husband would always remain the gallant naval officer I fell in love with?

Only I do know, don't I?

I would have gone on living in London. Begun to publish

books. Met Michael. Married Michael. Settled in his home on the banks of the Thames. Like Ratty and Mole, nestled safe and secure under the willows, living happily ever after.

But there will always remain one unanswerable question. Would fate still have intervened? Sweeping my hopes and dreams away on the current like so much flotsam?

Chapter Four

I HEAD BACK to the elegant spa city of Cheltenham, where my father chose to live as a widower, both for its convenience and charm. I've come to love the area too—the sense of stepping back in time as I drive through villages of soft yellow stone cottages nestled amid the rolling, mellow hills of the Cotswolds. I make good time, and stop at Marks and Spencer to purchase salad fixings, crispy bread, and fresh eggs for an omelet, as well as a packet of custard tarts, Daddy's favorite snack.

"Did you get the girls settled?" he asks as we finish up our simple supper.

"Turns out Penny is in Edinburgh, meeting with a potential new illustrator, so they're on their own. Playing grown-ups. I'm hoping it will encourage them to get on better together. As well as instill some sense of maturity."

"Don't be too hard on them, Georgie Girl. You grew up in a very different time. There was little choice but to be resourceful in postwar Britain."

"I know, I know, but it doesn't stop me wishing they could learn to be more self-sufficient. At least growing up in the fifties gave me a sense of independence, don't you think? I was far better able to take care of myself from the time I left school at seventeen than they are now, aged nineteen and twenty-two."

"You were that," he concedes, munching contentedly on a tart.

"Remember how I snatched the first opportunity that came along, wangling my way into that fledgling television station in

Newcastle? I reckoned it would be a good way to hone my writing skills."

"Chief bottle-washer was what you were at first, as I recall."

"But I caught the eye of a scriptwriter who was happy to write me a sparkling introduction to a pal of his at Twentieth Century Fox in London. And off I went to seek my fortune."

"You didn't give your mother and me much choice in the matter, did you? Just piled your worldly belongings into *my* car and drove off to the big city."

"I must have been a pain in the arse in those days."

"Just a bit."

It's a description Paul has attached to me many times during our marriage. To be fair, I suppose, I've made so many unintentional missteps along the way. If I hadn't insisted on keeping my maiden name because of my career, Ellen might have softened. If I hadn't brewed tea every afternoon at various Wharton gatherings, I might not have been considered an arrogant snob. If I hadn't insisted on a series of Mozart concerts for the family the year Orchestra Hall was built instead of the usual University of Minnesota ice hockey season tickets, I might not have been labeled a stuck-up Brit with attitude.

Would it have been so hard to change my name? Drink coffee all day like everyone else? Attempt to meet the sports-mad family halfway?

When we've finished washing and drying the supper dishes, Daddy and I wander into the living room. He dials his radiogram to a live concert at Wigmore Hall, and we settle down for a good listen. I throw open the French windows to the large communal garden. Soft, warm evening air wafts over us.

"Look." Daddy points to a handsome dog fox sashaying nonchalantly across the lawn, flaunting his thick red brush. He disappears into a dense hedge, and a few moments later reappears on top of the garden wall. "He's a regular. Utterly adapted to city living. Nothing but vermin, really."

But I'm entranced. The fox perches for several minutes, his yellow eyes gleaming in the dusky light. "*Look at me,*" he seems to say. "*Am I not a magnificent creature?*"

"Daddy," I ask, shaking myself from my reverie, "before I start making arrangements tomorrow, are you still sure you want to go ahead with this expedition to Italy? I'd be perfectly happy staying here with you for a few more days." How I would enjoy writing *The Cross Keys Fox,* the story of a suburban fox perfectly at home in his suburban garden. I tuck him away for the future.

"I'm sure," he mutters, pouring us both a drop of brandy. "But nothing will be the same."

"Of course not." But what does he mean? The place itself? Or the child on the sledge, all grown up now?

"I expect Castello di Miramare will be the same," I say, using the Italian pronunciation. "I've always wanted to see the place."

"Because?"

"Because after you finished your leave and returned to Italy, Mummy and I suffered through a bitterly cold winter and chronic food shortages while you were billeted in that place that looked like a fairy-tale castle."

Daddy stares at me, his dear, beloved blue eyes a bit unfocused. "All well and good, but I worry you won't feel the same way about me afterward. After we get there."

"So, you had a lady friend?" I tease. But when I catch the fleeting expression of anguish on his face, I wish I could swallow back the words. I've clearly embarrassed him horribly, as well as myself. "I'm not a fool—somehow I just never thought—it never occurred to me—I'm sorry, Daddy."

But then the hazy film of childhood memory unspools. It was

a wet Sunday afternoon. Words were shouted that I didn't understand. My mother bundled me into a taxi, leaving Daddy in the middle of the street, rain-drenched and alone. We went to my friend Ann's house. While the grown-ups huddled in another room, I told Ann that when my parents got a divorce I was going to live with my father. How did I even know the word "divorce" back then?

It reminds me of my conversation with Louisa and Annabel this morning and makes me edgy. Mum raised me alone all through the war and beyond. Was I really so fickle, I was ready to throw her away like a worn-out dolly for a newer, shinier parent I barely knew?

This gives me real pause. There must surely have been a serious argument between them. Could it have happened? Could my parents have actually chosen to live apart? Just as I had decided to leave Paul years ago, before fate stopped me dead in my tracks?

And how in hell is all this connected with Daddy's sudden need to go back to Trieste? Why does he fear I'll judge him differently when we get there? It doesn't make sense.

Thankfully, he seems to have lost track of the conversation. "By the way, darling, Paul phoned while you were driving the girls up to town. Seemed a bit annoyed that you were dropping them off in London in order to go gallivanting around Europe with me."

"You told him we were going to Italy?"

"May have mentioned it."

"Well, there's plenty of me to go around. Paul will survive a couple more weeks without me. I'll give him a call before I go to bed and explain the situation."

"Everything all right with you two?"

What can I say? Daddy knows me so well. Where he's concerned,

I'm mostly an open book. He's able to read my "happiness" gauge to within a fraction of a degree.

"More or less, Daddy. More or less."

After my father goes to bed, I think about Paul awhile before making the call. The early days were intoxicating, like too many glasses of bubbly. His dark good looks, solidness, and sensitive nature had beguiled me. And the dashing naval uniform hadn't hurt either. Perhaps we were altogether too easily able to impress each other. Paul provided parties with commanding officers, cocktails aboard visiting aircraft carriers from around the world, long jaunts up and down the California coast in his T-bird. Up my sleeve were visits to film sets, dinner with Sean Connery, and my marketable British accent, which opened up so many doors in those long-off days.

It wasn't until much later that I bumped up against his mother, and my life drifted off key.

Chapter Five

THE TRANSATLANTIC CONVERSATION with my husband is not a great success. The telephone is a wall contraption on a long cord in the entry hall of Daddy's flat. After I dial the number, I sit cross-legged on the carpet and wait for Paul to pick up.

I'm greeted with, "What the hell are you up to, Georgina? You've been gone two weeks already."

"Daddy asked me yesterday if I would take him to Italy," I try to explain.

"So this gave you license to dump *our* kids in London, without even consulting me?"

"For crying out loud, Paul, they're old enough to vote!"

"You of all people know damned well it isn't safe. There are still terrorist threats—random attacks—hardly ever any advance warning."

I squeeze the receiver tight, wishing it were Paul's neck I had hold of. *You just had to remind me about the Irish Republican Army, didn't you?* "The girls are staying at Penny's," I tell him. "They know the city well enough. You can't keep wrapping them up in cotton wool forever. Nowhere is completely safe anymore, Paul. You know that."

There is such a long silence, I'm tempted to cut us off and blame British Telecom later. But I know we need to get clear exactly what I plan to do and when the girls are due to fly home.

"So where exactly in Italy are you going?" Paul finally asks.

"Trieste."

"Your dad was stationed there after the war, wasn't he? So this is just a sentimental journey. Why can't it wait? The poor old guy just had a heart attack. Have you even consulted his doctor? Should he even be traveling?"

My head begins its usual dull ache in response to Paul's salvo of questions. "Are you quite finished? Does it not occur to you that this is precisely why we should *not* wait?"

I don't bother mentioning Daddy's middle-of-the-night search for an ancient photograph and a tatty red star, neither of which I had ever seen before. God only knows what Paul's response to that would be.

"Georgina, I really expect you to come home with Lou and Annie like we planned. You've got responsibilities here—Mom's get-together coming up, for one thing."

"The girls will be back one week from today. Plenty of time to go up to the lake with you for the Labor Day holiday. I doubt I'll be missed much."

Our old mutt Peanut barks somewhere nearby. My eyes sting slightly. Missing the dog, but not my husband. What a state of affairs.

"And by the way, there's something else, Paul. Annabel has news for you. No more college. She's withdrawn herself."

"What!"

I uncross my legs, lean my back up against the wall, and rest my pounding head on my knees. Paul's complaints continue to wash through the phone line. Eventually I hear, "I'll call you tomorrow," followed by the welcome click and buzz of the disconnected line.

Exhausted, I get myself to bed, but I lie awake for a long time. A sentimental journey, Paul called this venture of Daddy's, but the mementos he unearthed suggest something else entirely. Idly,

I ponder the parentage of the child on the sledge, which in turn makes me determined to fly my father to Italy as soon as possible. Get this mystery sorted, whatever it is. The farther away I get from my husband the better, since it's clear that any civil conversation we try to have is drifting out of reach.

NEXT MORNING, I WALK briskly past the crescents of elegant Regency homes into the Montpellier Spa area, headed for a travel agent I use frequently. Normally, I would stop for a coffee, shop a bit, browse in the galleries, and admire the classical French architecture and carved caryatides, but not today. In short order, I order a goodly amount of lira at the bank, purchase two first-class plane tickets to Venice, and arrange a hire car. I select a rather posh hotel, the Savoia Excelsior Palace, situated on the waterfront in Trieste. At least we will start our mysterious venture in grand style.

Two days later, having packed, canceled newspapers and milk deliveries, checked several times on Lou and Annie, and tried my best to reassure Paul that my plan is to be back home by the middle of September, I battle traffic on the motorway, Daddy in tow. The drive to Heathrow gets worse every year, exacerbated by the August school holiday crowd. Daddy no longer insists on driving, but sits rigidly in the passenger seat with his seatbelt fastened, gripping the armrest whenever an articulated lorry screams past.

"When do the girls get home to Minnesota?" he asks.

"Only four more days left in London. Sounds as if they're having a grand time."

"Any idea yet what Annabel will do next?"

"'Next' being the operative word. It's always a guessing game with her. Obviously sending her to college was a complete waste of time. Paul just doesn't want to admit it, especially to me."

Daddy nods. He knows his son-in-law well enough to understand.

"You know, the only place she expressed any interest in last year was a small art school in the Cities."

"What was so bad about that?"

"Nothing, except it's a two-year college, and Paul wants her to get a four-year degree. So, guess what happened next? Ellen made sure she got her into St. Olaf by making a huge donation to the Alumni Association."

"Oh, my goodness." Daddy grunts his disapproval. "Still, didn't hurt you to avoid higher learning, did it?"

"True enough, but unlike my girls, I always knew what I wanted to do."

"From when you were a little girl. As soon as you mastered your letters, you began filling your exercise books with stories. Especially in the dark of night."

He remembers. I so cherish the times he gathered me out of bed to save me from one horror or another. How I sat at the kitchen table scribbling away, while he calmed himself down with whiskey and ciggies.

"And Louisa?"

I release a long sigh. "She's certainly ticking all her grandma's boxes. But she has no real idea what she wants to do. Apparently it's all so much harder for youngsters to figure out these days."

"Lou is a bit of a homebody, isn't she? Maybe she'll be quite content keeping house, raising lots of babies."

"Paul would love that. Lots of grandbabies, just down the road and around the corner for him to spoil rotten whenever he feels like it."

"Georgina, do you regret not having a boy?"

"What!"

"You heard me. A son."

"Christ, Daddy, no. The answer's a definite no. You sound like Ellen. She got this mad idea Paul required an heir. All I wanted was healthy babies. I love my girls. But two children were quite enough."

All the time I'm saying this, I'm bracing myself, hands slick on the steering wheel, anxious to maintain control of the car if he confesses to fathering the child on the sledge. After a minute or two, I dare to take my eyes off the road and glance at Daddy. To my astonishment, he apparently has nothing more to add, and is very obviously pretending to take a nap.

Fine. I take a deep breath, and let my mind drift back to my daughters. In a way I'm relieved Annie asked the divorce question the other day. Clearly, I need to face up to the fact that the state of my marriage is being discussed openly back in Minnesota. The time has come to be completely honest with myself. *If* I were to leave Paul, I would like to relocate back to England. Easy enough, since I kept my British citizenship. But one day Louisa and Annabel will surely acquire husbands and children. Would I then want to be so far away? But, I remind myself, my own parents were an ocean apart from their grandchildren, yet we managed regular and constant visits to one another, including spending every summer at my parents' holiday cottage by the sea. Why couldn't our tradition continue in the future?

When the signs for Heathrow loom, I clear my mind and concentrate on getting us to the airport in one piece.

AFTER A FLURRY OF boarding procedures, we settle into our roomy seats and sip chilled champagne while the main cabin passengers enter. Daddy is delighted with the first-class comforts, and after a few minutes, the wine loosens his tongue.

"Beats the way I traveled to Italy the first time," he says. "Jammed in an overloaded troop carrier, part of an enormous convoy, snaking along the coast of Africa." He pauses. "Heading for Sicily. Into the jaws of death, like the Charge of the bloody Light Brigade."

After all the years of silence about the war, this outburst amazes me. Daddy gazes past the narrow airplane portal, past fifty-odd years, back to the rumble of another life, gone but obviously not forgotten. And he continues on.

"Later, the poor sods, waiting to board the landing craft, lurching in and out of lavvies, all a slop of vomit, piss, and shit. Sorry, darling." I squeeze his fingers. "The heat and stench were overpoweringly awful. My lungs ached for fresh air and nicotine. When I got on deck, there was fresh air, all right. Rough seas and gale-force winds. But no smokes. Complete blackout topside. Even after the men slithered down the nets, rock-hard with sea-spray and slippery as hell. Hundreds of blighters packed in the flat-bottomed boats, soaking wet, and no place to be sick but over each other."

These recollections horrify me. Spoken out loud, in such detail. Why didn't I know this? Couldn't I have taken the time to read about the Italian invasion? All anyone talked about afterward, as I recall, were the D-Day landings, which completely overshadowed the liberation of Rome.

"When our ships' guns sprayed the shore with shells, we could see the first wave of landing craft heading in. Lambs to the slaughter. Lambs to the bloody slaughter."

I fish around in my bag for some Kleenex and blow my nose.

"When I was small, I used to wonder if you had killed anyone. Silly, really, I suppose."

"Very silly, Georgie Girl. But not a topic one can drop into everyday conversation."

"You are now."

"I suppose." Daddy spins the empty glass between his fingers. "For years afterward, all I did was focus on finding ways to file all that away. Bury it deep. Certainly not ever talk about any of it."

Our stewardess collects the glassware. Shortly afterward, the plane hurtles down the runway. Taking me further from Paul and our miserable marriage; closer to comprehending more of my soldier-daddy's life in the years before I knew him; closer to understanding his great fear of coming home; closer to learning the identity of a long-ago child, the significance of a tatty red star.

Needing reassurance, I reach for his hand again, seeking out the thread of connection between us. "You still haven't told me exactly why we are going to Trieste. Or what it was you recently heard that made this trip so important?"

The plane lifts into the air. The wheels retract.

"No going back, darling. You'll find out soon enough."

But what, I wonder, will happen if soon enough turns out to be something I would rather not find out?

JULY–
DECEMBER 1945

Chapter Six

IT WAS IN July when Captain Drummond first saw her. Up on the Karst, a sparsely vegetated, bleak outcrop plateau of the Julian Alps, high above Trieste, a city clinging to the edge of the Adriatic Sea. His men were on foot, patrolling near the newly negotiated demarcation line between the Allied Occupation Force and the Yugoslav Fourth Liberation Army. Zone A on the Italian side for the Allies. Zone B on the Slovenian side for Yugoslavia. Their mission was to rout out pockets of vicious fascist Italians unwilling to surrender to the Allies, some of whom had been reported hiding in the nearby village of Rupingrande. Their orders, to disarm and arrest them any way they could.

As they skirted a line of trees, faint laughter filtered through the leaves. Drummond gestured for his men to stop, then pushed silently through the undergrowth alone to investigate. There was, he thought, something eerily compelling about the Karst, a flinty place of gushing underwater streams and potholes gouged out of the limestone over millennia. Several minutes later, he found himself gazing at one such pool, dappled in leafy shadow. A dozen women and almost as many children were splashing and spraying one another with water, giggling and laughing, intermittently soaping dirt and grime from each other's backs.

Piles of filthy clothing littered the edge of the pool. Drummond recognized the green caps worn by both men and women Partisan fighters, as well as Tito's Yugoslavian regular army. In the mottled half-light, the red felt stars sewn to the caps reminded him uncomfortably of splotches of blood.

One by one, the women clambered out of the water and began to rub the youngsters dry. Best leave them be, he decided. His mission was to neutralize the fascist holdouts, not interfere with the Jugs, who were nominally on the side of the Allies, despite the recent forty-day standoff in Trieste before the zones had been worked out and crisis averted.

As the captain turned to retrace his steps, the last of the bathers emerged. A moment sooner and he would have missed her. Water cascaded over her shoulders, breasts, belly, streamed down her thighs, spattering the grass like drops of dew. She grasped handful after handful of long black hair, wringing the tresses out. Then, lazily, like a satisfied cat, she seated herself on the side of the pool, stretched out her legs, hefted the hair over her shoulders, and began to comb it through. He was mesmerized. Lines he'd learned to love at grammar school flooded his heart. Lord Byron, he was pretty sure.

> *She walks in beauty, like the night*
> *Of cloudless climes and starry skies;*
> *And all that's best of dark and bright*
> *Meet in her aspect and her eyes:*
> *Thus mellow'd to that tender light*
> *Which heaven to gaudy day denies.*

Long moments later, he stole backward through the undergrowth, feeling distinctly disoriented, his breath a series of short, painful gasps. What disturbed him was the awe he felt, stumbling across what could only be described as a scene from an impressionist painting—specifically Degas's *Women Bathing*, which he had so admired in London before the war. On his honeymoon, as it happened. The sensation was all the more astonishing because in recent years he had grown accustomed to blundering over dead comrades, mangled civilian corpses, and rotting carcasses on a near-daily basis. Never such a scene as this—such a vision of beauty in all her dark and bright appearance. As he emerged from the trees, he already found himself half believing it had been a mirage of some kind.

"Everything as it should be, Captain Drummond, sir?" asked Corporal Larkins.

As it should be? Words failed him. For the first time since getting through the bloody war, he had absolutely no idea.

Chapter Seven

S EVERAL DAYS LATER, the captain was in his office, situated on the ground floor of Castello di Miramare, the Allied Eight-Army Headquarters since early May. A dull ache bloomed in his gut. Down the hallway, someone jabbed away laboriously on typewriter keys. Whenever the bell on the carriage return pinged, the pain worsened.

One of the intriguing things about Miramare was that every room had been constructed so as to provide an ocean view. The Hapsburg Archduke Maximillian had been a naval man, and consequently designed his castle so that he could imagine being on a ship at sea. From his own particular window, the captain looked down at the small collection of sailboats corralled into the castle's small, protected harbor. The sun was burning the waters of the Adriatic a deep gold, and Drummond decided then and there to cut the day short, check out a boat, and go sailing for a while. Good for indigestion, he reckoned.

Then the phone rang.

"Spot of bother in town, Captain Drummond," said the voice across the line. "I've a peasant here yattering on about goats gone missing from his village. Rupingrande, I think he said. Somewhere on the Karst."

Rupingrande. Very close to where he'd come upon a particular naked woman stepping out of a pool. But he didn't need to think about that. There was absolutely no point. Drummond reached for the packet of Alka-Seltzer on his desk. Tossed two tablets in a glass of water. Watched the bubbles fizz.

"God Almighty, who do they think we are?" he shouted down the phone, before gulping down the concoction. "All right, all right, tell him I'll take a look, see what I can sort out. But I'll need an interpreter. Preferably one who can speak Slovene as well as Italian, if that's possible."

With one last rueful glance at the sailboats bobbing on the water, the captain picked up his cap. Stuck his swagger stick under his arm. Checked that a packet of cigarettes was in the breast pocket of his battledress blouse. And strode off to the motor pool in search of Corporal Larkins, his batman, driver, and all-around general factotum. A strapping, red-headed fellow from the captain's hometown, Larkins had asked for the job before the regiment shipped to North Africa. Even if Drummond sometimes felt as if he were back in the nursery under the watchful eye of Nanny—kit at the ready, pressed uniforms, polished boots, hot tea—the captain wouldn't have it any other way. When Larkins's dander was up, there was no better soldier to have at one's side under fire.

An hour later, after stopping to pick up the interpreter in Trieste, Larkins was rattling their Land Rover away from the sea, up the steep, curving road onto the Karst. Along the way, black-garbed women and expressionless old men, faces etched by wind and sun, gazed sullenly from stone cottage doorways, orchards, and vineyards. It was too early for these countryfolk to have figured out where their best interests lay. Coming as they did from such varied ethnic backgrounds—Italian, Slovenian, Croatian—the captain sometimes wondered if they ever would. Poor souls. Not their fault. Victims of circumstance.

As soon as they entered Rupingrande, the villagers huddled around the vehicle. Not particularly menacing, although the odor most certainly was—Drummond detected stale sweat, ripe cheese, and livestock among the melange.

"They insist goats are disappearing at night," translated the interpreter.

"Ask them if they're sure it isn't the fascists they've been hiding."

After some unintelligible back-and-forth, the interpreter said, "They definitely claim it's Tito's lot who are responsible."

"Aren't they all moved into Zone B now?" asked Drummond. "The Slovene side."

When his words were translated, one of the villagers, a stooped old man, rattled off a stream of what Drummond was sure were Slavic oaths, dragged his foot through the stony ground to make a wobbly line, gesticulated wildly, and lobbed a glob of spittle at the Land Rover.

"He's complaining they don't know if they live in Italy or Slovenia anymore," explained the translator. "And they don't have any say in the matter."

"True enough," agreed the captain, as the old man began shuffling along the rutted track, beckoning them to follow. Larkins inched the Land Rover forward. Beside him, Drummond cocked his revolver, while the interpreter sat quietly behind them in the back seat.

Not more than half a mile beyond the village, they came upon a compound of motley tents. A fire burned, the unmistakable smell of roasting meat filling the air. The old man gestured with a gnarled finger before beginning his slow trek back into Rupingrande, obviously not anticipating the return of any goats.

Drummond and the interpreter got out of the vehicle. "Stay at the wheel, Larkins," the captain ordered. "Keep her running. We may have to leave in a hurry. I'm not about to get killed over a few stolen goats."

"Yes, sir." Larkins grinned, but his sharp eyes were nonetheless peeled for any trouble.

One of the tent flaps opened. A small boy, lean but supple, slipped out, blinking in the bright sun. Jammed on top of his fair hair was a child-size Titovka cap. Drummond laughed out loud. Until the child was joined by a woman brandishing a German Luger. *The* woman. The image of her wringing water from her hair flooded his mind, flooded his cheeks. Even dressed in men's trousers held up with a length of rope, she struck the captain as quite wondrous.

"What you want?" she asked in English. Her voice rumbled out of her throat, as if she were digging up each word from deep in the earth.

"Captain Drummond, Allied Command. Put the gun down." Hoping he wasn't making a grave mistake, he laid his own weapon on the bonnet of the Land Rover as a show of good faith.

She obeyed, utterly self-confident. He was starting to recall every inch of this woman's body. The face in sunlight, however, was new. Eyes pale as the limestone Karst. Cheekbones high as the mountains beyond the plateau. A full mouth and determined chin.

"You *are* one of Tito's lot?" he asked.

When she didn't respond, he stepped closer. The child grabbed her hand. Her boy, he supposed, although their features bore no similarity whatsoever. And why should it matter to him? Only it did.

Drummond bent down to the boy's level. "Not to worry, son— we are not here to cause trouble." *Stupid ass,* he thought to himself. The little blighter won't understand a word.

Then he shouted over to Larkins, "You got any sweeties?" His corporal had already established a lucrative relationship with some of the Yanks, and he regularly cajoled them out of bags of candy for the local kids—treats Drummond's little girl in Britain had never seen or tasted in her young life, the captain had noted with rancor.

"Yes, sir." Larkins held up a bar of chocolate. The child gazed hopefully at the woman. She nodded permission, and he marched toward Larkins. The lad was every inch a little soldier, straight legs and arms swinging, but licked his lips with anticipation all the same.

Drummond continued. "The rest of your group too?" He opened his arms wide, encompassing the entire encampment. "All Tito's people?" There was quite possibly a husband lurking too, armed and in no mood to take orders from the British. Still she held her tongue.

"Stop stealing the local livestock," the captain barked. "That's an order."

He knew instinctively that she would never admit to taking the goats, but he had to assume his command would be followed. The Yugoslavs didn't want trouble at the moment.

"And it would be a good idea to move your tents further inland, soon as you can. Make certain you are on the correct side of the Morgan Line. If you are not sure, send someone down into Trieste and we can get you an official map."

He had to admit there was much to admire about Tito's rag-tag army—against all odds, they had kicked the Germans out of Yugoslavia, then followed up by pummeling them to a standstill in Trieste before the Allies even arrived. But the less involved Drummond was personally, the better. The Yanks already had their knickers in a twist over the possibility that the Soviet Union might gain control of the port of Trieste through their Yugoslavian comrades, thereby obtaining an outlet into the Mediterranean.

"Will you do that?" the captain asked.

The woman stared at him with her pale gray eyes. She ran her fingers through the mass of hair, tumbling down her back. And finally, she spoke.

"We leave next day or two. You will not be troubled by us more. Go back to your castle by the sea. Plot and plan what is to be done with Trieste."

Drummond did indeed crave to get off the Karst. A night in the officers' club. Oblivion through whiskey. Above all, burial of the past five years' horrors. But whether he craved getting away from this woman, whose mouth he longed suddenly to kiss, was a different matter altogether.

"Goodbye, Captain Drummond of Allied Occupation Force," she called after him.

Chapter Eight

BACK AT CASTELLO di Miramare, the captain went about the monotonous daily business of occupation. Identifying areas still mined. Organizing land and sea mine clearance. Mopping up pockets of resistance, mainly hard-core fascists. Patrolling the city streets. Enforcing curfews. By no means was he plotting the fate of Trieste, as the woman had suggested—far beyond his rank and pay grade. But he was well aware that telegrams continued to fly back and forth between London and Washington, both governments desperate to keep the city out of the hands of the Soviets.

He wondered if the tent community outside Rupingrande had indeed broken up and moved into Slovenia proper, as the woman had said. There would then be no earthly reason to set eyes on her again. Which would be a good thing. Out of sight, out of mind.

Sometime later, Larkins appeared in his office, bearing a distinct bulge in the front of his shirt that was, without question, wriggling and squirming.

"What in God's name is that, Larkins?"

"A kitten for the little 'un, sir," Larkins replied, producing a writhing ball of black fluff.

There were stray cats all over the city, not that the locals seemed to mind. They actually left food out for the wretched creatures—off their own plates, when they had little enough for themselves. Damned fools.

"That little nipper we met up on the Karst," Larkins went on. "Needs a bit of something to cuddle, don't you think?"

The captain knew exactly who Larkins referred to, but letting on was more than his pride would allow. He swiveled his chair to look out over the sea and fumbled for a cigarette.

"Sir, I just heard those Partisans are all gone over the line into Zone B, except the woman with the Luger and the kiddie—she left her comrades and moved into another village about twenty-five miles west. Can't rightly pronounce it, but got the name written down."

The captain swung around. "How the hell did you find that out?"

"Lieutenant Ward took a patrol out. Asked about a bit."

Drummond watched the kitten scrabble out of Larkins's shirt and crawl onto his shoulder.

"You're too soft for your own good, Larkins."

"Yes, sir."

What would he have done without Larkins, he wondered? Through thick and thin together since Tunisia. Larkins's ability to make the best cup of tea had been the only thing to get Drummond through the ordeal of holing up in the Anzio farmhouse they'd had to kill seven Germans to seize and occupy. Four months of it, under the worst shelling imaginable.

"So, fancy a ride, sir? Quiet around here for once. Bit of a run, like?"

Drummond burst out laughing. "Talking of runs, do you remember our ride into Rome? We made it into the Eternal City in high style, didn't we? The conquering heroes, me driving that bloody great German Mercedes that you and your mates found buried in the farmhouse pasture. In pristine condition too. Never thought we'd see that day, did we?"

"Supposed to land at Anzio and take Rome fast as you like, weren't we!" replied Larkins.

"That was the general idea. Except there was a bit of a four-month cock-up on the part of the generals."

"You made a joke, sir!"

"Suppose I did! We kept the car quite a while, didn't we, till Mark Clark's adjutant got his beady eyes on it. Then rank and Yankee ingenuity won out!"

"So, what about another run today, sir? This little mite's getting antsy." Larkins slipped the kitten back inside his shirt.

"Why not. At least black cats are lucky."

"That's it, sir. We'll call him Lucky."

A SHORT TIME LATER, they had bagged a jeep and driven up onto the plateau in warm sunshine. Drummond unfolded the newest map he had of the Karst and laid it out on his knees. "Give me the name of the place we're looking for."

Larkins handed over a scrap of paper.

Drummond peered at the map, searching for somewhere called Opatje Selo—barely a dot, as it turned out, and sitting slap bang on the thick black line of demarcation, no less. "Christ, Larkins, it's in Slovenia. We're heading straight into Zone B because for some damned reason the Morgan Line bulges here." Drummond slapped the chart. "It's definitely not in our jurisdiction."

"Want me to turn 'round, sir?"

Drummond rubbed his chin. There were still plenty of crazed fascists lurking in the area. He could always use that as an excuse if they were challenged for overstepping zones. He unholstered his revolver and held it on his knees. "Keep going."

They continued to hurtle along an ancient, bumpy road. Opatje

Selo was little more than a cluster of homes roofed with red tile, an easy enough place to miss. Larkins pulled up beside a couple of shops on what appeared to be the one and only street through the place. He cocked his weapon but held it by his side when they got out to explore, trusting there would be no Jug patrols in such an out-of-the-way place.

A large, cobbled square was just a few yards across the road. Several women were standing around the water pump, including the woman he had come to see, whether he was prepared to admit it or not. Her ragged uniform was gone. In its place she wore a frock of the palest blue cotton, faded from many washings, cinched at the waist, and brushing her knees. A breeze caught the hem, lifting it slightly, exposing a firm, tanned thigh—with which, of course, the captain was already achingly familiar.

She turned, alert and curious, when she heard the two sets of military boots scrape over the cobblestones. Her companions straightened up, looking anxiously at one another.

"You lost, Captain Drummond?" she called. "This is Zone B."

"I am aware of that," Drummond replied.

"Well, what you want?" she asked, eyeing his weapon. "We say goodbye. You not hear me?"

Unbidden, a fragment of a Shelley poem shimmied through his mind.

> *All things by a law divine*
> *In one spirit meet and mingle.*
> *Why not I with thine?*

It was ridiculous. Beholding her again might cause the words to spin a web of magic around his heart, but why in God's name would she want to mingle her spirit with his? They might as well be from different galaxies, never mind different countries, different languages, different philosophies. Just as the villagers began to drift away, the child darted out of one of the lanes leading off the square, waving. Drummond quickly holstered the revolver. "Hello there, son. Remember me?"

The boy nodded. So he did understand English.

"What's your name?" the captain asked, lifting off the green Titovka cap and mussing the top of the boy's head.

"Józef."

"Good name. Strong name."

Józef clenched his fists and flexed his muscles, Tito's little soldier to a T. His huge eyes were the color of Larkins's tea—a starkly brown brew, steeped to perfection—and his hair brought to mind a field of wheat back home. Who was the boy?

"My man here has something to give you."

But when Larkins knelt down in front of Józef, the child suddenly started giggling. He traced his fingers over the mass of freckles, spattering Larkins's cheeks. Then he tugged off Larkins's beret. Patted his hair. "*Mati, rkeckast!*"

For the first time the woman came close to smiling. "My son has not seen before red hair," she explained.

So, she was indeed his mother. The captain was absurdly pleased, but he couldn't have begun to explain why.

"Aye, that's me, Józef. A ginger-top!" Larkins roared with laughter. "And look here." He pulled the kitten out of his shirt like a magician. Two big, yellow eyes like round suns glinted from the tiny ball of black fur.

Beaming, the child held out two grubby hands to receive the tiny creature.

"Captain Drummond here named him Lucky," Larkins told him, "because back home where we come from, black cats are lucky. What do you think, eh?"

"Lucky!" The kitten purred like a little engine in Józef's arms.

"And how am I supposed to feed it?" asked the woman, smacking her pail down on the cobbles and deliberately slopping water over the captain's boots.

He pointed at a nanny goat with a bulging udder, tethered in the shade of a tree on the other side of the square. "Perhaps Józef can learn to milk that Italian goat." *Hah. A point for me,* he thought, watching her blush slightly.

"My corporal can show him how to do it."

Larkins looked somewhat bemused, but when Józef reached for his hand and urged him toward the purloined goat, he rolled up his sleeves. "We'll give it a try, won't we, Józef?"

Alone with the woman, Captain Drummond was suddenly tongue-tied. He fished around in his pocket for a packet of cigarettes and offered her one. She shook her head.

"So, you just happen to find us. And came all way to give Józef cat?"

The captain lit a cigarette and drew the nicotine deep into his lungs, avoiding her question.

"What's your name?" he asked.

"You interrogate me?"

"Just answer my question."

"My name is Alenka."

"Alenka." Drummond let the sound roll around in his mouth. On his tongue. Savoring this new knowledge.

"I hear the Allies decide to do investigating on the west side the Morgan Line. Your side. Place called Basovizza? Is correct?" She waved her arm in the direction they had just come.

He was not supposed to talk about the Allied inquiry into atrocities committed by the Jugs during their forty-day occupation of Trieste. It was supposed to be strictly secret. But he did want badly to stay beside this woman, to breathe her heady scent for as long as possible.

He glanced over at Larkins and the child, struggling now to get the nanny goat to stand still. Why not stay around a bit longer? Let Larkins continue to spoil the lad for a while. Make the drive worth it—for them both.

"I imagine you can probably guess what we are going to do."

"You *do* interrogate me."

"I don't have to," he responded. "We soon discovered Tito's Fourth Army hauled the unlucky Germans who hadn't made it to safety into the Piazza dell'Unita. Roped them together, most of them already bloodied and battered. Instead of cataloging them and transferring them into POW camps, they summarily condemned them to death."

"Yes, is true. Some shot then and there in piazza."

"And others seem to have disappeared without a trace." He paused. "Which is why we are about to remove some of the debris from the Basovizza mine shaft. We've been told your lot threw German prisoners into that foiba?"

Alenka's clear gray eyes raked his face. Below the high cheekbones, her chin jutted out determinedly. Perhaps ominously. He wondered if she had her Luger concealed somewhere beneath the frock. Drummond allowed himself a moment to imagine just where that somewhere might be.

"What exactly will we find?"

She thrust her hands on her hips. "If you dig down far enough, Captain Drummond, past the fresh corpses, you will find the remains of bodies *not* wearing Nazi uniforms. You will find my husband, Darko Marusic, Political Commissar of Communist Slovene Party, Trieste. Twenty-eight years old. Ambushed with other Partisans on the Karst, November 1943. Then the Germans march *their* prisoners to Basovizza, and one by one hurl them into mine. Alive. All in this village, our village, marched there too, and forced to watch."

Christ Almighty. A murdered husband.

The captain pulled back his shoulders. He had never asked for this sodding job in the first place, this relentless cavalcade of horror and depression. Lost for words, he turned away. His batman had succeeded in milking the goat into a container of some sort. It looked like an empty hardtack tin. Lucky was lapping up his meal, and Józef was yattering away to Larkins in a mixture of Slovene and English. But Alenka was not finished with him. She stepped close to the captain, shaking her finger in his face, her cheeks blazing with anger.

"What was done this spring—was how you say—an eye for an eye."

Chapter Nine

AS THE CAPTAIN had earlier admitted to Alenka, there was to be an Anglo-American fact-finding mission into the alleged atrocities committed by Tito's army in the Italian village of Basovizza last May. Well, it was Italian then—and was still Italian according to the demarcation zone, but like the old man in Rupingrande had pointed out, "nobody is really sure where they live anymore."

On a late September day, Captain Drummond's Land Rover escorted a convoy of Americans with mechanical scoops and earth diggers, along with two British three-tonners filled with armed Tommies, up to the Karst. As the road grew steeper, they were reduced to a crawl. Engines whined. Tires skidded. Gears screeched. But once on the plateau, they picked up speed again. On the outskirts of Basovizza, he waved the Americans off to the right. They were to follow clearly marked signs along a narrow lane to the mine in question. Orders from Brigadier Eve, in overall charge of Allied Command, were to remove as much debris as possible in the time allotted, but to exercise care in consideration of what they were almost certainly going to find when the contents of the mine were exposed.

The British heavy lorries continued into the village proper. Basovizza wasn't large. No maze of streets and blind alleys to worry about—therefore, less possibility of snipers. The place seemed quiet, but there was an undercurrent of tension. It was pretty clear they were being watched. Curtains tweaked behind dusty windows. Detecting when civilians posed a threat, deciding when or when not to shoot, was the most difficult judgment facing an army of occupation.

The lorries disgorged thirty-odd soldiers, who promptly set up an armed perimeter around the houses. A few children emerged, hoping for handouts. Larkins tossed them pieces of the American candy and chewing gum that he was still getting from the Yanks on a regular basis.

The captain opted to hold the investigation outdoors. There was a vacant field of grass adjacent to the church which would suit his purpose well enough. Much safer, given the nature of the assignment. The weather was warm, the air loud with insects, the sky a pale blue—exactly the color of the dress Alenka had worn when he saw her last. It would be hot by afternoon. The tops of the mountains loomed through a light film of mist. Drummond told Larkins to commandeer half a dozen tables from the local café, and all the chairs available, while he went in search of the mayor.

One of the children, chewing furiously on a ball of pink gum, led him and the translator to a larger home nearby, whitewashed, with a red tile roof. He knocked. Immediately, an elderly woman clutching a broom opened the door. He stepped into the cool, tiled entryway, removed his cap, and laid down his swagger stick.

"Captain James Drummond, on behalf of Allied Command."

The mayor rose from a wood-carved chair beside a tiled mantelpiece, matching the entry. Probably in his fifties, dark skin, thick black moustache. His nod was curt, but he offered his hand. So, he was prepared to cooperate. Good. Helped the captain figure out whether or not there was likely to be any trouble.

"We are here to conduct an investigation into the actions of the Yugoslav Fourth Army during their recent occupation of Trieste," Drummond explained.

He waited patiently for the interpreter to translate. "Does he understand?"

"Yes, sir."

"Every inhabitant in the village must attend this inquiry. In the open field beside the church. Right away."

After listening intently to the interpreter, the mayor nodded.

"Any stragglers will be rounded up."

The mayor nodded again. He gave little away.

"Thank you for cooperating, sir. Difficult time for us all."

He was a hard chap to read, thought Drummond, but surely, no matter the allegiance of these people, they would want to move on with their lives after the horror of the German occupation.

A short time later, an assorted group of about fifty had assembled, muttering amongst themselves. Most of the women wore black peasant garb, but one or two of the younger amongst them had on old-fashioned skirts and blouses. The men were all old—no sign of healthy males anywhere. Many of them had been shipped to Germany to work in factories, and were only now straggling back to home countries—those who had survived, anyway.

Captain Drummond sat himself behind one of the tables, set out his cigarettes and a pad to jot notes if necessary, and spread open a detailed layout of the village and the surrounding area. The other tables were set up with typewriters and a mound of paper to officially record the proceedings. Two British typists, two American typists. The mayor addressed the people in both Slovene and Italian to explain the purpose of the gathering.

First to speak, and obviously revered by his flock, was the local priest. "On behalf of my congregation, I will tell you what happened here. The prisoners brought up from Trieste by the Yugoslav army were collaborators, Italian fascists, German military. We had no say in this matter, but still we supported Tito in what they were doing. Wholeheartedly."

His people nodded agreement.

"Over the course of about one week, the Yugoslav Fourth Army questioned roughly four hundred collaborators and political prisoners right here in this field. Then they mowed them down with machine guns."

Drummond winced. He knew well enough what mown-down bodies looked like. The Germans had a taste for this form of execution too—they had left this particular calling card all over the countryside as they retreated from Italy, pursued by the Allies. He lit a cigarette. "And then what happened to them? Where are the bodies now?"

The priest gestured down the road. The moan and whine of the heavy equipment could clearly be heard. "Thrown in the foiba."

"And the Italian fascists?"

"The Yugoslavs let us interrogate them." The audience nodded in agreement again. "We accuse them of their crimes. All fair and just. Each charge verified by at least three different people."

"And the crimes were?"

"Torture of our relatives. Murder of our families. The burning down of our homes, all over Karst. Always the prisoners admit their crimes."

I bet they did. When the priest explained that they had all been shot and added to the already-massacred in the foiba, the captain wasn't surprised. Just sickened. "I suppose you never thought to give them a decent burial?" Drummond asked, staring pointedly at his clerical vestments and the huge silver cross dangling round his neck.

The old men spat. The womenfolk hissed. The priest didn't say a word.

"What about the captured Germans?"

A young woman rose from her seat. "You want to know, Englishman, what Tito people did to them? I tell you. They tie them together, two by two. Like animals in ark of Noah. They march them to foiba. Shot one of each pair in head. Then we watch them fall deep down in pit." She laughed.

The sun beat down. The typewriters clattered. The captain smoked till his throat was raw.

But at last he was done. They had got what they came for: a detailed account of exactly what Tito's Fourth Army had done up here. Thanking the mayor for his cooperation, he made it clear that if any charges were brought it would be against the Yugoslav Fourth Army, not the villagers of Basovizza.

How much of the damned slaughter pit they would get to excavate was anybody's guess. Orders were to wrap up the inquiry as fast as possible. Privately, Drummond suspected the whole thing would end up a whitewash. The powers-to-be would not want to ruffle the feathers of the Soviet Union, still considered a victorious ally of the war, by making war-crime charges against their comrades, the Jugs.

Before heading back to Trieste and the welcome relief of several stiff whiskeys at the club, the captain had Larkins drive him to the Basovizza Foiba to see how the Americans were progressing. His counterpart, a Lieutenant Dick Harvey, was overseeing the excavation.

After parking, Drummond picked his way over the flat, barren landscape of windswept, scraggy trees, a scrubland of rocks, and discarded, ancient mining equipment that had been used variously since the beginning of the century to search for coal. A smell of diesel hung in the air, and very noticeably, not a bird sang in the miserable place.

Harvey's men had removed a substantial amount of earth. As Drummond kicked through the debris, it became obvious the mine shaft had also been used as a local garbage dump.

Possibly to help conceal the bodies below. It was a disgusting mix of soil, tree branches, metal containers, rotted food, even what looked like human feces.

Drummond spotted something gleaming in the mountain of waste. When he leaned down for a closer look he recoiled in horror, thinking it to be a human eye. On closer examination he realized it was a glass eye, an artificial eye, buried in a clod of rock-hard shit. It gazed at him in pleading despair. The white portion was realistically tinted with fine pink veins, the black pupil surrounded by a dark green iris. It would never be known who it had belonged to, but considering the cost of acquiring such a professional prosthetic, it would most likely have been one of the luckless Germans. The whole place was thick with untold stories.

Drummond walked over to the edge of the pit. A rope ladder was anchored to the ground and dangled limply into the gaping cavity. He removed his cap. Stared into the darkness.

"What passing bells for these who die as cattle?"

The poet Wilfred Owen had written those words toward the end of the Great War. To what end? It had turned out not to be the war to end all others. Far from it. Here was the proof.

Despite the blazing hot afternoon, Drummond's skin felt suddenly icy cold, and he tried to rub some warmth into his bare arms. Alenka had said her husband's body was down here somewhere. Further down. Far down. What was his name? Darko Marusic, the captain remembered. But after two years of deterioration, it would be well-nigh impossible to identify his body, except possibly through remnants of clothing or certain emblems. And that was only supposing they could stay longer to excavate more thoroughly, which almost certainly wasn't going to happen.

Harvey was approaching, a sheaf of papers in his arms. Wanting to make a report on the day's work, presumably. Was what they were doing in the short space of time they'd been given enough to claim justice for all the dead? Hardly. Far too many bones deep underground. At most, it might offer justice to the most recent victims slaughtered in revenge. But not for the Darkos of this world. Not for Alenka. Not for their boy. Left with nothing at all to bury.

Chapter Ten

THE FAT FILE, stamped *TOP SECRET*, lay on Drummond's desk. The joint British/United States inquiry. He and Lieutenant Harvey had worked hard on their portion of the report, but they both agreed it was sugarcoated. It essentially declared the local population had kept their heads down, and the Jugs had performed well in getting Trieste functioning again during their forty-day rule. The British Psychological Warfare Branch even reported that the Jugs' behavior and discipline were consistently "good," particularly the respect shown to Allied officers.

A mixed bag, clearly belying their own feelings and findings. Tito's forces had used multiple foibe on the Karst as mass graves for political opponents and collaborators, not just the mine shaft at Basovizza. Exactly as the young woman had reported to Drummond, the medical examiner had confirmed forty German corpses in uniform, roped together in twos, one shot to the head administered for each pair of prisoners. But as they had feared, in an effort to keep the Yugoslavs happy, many of the facts had been swept under the rug.

Larkins appeared in the office. "Slow day, sir?"

"As it happens, yes. Report done. Ready to turn in."

"Time to play then, sir."

"Play?" The captain tried to shake his head clear of the horrific sights they had recently uncovered. He and Harvey had supervised the recovery of the German corpses from the mine shaft. Tedious, mind-numbing work. They had eventually buried the bodies individually in wooden coffins in a nearby field. Then, as expected, came the order to stand down. Close up the mine. So, there Alenka's husband was to remain forever.

"Thought we could show the little nipper how to play a bit of footer," said Larkins, producing a round leather ball from behind his back.

"You didn't get that off the Yanks!"

"No, sir. They know nothing 'bout proper football."

Captain Drummond realized he should caution Larkins not to get too attached to the lad. Sooner or later he would be moving on, going home to England. Yet the captain recognized it was the poor chap's way of filling a void in his life. His own wife and son had died in a bombing raid on the Tyne shortly after he and Drummond had reached Tunis in North Africa.

Drummond was thoroughly fed up. The whole business up in Basovizza had left a bad taste in his mouth. Another trip to Opatje Selo was tempting. To hell with the village being in Slovenia. He was willing to overlook that particular fact. If necessary, he could claim to be chasing fascists still on the loose. He didn't know what he thought about the international situation anymore. Why couldn't they all put their weapons down and go home? The end of the war just seemed to be making things worse. All he *did* know was that he had an overwhelming longing to settle his eyes on Alenka again.

ALONG WITH A HAMPER of American food wheedled from Larkins's pals in the US commissary, they signed out and sped off, breaking the rules once again. In Opatje Selo, Larkins parked the jeep in the shade of some trees behind the local church, where there was a scrap of grass large enough for a game of football. He reminded Drummond of a benign version of the Pied Piper—within minutes of setting up makeshift goalposts, he had attracted every child in the village, including Józef. Larkins taught them how to dribble, kick, and, for the most part, keep their hands off the ball.

The village women soon gathered, settling on the ground to watch their children. It seemed they were prepared to accept two foreign soldiers showing up in their village uninvited. How exactly had Alenka explained them? Drummond wondered, as he hauled the hamper out of the vehicle and walked over. "Enjoy," he muttered, presenting the women with the food before spinning on his heel.

For a moment, he wished he could wander about the plateau for a while. Considering the precarious situation he had put himself in on the wrong side of the Morgan Line, however, he climbed back into the jeep. He thought about his own child at home: Georgina, born after he was shipped abroad. Four years old now. His eyes pricked, and his throat felt parched as the North African desert. He was rubbing his eyes when he felt a tap on his shoulder.

Instinctively, he knew it was Alenka. No adversary's touch would cause such a surge of joy. Did this woman have any idea how much he ached for her? He, a married man, *and* a father. But he couldn't help himself. He didn't care if she shouted at him again. About her husband. Or Basovizza. Or any damned thing, really. He simply longed with all his being to be close to her. Possess a tiny piece of her.

"You again, Captain Drummond. What you think about so hard?"

He busied himself with a cigarette till he was sure he was composed enough to respond. "Watching the children makes me think of my daughter. I have never met her."

Alenka held up a carafe of wine and two thick tumblers. "I join you?"

Was she really proposing they share a drink together? His heart thundered so hard in his chest it caused real pain.

"What will your neighbors think?" he asked, stalling for time. He was bending all the rules these days.

"They will not take notice. They like Yankee food too much."

Before he could stop her, she had climbed into the jeep beside him, apparently not caring what anyone thought. She poured wine for them both. "Those thoughts?"

Drummond tossed his cigarette butt out onto the road. "I get leave the end of next month. Three weeks. First time in England since the war began. I will meet my little girl then."

Alenka's pale gray eyes seemed to see through his skin, through his flesh and blood, and get into his mind. "And you are not knowing how it will be."

"I'm worried." His voice sounded shrill in his ears. Almost hysterical. Damn it. What a fool he was.

"I think when you see the child, it will become easy."

Alenka had not mentioned his wife, he noticed, dragging on a fresh cigarette. But the fact was that meeting the child's mother again worried him too. Over the course of the long, long war, Mary had ebbed in his memory like a receding tide. It felt sometimes as if there were nothing left but a black-and-white image in a silver frame of someone he had married years ago, holding a child he had never met. The years in between had been fashioned by forces so extreme, he didn't know how he was going to step away from the brink of his here and now into his yesterdays.

"Tell me about this England. Your home. Where it is?"

He realized how little thought he had given it recently. "My house is one of many in a stone-built terrace. In a city called

Newcastle. On the northeast coast of England. But my favorite place is a cottage by the sea for holidays. Although for most of the war, my wife could not take our daughter to the beach. All mined and tank-trapped, in case of an invasion."

They sat quietly for a while with the tumblers of wine. It felt so normal. Drummond had never been so close to her. The heady scent of sea spray and pine forests filled his nostrils, making him dizzy. The children raced after Larkins up and down the patch of grass, lost in the simple pleasure of playing. How many of them had fathers still alive?

"Does Józef remember his father?"

Alenka shook her head. "Not so much. He was young. When Darko is murdered, I run into the mountains of Slovenia. Join Partisans."

"With Józef?"

"Of course, with Józef. I would not leave my son behind."

"He doesn't look like you at all. Did he take after his father?"

"No. My husband was dark-haired, like me. It was joke we shared, where Józef came from." But her eyes were sad when she said it. "We loved each other."

Of course they had. The captain had loved his wife long ago, when they married. So why did the words she uttered cause his stomach to curdle? Just as well he was going on leave. Away from Alenka. Far, far away.

"Tell me what you did in the mountains. With the Partisans?"

"I am nurse. So, needed badly. Worked in Franja Partisan Hospital, near Cerkno. But we learn to shoot too. Operate machine guns. Even how to lay a minefield."

Drummond hated mine-clearing, another one of his "mopping-up" duties. More than anything, he hated the randomness of it. The area was still riddled with unexploded ordnance.

The Allies had always mapped their fields, but not so the damned Germans. Or the groveling wops, who had readily done their German masters' bidding. What odd allies they had been, the Germans and Italians, while it had lasted. Drummond detested both, but the Germans were straightforward in all they did, be it their remarkable military ability and discipline or their unbelievable cruelty. The Italians, on the other hand, swayed in the wind too much for his liking, accepting for the most part their former ally's occupation, even turning in their own countrymen when expedient.

"Many nurses come to hospital with children," Alenka continued. "So, we set up school. In funny way, the hospital peaceful. Hidden in ravine, protected by steep cliff walls. Stream at bottom for children to play in. Best of all, we not ever discovered."

What an incredible life this woman has led. If the Germans had invaded Britain, it would not have taken long for a resistance movement to spring up there too. Of that the captain was sure. How would Mary have responded? Played it safe, or fought back? He could not quite picture his wife lugging Georgina onto the wild, heather- and gorse-covered moors of northern England, handling weapons, blowing up bridges and railway lines.

"Many nationalities come to hospital. Many Allied airmen. So, I learn English. The children too. Good, no?"

"Truly remarkable."

He went back to the now-fanciful idea of an occupied Great Britain. The British were notorious for not learning other languages, the argument being that there was no need to bother since everyone else in the world spoke English. But presumably it would have been vital to learn some German under an occupation. How would that have played out, he wondered.

"Tell me, Alenka, why you and Józef came to settle in this particular village?"

"My house here." She gestured vaguely behind the church. "Been in Darko family for generations. After war over, women with children could go home if not needed more. And for Józef sake, I decide time to come home to Slovenia."

"Except it's not a separate country. Very much part of Yugoslavia."

"Of course. What we all want. Strong nation, all together one." Alenka smiled. "By the way, so is Trst. What you call Trieste. Or soon will be."

Captain Drummond lit another cigarette. "Don't be too sure about that, Alenka. I'm worried the city could become a real flashpoint between the three world powers. Personally, I've no wish to see another war fought over the strategic port of Trieste."

She touched his shoulder again, eyes bright, inquiring. "You believe this, do you?"

"I really do. You must take care."

All the time he spoke, he was conscious only of her warm hand, radiating through his battle-dress blouse.

"Maybe you right. I do not argue. Not with armed Tommy!" Suddenly a deep chuckle gurgled up from her throat. "Even if the Tommy is park on wrong side of line with Yugoslav Partisan in his driver seat!"

Chapter Eleven

THE CAPTAIN REELED out of the officers' club and
clambered into his waiting jeep. He waved a chit under
Larkins's nose. "Blighters are making me pay my mess
bill! Before my leave next week."

"Yes, sir, Captain Drummond, sir."

"You know what this means?" Drummond slurred his words.
"What we need to do?"

"Sell some loot?"

"Exactly." Officers sold off "spoils of war" in much the same way
the ranks bartered their ciggie rations around town. Blind eyes
were turned when necessary.

Larkins drove through the Piazza dell'Unita, empty of anyone
but a few troops maintaining curfew. Rattled over the railway tracks
that ran along the waterfront, where hulking warships loomed like
beached whales alongside the quays. Sea spray peppered their skin.
A lone seagull, unaware that it was night, screeched and dipped
overhead.

After the four-mile drive along the shore out of the city, Larkins
parked in the grounds behind Castello di Miramare. The stables
and coach house had proven a treasure trove for the British, filled
as they were with vast amounts of property stolen from the Jews
by the Germans during their occupation of Italy—china, crystal
glassware, candelabra, rugs, all abandoned when they were forced
to flee Miramare in the spring. What artwork had been found the
Allies housed separately, awaiting examination by art historians

in hopes of eventual return to museums. Private owners too, if they had survived, although the news of the extermination camps filtering in made that seem less and less likely.

Larkins lit a lantern, and the captain opened the lock with the combination of numbers he had memorized. Together, they loaded the jeep.

"Drive it up to the hills," muttered Drummond. "Flog the lot. Don't take less than a hundred quid. They're villains, the wops, with their black-market rackets. Whatever is left after I pay my bill is yours to keep."

"Yes, sir. Thank you, sir."

Drummond heaved himself awkwardly into the jeep, hampered by the amount of alcohol he had consumed. "Get me back to my quarters first, Larkins."

"Hold on a jiffy, Captain."

Larkins dived back into one of the horse boxes and dragged out a child's sledge—never used, polished runners, glinting in the lantern glow.

"Permission to drive over to Opatje Selo later, sir?"

"Larkins?"

"This beauty is just the ticket for the nipper, Józef. *And* his pals. Play in the snow, like."

Why not? Too bad he couldn't take it home for his own child. But that would be no easy task on the long train rides through Europe!

CAPTAIN JAMES DRUMMOND SLOUCHED deep inside his khaki greatcoat. The train was freezing cold. No heat at all. Rain streaked the soot-grimed windows. The carriage was a fug of cigarette smoke. Deep in the captain's pocket was the pass granting him three weeks' home leave, November 30–December 21.

When the train pulled into Newcastle Central Station, he heaved a kit bag, splattered with numerous unidentifiable stains, off the overhead rack and stepped onto the platform. The cavernous building was deserted. He slogged over the pedestrian bridge spanning the railway lines, boots ringing eerily through the rafters, startling to life a few dusty, pink-eyed pigeons.

He had written a letter to Mary explaining about the leave, but had no idea whether it had reached England ahead of him. In any event, he could not show up in the middle of the night. It would scare the living daylights out of his sleeping family.

When he realized this, a profound sense of relief swept over him. A reprieve of sorts. He wasn't ready. Not yet. Almost five years since he had seen his wife. And their child, an enigma. Surely, he reasoned, a few more hours would not make any difference. Especially if they were not aware of his impending return. He realized he stank. Sweat. Vomit from seasick servicemen during the Channel crossing.

Shaking a few English coins from his pocket, he paid for a wash in the station lavatory, reserved for gentlemen. The tiled bathroom was small but surprisingly clean. Sloughing off the filthy uniform, he sank into a tub full of hot water. With the miserable scrap of soap, he scrubbed his body raw. How long could be stay hidden in the cubby-hole? An hour? A day? A week? Three weeks? But when the water grew cold, he dried himself off and found a reasonably clean uniform in the kitbag, dutifully pressed and packed by Larkins.

When dawn broke over Newcastle, his ragged, war-weary city, the captain hoisted the bag onto his back and trudged through the streets, deliberately avoiding Grey Street and the bank he would have to return to when he was demobbed late next year. The reality filled him with dread. How would it be to shuffle papers and add up columns of figures in a stuffy room after commanding a company of men, being responsible for tactical decisions involving life and death, supplying ground logistical support in the midst of battle? He feared the benign safety and boredom of the office would suck him in. Close over his head. Drown him. He plodded on.

Up Northumberland Street. Along Osborne Road. Past the Royal Grammar School. Through Brandling Park. Down Eskdale Terrace to Number Twenty-Five, the iron railings around the small front garden long gone for guns. An empty glass bottle stood on the doorstep. In the distance he caught the rattle of the milk cart and the steady clip-clop of its horse.

Captain James Drummond kept walking. Away from his home. He walked another mile onto the Town Moor, a vast area of common land, where freemen of the city still had the legal right to graze cattle. It was such a long time since he had been privy to open space, unimpeded by trees, walls, or the possibility of sniper nests. But at the same time, the quiet was a bit unnerving. No rumbling tanks; no roaring planes; no exploding mines.

He stretched out on a wooden bench. Used the kitbag for a pillow. With a couple of hours' rest, maybe he could find the courage to go home, step into the past, and be who he was before the blood, pieces of flesh, and mutilated bodies informed his dreams.

Why hadn't he insisted Larkins accompany him home to serve as a sort of buffer? Larkins knew how to take care of him, protect him. Larkins understood him. Only Larkins had been oddly reluctant to return with him. Was it simply the tug of Opatje Selo, the opportunities to spoil the children who had survived the war? Drummond wasn't sure.

Finally, he slept.

SEPTEMBER 1994

Chapter Twelve

WHEN WE REACH Trieste, I have little trouble finding the Savoia Excelsior Palace on the waterfront promenade. Its sheer size makes it an easy landmark. As I pull alongside, a doorman immediately appears and arranges for our luggage to be carried inside.

"Good grief, Georgina. My officers' club was right here! In this building!"

"I had no idea. Expect it will look a bit different now, fifty years on."

I take my father's arm, and together we climb the shining marble steps, negotiate the revolving doors, and cross the hotel's black-and-white marble floor. While Daddy reacquaints himself with the ornate pillars surrounding the lounge area and the even more ornate gold ceiling, I check us in at the reception desk.

"Right here. British officers' mess," he is explaining to a rather bemused young porter. "End of the war. 1945."

The poor fellow looks as if he doesn't understand a word, but nods enthusiastically all the same. If I recall correctly from what Daddy tried to explain to me on the drive from Venice, this area was occupied by Germans, then briefly fell under the Yugoslavs, followed by American, British, and Commonwealth troops, right up till 1952. It is probably a part of history the locals would prefer to forget.

I insist on a suite, so that in the event of a nightmare, I can reach Daddy quickly. Luckily enough, I get us adjoining rooms

75

overlooking the sea. Each has a large bed, as well as a comfortable sofa with lots of pillows, a good reading lamp, and prints of Trieste landmarks on the walls. The furniture is dark and substantial, and the wood floors are covered in thick oriental rugs. An eclectic mix, which appeals to me.

Michael would have appreciated it too, but I brush that thought aside. This is not the time to wallow in my what might-have-beens. It is a time to help my father solve whatever matter has suddenly propelled him back to this city by the sea.

After such a long day, we are both tired. I call room service and order prosciutto, salami, cheese, and olives, along with a basket of bread and pumpkin-seed oil and a bottle of local wine. After the waiter has thrown a white cloth over the table on our balcony and set out the simple feast, we toast one another—"Happy days"— and start munching appreciatively. "So, what do we do tomorrow, Daddy? What's first on the agenda?"

"Not sure, darling."

"The ball's in your court, you know. We're here at your request."

Just as I finish speaking, the sun sets into the Adriatic, and Castello di Miramare springs abruptly into being at the far end of the bay, illuminated with floodlights. What a glorious surprise. I'm spellbound. When I was a little girl, I believed my daddy lived in a fairy castle. I can see now I'd got it right all along! I half expect the Queen of the Fairies to wave her wand and magic us over the water, into her kingdom.

Daddy is less inspired. "Wasn't lit up like Disneyland when I lived there," he remarks. "It was still smothered in camouflage netting when we marched in."

"Does it upset you? Seeing it like this?"

"No, not really. In fact, I think I'd like to go and see it again tomorrow."

76

"Me too."

For a while then there's silence, the two of us simply sitting and watching the waves beyond. When a briny breeze blows in from the sea, we reluctantly leave the balcony, turning in shortly thereafter.

BUT NOT LONG AFTERWARD, my father has one of his nightmares. Clear and distinct. And for the first time that I can remember, a specific name is added to his desperate cries.

"Stop! Józef! Stop!"

I reach him quickly through the adjoining door. Daddy is sitting on the edge of the bed, breathing heavily. The lamp is on. I notice immediately the picture of the inscrutable sledge-boy, protruding from a heavy leather tome on the bedside table: *Poems of Byron, Keats, and Shelley.* I bought the book for Daddy in 1967 for his birthday.

I pour us both glasses of water and settle beside him. "Who is Józef?"

"Józef?" he mutters.

"You were shouting that name." I reach over and pull the photograph loose. "Was this little boy called Józef?"

"Yes." Daddy nods his head. "That is Józef."

"What happened to him?"

"Happened?" He tugs on the sleeve of his pajamas, as if trying to reassure himself he's still here.

"You were begging him to stop."

"Stop?"

Exasperated, I try a different approach. "Something momentous *must* have happened for you to dream about him—to keep his picture all these years."

"You know, dear Georgie Girl, I don't think after all there is any going back."

"But that's precisely what we're doing in Trieste, isn't it? Going back."

Daddy sips from the glass of water I gave him. Puts it down. Takes hold of my arm. "Can we talk tomorrow, darling? When I've had time to think. I'm very tired. I don't want you to be ashamed of me."

"Nonsense." I help him back to bed and kiss him goodnight.

But he said more or less the same thing the night he rifled through his old suitcase. Is Paul right? Have I made a bad decision, bringing my father here? Obviously, Józef is part of this strange journey into the past. But Józef has been hidden away, unacknowledged, for fifty years. So what in hell happened to cause this sudden mad dash to the place where Daddy served out his time in the army?

For the first time, I scrutinize the old snapshot properly. There is no likeness to Daddy, or anyone else in our family. Bemused, I slip sledge-boy and his secret back between the pages of the book of poetry. If Daddy was using the picture as a bookmark, I have certainly lost his place.

Waiting for him to fall asleep, I curl up on the sofa and think about how I was able to push my own secret far into its metaphorical suitcase. A time in my life that is gone forever. Yet, scenes still flicker unbidden when I least expect them, as if I have blundered into the heart of an old film.

PENNY AND I WERE in the conference room at Moonbeam Mountain Publishers, waiting to speak with the illustrator of my third book, whom I had not yet met. The galleys were spread out across the table. It was a simple enough tale, about a little boy who discovers in the middle of the night that all the polar bears on his pajamas have run away. I was delighted with how the illustrator had interpreted my words through his art, and in the process captured exactly the essence of the world I had imagined for my character.

When Michael O'Hannery entered the room, I quite literally went weak at the knees. Such a cliché, but it describes my reaction perfectly. He was taller than me, rugged in a gentle kind of way, if that makes any sense; thick, chestnut-brown hair swept back off his face, curled around his collar. He wore faded blue jeans and a heavy plaid shirt, with a duffel coat flung over his arm. Laugh lines burrowed around his hazel eyes, sloping downward to a mouth so inviting, I struggled to maintain a professional demeanor. Though he greeted Penny with kisses on both cheeks and simply shook my hand, the room fairly sizzled with an instant frisson between the two of us.

The discussion that followed pretty much took place in a fog as far as I was concerned. Apparently the galleys were approved and dispatched to the printer. Penny excused herself to attend another meeting, but Michael invited me to have lunch—much to my relief. Already, I couldn't bear to let him go.

All the time we strolled up Marylebone Lane toward George Street, a snatch of song played in my head: "*On a wonderful day like today . . . I could kiss everybody . . .*" I wanted to frisk along like a lamb, shouting the words at the top of my lungs. Me, a fortyish, married mother of two. I was utterly besotted.

In the George Bar of Durrants Hotel, we toasted the success of our first picture book collaboration with a bottle of champagne. I was unfamiliar with the watering hole, but totally charmed nevertheless—intimate atmosphere, wood-paneled leather settees, a roaring fire, old oils, candlelight even in the middle of the day.

Michael asked me endless questions about my stories—where they came from, how I began, how they unfolded, how the settings became characters. All the while he listened closely to what I had to say, giving me his full attention, gazing steadily into my eyes.

Which, in a peculiar way, caused a heavy ache in my heart. For so long, every member of the Tribe Wharton had made me feel unremarkable. Irrelevant. I was constantly referred to as "Paul's wife" or "our Brit," never introduced as a writer. And of course, the coup de grace from Ellen: "When are you going to write a book for grown-ups, dear?"

When the barman rang time, I was obscurely sad. I didn't want the afternoon to end. Nor, apparently, did Michael O'Hannery. "I want to show you something special, Georgina—a particular painting," he said, guiding me across the street from Durrants to the Wallace Collection.

Once inside the art gallery, we wandered through several exhibition rooms until we came face-to-face with the canvas Michael wished to share with me. "*The Swing*, by Fragonard," he announced, slipping his hand easily under my elbow. It felt like the most natural gesture in the world.

The sensuality of the oil was not lost on me. I was beguiled. A tall, blonde woman on a swing kicked her slipper into the air. Had Michael brought me here because there was a certain likeness between myself and this woman from a time gone by? The champagne I'd drunk at lunchtime still fizzed through my veins, firing up every nerve ending in my body. Never had I felt more alive.

There is, in fact, an entire story painted on the canvas, and a decadent one at that. In the background, entwined cupids rather daringly caress a beehive; an angel sculpture gestures "*keep the secret*"; a small dog barks "*danger*"; in the background, behind the woman, a man who can only be her husband pushes the swing, oblivious to what is happening all around him.

Her lover, although half hidden in shrubbery, is still at the forefront of the painting, offered a privileged view of his lover as the force of the swing whips her voluminous skirts above her knees. His delight is shown by a symbolic doff of his hat.

"Otherwise known as *The Sting of Love*," Michael whispered in my ear.

This man, whom I had only just met, was making it abundantly clear how he felt. Truth be told, I was flattered. But my tongue was glued fast to the roof of my mouth. I was unable to make any indication that I understood the subtext of the painting beyond a slight smile.

When the gallery closed, we stood side by side on the front steps in the twilight. A hum of city traffic with its cacophony of horns churned distantly up and down the Edgeware Road.

"Is it time for you to leave me, Georgina?"

Helpless to obey the sensible, middle-aged-married-lady part of my brain, I blithely responded, "No, not yet." We strolled hand in hand through the late-day crowds, past Selfridges, down Park Lane, through the winding mews of Belgravia, toward the river.

Stars popped through the sky like sparklers. We leaned over the parapet, side by side, gazing at the greenish hue of the Thames. The tide ran fast, and pebbles washed against the shore.

Michael cupped my cheeks in his hands and kissed me for the first time. "I believe I loved you before I met you, Georgina Drummond. Drawn as I was to a wistful, willful, nostalgic woman . . . yearning for a certain missing something . . ."

The light from the river-walk lamps spilled like puddles of syrup onto the pavement. I longed to touch Michael's clean-shaven face. Curl my fingers through the hair that looped over the collar of his duffel coat. I wanted that man as I had never wanted before. But now it was time to bid him a hasty goodbye as custom dictated. Now was the time to fly back to my family as fast as possible. Now was the time to break the spell that he had somehow cast over me.

"I am married," I muttered. "A mother."

FOOTSTEPS OUTSIDE IN THE corridor snap me back to reality. I'm in the hotel suite in Trieste. Keys rattle. Voices shout. A door slams. But Daddy is asleep now, snoring softly. Keeping his secret. For now. For how long?

I tiptoe back to my bedroom, keeping a secret of my own.

Chapter Thirteen

DADDY IS DETERMINEDLY glossing over his nightmare, claiming he can't remember a thing about it, which I don't believe for a minute. He adamantly insists he is ready to drive along the coast to the once-upon-a-time British Eighth Army Headquarters, so I don't argue. I've wanted to see Castello di Miramare for myself ever since I was a little girl, when he sent me drawings of the castle after he returned from his first leave home.

Drawings of fairy turrets; magic staircases; a throne room; seagulls on a ceiling; garden statues; a fountain; crashing waves. I had glued each of the pictures carefully in a scrapbook. At bedtime, I'd tell myself stories about the princes and princesses who lived in the castle. When I was older, I lost the scrapbook. One day it mysteriously disappeared from my desk while I was at school. When I burst into tears, my mother told me to "grow up."

We don't need jackets—it is warm and sunny, and there's no sign of the infamous bora wind that pummels the city late each year. By the time it arrives, of course, I will have my father safely back home in England.

I deliberately avoid quizzing Daddy about Józef, deciding it is better to wait until we can sit quietly to have that conversation. Perhaps this evening. Having no real idea what his role was here, I'm more concerned that coming face-to-face with Miramare will prove upsetting for Daddy. When we approach the fluffy, white fortress on its rocky spur of limestone through a crenulated gatehouse, it is exactly as he had depicted it, save for one detail—the narrow approach road is lined with motor coaches.

"Why, it's nothing more than a tourist attraction now!" Daddy sounds offended rather than dispirited by what he sees.

"Well, at least it hasn't been turned into a Hilton Hotel! Or a convention center!"

I find a parking spot, and we walk around the fountain to a low stone wall where we can drink in the view: the vivid, steel-blue Adriatic and the gracious coral-tinged buildings, shimmering along the city waterfront at the end of the bay.

"Are you up for this visit, Daddy?" I ask, taking hold of his elbow. "We don't have to go inside the castle, you know."

But he plods over the gravel without a word, so we enter the portico and push into the entrance hall. The ticket office is to our left; I quickly pay our entrance fee and purchase a brochure. We continue on through the office and bookshop as indicated with arrows, and step first into the main atrium. There is the magnificent, carved wooden staircase that I remember from Daddy's sketches. He is momentarily overwhelmed, as I had feared. "Take your time," I whisper. "When you're ready to leave, just let me know."

We wander through the apartments of Emperor Maximilian and his wife Carlotta, furnished, according to the brochure, exactly as they had been when the they lived in the castle.

"It surely didn't look like this when you were here?" I remark.

"Oh, my goodness me, no," Daddy replies. "The place was bare, other than a few desks and chairs the Germans had left. When it was obvious by the middle of the war that the Germans were going to occupy Trieste, the local people managed to remove all these furnishings. Hid them God knows where, much as England emptied our museums before the bombing started."

"Yes, it explains right here that restoration began in 1955 after

Trieste was handed back to Italy again," I say, waving the booklet around. "Most of the furnishings were recovered."

But Daddy doesn't have time to read it. "You wouldn't believe what this place looked like in my day. Boxes of files spilling over with papers; overflowing ashtrays; half-drunk cups of tea littered about on every available desk or table; hobnailed boots scuffing these magnificent floors."

"Oh, I think I can!"

"But I bet you didn't know the castle always had a reputation for bringing bad luck to its owners."

"Tell me."

"Archduke Maximilian of Hapsburg, brother of the Austrian Emperor Franz Joseph, started building Miramare in 1856 for his beloved bride, Carlotta."

"Would you call the architecture Gothic Revival?"

"Believe so," Daddy says with a nod. "Shortly afterward, Maximilian was declared Emperor of Mexico and never saw it completed. Sadly, he was put up against a wall in Mexico and shot. Carlotta went mad. Understandably."

Poor woman. How sad. Mexico seems such a peculiar acquisition on the part of the Hapsburg Empire, even for those days.

"And believe it or not, the unlucky Archduke Franz Ferdinand stayed right here in Miramare in the spring of 1914, and you know what happened to him later that summer."

Indeed, I do. He and his much-maligned wife were assassinated in Sarajevo. The harbinger for what quickly turned into World War I.

"Much later, the Duke of Aosta moved into the castle. But five years after that, the poor sod was ordered overseas by Mussolini, to be Viceroy of Ethiopia. Bad move. He never made it home."

"The castle does have its share of tragic tales."

"Well, tragic or not, we set up Eighth Army Headquarters here in the summer of '45 without much incident."

Suddenly he stops. Scratches his head. "Good God."

He snatches the booklet out of my hand and starts reading. "Room 7. Carlotta's sitting room," gasps my father. "Well, I'll be damned!"

Light blue silk hangs from the walls. An antique fortepiano takes pride of place. I much admire a chest of drawers, decorated with bronze plaques of flowers, leaves, and various figures. Daddy shakes his head. "All the time this was my office, I had no idea who had been here before me."

We allow a group of French tourists to pass us. Daddy needs time to digest this discovery. And I need time to try to imagine his life then—a young soldier, living and breathing in this beautiful room with its view of the sea after surviving six years of war. So long away, he had not even met his daughter. Me.

Up on the first floor, we drift through reception areas; the throne room, where a painting of Maximilian, decked out in a brass-buttoned frock coat, hangs on the wall; and various drawing rooms, filled with Chinese and Japanese furnishings that hold no appeal for me. But I'm still impressed that it all survived, cared for by the local people, who had fortunately possessed a healthy respect for their own history.

All throughout the castle, the ceilings boast magnificent, sunken wooden panels, but it is in the dining room that Maximilian decorated the coffers with seagulls. Wings outstretched, each bears a beribboned scarlet scroll with Latin description, painted in gold. The Seagull Room. Just as Daddy had depicted it for me.

Beyond the upper floor gallery is a closed-off area, obviously under restoration. A sign states in several languages that the restoration is scheduled for completion in 1996.

"The Duke of Aosta apartments," Daddy explains. "When he decided to move into the castle, he installed a modern bathroom." He chuckles. "Lucky for us! We put his posh bathroom to very good use, I can tell you. Pity I can't show you."

"Can you show me your billet?"

"Doubt it. Doesn't seem to be part of the public tour."

And it isn't. But he does indicate a winding staircase, with ornate, hand-carved wood banisters, curving up to the third floor. Presumably the servants' quarters in Maximilian's day.

"Nice and quiet up there. I got to play my gramophone to my heart's content. No bother to anyone."

There are acres of garden, too much for us to explore. Daddy is leaning quite heavily on my arm now. "Don't know about you, Daddy, but my feet are aching. How about going back to the hotel for lunch now?"

He gives me a relieved little smile.

But as we start driving away, Daddy points out the stable area, nestled in a grove of trees. "Can we pull up over there for a few minutes?"

"Why?"

"I'll show you."

Somewhat reluctantly, I park again. My tummy is growling for food, and my feet really are sore. Daddy pushes open heavy wooden doors.

"Are we allowed in this area?"

He shrugs. "No notice anywhere saying we can't, is there?"

He's getting irritable, but I'm unsure why. We wander along a row of empty horse boxes. The interior is cool, and rather gloomy. Eerie, in fact, as if haunted by ghosts hovering in the rafters. I shiver; someone walking over my grave. I button up my cardigan.

"Why on earth did you want to want to stop here? There's nothing to see."

Daddy walks ahead of me slightly. Then he turns around to face me, causing me to pull up short. "When we first set up headquarters and had a good look around, we discovered the stable stalls, piled high with stolen swag."

"Do you mean the castle furnishings?"

"No, no. I told you, the Germans didn't have a chance to get their hands on that. What we discovered had all been stolen from Italian Jews during the German occupation. They'd systematically robbed the poor souls, prior to arrest and deportation. And later, the stuff was abandoned here in their rush to escape in April 1945."

"What happened to it all?"

"My dear girl, we helped ourselves. Mostly to pay off mess bills."

"All of you?" *The spoils of war,* I suppose. I feel sick. "How could you?"

"Larkins, my batman, found the sledge here," adds Daddy.

"What?"

"Józef's sledge. The one he's sitting on in the picture."

"Your servant stole it!"

"Georgie Girl, no one was ever going to come back to claim it. The Nazis had turned an old rice mill in the city into a transit center for the Jews, before they were shipped north to the death camps. Then, not satisfied, they added their own crematorium. Need I say more?"

The atmosphere in the stables is turning rancid with an odor of death and decay. A lump is wedged hard and fast in my throat. I can't swallow. Anything to do with the Holocaust makes me want to weep, ever since taking the girls to the Anne Frank Museum in Amsterdam, soon after they had both read the diary. Just as I knew I would, I'm starting to cry. "I'm getting out of here now."

"Darling, I'm sorry. I didn't mean to upset you. But quite suddenly, when we were driving past, I had such a vivid memory of Larkins holding up the sledge—"

I almost trip in the bright sunlight outside. Dig for my sunglasses. Move quickly toward the car—shuddering—not looking back. Wishing I didn't know where the damned sledge came from. Or how my father had paid off his mess bills.

But when Daddy doesn't appear for several minutes, I start to panic. Has he fallen? Suffered another heart attack? I'm just about to go back for him when he emerges, closes the door to the stables carefully, and stumbles into the car.

"So, was the boy pleased?" I mumble, when Daddy gets himself settled beside me.

"About what?"

"About the sledge, what else?"

"No idea." Out of nowhere, his voice suddenly sounds blithe and breezy. "Larkins was the one who delivered it." Is he implying Józef was of no consequence, after all?

"But the boy was important to you? Right? Who was he? Tell me why you had his picture hidden away?"

But for the entire drive into Trieste, Daddy closes his eyes and ignores me. His pretending-to-take-a-nap trick. Just like he did in the car, driving to Heathrow, when he didn't want to discuss any further the pros and cons of having a son. In an odd way, I'm relieved; the silence gives me an opportunity to go over in my head the bizarre conversation that just occurred. And the realization that I know nothing at all about this time in his life. Was it wrong, what they did? "To the victor belong the spoils." Who was it who said that? I can't remember. But I'm sure I came across the quote in America somewhere.

Just like a jack-in-the-box, Daddy springs to life when we reach the hotel. Hops out fairly smartly, shields his eyes from the bright sunshine, then waves his arm to a point high above the city. "Up there. The Karst." All I see is the city, clinging tenaciously to its steep hillside, topped with a mantle of low-lying, blue-gray clouds. What am I supposed to be looking at, for goodness's sake?

"Where Józef lived," Daddy snaps, as if I'm somehow supposed to know this.

"Come on, you, inside," I snap back, rapidly losing patience.

When we are seated in the dining room with its lovely view of the Bay of Trieste and Miramare, cold glasses of prosecco in our hands, I continue the interrupted conversation. "Daddy, *please* talk to me. How—why—did you know him—this Józef?"

Daddy swirls his wine around the glass, pondering my question for so long I think he's lost track of it. The waiter serves us with fresh-caught John Dory, baked in lemon caper dressing, with a watercress salad.

"He was a little Yugoslav lad," he finally blurts, "part of a group of Partisans I had dealings with. Jugs, we called them in those days, because Yugoslavia was still spelled with a *J*. One of my many roles was to keep the peace between them—the Triestines as well as the peasants in the hills, who were a real ethnic mixture, I can tell you. Slovenes, Austrians, Croats, Italians. The worst task we got was investigating the Yugoslav Fourth Army atrocities. During and after the war."

"I had no idea what you did."

"Why would you? How could you? You were just a little girl when I came home."

"Well, I don't just mean me. I don't remember *any* conversations with Granny, Auntie Margaret, our neighbors. Weren't they interested in why you had to stay on so long, after the war was over?"

He looks at me. Really looks at me. It's disconcerting, and I gulp a mouthful of wine. "It upset your mother. She preferred to pretend none of it ever happened. The whole North African/Italian campaign. But especially my ending up billeted in Miramare. I suppose she imagined me living the 'Life of Riley.' Plenty of food. Free ciggies. Booze."

As well as plenty of Jewish belongings to plunder whenever you felt like it. Did you tell Mum about that?

"Let me guess." I say instead. "Keeping disparate groups from killing each other, investigating atrocities, was not exactly the 'Life of Riley.'"

"No." Daddy tugs on his cuff. "But everyone in England wanted to 'get back to normal' after the war. 'It was terrible everywhere.' 'It's over now.' 'Forget about it.' It's all I heard for years afterward." He shakes his head. "Easier said than done, of course."

His cheeks have taken on a sallow cast, and his voice quavers ever so slightly. Despite what he was told, he very much has not forgotten or got over it, no matter how hard he may have tried.

"Maybe a rest after such a busy morning? I can do some sightseeing on my own."

Daddy relaxes, and after we finish eating, I accompany him upstairs. My plan is to look around this Karst area. If I can find the village where the picture was taken, someone might recognize the boy. Or, the grown-up boy might still live there. Who knows? And if he does, maybe he'll be able to explain to me how a British officer, part of the Allied Occupation Force, came to have a picture of him.

While Daddy is in the bathroom, I slip the snapshot of Józef into my handbag. I feel like a sneaky seven-year-old. But I don't care. I'm sick of waiting. I want answers. Now. Not when Daddy decides he is ready to level with me. Patience is not one of my virtues.

Why did Larkins give *that* particular boy the sledge, when there must have been dozens of little Jugs running around? And why did Daddy keep *that* snap of *that* boy on *that* sledge all these years?

Chapter Fourteen

Aften getting directions from the concierge, I drive up a steep, modern road toward the Karst, which he explained to me is a flat piece of land above Trieste. I reflect how different it must have appeared in 1945—certainly, there would have been no ugly suburban homes, clustered around industrial parks. But once I reach the plateau—a narrow strip of rather barren countryside—there is a sense of melancholy time-lessness. Whether it is me on the Karst now—Nazis fifty years ago—Roman centurions a thousand years ago—the jagged gray crags, vineyards, olive groves, and goats and sheep tugging sparse grass all probably looked exactly the same.

I drive aimlessly, searching for wells in the various hamlets. Road signs are in Italian and Slovenian, so I'm not even sure which country I'm in half the time. But I do vaguely recall that Slovenia fought a ten-day war of independence not long ago, to separate itself from the now rapidly disintegrating nation of Yugoslavia.

My sense of direction is not very good, but according to a sign-post, I have reached a village called Basovizza. Rows and rows of red pennants are strung across the main street, flapping sporadi-cally in the breeze. For some sort of fair, I suppose. It's a dusty place, a few red-tiled homes clustered together around small patches of cultivated gardens; a church stands in the distance, with a round stained-glass window above the main door. I park the car, sling my handbag over my shoulder, and stroll around in an increasingly fruitless search.

When I come upon a modest café, I decide to get a cup of coffee and ask if anyone can identify the village well in the snapshot for me. I sit myself down at a trestle table, facing the street. But as soon as the proprietor slouches up, I am less certain of my plan. He looks me up and down, taking in my stylish clothing, the expensive handbag. "American?"

"Pardon me?"

"Dollars?"

Then I understand. He wants to be paid in dollars. For a cup of coffee! But he probably has some sort of monetary racket going. Who knows? If I have strayed into Slovenia, dollars might be more valuable to him than the local currency, whatever that may be.

Apprehensive about the café now, I nevertheless nod and order a cappuccino. When the proprietor comes back with the coffee, I produce the picture, point at the well, and try to mime the question of where it might be located. What a charade. He shrugs and retreats. As soon as I finish my drink, I regret it—I'm suddenly dying to go to the loo. I don't even know how to ask, but the need is urgent, so I force myself inside. The place is dimly lit. Through the gloom, I can see only one occupied table; four or five men of varying ages, playing a sort of card game. But for the life of me I don't see a woman anywhere. I try hard not to let this worry me, so desperate am I for a wee.

The owner, hovering behind his bar, gestures to the back of the building. "Out there."

Damn him! He spoke English all the time and let me make a complete fool of myself. My face burns, but I move with as much dignity as I can through a wooden door into a walled-in yard. High walls. Very high. Sudden claustrophobia, not a condition I usually suffer from, envelops me. I'm seriously regretting making this trip. What possessed me to embark on such a fool's errand by myself?

It is obvious where the facilities are. All I have to do is follow the tell-tale smell into a shed with an ill-fitting door. A primitive water closet indeed, but needs must. I pull down my knickers, grateful I am wearing a skirt—less to keep from trailing on the tacky floor. Squatting over the toilet seat, I relieve myself as fast as I can. When I have found a tissue in my bag to wipe with, I step outside quickly.

Only to find I am surrounded by the card players, leering at me as I emerge. Christ Almighty, they're going to rob me. My wallet is stuffed full of sterling and lira, as well as the dollar bills with which I paid the owner of the café—who probably orchestrated this holdup in the first place.

Losing any bravado I might have mustered, I manage to slip Józef's photograph into my pocket for safety before tossing my handbag on the ground. I am hoping desperately they will take the money and leave me alone. Out spills my favorite Revlon lipstick, several Playtex tampons the girls have left behind, and a roll of film that will never now be developed. Horrified, I watch these personal items disappearing into a mucky gutter.

"Take the bag," I beg. "Just take it."

But they keep their hands by their sides. Inch closer to me, *not* my discarded bag. A fleeting image of Daddy's monkey-head swagger stick flashes before my eyes. What I wouldn't give to have a hold of it now. To crack each of their stupid heads in turn.

"*Ameriska!*" they yell. "*Anglescina!*"

"*Nasprotrik,*" snarls an ancient, wizened old man. "*Izdati.*" He grabs my hair.

Then another of the men, younger and taller, spits in my face. "*Izdajalecs.*"

Other than the fact that they have me clocked as either American or English, I have absolutely no idea what they are saying, except that it's pretty clear they are seeking some sort of revenge. But for what? I swallow back a sob. Try to swipe my cheek free of the disgusting spittle.

"Help," I yell, vainly hoping the owner will come to my aid. "Help."

But clearly that foul piece of shit knows exactly what is going on. He won't raise a finger to help me. This is a vendetta I do not understand.

Then, quite suddenly, it turns into something else entirely.

They are pushing.

Poking.

Prodding.

The smell of their excited, edgy sweat overwhelms the smell of the loo. Bile gathers in my stomach, a cauldron now, boiling and bubbling. *Toil and trouble, indeed,* flits inanely through my mind.

When I feel an erection hard against my hip, the contents of my belly make a break for it. I spill vomit all over the monsters, absurdly wishing it contained adder's fork and blind-worm's sting. Really! *Macbeth* at such a time as this! I'm going completely mad.

Momentarily startled, they back off, yakking away. I cannot understand a word.

I grab my bag and race blindly through the café. Out to the road. Drag open the car door. Flee. When I am certain I am out of reach of the bastards, I park, make sure the doors are locked, and rummage for my secret stash of ciggies.

Did they attack me because I'm Anglo-American? Weren't we the heroes? Rescuing these people from the Nazis? It appears not. Not in this neck of the woods, anyway.

After smoking a cigarette, I wonder if I shouldn't try to find a police station and report what happened. But what did actually happen? I was threatened, but no actual crime was committed, other than scaring the living daylights out of me. No theft. No rape. Then I think of my nonexistent abilities in any European language, which would inevitably elicit another pantomime of incomprehension, before it turned out the officer, like the café proprietor, understood English perfectly well.

Instead, I lay my head on the steering wheel and take deep breaths. Then I retrieve the snapshot of Józef from my pocket and look at it for the longest time. Rather than waiting for my father to explain in his own sweet time who this child is and why he's so important, I had filched the damned photograph from his room and gone haring off like a maniac, never imagining for one moment that I might be cornered and attacked on my first afternoon in Italy.

As I drive myself off the Karst, my panic turns to pure anger. How dare the brutes frighten me like that? I spot a shabby strip mall, not unlike those in the American suburbs, a world away from the glorious Hapsburg buildings in Trieste just down the road. Striding into a general store with my head held high, I stomp up and down the aisles until I have blown off enough steam. Fortunately, there doesn't appear to be anyone else shopping, otherwise I would probably be arrested for acting so oddly. And being a foreigner, to boot.

The merchandise is tawdry, but when I spy a bright turquoise tote of imitation leather, as unlike my old handbag as it is possible to find, it makes me burst out laughing. Either one of my girls would love it. They will no doubt fight for possession of it later.

Back outside in the parking lot, I transfer my makeup, reading glasses, wallet full of money, Józef's photograph, and the notebook in which I jot down story ideas into my garish new purchase. On the way to the hotel, I toss the filthy handbag out the car window with glee. I am feeling better already. It's extremely gratifying to behave like a hooligan once in a while. Shades of my grunge girl, Annie!

Safely back in my bedroom, I run a scalding hot shower, empty an entire bottle of shampoo on my head, and scrub my scalp till it's raw. My skirt and blouse, linen jacket, bra and knickers—even my sandals, sticky with unidentifiable substances—are all stuffed into the bathroom receptacle. Never to be seen or touched, or thought about, ever again.

Chapter Fifteen

S O, WHAT DID you get up to this afternoon, Georgina?"
Daddy asks skeptically. "You've been uncharacteristically
quiet this evening."

We are enjoying after-dinner coffee on the small patio outside
the Caffè Thommaseo, facing onto the seafront. I scoop frothy
cappuccino into my mouth and ignore my father. Lights on the
masts of the yachts anchored in the bay shine silver shadows over
the water. Faintly, I catch the lap of waves against the hulls.

"Well?" He's not letting me off the hook.

"Actually, I drove up to the place you pointed out this morning.
The Karst."

"Thought as much." My father eases forward slightly and rests
his elbows on the tabletop. "Was there really any need to go tear-
ing off there alone?"

"I wish I hadn't."

"Why is that? Did something happen?"

I have no intention of telling him the entire story, but I want
to speak of it a little, to settle any leftover jitters. Earlier, I even
thought of phoning Paul, but in the end I didn't, dreading that
the conversation would simply end with him haranguing me
that "none of it would have happened if you were home with me
where you belong."

"Tell me, Georgie Girl."

"I stopped for a coffee. Ran into some men who got angry because I was Anglo-American."

"How did they figure that out?"

"The proprietor asked me to pay in dollars."

"Did they try to hurt you?" Daddy is pulling on the cuff of his jacket now.

"No. No, they didn't."

"Are you sure?" His face is a crease of worry.

"Well, my self-esteem is bruised." I manage to laugh.

"Where exactly were you? Try to remember."

I have to think for a moment or two. "Baso . . . something . . . Basovizza, I think the road sign read."

While I'm telling Daddy this, a rumple of memories creep one by one across his dear face. "Dear God, girl. No wonder you ran into trouble. They're a defensive lot up there. I knew them well. It's where I had to carry out the investigation into the Jug atrocities. I told you at lunchtime."

"But what has that got to do with harassing me? Wasn't it a good thing the Americans and British were probing into such things?"

"Not in their eyes. They were avid supporters of Tito, during and after the war. In May '45, that village was involved in murdering Germans who were technically POWs, political prisoners, or anticommunists."

"Oh, my God." It was beginning to make a mad sort of sense.

"What most infuriated those people was that when the Allies drew the Morgan Line of demarcation to separate Italy from Slovenia, Basovizza ended up on the Italian side. It seems they have neither forgiven nor forgotten. Resentments get passed on generation to generation."

"But the Allies were only trying to do the right thing."

"With the benefit of hindsight, I'm not so sure we were. But at the time, America was obsessed with keeping Trieste out of the hands of Tito and the Soviets. It was a vitally strategic port in those days."

"There were red flags flying over the main street, Daddy."

"Well, there you are, then. They obviously still support a united Yugoslavia, however impossible that is now. The whole country has exploded." Daddy thrums his fingers in a ragged confusion of noise on the top of the table. "I'm sorry you ran into the blighters. It can't have been pleasant."

No, it was not. Not pleasant at all. An old man grabbed my hair. Another spat in my face. Lust and hate seeped out of their pores.

"But perhaps," he adds, his tone becoming abruptly unreadable, "the entire drama could have been avoided if you hadn't decided to 'borrow' my photograph of Józef. Did you think I wouldn't notice?"

He relaxes back in his seat again, but I can't tell if he's annoyed with me or not.

"I'm really sorry, Daddy. But I got very upset when you told me how the child got his sledge." I place the snap between us on the table. There is a lump stuck in my throat again, and it won't go away. "It seems—well, wrong, somehow—immoral—not caring about who it belonged to before." Brutal images stream through my head—Nazis breaking down a door; piling furniture, dishes, rugs into a lorry; at the last minute spotting the sledge and snatching it from the arms of a small boy. What happened to *that* child? Before his sledge ended up at Castello di Miramare.

"Immoral, I agree. But not caring and not being able to do something about it are two very different things, Georgie Girl. If I had not allowed Larkins to appropriate the sledge for Józef—a little chap we knew well, as it happens—it would still have ended up with strangers."

While doing a series of school visits in Virginia, I'd gone to the Holocaust Memorial Museum in Washington, DC, by myself, soon after it had opened. When I encountered the compelling mass of discarded shoes, in every shape and size imaginable, I had to stop and sit for half an hour, so tangled were my thoughts. So many human beings had walked in those shoes, played in those shoes, polished those shoes, and now the shoes were empty forevermore.

"You had the mad idea you could locate the place where the snap was taken?" Daddy continues.

"It is why we're here, isn't it?" Unbidden, my voice rises to a squeak.

"Is it?"

"Yes, Daddy!" I attempt to lower my voice. "To find the boy on the sledge."

"Because you think he might be my son?"

"Is he?"

"No, Georgina. Józef is not my boy."

"I suppose it isn't really any of my business."

"I suppose not." Daddy gets up slowly and pats my shoulder. "But enough for now, darling, all right? I'll go and pay our bill. And avail myself of the facilities."

Enough for now, indeed. I'm drained. What a fraught day it has been. I gaze across the seafront at the star-spangled water, wondering why my parents never had another child. There was certainly a glut of new babies all through the late forties as the armed forces systematically demobilized.

I think back to that time, after Daddy returned to England for good. When he didn't wear his uniform anymore, but instead put on a gray suit and went off to an office in the city every day, carrying a briefcase. Was he happy? From a childhood perspective, I believed he was. We functioned like any other family—picnicked in the park, built castles on the beach, swam in the sea, celebrated birthdays in Fenwick's Tearoom. But Daddy most definitely was not happy the nights he had his nightmares. When he would plonk me down on a kitchen chair to keep him company while he drank his whiskey and smoked his cigarettes. Where on earth was my mother those nights? What was she doing? Why did she never talk to me about those times?

Risking a quick smoke before Daddy returns, I slip a cigarette out of my gaudy new tote and light up greedily. Just as the nicotine hits my lungs, I'm suddenly deluged with a cloudburst of remembrance, coming from god knows where, but literally drenching me in details from a particular day in the past.

I had come home from school early for some reason. When I dashed upstairs to change out of my school uniform, I realized my parents were in their bedroom. The door was shut tight, but angry words were spilling into the hallway. I knew I should go downstairs. I knew it was wrong to listen to private conversations. But my curiosity got the better of me, as it usually did. I stayed in the hall to listen.

"It's time we had another child," said Daddy. "Before Georgina gets any older."

"No."

"But Mary, it would be wonderful for all of us. Wouldn't it? A way to bring us closer together. We have been apart so long."

"No."

"And I wasn't even here for Georgina's birth. I would love to be able to share such a happy time with you now."

"Georgina. Georgina." The bitterness with which she said my name frightened me. "I raised our daughter on my own for five years. Never knowing if you would even survive. We had a routine. We had our ways. We were settled. But now all she wants is you. Not me. You!"

"Mary, Mary, we're still getting used to one another. Georgie Girl loves you. I know she does."

"Stop calling her that ridiculous name, James. She was christened Georgina." Mummy paused. "You want me to get pregnant, sick, fat, depressed, all so I'll have someone else to occupy me while you indulge your precious 'Georgie Girl'!"

"Of course not. That's ridiculous."

"No, it isn't." There was a break in my mother's voice that was unbearable. I felt as if I had jumped into the deep end of the pool at school and forgotten how to swim.

"We talked about wanting a large family when we got married. Don't you remember?"

Mummy mumbled something I couldn't make out.

"What made you change your mind, Mary? Please tell me. So I can understand."

"No."

"For Christ's sake, stop saying 'no' all the time."

"Well, stop asking." My mother was weeping.

Footsteps muffled over the carpet. I scooted behind the laundry hamper and crouched down low. Daddy stormed out of the room. He had no idea I was even in the house.

When I heard his car door slam outside in the street, I went down to the kitchen and made a pot of tea. Granny would do the same thing for Mummy, to settle the nerves, she always said. Somehow, I managed to carry a brimming cup upstairs without scalding myself. Mummy was lying in bed, underneath the eiderdown.

"I've made you some tea," I whispered.

"Thank you, Georgina. Put it down."

"Mummy?"

"Not now. Please leave me alone."

Instead, I tried to climb up beside my mother for a cuddle. But she pushed me aside. What happened next? Did I whine and fuss? Throw a tantrum? Try as I might, I can't remember.

Slowly, the recollection starts to ebb, fading into the mists of memory. The Mummy and Daddy of my childhood grow fainter, hovering just out of reach before completely disappearing into long ago and faraway. Just as my father steps out from Thommaseo's brightly lit interior, to sit next to me again on the patio.

"Caught you," he remarks, sneaking the cigarette from between my fingers. "Hard to stop, isn't it?" he adds, knocking the accumulated stem of ash into the ashtray.

"I *am* trying."

"You were off with the fairies, as we used to say. What were you thinking about so hard?"

"Nothing much. Just wondering why you and Mummy never had another child. That's all."

"That's all?" He pulls hard on the remains of the ciggie. "Well, I suppose it hardly matters now."

Does he mean it hardly matters that Mum refused to give him another child? Or that he is smoking the remains of my cigarette? On reflection, perhaps in his mind both things don't matter anymore.

"I would have liked a sibling," I say, gathering up my jacket and tote for the short walk back to the hotel.

He stubs the cigarette out slowly. Frowns slightly. "Are you sure about that?"

"What do you mean?"

"Remember your little green goblin? Used to show up when you were struggling to share. Especially your books. You called him George, as I recall. Made me draw you pictures of him, perched on your shoulder."

"And Mum told you to stop. She said they would give me bad dreams."

"Is your green goblin still around, Georgie Girl?"

I take his arm in mine. "Well, grown-up me manages to control her jealous streak most of the time." We stop outside on the pavement for the traffic light to change. "Although I confess, I'm still not particularly good at sharing."

"That's what I'm afraid of," he says.

"Meaning?"

"Oh, I don't know." Daddy pulls his arm away.

"Of course you do," I scold. *Subtleties be damned.* "It's high time you told me exactly why we're in Trieste!"

JANUARY –
MAY 1946

Chapter Sixteen

I N THE END, storms in the English Channel delayed
Drummond's return to Italy by almost ten days, well into
the New Year. Afterward, it seemed to him that the time back
home in England had been largely spent in an impenetrable gray
fog, interspersed with a few vivid scenes seared into his mind—

*The metallic echo of their feet in the street, his first evening home.
Mary's incessant chatter, in an effort to keep the air around them filled
up. The fug of stale smoke, sooty coats, and human sweat when they
pushed open the door of the Brandling Arms. His automatic request
for a double whiskey.*

*"You'll be lucky, mate," scoffed the bartender. "You're not in the
mess now!" Settling for a pint of weak, watery Newcastle Brown Ale.
Bribing the man with two half-crowns to wangle a gin and tonic
for his wife. Conversations in the pub with weary people he barely
remembered, resentful that nothing had got better since the war ended.
Spending much of the evening resting his hands on the edge of the
sticky table, clenching his fists, staring vacantly into his pint.*

*Mary reaching for his hand on the short walk home from the pub.
Forcing himself not to pull away. Knowing that soon they would
have to get into bed together. Mary expecting him to make love to her.
Struggling to find some part of his past with her to relate to. When
she undressed, his horror on realizing how much thinner she had become. Wanting to be kind. Sympathetic. Consoling, for the years of
the war, but feeling only an awful embarrassment that he had been
unable to do anything for her. Managing somehow to come together in*

an awkward mating dance of intimacy. Afterward, wanting to weep. Wanting to escape to the club. Wanting to put himself in the capable hands of Larkins. Wanting to take one of Larkins's runs to Opatje Selo, the forbidden village he must never return to again.

Mary's mother suggesting he take Mary away to a hotel for a couple of days. A second honeymoon of sorts. She would take care of Georgina. But what would they talk about? What would they do all day? More especially, what would they do at night? Shamefully, he used Georgina as an excuse. If they were to go and stay in a hotel, the child must accompany them. It wasn't fair to leave her at home.

Mary herself being enormously upset by this. The suggestion coming to naught. Sharing the bed getting no easier. Waking in a cold sweat in the midst of an attack, dragging Mary onto the floor to save her from incoming mortar shells. Terrifying her. Trying to apologize for his behavior. Promising that things would get better. "I hope so, James," Mary said. "This war has stolen away our lives."

Dark, dreary days. High winds. Sleet storms. Snowstorms. Watching Mary dragging Georgina through the snowy streets on a dust-bin lid. Imaging another mother and child, in another country, sledding on a pristine sledge.

Taking Mary and Georgina to see Cinderella, *a pantomime at the Theatre Royal, Newcastle. The child sitting between them. Depending altogether too much on his Georgie Girl, who had barreled into his arms. Loving her deeply. Alenka had been right about his child—"when you see her it will become easy"—but it was so very far from easy when he saw his wife.*

Without a word being spoken, both James and Mary understood, when the visit drew to a close, that it was a relief for them both.

WHEN DRUMMOND'S TRAIN ROLLED into the Trieste train station, Larkins loomed head and shoulders above the crowd milling about on the platform, his ginger hair and freckled face a welcome sight.

"Good leave, sir?"

"Fine, thanks. Just fine."

Larkins tossed the kitbag over his shoulder, and they marched out to the parked jeep. "Where to, sir? The club?"

"No, Larkins. Miramare. I need to soak in a bath. Getting from Newcastle to Trieste on postwar trains is no joke, I can tell you."

Slushy streets hampered the drive through the city. The air was frigid. Drummond hunched into his greatcoat, its fetid smell emitting a certain heat. He had refused to let Mary try to remove the accumulated muck. The coat represented the story of his war, every smudge, smear, and bloody stain on it. Larkins understood that without being told.

"So, what's been happening while I've been gone?"

Larkins laughed. "Oh, spot of bother in the city, last few nights. The ranks got too cocky 'bout flogging their free cigs in the back alleys. The MP's got wise. Pounced. Confiscated the lot. Then they let the offenders go."

"I bet I can guess what happened next."

"Yes, sir. MP's kept the swag. Sold it on later to their own pet buyers."

"I suppose we are all a bunch of crooks in the end," Drummond noted.

"Aye, sir. Suppose we are."

They reached the castle and parked. Larkins heaved the kitbag up the stone staircase to what used to be the servants' quarters on the third floor, but now provided housing for British Eighth Army officers. The lucky ones, anyway.

Larkins unlocked the door to his room. It took Drummond

aback to realize how much he had missed its monk-like quality. Its promise of solitude. A single bed on a wrought-iron frame. Blankets folded neatly. Fresh-ironed sheets, smelling of sea spray. Piled on his desk, old favorites: poetry by Graves, Aldington, and Sassoon, novels of Forster, Ford Madox Ford, and the like. For current light reading, he'd been much taken with Agatha Christie's *And Then There Were None*—a perfect way to pass the long train journey. On top of a small dresser were his precious gramophone and box of records. An overstuffed easy chair sat beneath the window. A quick glance outside offered a full moon, glittering over the black sea.

Drummond bathed while Larkins unpacked and sorted his laundry. On his return, barefoot and much cleaner, Larkins thrust a small snapshot into his hands. "For you, sir."

He gazed at a picture of the boy, Józef, in the snow, sitting on the purloined sledge. Despite a thick wool balaclava pulled over his head, Drummond was certain he spotted the Titovka cap peeking out. *Bet he sleeps in that damned hat!*

"You should keep this, Larkins. The lad's your biggest fan. Course, it's only because of your mop of red hair!"

"Got a copy, sir. Thought you would like a bit of a keepsake too."

What Drummond really wished was that Alenka was also in the photograph. Through the drawn-out, bleary time in England, he had fought against his need to bury his face in her neck and smell the sea and pines. The need to grasp her long black hair. The need to feel the heft of it in his hands.

"You obviously had no difficulty getting the sledge delivered," he remarked, rifling through a drawer for cigarettes. He lit one, and the sharp smell of fiery sulfur settled him somewhat.

"None at all, sir. They've a ton of snow on the Karst already.

Shortly before Christmas, I drove up there far as I could, met Józef's mam—your friend—outside Opatje Selo."

Drummond spun around. *Cheeky devil.*

"I loaded the sledge with supplies for everyone in the village, courtesy of our Yankee friends," Larkins went on, his expression one of bland innocence.

"Well, why not? The Americans have more food than they know what to do with."

"Enough to eat at home now, is there?" asked Larkins.

"Hardly. You should have seen the scrawny chicken I persuaded a local farmer to part with. Even better, my 'loaves and fishes' miracle performed on Christmas day before a houseful of relatives!"

"My mam writes rationing has got worse since the war ended. Don't seem right, somehow."

"No, it most certainly does not." The captain gave a disheartened sigh, recalling ration books and food shortages, and the meals Mary had tried to put together as a consequence.

"Well," Larkins said, swerving onto safer conversational ground, "that's you all settled. I'll wake you in the morning, sir. Your uniforms are all hung up, clean, and pressed. Nighty-night, then."

"Thanks, Larkins."

When the thudding clomp of Larkins's boots receded down the stone staircase, Drummond poured himself a whiskey and stretched out on his bed. He closed his eyes and wrapped himself in the comfortable solitude his monastic cell afforded. For a while, at least, no more struggling to become the man he once was; no more struggling to hold conversations with people he barely knew; no obligation to reduce his war to palliative soundbites.

If only he could remain hidden for hours, days, weeks. The same desire he'd experienced in the station bathroom only a few short weeks ago overwhelmed him: to be left alone. Beholden to no one. With just his music and poetry, both of which were pearls on a string of beads, providing sounds and images for his own personal delight.

His wish was granted. In the clutches of the snowy winter, the business of occupation had slowed. Mine-clearing on hold. The Yugoslav Fourth Army cooperating, compliant with requirements of the Morgan Line. Tito apparently communicating with London and Washington. And Moscow, of course. Drummond was beginning to realize what a wily fox the man was. If it took Marshal Tito's playing one world power against the other to maintain some sort of stability, so be it.

Chapter Seventeen

ONE RELENTLESSLY SLEETY morning weeks later, Larkins roused Drummond as usual with hot water for shaving and a freshly pressed uniform. As Drummond rose, groaning, to a sitting position, Larkins took in last night's debris all over the floor—overflowing ashtrays, empty bottles, even a broken gramophone record—with tuts of displeasure.

"No excuse, Larkins. But save me the Mary Poppins lecture today, okay?"

"Right you are, sir. Permission to make a request?"

Drummond hunched on the side of his bed, rubbing a sore head. "What?"

"Out with some Yanks last night. Seems they've gone and made a deal. Well, commandeered, more like, one of the local picture houses—"

"So?"

"So, every Saturday morning for the rest of the winter, they're going to show cartoons for the local kiddies."

"What the hell are—"

"Films, but not with real people in them. Just lots of drawings all squashed together."

"Enough, Larkins, enough." Drummond stumbled over to his desk and downed two aspirins with a glass of stale water. "So, what is it you want from me, exactly?"

"Just your okeydokey to fetch the kiddies from Opatje Selo to enjoy the treats."

"Which is nothing more than an excuse to see Józef and his pals. And completely ignores the fact that they live in Zone B."

"Yes, sir."

Drummond flopped on the bed again, groaning loudly. "What about the roads?" he muttered, stalling for time. "There's still plenty of snow up there. And it's a good twenty-five miles to the village."

"So I thought, if you requisition me a three-tonner, I could manage easy. There and back." Larkins grinned. "Loads of room for the mammies too, if they want to come along."

By which he meant Alenka. *God, I'm letting him get away with murder these days.* His pal Harvey would call Larkins a real smart-ass and give him a kick in the pants.

Drummond lay back on his bed. His head ached and his throat hurt. Larkins's scheme was completely crazy. Completely unnecessary. He should refuse. He should make sure he never saw Alenka again. He should steel himself from the longing that ate away at his insides.

"Sir?"

Drummond rubbed his eyes. Picked up a piece of the shattered record. Tossed it in the waste-paper basket. His life was a bloody shambles.

"Yes, very well, Larkins. Why not?"

Larkins whipped a chit out of his shirt.

Drummond scrawled his signature, assuring himself that Alenka would have no interest in this silly cartoon business anyway. Assuring himself that soon enough he would be demobbed. Shipped back to Blighty. For good. And that would be that. His longing for her firmly and forever out of reach.

BUT A WEEK LATER, he woke up in a sweat. Rubbed his eyes. Stared at the clock. It was Saturday. Larkins was already on his way to Opatje Selo. What if the mothers did come with their children? What if Alenka planned to ride in the truck too? If he could just see her once in a while, would he be satisfied? Would it be enough? He couldn't expect more. It was out of the question.

Drummond half-heartedly commanded himself to stay in the castle. Write a conciliatory letter to Mary. But how to begin to explain how difficult it had been to return home? How to explain his war—what he had seen, what he had done, how it had changed him? He worried that in attempting to blot out the war, he was blotting out his entire life thus far, but did Mary even want to know? He didn't think so. All she wanted was the old James, whoever that man was. He didn't know him anymore.

The captain pushed off the damp sheets, bathed, shaved carefully, dressed in his most presentable uniform, and ordered a vehicle to be brought around from the motor pool. Unfortunately, only a jeep was available. The weather was miserable, so he would likely get soaked to the skin. A light drizzle was showing signs of turning into snow at any moment. But he didn't care. He drove fast, trying to blot out all the reasons he should remain at Miramare.

On the outskirts of Trieste, the captain realized he had no idea which cinema was hosting the children's show. Damn. Damn. Damn. He drove himself to the American officers' club in the Hotel de la Ville and signed himself in. By great good luck, Dick Harvey was slouched on his usual stool up at the bar. They'd become good pals since they worked together on the Joint Task Force last year, overcoming, among other things, the barrier of a common language.

"Howdy, Jimmy," the American yelled drunkenly across the otherwise empty room. "Join me?"

Why, he wondered, did the Yanks have such a compulsion to shorten everybody's names? They probably addressed their supreme commander as Ike to his face!

"What's your poison, Jim?"

"Whiskey, please." Hanging up his cap and Sam Browne belt, he joined Dick at the bar.

"Sorry about the brawl in here the other night," Harvey said, slapping Drummond on the back. "Bit like the Wild West sometimes, I guess."

Drummond rolled his eyes. He had been Dick's guest in the American mess, and one of the officers had taken an instant dislike to him. "Not sure how the British army would have reacted to the murder of one or their own. Or the fact that your lot don't check your weapons at the door. But I know how I feel about being held at gunpoint by a Limey-hating Neanderthal!"

"Yeah, for sure, the guy's off his nut. Confined to barracks for a few days."

"Glad to hear it."

"But what brings you back here? Nothing better to do in this fucking hellhole of a town?"

"Where are your lot putting on that show for the local kids? One of the cinemas in town, I believe, but I forgot which one?"

"Can't see you watching cartoons, Jimmy!" Dick roared with laughter and slopped half his drink across the marble counter. "Not your style, you with your highbrow operas and such-like!"

Drummond ordered two more drinks. "Can you help me out, Dick?"

"Sure thing. In the north of Trieste, by the railway station. Near the Café San Marco. At least I think so." Dick gulped more whiskey.

"Thanks."

He kept his pal company a few more minutes, then made his

excuses, collected his belongings, and retrieved the jeep. So accustomed to being driven around by Larkins, he wasn't entirely sure where he was going. He got lost twice before spotting signs for the train station. By the time he located the cinema, he was sweating with frustration, and the whiskey sloshing around in his belly, reminded him he had forgotten to eat any breakfast.

He found the café, which had a clear view of the picture house, and ordered a plate of pasta to sop up the booze. Through the steamy window, he watched lines of children streaming inside the cinema. They were bundled against the damp cold in an odd assortment of clothing that had survived the war, no doubt passed down from child to child till they fell apart.

At last, the British lorry hove into view. When Larkins lifted up the back tarp, about two dozen kids pushed and shoved to get down. Where had he found them all? One by one, they jumped into his open arms, whooping with joy. The captain elbowed a circle of glass clear of steam, desperate for Alenka to be among the crowd. He thought he recognized some of the village women to whom he had given the picnic basket—a lifetime ago.

And then he saw her, leaning over the back of the lorry, enveloped in a huge black coat, crimson muffler, and woolly hat. *She came.* His palms were sweaty, and his heart raced with the need to run to her. Drummond almost knocked over his half-consumed meal. "Be right back," he shouted to the waiter, and tore out of the café.

"Sir?" Larkins spun round in surprise. "Where's the emergency?"

"No crisis, Corporal. Everything is fine. Just thought I'd come into town for the day."

Larkins raised a quizzical ginger eyebrow.

How idiotic he sounded. Trying unsuccessfully to control the flush spreading across his face, the captain offered his hand to

Alenka and helped her down. "Are you going to the show with Józef?" he muttered.

She shoved her hands inside the pockets of the bulky coat. It was so large; it must have belonged to her husband. "I do not have to."

"In that case, perhaps you would like a cup of something hot to warm you up? Or something to eat?"

"That would be welcome." Alenka kneeled to give Józef a hug. "Be good boy, yes. Enjoy Yankee film."

Nodding, Józef grabbed a firm hold of Larkins's hand. When they pushed open the door of the theater, discordant strains of music poured into the street, making the captain flinch.

When he had settled Alenka at the table beside the window, he asked: "What would you like?"

"Soup, please."

He waved the waiter over and ordered a bowl for her, along with a jug of wine and two glasses.

"How was your little girl?" she asked, shrugging out of the coat and pulling the damp woolen hat from her head. Immediately, the mass of black hair spilled down her back.

"You were absolutely correct," he replied. "It was as if I had always known her. As if she had always known me. Quite extraordinary, really."

"I am pleased for you, Captain Drummond."

Slowly, he allowed himself to relax. "Thank you. That means a lot." He poured the rough red wine for them both.

"You have been back a while now. How was the leave?" Alenka continued, raising the spoon to blow on her soup.

"Not easy. My country is shattered. And not just physically. The people are dispirited. As if they had lost the war. No coal for heating. Less food than during the war." He paused for a minute, clenching his fists. "And now I hear through the grapevine that the United States is planning a huge recovery program for Europe. The countries that lost, that is. No doubt it will take Great Britain fifty years or more to repay our American loans." His voice was bitter.

"Perhaps time your country try to be communist? Like us. *Bratstvo I jedirstvo*. Brotherhood and Unity."

"Do you really believe in all that? Does it work?"

"I hope. We fought two wars at the same time to get it—the civil war against the Royalist Chetniks *and* the war against Hitler's occupying fascists. But all free and equal now, how you say, fifty-fifty."

"As an idea, it all sounds very nice. I can't help thinking it's an illusion."

But what if she was right? Drummond remembered the various cock-ups during '43 and '44. Too much time wasted backing the Royalists instead of Tito's army, simply because the United States feared a united Yugoslav Communist government sitting on Stalin's doorstep. But truth be told, Great Britain had just voted in a socialist government of their own. He hardly knew what to think any more.

He reached for a cigarette. "At least the Salvation Army provided me with free ciggies while I was home."

Alenka laughed. "See? Even. Fair shares for all. But you smoke too much, Captain."

"I know," he murmured, dragging deeply.

"I want to ask you, about Basovizza investigation?"

"All finished. Closed, now. No action taken against Tito's army."

"What do *you* think of that?" Alenka asked.

The captain shrugged his shoulders. "Well, I believe Tito has realized that bloodletting is counterproductive. And he needs participation and support throughout the Yugoslav federation if he's going to make your brand of democratic socialism work."

Alenka scooped up the last of her soup, nodding happily.

"Would you like some more?"

"Please, yes, I would."

The waiter brought another serving, as well as a loaf of bread, which they shared. An excuse for Drummond's fingers to hover close to Alenka's. But before he knew it, the womenfolk and their children began flooding out of the cinema across the road. How had two hours passed so quickly?

"Must you leave now?"

"Captain Drummond, of course I must."

"Will you bring Józef to the show next Saturday?"

She nodded, standing up. He helped her slip into the long black coat, and was rewarded with the intoxicating aroma that clung to her skin.

"Thank you for meal." Alenka brushed his cheek with her fingers. A spasm of desire shot through his body, almost knocking him to the floor.

Long after her departure, the captain remained seated at the table beside the window. Letting the lingering smell of her seep into his own skin. Letting her throaty voice rumble around in his mind. Letting the touch of her hand on his cheek melt his heart.

Chapter Eighteen

EVERY DAY NOW, the captain's spirits lifted. There was something to look forward to, after all. In the evenings he spent more time in his room rereading his favorite poems and less time in the officers' club. He was reading American literature for the first time in an effort to better understand the Yanks: Faulkner, Zora Neale Hurston, Fitzgerald, Hemingway. Dick Harvey had promised to try to get him some books on the American Civil War, about which he knew next to nothing, as it had not shown up on the history syllabus during his time at school.

The following Saturday, he again drove himself into Trieste, and waited impatiently for Larkins to deliver his passengers from the Karst. He had signed the requisition form again with glee. The weather had warmed considerably during the past few days, and the streets were dry. A watery sun pushed its way through the clouds. Larkins should have no problem with the roads.

The captain strode up and down the street, feeling like his clumsy, shy, fourteen-year-old self when he had dared ask a girl to go for a walk with him for the first time. When the lorry rattled to a stop outside the picture house, he realized he had been holding his breath for most of the time. Alenka jumped down, almost tripping on the long black coat. Waved him over.

"Captain Drummond, Józef want me to go into film today. He has talked of nothing else, all week long."

"Fine. I'll join you."

He recognized that he had not actually been invited, but he

didn't care. Besides, he would put up with just about any childish drivel to sit beside Alenka for a couple of hours. Especially in a darkened picture house. God, he was behaving like a lovesick boy.

"Of course." Alenka's gray eyes twinkled knowingly.

Larkins lined the children up in a crocodile of twos and led them into the theater. Józef, Alenka, and the captain followed. It wasn't a large place, almost completely filled with the Trieste children, and looking decidedly shabby after all the years of war. Worn flooring, broken lights here and there, walls in dire need of a coat of paint. They found seats in the back row. Alenka hoisted Józef onto her lap to see the screen better. When Drummond doffed his cap and placed his swagger stick down, Józef reached for it. "What is strange animal?" He rubbed the head of the leather stick with his fingers, as if it were a talisman of some kind.

He laughed. "A monkey. Do you know what a monkey is?"

Józef shook his head so hard his Titovka cap almost fell off.

"I had it made in a country called Egypt," Drummond explained. "Many monkeys lived in the country hundreds of years ago. So, the people respect and honor them still."

"It is heavy."

"It is. So I can hit bad men over the head."

Józef's brown eyes grew huge. "Here?"

"Not here, Józef."

While they were talking, an American GI loped up and down the rows, passing out paper sacks to all the children.

"What is *hudoben* smell?" asked Alenka.

"Mati, it is good," Józef said. "Popcorn. We ate last week. The Yankee tell us nobody in America can watch a movie without it." Józef accepted a bag and handed it to his mother. "Try."

Alenka shook her head.

Drummond sniffed. "Damn and blast. Real butter." He gazed

at the children, munching away happily. Sometimes it made him incredibly angry that the Americans had a seemingly never-ending supply of good food. He gritted his teeth, recalling Georgina's weekly allotment of butter, barely enough to scrape over one slice of toast, almost a year on from the war.

When all the popcorn was distributed and the kids had settled down, the lights in the theater dimmed. The film, called *Fantasia*, consisted of various animated characters moving to classical music. Not just any music, but pieces by Stokowski, Tchaikovsky, Beethoven. Drummond sat back in his seat, astonished. *Dick Harvey, my friend, you should be here today.* Let him see just how much class this Mr. Walt Disney could produce, when he set his mind to it.

Alenka watched the screen, rapt. The soldier was achingly aware of the proximity of her shoulder, arm, thigh, to his own body. Her hair was piled on top of her head today, but one loose strand had drifted across her cheek. He wanted to reach over and fasten it behind her ear. But before long, he was rewarded in a different way.

When Schubert's "Ave Maria" began soaring into the rafters of the darkened theater, Alenka reached for his hand. It was involuntary, but it didn't lesson the intense pleasure he felt. There was something so erotic about her warm, moist palm resting on his knuckles. Whenever a particular bar of music resonated, Alenka squeezed his hand hard. Nothing in his life had ever felt so sensual.

When the credits rolled and the lights went up, she snatched her hand away, but Józef was already off her lap, stomping and clapping right along with the rest of the audience. Drummond wondered if the children were more intrigued by the animation or the music. For himself, it was a revelation. What a brilliant way to introduce children to classical music. He would have to tell Georgie Girl all about it in his next letter. Mary would find it odd he had attended a motion picture made for children, but never mind.

Outside in the sunshine, he begged, "Stay a while longer, Alenka. I'll drive you home later."

She hesitated.

"Both of you, of course," he added hurriedly.

But Józef was tugging on his mother's coat. "No, Mati, I want to ride in lorry with Mr. Boss Man."

"I think, Józef, that it is Captain Drummond here who is Boss Man."

The captain swept the Titovka cap off Józef's head and ruffled his hair. "I would not be too sure about that, son. Corporal Larkins here pretty much runs the show!"

Larkins beamed as he lifted the children, one by one, into the lorry for the ride back.

"Captain, I cannot let Józef go home by himself."

Did Alenka look disappointed? He couldn't really tell. But it was all right. Fine. Because during the coming days he could happily recollect the sensuous heat of her hand on his in the theater, and the tenderness of that same hand on his cheek last week in the café, any time he wanted. What more could he possibly ask for?

Drummond slipped a cigarette between his lips and cupped his hand around the flame of the lighter. He drew a satisfying mouthful of smoke into his lungs as he watched the British lorry pull away. Until next week. And the week after that. And the week after.

Chapter Nineteen

THE CAPTAIN'S DREAMLIKE Saturdays eventually came
to an end when the snow on the Karst melted. With the
springtime thaw, the methodical business of occupation
heaved into motion again. Not least of the chores was mine-
clearing. Drummond would line up groups of Italian POWs, dis-
tributing to each poor bastard a steel probe or bayonet. Through
an interpreter, he instructed them to crawl on their bellies through
each designated area, inserting the rod carefully into the ground
ahead of them. If they made contact with a buried mine, they were
to clear away any dirt and remain absolutely still. At this point, he
would send for a disposal expert. As the Allies had fought their
way up Italy, they had mostly herded flocks of sheep into suspect
areas to do the job of clearing German mines. Now it was the turn
of the Italian prisoners, all of them hard-core fascists who had
fought on with the Germans after Mussolini surrendered, killing
their own countrymen as well as Allied forces. Drummond had
absolutely no time for them.

After he had set up today's hodgepodge crew of POWs, he released them to Lieutenant Ward and sat in the jeep on the edge
of the grove, smoking cigarettes and thinking about Alenka. He
was aware that she was only a couple of miles away, tucked in on
the other side of the Morgan Line. Where was she at this precise
moment? What was she doing? Who was she talking to? When
might he see her again? He relived each momentous Saturday—
first those spent in Trieste, then the times he had ridden back in

the lorry to Opatje Selo after the American cartoon shows. While Larkins and his pal Jobson had entertained the youngsters outside with games of football, hide-and-seek, and tag, Alenka had opened the distinctive blue door to her home and offered glasses of wine. A black-and-white photograph of her husband, Darko, took pride of place on a wooden dresser in the living room; a poster of Tito hung beside the front door. Drummond supposed it might be mandatory now to display an image of the "great leader." One afternoon, he tacked up a snapshot that he'd spotted in an old magazine: Tito meeting Churchill in Naples in 1944. Alenka had roared with laughter and written "COMRADES" across the cutting.

Her more serious observations continued to astound him with their prescience. "I think you stranded, Captain," she had remarked the last time he saw her. "Stuck like a shipwreck. Waiting for the time you go home." That was exactly how he felt.

In all the years of fighting his way back and forth across North Africa, slogging through Sicily, toiling up the Italian boot, all the way to this nowhere place abutting Tito's Yugoslavia, there had been plenty of women for the taking. Rarely had he been tempted. Certainly, never with this maelstrom of emotion that was battering him now.

As the sun rose to its highest point in the sky, something began to itch under the captain's skin. Beyond the hum of insects, beneath their drone, was something else. Another noise. Unsnapping his holster, he left the vehicle, moving into the grove.

Weeds grew up between the rows of trees, sodden and mashed by the winter snows. Mounds of unharvested, rotting olives strewed the earth. To his left, in the distance, the prisoners were similarly strewn on the ground, eating their rations. God, he thought irritably, they were fed well. Too well. Better than they had treated their own prisoners during the war.

Was he spooking himself unnecessarily? Maybe. But his nerves were stretched thin as razor wire. Sweat pooled under his armpits. Trickled into the small of his back. He stopped. Cocked his ears. There it was. Faint but unmistakable.

". . . shall have a little fishy . . ."

One of Larkins's songs. But definitely not Larkins's voice. He strained his eyes. Through the hoary trees, he could just make out a small figure with a green Titovka cap perched jauntily on the familiar head of wheat-colored hair. *Please, God, no*, his mind raged. *Don't let it be.*

". . . on a little dishy . . ."

What the hell was Józef doing by himself, in the middle of an area riddled with land mines? He was getting closer now. Waving a fishing net over his head.

"Józef. Stop. Right there."

"Hello, Mr. Captain."

"Don't move, Józef. All right? Just stay quite still."

"I show Mr. Boss Man what I catch for Lucky." The child held aloft a jam jar, fitted with a string handle. Water sloshed on the bare ground. "A little fishy."

"NO! JÓZEF! STOP!"

". . . have a fishy when the boat . . ."

Just before the last moment lurched away into the captain's past, the midday sun glittered through the leaves of the olive trees, almost blinding him. A bird sang. Then the explosion splintered the air. Violent. Savage. Scorching. A mountain of dirt and soil spouted skyward before thudding back to earth. And Drummond began running, running, running toward the fallen child.

Somewhere behind him, Larkins screamed, "Sir. Don't. Please! Mines."

But he did. The captain kept running. This was all his fault. Had to be. Somehow.

"For fuck's sake, don't," cried Larkins.

The harder he tried to run, the more sluggish his legs felt, as if he were wading through molasses. Until his boot struck something soft on the ground, and the world sped up again.

Amazingly, the green Titovka cap still clung to the head of fair hair. Eyes, brown as well-steeped tea, still open. The small mouth, wide in a silent "*oh*" of incomprehension. But the remainder of the body was mutilated beyond repair. Instinctively, Drummond knew he was standing over a corpse. Only one small, brown minnow was still alive, gasping for air in a spreading pool of blood.

If he was conscious of anything, it was the visceral need to blow up every German soldier he could lay his hands on. With their own damned mines. All the way to Berlin. Alenka and her comrades had it right, during their forty-day rule of Trieste. An eye for a fucking eye.

Captain Drummond doubled over, struggling to breathe. His heart beat wildly. He thought he might be having a heart attack. He hoped he was. *Let me die,* he beseeched—some deity or other—so he wouldn't be haunted by the sight of this dead child, nor the sensation of the child's head against his boot, for the rest of his life.

Then came the noise of an engine gunning toward him. Larkins, driving the jeep into the grove. Brute force. Smashing trees. Oblivious of the very real danger to his own life.

Just in time, Drummond stomped the fishing net and its wooden pole to smithereens. Kicked the jam jar into the scrub. Not only had Larkins helped Józef make both, he had taken him fishing several times. The captain saw no reason his corporal need ever find out what the child had been up to before he died.

"Is it one of the wops?" shouted Larkins, careening to a stop.

"No. Not a wop."

"Well, who the . . ." He looked down, his eyes catching the green cap, and the color fled from his face. "Please Jesus, don't let . . ."

"I'm sorry, Larkins."

"Is he alive?" Larkins sank to his knees beside the mangled child, struggling to find a pulse. "We'll get him to our hospital. Now. No time to lose."

Drummond shook his head. "He had no chance."

Larkins gathered up the ripped-open, bloody body and struggled to his feet, his mouth twisted with pain. "Fucking, fucking, fucking Germans!" he screamed. "The war's supposed to be over and done with. We're supposed to have won."

The captain said nothing. There was nothing *to* say.

His corporal, clutching the lifeless body in his arms, began bawling like a baby. "What can we do?"

"It isn't as if we have a choice."

"No, sir," Larkins sobbed. "Suppose not, sir."

"Carry the little lad. Get in the jeep. I'll drive."

When Larkins had eased into the passenger seat, cradling Józef, Drummond slammed the vehicle into reverse, stopping only long enough to order his lieutenant to get the POWs back to their prison camp.

Not long after, he halted outside the house with its familiar blue door. What the hell was he going to say? Or do? This was a million times worse than spewing out bereavement letters, ad infinitum, all through the war.

"Wait in the jeep, Larkins," ordered Drummond.

"No, sir." The corporal stepped out of the jeep, his bundle tight

131

against his chest in a vain effort to keep the intestines from spilling. Already, the soaking, drenching blood was spreading its ferrous odor all over his uniform. "She's a nurse, sir, maybe there's something she can do."

Oh, dear God, the poor fellow surely doesn't still think she can bring him back to life.

Drummond banged on the door with a fist. Kicked it hard with his boots. Banged again.

"Where the hell were you?" he bellowed when Alenka opened the door.

She stared blankly at the captain. At Larkins clutching his burden. Not understanding.

"The whole damned grove was marked off. Marked for—"

"What?"

"Why weren't you *watching* him?" Drummond howled. His throat ached so badly it felt as if he'd swallowed broken glass. "Where in God's name *were* you?"

He shoved past her, into the house, and indicated Larkins should lay the child on the cloth-covered table. His corporal quickly pulled the edges of the tablecloth over the gaping guts, then stood beside the corpse, his legs spread apart for balance, eyes straight ahead, on guard.

"Let me see. Must see." Alenka shoved past Larkins. "He cannot be dead. Cannot be."

She tore aside the tablecloth, stared, and screamed. And screamed, and screamed.

Drummond found a white, ironed bedsheet in the sideboard dresser. He glanced at the photograph of the child's father, Darko, before spreading the sheet gently over his son's body. It smelled of fresh, open air.

"Corporal, wait outside for me," he whispered.

"Are you sure, sir?" Larkins's eyes were swollen red. He started to shake his head.

"Please, Larkins. I'm sure."

Reluctantly, Larkins closed the front door behind him.

Drummond turned to Alenka, and tried desperately to explain. "We were conducting a land mine sweep in an olive grove. It was cordoned off. Everything as it should have been—"

She turned on him like a raging bull. Beat his chest. Pulled his hair. Kicked his shins. Flailed and flailed, wailed and wailed. Every slap, smack, slam cathartic. The captain never wanted the pain to end.

AT SOME POINT DURING the long afternoon, an older woman slipped into the room. Ignoring the searing grief roiling the air, she took the child in her arms, muttering that she was taking him next door to prepare his body for burial. An all too familiar ritual for these people through the bitter years of war, realized Drummond. Footsteps came and went outside, but no one else entered the house.

Larkins was still outside in the jeep, clutching the steering wheel, staring hard at the blue door, as if sheer willpower could bring the child back to life. But after an hour or so, he started the engine and idled just long enough to give his captain the opportunity to leave. Then the tires thumped sluggishly down the gravel lane, a dirge of sorts. When it died away completely, Drummond trusted that despite his own grief, Larkins would drive back to Castello di Miramare, make the necessary report, and account for his officer's absence.

Too weak to keep up her furious barrage any longer, Alenka crawled on her hands and knees up the steep wooden staircase.

He followed, terrified she might try to harm herself. To his re-lief, she collapsed onto a bed, her sleep immediate and deep. But her breath was shallow—so shallow, the captain feared for her life. Over the years of the war, he had seen plenty of men die in just such a way. Not daring to leave her for even a moment, he sat bolt upright on a wooden chair, wide awake, to keep a lonely vigil all through the night.

Chapter Twenty

NEXT MORNING, THE captain stretched his aching body. Rubbed the stubble of beard sprouting on his chin. Became aware of dirt embedded in every crease of his skin. His own sweat was fetid. Splatters of Józef's blood, he saw, had dried into brown stickiness on his clothing. It repelled him. He should find somewhere to wash. But, quite unable to stop himself, he instead moved toward Alenka.

The room was still deeply shadowed, except for a ray of dawn light sliding through a single shutter slat, causing sparkles to dance in the mass of her hair. How he longed to capture each twinkle, to treasure them always. Smooth as pebbles rubbed clean by water, Shelley's "Love's Philosophy" slipped achingly through his mind.

And the sunlight clasps the earth
And the moonbeams kiss the sea:
What is all this sweet work worth
If thou kiss not me?

He simply had to touch the lips he had craved to kiss since she'd leveled her weapon at him that first morning. With an exquisite, throbbing fear, he dared to kneel beside her bed. At no point throughout the entire war had he felt such trepidation. He fully expected her to draw that Luger from under the pillow, to exact revenge for the death of her son. If this was his fate, so be it. He could not deny himself. He reached with his forefinger to gently caress first the top lip and then the lower. Soft, full, warm, and alive.

When she opened her pale gray eyes, the lids swollen and bruised from weeping, and caught sight of him, a sense of calm relief inched its way across her face. "You stay all night with me," she murmured, before pulling him toward her. Grasping the finger that had just traced her mouth, she ran a delicate, wet tongue from palm to fingertip, and then slipped the finger into her mouth. Captain Drummond wept.

Then she rose, and shed her frock and undergarments. There before him, miraculously, was the body he had held in his heart for so long. Unable to move, he simply drank in the smooth-skinned, sun-kissed body; the full, ripe breasts; the thick bush of black hair between her legs; the supple thighs; the slender feet.

Alenka unbuttoned his bloodied shirt, folded it with care, and laid it on the wooden chair where he had kept watch through the night. "Józef," she whispered, stroking the fabric with the palm of her hand. Trembling slightly, she very, very slowly unbuckled the captain's belt, unbuttoned the khaki trousers, and let them fall to the bare wood floor.

Lying on the tangle of sheets, he rolled a hand into the heavy black hair and drew her close, feeling the beat of her heart. The relief of the first kiss was like balm on a festering wound. He lowered his head in gratitude. Pressed his lips to the hollow of her throat. Rested there, inhaling the scent he loved beyond all else.

And when they made love, their cries were a mingled combination of grief and gladness. A validation of the child's short life, rather than a disregarding of his death. Hoping that Alenka could understand what he was trying to say, he held her in his arms, moved to whisper, "*To soar from earth, and find all fears lost in thy light—Eternity.*"

BY AND BY, LIGHT washed through the room. Muted voices outside called to one another. Well water pumped and splashed in the square. A tardy rooster crowed nearby. And the drowsy captain became aware of discreet tapping on the front door downstairs. Grappling awkwardly into his trousers, he opened the shutters and stepped onto the balcony. His jeep was parked in the lane, and Larkins was holding up a clean, pressed uniform.

Quietly, so as not to wake Alenka, he crept down the stairs and opened the door. Lucky darted through his legs into the kitchen, dangling a dead mouse in his mouth. An offering for his young master. Józef. The reality of the child's death hit him again.

Larkins was clearly devastated too, every bit as shattered as when he got news of the death of his wife and child. His eyes were bloodshot, and he was desperately trying to keep from breaking down. But despite his sorrow, he had brought his officer shaving supplies as if it were a perfectly normal day at Miramare. And, of course, a packet of cigarettes.

Drummond was finding it hard to talk under the circumstances. He was standing in the doorway of Alenka's house, shirtless, in a village off-limits to British soldiers. He nodded his appreciation that Larkins had managed to perform his duties without conveying judgment of any kind, then tore open the cigarette packet and lit up to cover his embarrassment. "Look here, Corporal, I don't really . . ."

"No, sir. You don't. Not to me." Larkins scraped at escaping tears with his sleeve. "I'll pick you up in about an hour? Right?"

"Right."

"And I almost forgot—the mine-clearing is underway again. Lieutenant Ward in temporary charge. All in order, sir."

In the kitchen, Drummond washed as best he could, using a pail of water he found beneath the sink, and with the aid of a small mirror hanging on the wall, managed to shave. Once he was dressed in the clean uniform, he looked at his face in the mirror again, surprised that he looked the same. Still James Alexander Drummond, twenty-nine years old, blue eyes, dark hair, despite the fact that he and Alenka had made love that very morning.

He sat heavily on a chair. Was he supposed to feel guilty about it because Józef had died yesterday? Did Alenka feel guilty? He didn't know—they had barely spoken in their desperate need for each other. What should he do now? Go back upstairs? Wake his lover? Just thinking that word caused ripples of pleasure through his body. He was dithering like a schoolboy when his jeep rolled up outside the window again. *Damn it.* Surely it had not been an hour yet.

"Brought the priest, sir," muttered Larkins, walking through the door. "Thought it wasn't right, Józef's mammy should be left alone when we leave."

The captain nodded. How on earth had Larkins managed such a feat without a word of Slovene? But then again, all the women in the village would be aware of the tragedy by now, and would have visited the church. Larkins saluted and removed himself quickly.

The young priest hovered, awkward and embarrassed in the presence of a British soldier. Especially one who was on the wrong side of the demarcation line. Especially one who appeared to have stayed in the house all night. *Makes two of us*, thought Drummond, gesturing to a chair beside the table.

Soon after, Alenka trod down the wooden stairs. She wore a black cotton skirt with a white blouse, her mass of hair pulled back and tied with a piece of string. Her face was pale as milk. She greeted the priest. Filled a kettle on the stove. Took down a jar of Nescafé, stamped *US Army,* from a shelf over the sink, and spooned coffee into stoneware mugs.

She ignored Drummond utterly. Panic gripped him. Had the morning not really happened? The joining together of their bodies. The joy. The pain. He was out of his depth. His arms hung artlessly at his sides, not even his swagger stick to keep his hands busy.

Alenka placed two steaming coffees on the table, one for herself and one for the priest. The captain might as well have been invisible. She spoke to the priest in Slovene—shutting out Drummond completely.

He felt his face flooding with anger. Was she talking about him? How he had delivered her dead son home in the arms of his corporal? How it was all his fault? How he'd helped draw arbitrary lines all over the countryside? How he had dug up Tito's enemies at Basovizza? How he was occupying Trieste, which rightly belonged to Yugoslavia?

Lucky rubbed himself against the captain's legs, mewling piteously. He scooped the cat into his arms. "Looking for Józef, eh?" he breathed into the soft black ear, struggling to control himself. He filled a bowl with water and placed it on the floor.

Drummond lit a cigarette. Mustered the remnants of his pride. With his neck stiff and his back rigid, he turned on his heel, all the while wanting nothing more than to fall to his knees on the cold stone floor in front of her.

Beseech Alenka to touch him.

Speak to him.

Love him.

Chapter Twenty-One

THE BELL'S DULL death knell pealed through the damp air as they parked on the main street directly opposite the church. Insisting they return to Opatje Selo, Larkins in his usual efficient fashion had made it his business to find out when Józef was to be buried. Since he was cheated out of his own son's funeral, he said, he was bloody well going to attend this one. Despite the irregularity of it all, Drummond found it impossible to refuse. It seemed as if their roles were reversed now—a reversal the child had taken for granted, the captain bleakly recalled. Larkins had always been Boss Man to Józef.

Truth be told, the captain would agree to almost anything to glimpse again the woman he had so recently possessed. *"In secret we met, in silence I grieve, that thy heart could forget."* He lit a cigarette, welcoming the sharp bite of nicotine scratching his lungs. It steadied him against the very real fear that making love to Alenka had been nothing more than a far-fetched fantasy.

Approaching slowly through the village square, held aloft by four members of Tito's Fourth Liberation Army, was a plain wooden coffin, on top of which rested Józef's green Titovka cap.

He couldn't wrest his eyes away. The mangled body was as tangible to him as when he and Larkins carried the boy to Alenka five days ago. Drummond realized it would remain so. Imprinted on his mind forever. Together with the sight of the child coming toward him, holding up the jar of minnows, and his own desperate, futile attempts to make the child stop. Immediately behind the coffin walked Alenka, dressed in a short, black, sleeveless frock, a light lace shawl around her shoulders. Her glorious black hair was pulled off her face, knotted tightly, and covered with a small piece of lace. A straggling procession of comrades and villagers followed. Saddest of all were the children, bemused and bewildered by what had happened to their friend.

Captain Drummond and Corporal Larkins stepped out of the jeep. As the coffin passed, they snapped to attention and saluted. Alenka glanced toward the captain, and he felt the leather band inside his cap tighten around his head like a vise. Blinking away sweat as it dribbled into his eyes, he fought back the urge to move to her side. Take her hand. Comfort her.

To the comrades and villagers, they might as well have been invisible. Perhaps a good thing, since, at the very least, they had every right to order the foreigners gone. Or worse.

When the cortege disappeared into the church, Larkins cleared his throat. "Sir."

"Right. Let's go."

They crossed the empty street; pushed through the rough-hewn, centuries-old wood door; and sought a pew at the back of the church. The place was dim and cool, lit only by a few flickering candles and sunlight winking through the high windows. Effigies of Christ crucified and dripping blood hung all around the place, making the soldier uneasy, as did the pungent smell of frankincense and myrrh. So unlike his calm and orderly parish church at home. No comfy hassock to kneel on here, only the cold stone floor. He bowed his forehead into his hands and closed his eyes.

But he couldn't pray. Not for Józef. Not for Alenka. Not for himself. The mass was interminable. All in Latin, of course, unrecognizable despite his having suffered through three years of Latin at the Royal Grammar School. Beside him, a restless Larkins fidgeted. How the child had whittled his way into Larkins's heart. It was every bit as devastating to him as the death of his own child.

After what seemed a tiresomely long time, the funeral mass ended, and the congregation began moving up the aisle. When they realized the British soldiers had been there all the time, whispers hovered. Allied soldiers, not only involved in the child's death, but trespassing in a clearly designated Yugoslav area? *Go ahead. Do your worst. I don't bloody care*, the captain's mind raged.

But the footsteps kept shuffling ahead. When the coffin passed, he saw again from the corner of his eye the lonely little Titovka cap with its bright red star. Heard the louder feet of the Jug soldiers. Then the priest, swinging the damned censer. Making his eyes water. *Damn, damn, damn.*

When the church had emptied—even Larkins moved away to give him privacy—Drummond eased off his knees, into the pew. The sooty candlewicks had been extinguished, but a greasy smell of tallow fat lingered in the air.

Gazing at the grotesque picture of Christ hanging over the altar, he ached for comfort. Longed for a cozy, blue-eyed, blond, English Jesus, like the one depicted on the front of his daughter's book of Bible stories. For something, someone, to be there. But any faith he may have possessed had departed for good long ago, the day he stumbled into a field in central Italy and found two dozen schoolgirls shot in the back of the head. Growling, he roughly knuckled his eyes.

And then a soft breath grazed the skin on the back of his neck. Alenka. Like an absolution, she leaned close and whispered, "Now we bury Józef. You come, please?"

He looked up at her, bewildered.

"It is all right."

Wordlessly, he followed her outside, Larkins too. The

congregation was gathered around the small casket, preparing to accompany it to the cemetery. One of the children had been given the Yugoslav flag to carry; hoisting it proudly, he led the way.

Drummond and Larkins joined the back of the slow parade as it wound down a lane for half a mile or so. On either side, cherry trees were beginning to blossom and grape vines were greening into bud. The fresh air was a welcome relief after the stifling church.

The graveyard was protected by a sturdy, gray stone wall, and at the far end of a well-worn path was the family plot. Each gravestone bore the name—MARUSIC—going back generations. Except for the poor fellow, Darko Marusic, thought the captain. Deep inside the Basovizza Foiba. Never to receive a proper burial. At least his son would have one in his stead.

After more interminable Latin, more waving of incense, Józef was lowered into the freshly dug hole, the flag dipped in respect for the little warrior. A pain shot through the captain's chest. Alenka sank to her knees by the side of the grave. Soil clung to her bare legs. She kissed her fingers and leaned in to caress Józef's Titovka cap tenderly.

Instinctively, Drummond reached to help her up, but Larkins stepped in front of him. Abruptly, the Jugs formed a protective screen around Alenka.

"Best we leave now, sir."

The melancholic thud of spaded earth pursued them out of the cemetery, up the lane to the village, and into the comparative security of the jeep. Drummond sat in morose silence. He must control himself. His behavior was undignified. Unprofessional. He lit a cigarette, the nicotine slamming into his lungs. What the hell, he wondered, had Alenka meant by, "*It's all right*"? It wasn't all right. What was there to keep her in the village now? Memories of a murdered husband and a dead child? No, she would return with her old comrades further into Yugoslavia, where he had no jurisdiction. No authority to follow. All he would be left with was the single memory of their lovemaking. *"Pale grew thy cheek, colder thy kiss, truly that hour foretold sorrow to this."* He would never see her again.

The mourners reappeared, crossed the square, ushering Alenka back to her home.

"Sir, we need to leave. Don't want them suddenly deciding it was all our fault. Accusing us of not keeping the area clear." Larkins cleared his throat. "We've seen the little lad off to a better place. Nothing more to be done, sir."

"Very well."

Without warning, the corporal's eyes widened. "Christ Almighty. Right now!" Larkins threw the vehicle into gear.

"What the blazes?" Drummond tossed the ciggie, cocked his revolver.

A Jug was approaching, holding something above his head. If it was a grenade, he would have to shoot the man fast, before he lobbed it at the jeep. And what an international incident that would make: a British soldier wanders into Yugoslav territory against orders and murders one of Tito's men.

"Tommy," shouted the Jug, waving his arm around. He was outside the church now.

"Fuckin' hell," muttered Larkins.

Drummond leapt over the side of the jeep. He aimed his weapon directly at the man's heart.

"Terrano!" yelled the Jug, crossing the street.

"Stay where you are," ordered the captain.

"Terrano!" The soldier finally lowered his arm. In his hand was a small, round bottle of ruby-red wine.

"You damned fool. I almost shot you." Drummond kept the revolver cocked. "What the hell do you think you're doing?"

"Alenka send me. Ask you to drink to honor life of Józef."

Could he? Dare he? Risk his life to set eyes on her once more, before she left forever? But he was outside Allied jurisdiction. No protection but his weapon. He and Larkins could easily be murdered. Bodies never found. Disposed of in the Jugs' own inimitable way. *And,* it would give Tito an opportunity to stir up trouble again if he wanted to.

Use your common sense, man, screamed the words in his head.

"Sir, please," begged Larkins, sitting in the jeep behind him.

"Come. No harm," continued the Jug, striding closer until they were standing toe to toe.

Feeling this to still be a direct threat, Drummond braced himself to use his weapon.

But the Jug stuck the bottle under his arm and thrust out his hand. He was a brute of a man. No doubt a fierce fighter. His uniform was worn, but serviceable. A brace of medals adorned his chest. "We compatriots? Got rid of Nazis together?"

Drummond grimaced. *One damned way or another.* An image of the assassinated Germans, retrieved from the Basovizza pit, laid out in neat rows, loomed in his consciousness.

"We friends. Win together. Yes?" He could smell strong homegrown tobacco on the man's breath.

Captain Drummond replaced the revolver in its holster, and accepted the proffered hand.

"Come on, Tommy—"

Drummond backed away slowly. "Not possible."

He jumped into the jeep, Larkins let out the clutch, and they sped off, leaving their "compatriot" behind in the dust. Leaving Józef behind in his grave. Leaving Alenka behind forevermore.

SEPTEMBER 1994

Chapter Twenty-Two

DESPITE MY PLEA last evening that my father reveal the reason we are here in Trieste, we spend a good part of the day examining the famous mosaics in the San Guisto Cathedral on its high hill, studiously not talking about yesterday's visit to the stables at Miramare, the sledge-boy's parentage, or my near-calamitous trip to the Karst.

Daddy is irritable all day, complaining about the gaggles of tourists, the heat, the service in the café at lunch time. It's completely out of character, but reminiscent of how he was behaving when I arrived in England, weeks ago. I propose an early night, hoping that once Daddy is properly rested, we can get back to business. Why we are here. And what exactly do the snap of Józef and the felt star mean?

Daddy suggests a nightcap, so I call down for two brandies. When a waiter delivers our drinks, we settle into the comfy chairs in our nightclothes and wallow in the glorious view of the bay. Seagulls squabble and squall in the star-encrusted sky. They swoop so close to the open windows, I'm afraid they intend to join us. They are such a tenacious and permanent feature of this city; no wonder Maximillian decorated his dining room ceiling with the birds.

After our usual toast, "Happy days," Daddy sets down his glass abruptly. "Fetch my book for me, would you, darling?" he asks. "It's on the bedside table."

"Do you really tote this massive tome everywhere with you?" Hoping to make him smile, I pretend to struggle to pick it up.

"I do. All my favorite poets in one place."

I place it carefully onto his lap. "Would you like me to read some of them to you?"

But he says nothing. His eyes meet mine, steady now, as if he's mulling over how to respond. Surely the question isn't that difficult to answer.

"Don't you feel very well?"

"It's not that."

"Well, what then?"

"You said last night that Józef wasn't any of your business. Which is mostly true. But there is something I haven't told you yet . . . that is . . . that is very much your business."

"Well, well, at long last."

But he doesn't say any more. Simply ruffles his thumb through the pages of the book, driving me crazy. Just when I can't stand the noise any longer, he apparently finds what he is looking for. A flimsy, blue airmail envelope.

"You have to read this," he says.

But a vague recollection of a different airmail letter from a time long gone gusts through my mind, raising the hairs on the back of my neck. A warning of danger? I feel suddenly detached from the here and now, from the city scenes hanging on the walls; the rich smell of brandy; the Adriatic beyond the window. I'm here but I'm not. Waiting for what? What am I afraid of, all of a sudden?

"Please, read the letter," Daddy urges.

"I don't want to read your private correspondence."

"Georgie Girl, I want you to. I insist." A sudden tremor passes through his fingers, and the letter flutters onto the rug at his feet. "I've been trying to find the right time to give it to you. I tried the night Louisa and Annabel argued about guilt. But when we got to my flat, I couldn't pluck up enough nerve."

"Really? Because you're guilty of some crime?"

"A jury of my peers might certainly think so."

Oh, my God! Reluctantly, I lean over and pick up the envelope. The front is completely covered in scratched-out addresses of every home Daddy has ever lived in. Eskdale Terrace, where I was born and raised. And then on to the Wynding, our holiday cottage in Bamburgh for many years. From there, it somehow made it to my parents' retirement home on the River Thames in Gloucestershire, and finally to Cross Keys Court. How long must all this rerouting have taken? I'm astonished the letter wasn't tossed, mislaid, or otherwise lost along the way.

"Read it now, darling. Then we can talk."

I take a large slug of brandy. Then another. Outside, Miramare beckons seductively, like Lorelei on her rock. But I can't put off the inevitable. After all, I asked him yesterday to come clean and explain himself.

+366(0)1 417232619 Gornji Trg.
Ljubljana
Slovenia

10 March, 1994

Dear Captain Drummond,

I hope that you will receive this letter, and God willing, you are alive.

You knew my mother, Alenka Marusic, over many months after the end of WWII in Trieste, Italy. She never made any secret of who my father was, but over the years, she always forbid me to disturb you with such knowledge. However, she has recently now passed away, God rest her soul, and I found your name and address among

her papers. I take it upon myself to defy her wishes and impose myself on you.

Much time has passed, so I hope that this news will not come to
distress you. I am having a wife Ava, and two children. A son Józef
who is aged ten years. His name, you will recognize, I am being sure.
And a daughter, Mia, who is aged eight years.

In hopes you will respond to me.

And hoping this finds you in good health.

Greetings from your son,

Janez Marusic

A bolt out of the blue. I've always found the expression rather
silly, but now I completely understand. I'm riven in two, as if by
lightning. I push out of my chair and start pacing, desperate to
calm down and try to make some sense of this bombshell. The
sender's address is in Slovenia. Only a few short miles away. I rush
to the window, as if I expect the country to materialize before my
eyes and offer an explanation for what I have just read.

The irony of the situation isn't completely lost on me. Having
stewed over sledge boy's origins, I am now confronted with a double whammy. A genuine son. But someone else entirely.

"When on earth did you get this?" I ask, waving the letter in
front of my father's nose.

"Shortly before you brought the girls to visit." Bright red spots
erupt on his cheeks. At least he has the grace to be embarrassed.

I sit down abruptly. "Five whole weeks ago, and you never
thought to tell me!"

"It was difficult to absorb what the letter said. What it meant.
The shock was tremendous." He is tugging on his dressing gown
sleeve, and I reach for his hand in order to calm him.

"And I feared you would lose all respect for me if I told you the truth. That I would lose you."

"Lose me? Listen, Daddy, I need you too much for that to ever happen."

I don't add that other than Michael, he's the only person in the world who understands all of me. Every failing, fault, and flaw. Which is why, I realize, he asked about my green goblin, George, yesterday. My fingers itch for a cigarette, for the sensation of nicotine bombarding my chest with its poison.

"At least it's clear now why you wanted to come to Italy."

Daddy says nothing.

"You did respond to . . . to this . . . this son of yours?"

His shoulders sag, making him appear somewhat diminished. He shakes his head slowly.

"Because you're embarrassed?" I ask, Lou's *Don't you ever feel guilty?* outburst in the restaurant rattling repeatedly through my head.

"All I knew was I wanted to get myself back to Trieste first. And then . . . try to decide . . . how best to proceed."

"And this woman? This Alenka? She was real?"

"Oh, yes. She was real."

"And you loved her?"

"I did. And she loved me too. I know she did. Why didn't she let me know about the birth of our child? I don't understand. How could she not have written? She had my address."

"I'm in no position to answer that."

"Perhaps I should just have destroyed the letter from Slovenia. Let sleeping dogs lie, as the saying goes. Instead of burdening you with it. It wasn't fair."

I lay the letter carefully in his lap.

"Fair or not, you did burden me with it. Now I know you had

a passionate affair when I was a little girl. Now I know I have a brother as a result of this relationship, who turns out not to be the boy on the sledge. There is no going back from this. No going back at all!"

Chapter Twenty-Three

B ACK IN MY own bedroom, I drag on a pair of jeans and snatch up a flannel shirt, one of Annie's that I found abandoned in the bottom of my suitcase. I dash down the stairs and out of the hotel. Crossing the dual carriageway, where a railway line once ran, I cause several irate motorists to blow their horns at me before I reach the safety of the seafront. It is chilly, which fits my mood. I pull the hood of the shirt over my head and masquerade as one of Annie's grunge crowd.

What I would really like to do is walk for miles, but I barely know this city, listing its way up the steep hillside to the Karst. And after my experience yesterday, common sense prevails. Instead, I perch awkwardly on a black bollard and smoke a cigarette, staring at pinpricks of light twinkling behind shutters, reminding me of all the other lives that are being lived day after day in the world. Some happy. Some sad. Some simply existing. Where do I fit in? I've no idea at all.

Aided by my green goblin, George, Daddy's infuriating questions jangle around in my brain: *Why didn't she let me know about the birth of our child? How could she not have written?*

What in God's name was I supposed to say to that? *I'm your child. Me. Me. Your Georgie Girl.*

Unbidden, the blue airmail letter of long ago blows across my consciousness again, delivering a distant childhood morning in perfect detail. The sense of foreboding I felt earlier tonight was right on target.

It was the summer term of 1947, and I was home from school with an ugly case of chicken pox. Having finished *Five on a Treasure Island* for the third time, I was bored out of my mind. Mummy promised to pop around to the library to look for more *Fives* if I promised to stay in bed. Granny was helping out because of my illness, and I could hear her in the kitchen cooking luncheon. Probably horrid gray mince again—meat was still rationed, and what there was of it was quite suspect in my mother's opinion. On more than one occasion she had wondered if we weren't in fact chewing one of Mr. Lawson's beach donkeys!

When I heard the morning post plopping through the letter box, I could not resist getting out of bed, hoping my *School Friend* magazine had arrived. Instead, there was a flimsy blue envelope lying on the doormat, which intrigued me. I was just about to tip-toe downstairs when Mummy's key turned in the lock, so I peered over the banister instead. She spotted the letter right away and squatted down to read the envelope. After several moments, she picked up the unusual missive between finger and thumb, just the way she had the dead mouse she found in the pantry, and marched into the kitchen. There was frantic whispering, followed by an argument.

Of course, I was far too nosy to mind my own business. Not for nothing was Blyton's plucky, spunky Georgina, who could never let a mystery go unexplored, my favorite character. I sneaked downstairs.

The kitchen door was not quite shut. Granny was holding the letter over a stream of steam, pouring from the spout of the kettle. As if by magic, the flap of the envelope curled open. She turned to my mummy, sitting at the table. "Here, Mary. Read it."

Now I wished I weren't playing spies. What I was watching felt wrong, though I did not understand why. But I was frozen to the cold linoleum floor, quite unable to move.

Mummy pulled a flimsy, blue sheet of paper from the envelope. As she read, her face flushed the most awful shade of scarlet; then her head slowly drooped, even the curls in her hair seemed to sag, and a large teardrop fell onto the piece of paper. She handed it to my granny. I was frightened. I wanted to walk through the door for a quick cuddle. Why didn't I?

"No good can come of this, my dear," said Granny. "Best ignore it, don't you think?"

My mother said nothing. Just gripped handfuls of fabric in her fingers, till the skirt she wore was a wrinkled mess.

"Once this cat is out of the bag, there is no knowing what might happen. Think of Georgina. How this news could affect her whole life. I say, least said, soonest mended."

Mummy crouched in her chair as if someone had struck her.

"He won't find out, dear. How could he? He'll never know. Best get rid of the letter now."

"Very well." Mummy's voice was brittle, different to the way she normally sounded, like nothing I had ever heard before. She unfolded herself from the chair as slowly and painfully as an old woman plagued with aches and pains, and lighted a spelk from the pilot light on the stove. She clasped the letter over Daddy's ashtray. Held the flame to it. When the letter had burned to ashes, she did the same thing with the envelope.

"There, there, Mary. All done. We can go on just as before."

Perched on the bollard, I crush the end of my cigarette underfoot, trying to digest this scene from the past. I can only assume it was sparked by the arrival of the second blue airmail letter for Captain Drummond, forty-seven years after the first.

But Granny was wrong that day. Life couldn't possibly have

gone on just as it had before, no matter how much she and my mother hoped it would. Not with such a huge secret hanging over the family, surely? Their act of defiance must have insidiously affected how we lived together. I was the one Daddy turned to after every night horror. Did he speak names that my mother recognized, making it impossible for her to offer comfort? Adding to the guilt she already bore, the guilt of hiding his son from him?

The polizia begin checking cars parked overnight along the Le Rive. I worry they will decide to check on me too. A lonely, middle-aged woman, huddled in a hoodie, probably looks a bit suspect. My bum's getting cold anyway, so I ease off the bollard. But I am not ready to face my father yet. Not tonight, anyway. Because it's slowly dawning on me that I can in fact answer his questions. But for the life of me, I don't know what the hell to do about it. Do I tell him? Should I tell him? Because if I do, the truth will completely alter the memories he has of his long-lived marriage.

One by one, I tick them off in my head.

Alenka did contact you.

Your wife intercepted the letter.

Your wife read the letter.

Your wife burned the letter.

So, any decision you would have had to make in regard to Mummy and me went up in smoke in 1947.

Chapter Twenty-Four

Back in the hotel, I soak in a hot bath, enveloped in a
fug of steam, facing the fact that I haven't been any more
truthful in my marriage than my parents were. Swaddled
in the muggy warmth, loving the sense of weightlessness it affords,
I allow myself a self-indulgent wallow in the past.

After our first kiss on the riverbank in the lamplight, Michael
and I had stood close together, not touching, letting our eyes ask
all the questions our lips did not. My insides dissolved. I was warm
and wet, craving a man I had only just met. Had I gone utterly
insane? Crazy? Out of my mind?

Michael placed his hands on my shoulders. "We can do this the
conventional way—waste weeks playing games, sending flowers,
writing love letters, eating candlelit meals—or we can make love
now and work our way backward through the getting-to-know
parts later."

Crazy or not, I took Michael's hand and moved into our future.
No hesitation. Not for a moment. No sense of guilt, as I remember. Nothing had ever felt so right in my life before.

When we stepped over the threshold of Michael's flat in
Wapping, I was greeted by a spicy smell of nutmeg and clove.
Michael explained the brick walls were part of a once-upon-a-time
warehouse. I imagined sailing ships docked in the river, delivering their exotic cargoes to the royal courts of England. We made
our way hurriedly past jars of brushes, easels, drafting tables, piles

of books, vivid wool rugs, and scattered chairs, before we finally slowed.

Michael undressed me. Each button on my blouse loosed carefully. His arms glided behind me to unsnap my bra. He cupped my breasts, lowered his head to suck gently on my nipples. He slipped off my skirt and slid off my knickers. Laying me on his bed, he unzipped my boots and massaged my feet, calves, and thighs.

The moon poured through the wall-wide window. Haunting foghorns wailed downriver. When Michael peeled off his own clothing, he leaned over me, his breath warm on my ears, cheeks, lips. His skin was smooth, with the faintest odor of turpentine, linseed oil, and perspiration. I kissed him gently, and licked his neck. I was fully aware how many would choose to label me for the choices I made that night: breaking my marriage vows, causing potential harm to my children. Yet, I did not feel I was behaving badly. Rather, I was entering a separate world, quite apart from Paul, his family, and Minnesota.

Michael was hard and smooth. I rested my leg on his hip and guided him into me. He moved rhythmically with a gentle, wet swooshing sound, all the time gazing at me with his hazel eyes. Then he pumped harder. I gripped my knees around his waist. "Georgina," he cried, his voice overflowing with love. When he tipped slowly forward onto me as he softened, we held each other. A coming home of sorts for both of us.

The bathwater is cold now, my fingers white and puckered. I drain the tub; ease my unloved body, deprived of Michael for so long now, onto the thick, fluffy mat; and dry myself. I would like so much to be able to pick up the phone. I would like to be able to hear Michael's voice. To be able to tell him about tonight. What I've just learned of my father's secret life. What I've recalled of my mother's. But Michael was lost to me many years ago.

So, I gaze out of the window onto the now-deserted Le Rive. The bollard where I sat. The rolling dark ocean. I drink a glass of water. Take a sleeping pill. Lie down on the bed. Count imperceptible cracks in the ceiling. Trace lacy leaves on the wallpaper. But I am getting wider and wider awake. I need to speak with someone, or I will explode into a million pieces.

In desperation, I put in a call to Paul. But when the operator connects me, the phone rings and rings. He isn't home from work yet. Seven hours behind Trieste time. I remember that our new answering machine will kick in at any moment. I don't want to leave a message. Not of this magnitude. Just as I am about to hang up, Paul grabs the receiver, out of breath.

"Hello, Wharton residence."

"Hi, Paul. It's me."

"Well, what a surprise. What an honor. I assume you've arrived safely."

"I just wanted to talk to you."

"What's wrong? Are you all right? You're so damned far away."

"I had a bit of a shock—"

"What! Are you hurt?"

"*PAUL*. Please, let me explain."

"Okay. Sorry."

I hear him toss his jacket in a heap and slump into the chair beside our telephone, presumably ready to listen now. Peanut, our dear black mutt, click-clacks his paws across the wood floor to greet his master. I swear I can hear his slurpy licks across the miles.

"Daddy had an affair right after the war—"

"What?"

"Yes, with one of the locals, apparently. He—"

"I can't believe that. This is *your* dad we're talking about, right?"

"He just showed me a letter he received from Ljubljana."

"Where the hell is that? Doesn't even sound like a real place."

"Just listen, Paul. The letter is from the son of this woman . . . claiming Daddy is his father."

A huge snort erupts on the other end of the line. I imagine the cables running from Minnesota, under the Atlantic, across Europe, only to end up here in my hotel room, delivering his dismissive scoff into my ear. My mind travels home, to the hallway where I know Paul is sitting; into the sunken living room; up through the dining room; into the kitchen with the island counter grill; to the cozy den and screened porch. How little I miss it.

"It's just a scam, Georgina," he says, "plain and simple. The guy is out to blackmail your dad. Looking for an inheritance, most likely."

And he's off, putting his own spin on things. The way he always does.

"I bet these assholes get hold of lists of everybody who served there during the occupation. Find out who's still alive. Then, bam. Big rip-off."

"The thought never crossed my mind."

But Paul is rambling on. "The best thing for you to do is take the old man home. The sooner the better. Doesn't do any good digging up what might or might not have happened fifty years ago."

I don't bother to mention how confused I feel about learning I have a brother, because I know what Paul will say. *Forget this bull-shit. Everything will be okay when you get your dad home. You just need to get your priorities straight.* We never seem able to get below the surface of things.

"You've been gone weeks, Gina. It's like you've forgotten all about me. I don't think you miss me at all."

"Don't start all that again, Paul. I told you, I'll be home in a couple of weeks."

But the dismal truth is I don't miss him. Over time, it has become sadly easy to forget him entirely when I'm traveling. Which I suppose makes me some kind of an A-one bitch.

"Cheer up, Paul," I add. "Lou and Annie will be home tomorrow. Then you'll all be off to Wind Lake."

"Where you should be too. Back where you belong."

Back where I belong? Before he can harangue me further, I mumble a goodbye. His parting shot is cut off as I place the receiver back on its cradle with a sigh of relief.

Chapter Twenty-Five

WHEN I HEAR my father moving around, I poke my head around our adjoining door, groggy from the combination of brandy and sleeping pills. He is dressed but looks tired. I don't suppose he slept very well either, after finally sharing his overwhelming news with me.

"I don't know about you, Daddy, but I could use some fresh air this morning. How about a wander around the canal? Find somewhere for breakfast?"

I'm hoping it will be easier for us to discuss the contents of the Ljubljana letter outdoors. For discuss it we must. I can't stay in Italy forever.

An hour later, after a reasonably brisk walk across the magnificent Piazza dell'Unita to the man-made canal slotting its way into the city, we settle under the bright yellow awning of a small café. Daddy orders pots of hot chocolate and large slices of apple strudel.

"Strictly against doctor's orders," Daddy comments. "But I don't give a damn. I'm in the mood for sugar."

"I phoned Paul last night," I tell him, doing my best to keep my tone light. "He thinks your letter is a scam. Is there any possibility he could be right?"

"Absolutely not." Daddy's voice is firm. I have no reason to disbelieve him.

While we wait for our breakfast, I ask: "Did you tell my mother about your affair?"

He shakes his head ruefully. "I couldn't hurt her. What happened between Alenka and me was otherworldly."

Immediately, Michael weeps his way back into my middle-aged heart. A separate life. An otherworldly life. The same for us both. In my parallel life, I had floated like Fragonard's girl on her swing, caught in the sting of love.

For a moment or two, I'm tempted to share the story of Michael, how I too had an illicit affair, but it feels selfish. Today is not about me, or shouldn't be, but about discussing Daddy's stunning news as honestly as possible.

When the waiter places a tray of warm strudel and steaming chocolate on the table, Daddy takes my hand and squeezes hard. "Are you upset with me for not showing you the letter from Janez right away? Not telling you about my affair with Alenka?"

"I *am* upset. Mostly, about your questions."

"Questions?" Daddy looks baffled.

"You don't remember, do you? You asked me why this woman, Alenka, hadn't let you know about the birth of your child. Why she hadn't written. How on earth do you think that made me feel?"

"Oh, Georgie Girl. Please forgive me. I didn't mean it literally." He shakes his head, looking crestfallen, and mutters almost to himself, "How could I have been so thoughtless?"

I take a bite of flaky, sweet strudel and weigh my options. I can say to my darling daddy: *I have your answers. I know the truth. Alenka did write you a letter. It was hidden from you. And destroyed.* Or I can ignore that particular act of duplicity, and pose another question.

"Daddy, for the sake of argument, what if this woman had written with news of your son?"

"But she didn't."

"But suppose she had. Then you would have been forced into

telling Mummy everything. Forced to make a choice. Stay with us in England? Or run off to some godforsaken country behind the Iron Curtain?"

I can't stop talking. I have an urgent need to know what he would have done if the evidence had not been snuffed out in a puff of flame. When I finally fell asleep last night, I dreamed of Mum as her young self, standing in the hall of our old home in Newcastle. Holding that first thin blue sheet of paper sent from overseas. Waiting for Daddy to come home. Demanding an explanation.

"Would you have left us?"

I want to scream out loud: *—a letter came, —a letter was read, —a letter was set alight and burned in an ashtray.* The words prick my tongue, where they remain, unsaid. I'm at a loss for what to do.

Daddy holds the cup in both hands and gulps the chocolate greedily. "You know, Georgie Girl, lots of soldiers didn't go home after the war. They made their lives in Europe with women they had met."

A sad, pathetic anger lodges in my gut, like a shriveled-up plant starved of water. "Is this your way of telling me you thought about staying too?"

How different my life would have been, if my only recollection of this dear man was a cold winter morning in the backyard with my bunny. The black-and-white photograph of him, hung over the mantelpiece, fading gradually over time.

"No, of course not. That's not what I'm saying at all. I was a married man. I always knew we only had a finite amount of time together. Alenka and I said our farewells."

"Except, when you said those farewells, neither of you knew about the child."

"Ah, yes. The child."

"Quite! Which leaves my original question. If you had known about him, what would you have done? Please tell me."

But Daddy is far away, staring at the moored motorboats in the flat, oily water of the canal. Recalling his lover? Is she weaving her way through his mind, like a will-o'-the-wisp, as Michael does mine? Except Michael and I didn't know our time was finite. We didn't get to say our farewells.

I swirl crumbs of pastry around my plate. Do I tell Daddy the truth? My parents deceived each other. Daddy conducted an affair in Trieste. Mummy destroyed proof of his son. They both paid dearly for their actions. *What tangled webs we weave.*

Realizing I am not going to get an answer anytime soon, I pay the bill and suggest a stroll along the Molo Audace, stretching into the Bay of Trieste. It is a calm, trouble-free harbor now; not a battleship in sight, not a single armed soldier on patrol. So very different a place from when Daddy was here immediately after the war. But on cue, a distant rumble of mortar fire grinds across the water from Croatia.

Daddy flinches. "More conflict. Bloody pointless."

"Nothing ever gets fixed, does it?"

"No. Just a few awkward pauses, now and then."

We rest on a bench at the end of the quay, shoulders brushing together, listening to the water slap-slap-slapping against the stone wall.

"Georgie Girl—everything you know now—do you feel differently about me?"

"Perhaps you mean ashamed?" I suggest, laying my head on his shoulder.

"All right, do you feel ashamed of me?"

Shaken, certainly, at the very idea of having a brother, coupled with the admission of the obviously fervent affair with the man's mother. But I wonder if I don't owe him some slack, considering the brutal years of the war, when he must have lived daily with the realization that his life could be over in a flash. And besides, what right in the world do I have to play a holier-than-thou role?

"If I was ashamed of you, Daddy, it would be a case of the pot calling the kettle black."

"Really? Whatever do you mean?"

"I haven't been faithful to Paul."

Daddy is hushed for a while. Across the bay, Miramare shimmers in the morning sun. Sailboats scud over the water. Then he states emphatically: "Michael O'Hannery."

Well, I'll be damned!

When I lift my head to look at Daddy, I know my mouth is wide with shock, like a goldfish. They had only met once. My father had taken the train down to London for a few days, to treat me to a cornucopia of music at the Royal Opera House. And I had invited Michael—as my new illustrator, not as my lover—to meet us for dinner one evening.

"Was it that obvious?"

"Your friend was not very good at hiding his feelings for you." Daddy smiles. "And you did start spending rather a lot of time back in England, for quite a while."

"Did you tell Mum?"

"There seemed no need to upset her, since you had obviously decided, in the end, to stay with Paul. And the girls were still so young."

Yes, Daddy. I stayed with Paul, but not for the reasons you think. The girls were spared learning how close I had come to leaving their father only because of an unimaginable event, eleven years ago.

"For a long time after, I could barely hold myself together."

I had wanted so badly to marry Michael. Make a life together. I had flown home to find the kindest way possible to tell Paul I was leaving him, to consult with a lawyer, to gear up for what would inevitably be a nasty fight over custody arrangements—spearheaded, no doubt, by Ellen.

"Do you remember the sitcom *Butterflies*?" I ask. "It was British, but it aired in the US in the eighties? About a bored, middle-aged housewife, with a boring husband and two insufferable boys."

"Very well. The theme music was Albinoni's 'Adagio in G Minor.'"

"Trust you to remember that." I kiss his cheek. "At the end of each show, the woman trailed home from a clandestine, but entirely innocent meeting with a man to cook her family yet another meal. I connected so strongly with the character; I would find myself awash in tears of self-pity sometimes. Paul decided I was entering early menopause."

"Oh, dear girl." Daddy reaches for my hand and squeezes, rewarding me with the imperceptible twitch of our lifelong connection.

"You mentioned how young the girls were. But I'm not sure the situation is much different now. I *still* worry my daughters will never forgive me if I walk away from Paul."

"And you want to be part of their lives, you're just not sure you want to be part of the marriage anymore?"

"I'm afraid so."

The marriage. All twenty-seven years of it, caring for the children through moments of love, hope, drama, doomed expectations, disappointment, boredom, resignation. To get where we are today. Which is . . . ?

"I am not sure I'm the one to offer advice."

"I don't even know why I'm telling you this. But what we *can* decide is what to do next about Janez."

"Do next?"

"You can't drop Janez in my lap, Daddy, without any sort of plan! You have choices. Write and let him know you're in Trieste. Or I can drive you to Ljubljana. It isn't far. Or simply stop all this. Go no further. We have open tickets home. We can go back any time."

"I do worry it's too late. Would it be wiser to leave the past in the past after all this time? Perhaps if I had known sooner, before I got to be a tired old man." His sigh is so deep, he makes himself cough.

"You're an old soldier. Think of this as one more battle."

"Battle?" Daddy looks faintly amused. As if on cue, mortar fire in Croatia growls and grumbles over the water again. A not-so-subtle reminder that the world we live in has not changed very much.

"Sorry. Bad choice of words. But you chose to come here, which tells me you have a strong need to connect at some level. Recognize it as a chance to put things to rights. Don't give up now."

I'm not entirely sure I really mean what I am saying. My father, in attempting to right this wrong, will alter both our lives in ways I cannot yet imagine. But I yatter on, for reasons I do not understand. I am still dazed by what Mum did to keep secret the fact of her husband's newborn son. The cruelty of it. But what would I have done in such circumstances? Suppose Paul's old fiancée had announced she had given birth to his child? And a son, no less! I almost burst out laughing. Ellen would have been cock-a-hoop. A son and heir! Would I have acted in the same way as my mother? Is it what most women would have done under the circumstances? Can it be excused by the argument that my mother and grandmother had *my* best interests at heart? I don't know. I'm not sure I will ever know.

For a moment, I'm tempted to get it all out in the open. Enough of these secrets. Then I remind myself Mummy can no longer defend herself. And anyway, what possible good can come from speaking the truth now, when it would only hurt Daddy unnecessarily? What was it Granny said? *"Least said, soonest mended."*

"Tell you what. We'll go back to the hotel now, and you can write to your son."

"What—how—I can't—"

"Yes, Daddy. You can. Start by telling Janez about your feelings for his mother. What she meant to you. That you had no way of knowing she had given birth to your child."

"And let him know I'm here in Trieste?"

"Of course!"

JUNE –
SEPTEMBER 1946

Chapter Twenty-Six

THOROUGHLY DISPIRITED, DRUMMOND stared out of his office window, smoking. He would call it a day soon. Get Larkins to drive him to the club in Trieste. Drink whiskey all afternoon. Forget. All the things he did not want to think about. The recurring image of Józef's broken body lying on the ground. The bumbling visit home. The knowledge that sooner, rather than later, he would receive orders to return to England. It was six weeks since he and Alenka had made love. Did she care at all what had happened? Perhaps it never had actually happened. More likely, it was no more than a figment of his overwrought imagination. His mind continued to meander moodily, until a knock on the door interrupted his thoughts.

"Enter."

A baby-faced private, newly minted, newly out from England, stood there blushing.

"Well?"

"There's a woman outside. Says she needs to speak to Captain Drummond."

"Hand her off to Robinson. I'm leaving in a few minutes."

"She insists. Says it is to do with a death in one of the mine fields."

His chest bunched tight. She'd come. As he had let himself imagine she might, in rare, fleeting moments.

"Is she armed?"

"No, sir. But she is a Jug. Got a uniform on to prove it."

"All right. Bring her in."

The captain got himself into the chair behind his desk and groped a cigarette from its packet. Two sets of footsteps rang on the parquet floor outside. Two sets of footsteps entered his office. He drew deeply on the ciggie before daring to raise his head.

Alenka looked extraordinary, all the way down to the heavy, clumping boots. He hoped she had been searched thoroughly. She probably still had the German Luger hidden somewhere or other in the folds of her military shirt and pants.

"Do you want me to stay, sir?" asked the private.

He waved him away.

As the man's footsteps faded into the distance, Drummond met Alenka's eyes. "How did you get here?"

"On a farm cart, coming into Trst."

"Sit down." Drummond dragged on the cigarette again, rubbing his chest to loosen the painful knots that had formed.

She ignored him, remained standing. "You did not come to my house?"

"No. It wasn't appropriate."

"What does that mean? You came to funeral. You came to burial. But you take no wine with me?"

He gazed at the Titovka cap, perched on the mass of spiraled-up black hair. Thought fleetingly of the smaller Titovka cap buried in Józef's grave. He focused on the red star to avoid Alenka's flaring gray eyes.

"After we . . . after we . . . er . . . I had the distinct impression you did not want anything more to do with me." He stubbed his cigarette into an overflowing ashtray, then plunged into the question *he* wanted to ask. "What did you mean when you said 'It's all right'?"

Alenka stuck her hands in her pockets, looking wrong-footed for the first time.

"You said 'It's all right' in the church," he repeated. "You said those words to me."

She seemed to shrink slightly into the drab olive shirt she was wearing, and began a slow circuit of the room. Checked the view from his window. Examined a chart on the wall. Dear God, it was classified. Any sane officer would get rid of her. When she reached his desk, she picked up the silver-framed photograph and studied it closely. Drummond coughed, embarrassed. Not sure why—except his wife and child were trapped in the frame, caught in a moment long ago, helpless to defend themselves. But from what, exactly? Losing dominion over him?

"They are alive," she said.

"Yes."

"Darko and Józef not."

"No."

Alenka's eyes clouded. A deep frown furrowed her forehead. Convinced she was about to smash the picture of his family against the wall, Drummond braced himself for the sound of shattering glass. How ironic for it to have survived years of battle, only to be destroyed now by an anguished Slovenian woman after the war had ended. But instead, surprisingly, she clutched it close to her chest.

"I know why you not come to house. You thought if you ignore me, would force me to come find you."

It wasn't quite that simple, but as much as he had longed with every fiber of his being to accompany the Slav soldier back to her house on the day of Józef's funeral, military common sense had won out. And there was more. He had not wanted to seem to grovel. His pride still smarted from the way she had snubbed him in front of the priest.

"Actually, I expected you would have left the village by now. I assumed you would rejoin your comrades."

"And do you know why I did not?"

"No." He had no idea. This woman, who consumed him body, soul, and mind, was a complete mystery. But one he still yearned to unravel, piece by piece.

She leaned across his desk, brandishing the photograph of Mary and Georgina in front of his face. "You feel guilty? You feel shame of what we do before, Captain Drummond?"

He stared at the two people he had wronged. Mary, his wife. And his little Georgie Girl. Did he feel guilty? He ought to, because Alenka was referring to his one glorious, tantalizing taste of heaven.

"What do you want, Alenka?"

"I do not know." Instead of destroying his photograph, the fire seemed to fizzle from her.

She replaced it on the desk beside him. "I am sad. Angry. Days I cannot believe Józef will not walk through door." She finally sank into the chair opposite him. "You think me bad mother?"

"Why?"

"Because my son play loose in countryside." She lowered her forehead on top of the desk.

Mesmerized, he watched shivers shudder down her spine. Like a creature in pain, she made not a sound.

Drummond steadied himself enough to rise from his seat and kneel beside her. "I don't think that at all, Alenka. It was a frightful accident." He hugged her clumsily. "I am so sorry."

Selfishly, he was sorry for himself too. He knew the episode in the olive grove would never go away. It would haunt him for the rest of his life.

"Will you take me home, Captain?" she begged.

"Of course."

He opened the office door and told the private to fetch him a vehicle from the pool. No driver. Then he strapped on his revolver, checked the ammunition, refilled his cigarette case, grabbed his stick and cap, and escorted Alenka out of the castle.

He drove fast. Waves dashed against the shore, against ships; winds plucked mast ropes, pulled mooring ropes. They pushed through the city, onto the plateau. Rattled along the rough road to Opatje Selo. He glanced at his passenger occasionally, and to his relief saw her face had calmed. She now appeared resolute, as if she had reached a decision.

"Can we stop?" she asked.

"Where?"

"Just here."

He pulled off the road and parked the jeep as close as he could to a tumble-down stone wall, beneath an overhanging tree, for camouflage.

"Why?"

"I show you."

Drummond followed her over the wall and into a dense thicket. The farther they pushed through the brambles, the deeper a nagging fear penetrated him. God Almighty! She had planned this. A setup. Terror gripped his bowels. Any minute she would pull out that damned Luger and blow his head off, or she would lead him into an ambush. Revenge for Józef's pointless death. Revenge because Georgina was alive. Clear as day, he saw Alenka flourishing the picture of his wife and child.

The trail was narrow and overgrown, and he couldn't make out where the hell he was. They appeared to be moving rapidly down-hill for a mile or more. But rather than retreat from what was surely a lethal situation, as he had been trained to do, he followed behind her blindly, like Mary's little lamb.

His desire for her filled him with a need so sharp, it erased any thoughts he might have had to extradite himself from danger. *So be it,* he told himself. *I survived the bloody war. If my number is up now . . .* Gradually he became aware of a bubbling, roaring noise. Water, getting louder. And birds chirruping, lots of them. It seemed a lifetime before they eventually emerged into a large clearing, surrounded by steep limestone walls. On the far side was a waterfall, splashing out of solid rock.

He took a deep breath. Looked around. Raised his hands. Ready to surrender. Except—there were no Partisans. No firing squad. Just this woman before him.

So, why had she brought him here? What did she want? He clasped her chin gently in his hands. Gazed into her haunted gray eyes. He saw grief, certainly, but what else was there, he couldn't discern. She didn't move. Didn't speak. Just waited.

The captain placed his mouth on the nape of her bare neck, beneath the Titovka cap, and ran his tongue back and forth across her briny skin. The musical cacophony of water and birds was making him giddy. He unfastened her shirt and clasped a hand around her full, round breast. The nipple pushed urgently against his thumb, demanding attention. He lowered his head like a starv-ing infant. When a deep moan rattled in her throat, he nudged her quickly against one of the sheer rock walls, toppling her cap and releasing the hair.

"My Boadicea," he whispered against the racket of the falls in their ears.

"Who?" she gasped.

"A warrior queen." Drummond raised his head and kissed her mouth, hard. Explored with his tongue. She shuddered. Kicked off her boots and trousers. Wrapped her thighs around his waist. Frantic now, he unbuckled his belt and tore the buttons from the fly in his urgency. When he entered her, she was ready, welcoming, humming with pleasure. Having held back his dam of longing for so many weeks, his relief was immediate. *Thank you, thank you, thank you, my beloved*, rang the words through his head.

He clung to her, but Alenka slithered to the ground, took his hand, and led him to the waterfall. Removing the remainder of their clothing, they stood beneath the crystal-clear, sparkling water and caressed each other slowly. Much, much later, they lay on their backs in the clearing and let the afternoon sun dry their bodies.

"This place?" he asked.

"Partisan hideout from old days."

"I was convinced you were going to produce a couple of your comrades to finish me off."

"Did you?" A flicker of surprise flashed in her gray eyes.

"Made no difference, my darling. I would have followed you regardless, to the ends of the earth."

"So, warrior queen? Tell me of her."

"She was fearless. Like you. Fought off Romans, invading Ancient Britain."

Alenka rolled onto her side, rested her cheek on her hand. Smiled. "All this, Captain Drummond, and I do not know even your given name?"

With tingling fingers, he explored each hill and valley of her body—from the top of her head to the arch of one slender foot—before his tongue retraced the route—salty, salty, salty—all the way back to her waiting lips. Then he raised his head and laughed with joy. "James. My name is James."

Chapter Twenty-Seven

THE DAY THEY made love at the waterfall, Alenka implored James to find them a room in the city. A place further away from her memories of Opatje Selo and Józef's death. A place for them to meet until James was returned to England. Shortly afterward, with help from Larkins, Drummond found a place to rent in an old tenement building tucked in a narrow alley in the heart of Trieste.

IT WAS FULL SUMMER now, scorching hot, and Drummond wore his standard tropical kit daily; shorts with long socks. But still he sweated, mounting the stairs to their room on the second floor.

Before he could slip the old iron key into the lock, Alenka opened the door wide. Her hair was pulled off her face, into a thick braid that trailed down her back, exposing her high cheekbones. The frock today was a pristine green, resembling blades of English grass poking through the earth. Drummond was acutely aware that beneath the frock, she was naked. But he would savor the intensity of his desire for as long as he was able without actually touching her. He sat down at the table beneath the window. It was wide open, but the breeze was nonexistent. A sleek film of perspiration gleamed on Alenka's face, arms, legs.

"Wine?" She held up a bottle and two glasses.

"Please, darling."

"Busy day?" she asked, pouring drinks for them both.

"The usual. Umpteen political parties vying for power. Fighting each other. Heat doesn't help. Had to organize extra patrols, but tonight I am off duty all night long, thank God."

He savored his wine, aware of how young he felt again, in the best of ways. As he had been before the unspeakable demands of the war had transformed him into little more than a killing machine, void of feeling, because life as he had known it was gone. Now, miraculously, life was restored to him. He was alone with the woman he loved, in a room in Trieste. A world away from reality, where the strength of their passion for each other held at bay the enormous tragedy of Józef.

"James, before you a soldier, what did you do?"

"Do you really want to know?"

"I do. Tell me. So, when you gone, I can think of you in other life."

Drummond sighed. "I worked in a bank. My father had been the bank manager. Both my parents died before I had even left school. I understand the company had promised him they would watch out for me. Make sure I was employed. It was the Depression back then."

Alenka reached across the table to stroke his face. "You do not like it?"

"I hate it." He grasped her hand and held it tight. "Day in and day out, dressed in a suit, carrying a briefcase, bored to tears, driven mad by columns of numbers."

"Sound sad, James." She stroked his cheek. "Is there not something else for you?"

"Sometimes I think I'd like to stay in the army instead. Take a permanent commission."

"What does wife think of that?"

"I haven't broached the possibility with Mary. I have no idea how she would feel about being posted all over the British Empire."

Secretly, he was rather sure she would hate it. Never truly settling down again, uprooting their daughter from school. Personally, he believed it would be a marvelous experience for his Georgie Girl.

"Do you wonder what *my* life will be like?" Alenka asked.

"Of course I do, darling, of course."

"I have my house. And small pension from our government. Before Józef die, I was certain of plan. I would raise him there, maybe help with cooperatives in the area. But like you, I too feel—how you say—mixed up?"

He put down his glass and kneeled before her, no longer able to stand the knowing of her nakedness. "You do believe, darling, if things were different, if I had no other responsibilities, this is where I would choose to stay."

"I do, James."

He embraced her slender feet. Kissed each delicate toe. Stroked her calves, the inside of her knees. Spread open her legs. Lowered his head and worshiped at his holy grail. He licked and lapped her nectar slowly, while Alenka clutched his head, humming. He drew her forward on her chair to open her wider still, so that his fingers could probe, explore, penetrate, caress each inner fold and furrow—as she pitched and plunged—until she murmured his name—*James, James, James,* over and over and over.

Afterward, they staggered over to the bed, removing their clothing to lie naked atop the cotton sheet. Alenka reached for his hand and sucked his fingers.

"This is how I taste?" she asked, laughing. "Salt and honey."

"Yes, my most precious Boadicea. That is how you taste."

The streetlamp outside cast its warm yellow glow across the bed.

"James, do you remember when you say you thought I go off with comrades?"

"Of course I do. We were in my office."

"Do you know answer now?"

James turned to drink in his beautiful woman. "For me?"

"Yes! I stay because of you, James." She kissed his lips. "But I know you cannot stay for me. I know you must go home to your bank. To your tall house in big city. And cottage by the sea."

Dread settled like a stone in his gut. He didn't want to think about what he must do, when what he really wanted to do was stay in this place for the rest of his life.

"When I look at photograph of wife with Georgina, I know in my heart that if I let you love me again that day, it could not, must not, be forever."

During his leave, he had reminded himself every day that his responsibility was to Mary. It was not her fault that the long years of the war had faded her into little more than a pleasant memory. And above all else, there was his little Georgie Girl.

He moved above Alenka, resting on his elbows to watch her face. She cradled his hard, throbbing penis in both her hands. Unhurriedly, she eased him inside herself. They continued to gaze at one another, perfectly still, not moving.

"I never want to be separate from you, dearest love."

"I know, James," she breathed into his ear. "But it is not possible."

"Tonight, all is possible." Slowly, James began to glide back and forth. Teasing. Tantalizing. Tormenting. Desperate not to miss one undulating swell or ripple of her secret self.

"Now," she begged.

"Like this, Boadicea?"

"Please, please," Alenka begged.

He thrust deep, seeking sanctuary, losing himself in his safe harbor. He held tight to her, far into the sultry night. How was he ever going to find the strength to let go of such perfect happiness? How was he going to find the strength to face the future without her? A future in which the truth of her lost child would come crashing back in a tidal wave of horror for them both.

Chapter Twenty-Eight

L ARKINS DROVE THE captain along the coast from Miramare early. He didn't have to report for duty until evening—the whole picture-perfect day could be spent with Alenka in Trieste. The icing on the cake was that the Opera House was reopening with a production of Bellini's *La Sonnabula*. Remembering how much Alenka had enjoyed *Fantasia*, Drummond could not wait to watch her reaction to a live orchestra, live voices, live music on a live stage. For one mad minute, he even considered purchasing a ticket for Dick Harvey! As instructed, Larkins dropped him outside the Teatro Guiseppe Verdi; shortly thereafter, Drummond had two tickets safely stored in his pocket.

After this, he chose bread, meats, cheese, and fruit from the various market stalls, which were just now popping up in the city again. Although before the war he had never imagined "doing the shopping" in Brandling village for his wife, it now seemed rather silly. Why not? Yugoslav women had lived and fought right alongside their men. Why could the men not assume the more traditional roles when the occasion warranted it? With his arms full, and feeling rather smug, he wound his way through the maze of alleys behind the Piazza dell'Unita, to their lovers' haven.

He deposited his purchases on the table. "Surprise!" he cried, pulling the tickets out of his shirt pocket like a carnival man.

"What?" Alenka plucked the tickets from his fingers warily. "Opera? At Teatro Verdi?"

"Yes! We are going to sit on velvet seats, in a box, overlooking the stage. Side by side. For everyone to see!"

"No, James. We will *not* do such a thing."

"Of course we will, Alenka."

"And what would I wear?"

The captain pulled her into his arms, gulping greedily the heady aroma he so loved. "My darling, wear your uniform for all I care." He pulled back her hair and kissed the soft skin behind her ears. "It doesn't matter."

Alenka pushed him hard. "It does! For me it does!" Her voice had risen to a shout.

Belatedly, Drummond realized that just because he adored her in her Titovka cap; adored her in her worn cotton frocks; adored her in Darko's old black coat; adored her in absolutely nothing at all; didn't mean she wouldn't care what she wore on such an occasion. His cheeks flushed red, his mortified stomach turning.

"You think I have a wardrobe full of fancy gowns like some decadent capitalist woman!"

Alenka glared at him; desperate to avoid those suddenly piercing eyes, he turned to the kitchen table to uncork a bottle of wine, slice the bread, and arrange the salami, fruit, and cheese on a platter.

"I'm such a fool. I didn't mean to upset you. It's just . . . I wanted to give you a treat . . . because . . . I'm so proud of you." He gestured helplessly at the spread.

"Come and sit down, darling. Calm down. Enjoy some wine."

"No!" Alenka flung the tickets onto the table. "Is *you* want treat. So, *you* go to show in your fancy Tommy uniform. I stay here. A Cinderella *razcapanec* like in fairy tale!"

She was as brave as any man he'd ever fought with, yet he remembered the sight of her stepping out of the pool—exquisitely feminine, like an image from a Degas painting. How had he failed to take into account that his Boadicea was a woman, like any other that walked the earth? What the hell could he do to make amends?

Cinderella. He remembered taking Georgie Girl to the pantomime—Cinderella alone in the cinders, waiting for her fairy godmother to provide a gown, carriage, and white horses to take her to the ball. How enchanted his daughter had been by the magic. Of course!

"You won't stay home like Cinderella. After lunch, we are going shopping. I will buy a gown for you to wear at the opera."

"Do not act crazy, James. There are no such things for sale anywhere."

"Don't be too sure about that." As he well knew, the black marketeers skulking in the hills were all too ready and willing to trade suspect merchandise. Clothing was finding its way into the salons, in particular a place near the British officers' club that he had learned about through various reports landing on his desk.

"Really? Can we?" A reluctant undercurrent of excitement had entered her voice, though she was careful not to let it spark her eyes.

"We can." He grinned at her. "We have plenty of time to find you the perfect dress. Larkins doesn't collect me until evening." Smile widening, he whispered, "I have always wanted to play the role of a cinema idol, sitting on a wobbly chair in an elegant couturier, watching his lover try on frocks."

Did she even know what he was talking about? He had no idea. And he didn't care. They communicated in all the important ways, just fine. He eased away from the table slightly, and opened his arms wide. After a moment, Alenka slid onto his knees and wound her arms around his neck.

"I love you, James."

A SHORT TIME LATER, just as he had fantasized, the captain was seated in a fragile gilt chair, in the small salon he had learned of, tucked discreetly away in a tiny courtyard. No doubt it had made a good living during the German occupation, and now it had a steady clientele of Allied officers. Drummond watched the commessa, stern in her black saleswoman costume, sweeping in and out from behind a curtain, holding up various dresses for Alenka to choose from.

He did his best to ignore the whispers in his brain—memories of Mary's recent letter, where she wrote that Georgina was growing so quickly, she looked like a little ragamuffin in her ancient winter coat. That she, Mary, had barely been able to scrounge together enough clothing coupons to buy their daughter a replacement. His little English *razcapanec*, whom he adored.

Alenka made a selection, and was whisked into a changing room. A few minutes later, she appeared clad in a long gown of slate-gray silk that exactly matched her eyes. It clung to her body. *His* body. Every nook and cranny of it. He breathed in the smell of the soap with which she had bathed herself not an hour before. It had taken every ounce of self-restraint to stop himself squeezing into the hip bath beside her. He tried to concentrate on where he was, and not on the many ways he would possess her as soon as they returned to their refuge.

When Alenka spun around on the small, raised dais, he discovered the garment was backless. It began its sweeping plunge from her waist, trailing silkily over her sweet, round buttocks, thighs, all the way down to her ankles. Although he could not begin to imagine how it managed to stay on her body, he could imagine his arm looped over the back of her chair, caressing her bare shoulder blades, stroking his thumb up and down her spine, fondling the flesh, so readily accessible, below her waist.

She raised a questioning eyebrow as her fingers slid uncon-
sciously across the soft fabric. Despite the fact that he would have
enjoyed watching her try on half a dozen more outfits, he longed
with all his being for her to choose that one.

"Grazie, signora. Please wrap up the gown."

ONE WEEK LATER, CAPTAIN Drummond gazed over the elegant curve of the Teatro Giuseppe auditorium. Crimson velvet
seats. Gilt carved balconies. Five levels, rising to the domed ceiling. Painted, as far as he could tell, with half naked, frolicking
shepherdesses. Mingling with the warm air was a buzz of voices, a
scrape of violin bows, the scent of exotic perfumes, and the glitter
of sparkling jewels on necks, wrists, and ear lobes. Various Allied
uniforms were dotted throughout the house—American, British,
Canadian, Australian, New Zealand. A year or so ago, the uniforms would have been quite other. There had still been 200,000
veteran German troops in Northern Italy, as well as Mussolini's
50,000 avid fascists.

He turned to admire his beloved, seated proudly on a round
crimson chair in her capitalistic gown. Her hair was secured with
an assortment of silver pins. On her lap lay the small mesh purse
he had found for her when Larkins stopped one day in Barcola, a
little waterfront town halfway into the city from Miramare. The
shop was on the promenade, a tiny place owned by the frailest
couple he had ever encountered—the slightest breeze would blow
them away. *God help them when the bora blows*, he thought. The
merchandise had been meager, but when the woman had offered
him the purse from under the counter, he had known instantly
that it was at least a hundred years old. Probably a remnant of the

Hapsburg dynasty. He'd pressed a bundle of lira into her palm, and she had nodded gratefully.

Soon enough, the lights dimmed. The audience hushed. The conductor raised his baton, and the curtain rose, revealing a village square in Switzerland and a local inn. At the back of the stage towered a castle. The village chorus sang joyously of the engagement of an orphan named Amina to Elvino, a farmer. Only his former lover, Lisa, who owned the inn, appeared forlorn.

Alenka cooed with delight. James chuckled to himself, realizing she could understand almost every word, sung in Italian, as he struggled to keep up. But the gist of the story was clear, as were most opera plots. When the obligatory stranger, in this case, Rodolfo, entered, Drummond guessed he would eventually be revealed as the long-lost Lord of the Castle. When the lovers quarreled, and then made up, Alenka reached for his hand.

"Like us too," she whispered.

Not long after, a sleepwalking Amina came through Rodolfo's window, dressed in white. Ever the gentleman, Rodolfo left the girl alone in his bed rather than take advantage, but she was discovered, leaving her wedding contract with Elvino in tatters.

The curtain fell. The lights came up. Applause reverberated throughout the theater.

"Will be happy ending, James?" murmured Alenka.

"Yes, my darling, I am sure all will end well." He caressed her cheek. "Come with me. I have a surprise for you."

When Alenka rose, the slate-gray gown slithered over her breasts, belly, and thighs like a waterfall. No, not a waterfall, exactly—more like the water streaming down her body, the first day he'd set eyes on her. James stroked her naked back as he drew her into the anteroom behind their box and closed the curtains. A bottle of champagne rested in an ice bucket on a glass table beside a small divano.

Muffled voices droned beyond the candlelit alcove. He released the cork with a satisfying pop and poured. Sitting side by side on the sofa, the pair clinked glasses and drank the foaming, bubbling liquid, all the while gazing at one another over the rim of the flutes.

"Is perfect, James," murmured Alenka. "Perfect."

"I love you, my darling."

"With the music in my heart all this night, I pretend we go often to Teatro Giuseppe Verdi; sit often in box; wear often my gown; live together; grow old together."

Was it possible? Could they make a life together? How? Where? Nobody yet knew the fate of Trieste. It might take years for there to be any resolution. What the hell could he do? Write off democracy and join the Army of Yugoslavia? It was ludicrous. If he ever tried to go home again after that, he would be hung for treason. He considered the place where he knew her heart to be, longing to lay his head there and forget the future.

When the bell for the second act rang, they re-entered the box. James moved his chair closer to Alenka, so as to keep his hand on her smooth, bare back. A form of reassurance that at least for tonight, she was by his side. As the opera reached its climax, Amina appeared on the roof of the mill, sleepwalking again. The chorus gained strength as the girl descended without falling. Still asleep, she sang of her love for Elvino, and her grief at losing him. Alenka reached out for James's hand, but just as he had predicted, all ended well. A repentant Elvino placed the ring back on Almina's finger as she gained consciousness.

Alenka leaned forward on her chair and clapped and clapped, her face infused with happiness. She stood. Held onto the velvet covered balcony. Clapped some more. Gradually, the crowd

filtered out of the theater. James loved the sound of satisfied dev-
otees; it rang like a melody of music in his ears as it ebbed and
flowed with the departing audience.

"It was beautiful, *ljubcek*," reflected Alenka as they strolled
home, hand in hand.

He paused beneath a streetlamp to kiss her gently.

"I like happy endings. Lovers reunited. Live happy ever after. If
only we could sleepwalk together through our lives."

"If only we could." James picked the assortment of silver pins
from her hair and watched it pour down her beautiful bare back
like a dark, flowing river.

"But we know this special time must end," she whispered. "Don't
we, James?"

"Not tonight, my darling. Not tonight."

SEPTEMBER 1994

Chapter Twenty-Nine

WHILE DADDY COMPOSES what will no doubt prove to be a difficult letter, I take the opportunity to write to my daughters. Based on what passed between us in Penny's flat in London, it's obvious they are aware of the tension between their dad and me. If our marriage were to come to an end, they would be confused, hurt, and most certainly angry. From Lou, the rule follower, I'm sure there would be an inability to see any gray areas, resentment at having to divide her time between Paul and myself. From Annie, the rule breaker, I am far less certain what I would expect.

Home intrudes. In my head, the stovetop where I bet several mangled, dried up teabags lie abandoned—Paul has rather taken to tea drinking, but never quite mastered the intricacies of leaves in a pot. In the background, a steady patter of *Good Morning America* with Joan Lunden and Charlie Gibson. A jumble of dirty jeans, T-shirts, towels spilled onto the laundry room floor. I am glad I'm not there right now. It makes me sad. But now that Daddy is preparing to make contact with Janez Marusic, I assume a meeting will be arranged, and then I can get myself home and try to make some sense of my life. Sort things out.

How I might go about separating myself from the long marriage, I've no clue. I had it figured out once—that long-ago Christmas, when Lou and Annie were still young children, before fate intervened. I was prepared to request a divorce, as well as prepared for the inevitable hassle with Ellen, because life without my two ducklings was unimaginable.

My dearest Michael, just to reinforce our commitment to one another, had arranged for the pilot on my flight to Minnesota to announce over his intercom that he had an important message for passenger Ms. Georgina Drummond. *"No sooner they met but they looked, no sooner looked but they loved, no sooner loved but they sighed, no sooner sighed but they made a pair of stairs to marriage."* Despite his rather mangling Shakespeare's words of love, loud applause had broken out throughout the Northwest Airlines jumbo jet.

But everything is so different now. No lover waits for me in London. And it will be every bit as hard leaving Paul now, precisely because the two little ducklings are full grown. Each with a distinct voice, a stubborn disposition, and a fully developed sense of selfhood, coupled with the growing realization that their parents are not the paragons of virtue they believed us to be when they were youngsters.

Added to which, what will they make of a brand-new, never-before-heard-of uncle? My guess: Lou will be shocked, Annie intrigued. If I'm honest, I'm not sure how *I* feel about the out-of-the-blue discovery that I have a sibling. But I can't worry about this at present. One thing at a time. Both girls need to spread their wings. Hopefully their few days in London have had a liberating effect.

Annie, I write, *I don't in any way approve of how you removed yourself from college, but I do understand. It is not for everyone. Your old mum did okay without four years of higher learning. This is your chance to try different things. Meet different people. There is a whole big world out there you know nothing about yet.*

Lou, I am proud of all your hard work, all your achievements. It was such an honor to attend your graduation last May. But step back awhile—weigh your options before graduate school. Maybe travel a bit first, just not with your sister. I draw a smiley face, hoping she will take this advice the way I intend it.

I tell them Grandpa and I are enjoying a spur-of-the-moment holiday in Italy, making no mention of the real reason for the trip. After giving both the girls a few more tidbits about the castle where their grandpa lived for eighteen months and the coincidence of his once-upon-a-time officers' club being in the hotel where we are staying, I seal up the envelopes and wander downstairs to ask the concierge to airmail the letters to the United States.

Back in my room, I stretch out on the comfortable sofa, snuggled amongst the array of pillows, and begin reading the latest novel by Margaret Drabble, *The Gates of Ivory*. Her opening line hooks me as always: *This is a novel—if novel it be—about Good Time and Bad Time.* I chuckle. If I ever write my memoir, I will have to snitch Drabble's phrase and call the book *Good Time and Bad Time*. I am savoring the words and structure of this simple sentence when a heavy thump sounds from Daddy's room.

My book thuds onto the floor. I leap up and wrench open the door dividing our suite. Daddy is slumped over the desk. His face is doughy, turned to one side. There is a steady drip of blood seeping from a cut above his right eyebrow, caught, it seems, on the edge of a letter opener. He is breathing, but it sounds extremely shallow.

My brain won't function. It's running in circles—*Please, please don't have had another heart attack. Please, please don't be dead.* I feel cast in stone, like the statues we glimpsed from the windows of Miramare castle. But I come to my senses, grab the phone, and call down to the hotel desk. "Suite 526. My father has collapsed. Get an ambulance. Hurry. Please hurry."

I am afraid to move him, so I get down on my knees and rub his back gently. I have no idea if he can hear me, but I do my best to comfort him.

"I'm right here, Daddy. Your own Georgie Girl.

"I won't leave you.

"Be brave.

"Hang on.

"An ambulance is coming.

"We will get you to a hospital. They'll know what to do."

I try to wipe his brow, staunch the blood, make him presentable before help arrives. Stupid. Stupid. He is lying across the beginnings of a letter to his son, splattered with blood from the cut . . . *tell you first how I loved your mother, heart and soul . . . if I had known* . . . And here's the rub. He had no time to write more before he collapsed. Will I ever know what he would have done if he had known of this child's existence? If the letter from Alenka had not been destroyed? If it had not even been opened? If Mum had handed the thin, blue airmail envelope to Daddy across the tea-table that evening? What then?

All this swirls through my mind as I gather him up some belongings. I have no idea what is expected in an Italian hospital, but I pack a carry-all bag with his dressing gown, clean pajamas, toothbrush and paste, shaving equipment, and his various bottles of medicine. And, of course, his passport. I glance at his book of poetry. The enormous tome can wait. I will take it for him later, along with his reading glasses, if he asks.

Our rescuers are kind. They lay Daddy gently on a stretcher, then carry him to the lift, through the hotel foyer, and into a waiting ambulance. They gesture for me to get into the vehicle. I'm so grateful.

Blessedly, the Maggiore Hospital is in the city center, only minutes from our hotel. In a blur, we are whisked to the cardiac ward on the fourth floor. Daddy is connected to numerous tubes and beeping machines; I am told the heart doctor has been called and will arrive shortly. A nurse sutures his cut. His lids flutter open, but his eyes are unfocused.

I sit in a chair beside his bed, wishing my own heart would stop beating quite so fast. What if I had gone out for the rest of the day? What if I had fallen asleep and not heard his fall? I can't bear thinking what might have happened if I had not got him to the hospital so quickly. *There is no way I can get my head around the reality of living in a world without you, Daddy. Not yet.*

Matron comes over to his bed. She speaks English, thank heavens.

"Your father is in no immediate danger, my dear. Why don't you return to the hotel for now and try to get some rest?"

"Can't I stay?"

"In Europe we have strict visiting hours. But I have the telephone number if it becomes necessary to summon you back. There is nothing else to be done until the doctor has examined him."

"Matron, he suffers nightmares."

"World War II?"

"How on earth did you guess?" I ask.

"He looks like an old soldier." She nods knowingly. "My mother nursed all through the war and after. Very used to what we used to call shell shock."

"Oh, I see."

"Was your father stationed here? Is that what brings you both to Trieste?"

"He was, and it is."

"We will keep him lightly sedated. Best thing in the world for him. And the sedation will take care of his night terrors."

I nod. "Daddy, please just get better," I whisper to the world in general.

"Signora, I will be frank with you. It is obvious to me that your father has suffered a heart attack. He is not at all well. Perhaps there are family members you wish to contact." She caresses my cheek. "And in the meantime, we will do our best to take care of him. I promise you."

I know they will. But it doesn't make leaving my father's side to walk away down the ward any less difficult. With each footstep past every hospital bed, past every patient draped in an identical white blanket, I am reminded how frail Daddy has become. That our time together grows shorter by the day. That I have been advised to contact family members.

When I reach the double glass doors at the end of the ward, I turn and wave goodbye to my darling daddy, lying flat on a hospital bed, sustained by machines.

He can't see me. He can't hear me. He doesn't even know I am there.

Chapter Thirty

S AFELY BACK IN our suite, I snatch a cigarette from my stash and step onto the balcony to smoke. Today, the light is playing games on the bay—splashing up against the Molo Audace, the water is a dark, gunmetal gray, but offshore, it is a vivid turquoise, almost exactly matching my flashy new tote. Castello di Miramare stands sentinel on its promontory. The seagulls circle endlessly. Under different circumstances, I could soak up this view till nightfall. One of the things I have missed terribly living in Minnesota is the sight, sound, and smell of the sea. Lakes don't have quite the same allure for me.

Fortified with two cigarettes, I force myself over to the desk. If I am to heed Matron's advice about contacting family, I have to find the letter Janez wrote. And there it is, plain as day, propped against the reading lamp. From the date at the top of the page, I realize that it took almost six months to reach my father. But with Daddy ill again, why should I bother with the added nuisance of making contact with someone I never heard of? How much does it matter now?

As I chew this over, George, my mostly dormant but irascible green goblin, rouses himself, just as Daddy predicted. He does not often spark to life, but when I get anxious, defensive, or rattled, or when I am at odds with myself as to what to do for the best, he still has a nasty habit of announcing himself.

George proceeds to fill my head with fantastical doubts. Perhaps Janez has given up hope of hearing from his father after this long time? Perhaps he has moved without leaving a forwarding address or telephone number and can't be reached? Perhaps he has been struck down with a dangerous and virulent infection and must be confined to a sanatorium? Perhaps he has suddenly and tragically died in a motorcycle accident?

What a thoroughly horrid woman I am. A real bitch. But I don't care, not one blasted bit, because I don't want to share my father. Especially not now. I want him all to myself. Truth be told, I have always wanted him all to myself. Only-child syndrome, I suppose. So why did I encourage Daddy to write to Janez in the first place? I must have momentarily lost my senses.

Despite knowing perfectly well that the right course of action is to contact this man urgently, I tear up the letter from Slovenia instead, and watch the pieces float into the wastebasket with satisfaction. George, on my shoulder, claps his approval.

Now I am beginning to understand more clearly why Mum didn't want to share her husband. In a roundabout way, I have her to thank for burning the letter from his lover. Her way of making absolutely sure neither one of us would have to share him. Or, God forbid, risk losing him altogether. I give the wastebasket a good, satisfying kick!

Another thing I should do is phone Paul and the girls. They are staying at the lake for several more days. I have the telephone number, but the anxiety I feel when I anticipate speaking to Paul— trying to explain what has happened—exhausts me. I will have more news about my father's condition tomorrow, I reason.

It's Michael's voice I long for. Fair-minded, generous Michael, always able to take the long view. I close my eyes and conjure myself back in time onto his jetty, extending out over the River Thames. Whorls of fine sea mist swirl upstream from the estuary, phantoms dancing on the water. I taste the tang of pitch on the pilings, ever so faintly on my tongue. Michael says to me clearly: *"Put yourself in Janez's shoes. Doesn't it seem unfair for the man to never know his father received the letter; to never know he traveled such a long way in hopes of a meeting; to never know his father lies ill in a Trieste hospital?"*

I know, I know, I know. Michael would expect me to do the right thing. Michael would help me do the right thing. But he's not here. And without him, my egoistical goblin remains in charge, whispering seductively in my ear, *"Forget all about it. You don't want to do it. You don't have to do it."*

Disgusted with myself, I traipse into my own bedroom and sit beside the telephone, waiting for word from the hospital. Soon enough, the phone rings. *Oh, dear God, please don't let this be bad news.*

"Signora Drummond?"

"Yes."

"Dr. Giovanni here. I have just examined your father. Would you like to meet me tomorrow morning at the hospital so we can talk directly to one another?"

My worst fears swim dizzily in my head. "Please just tell me." I twist the cord of the telephone round and round my wrist.

"Your father did suffer another mild heart attack earlier today, just as Matron suspected." He pauses. "I understand you are an American?"

"I live in the States, but I'm a British citizen."

"If your father lived in America with you, I expect extensive and invasive measures would be considered."

"Probably," I agree.

"Not so in Italy. His heart is far too weak. I have ordered some more blood tests and a chest X-ray, but I do not see any point in doing another coronary angiogram at this stage. The results will just verify my diagnosis. I managed to reach your father's general practitioner in England, and based on your father's history, we are of one mind. Our advice is to keep him happy and comfortable to enjoy the time he has left."

Time he has left? My head empties of words—I watch them march away across the floor in a determined line, never to be spoken. But somehow, I manage to ask, "Can you tell me how long my father has to live?"

"It is impossible to say."

I unwind the plastic cord from my wrist slowly. Stare at the red welts. I can't tell if they hurt or not.

"Are you still there, señora? Are you all right?"

"Yes, doctor. I'm here. Should I not have agreed to bring my father on this trip to Trieste?"

"That depends on how important it was to him. Matron mentioned he was stationed in the city after the end of the war."

"He was."

"Then I think whatever his motivation, it was the right thing to do. Often when people sense that the end of life is close, there is a great emotional need to 'square things.' Is that how you say?"

In spite of myself, I manage a little laugh. "It is indeed."

"I will be in touch when I get the laboratory results and his chest X-ray reading. There will no doubt be adjustments to his medication. And I will definitely want to keep him here for several more days."

"Thank you, Doctor. Thank you very much."

I place the receiver soundlessly in its cradle, as if that might be sufficient to erase the conversation. Wishful thinking. My daddy is nearing the end of his life. What I have dreaded since his first heart attack. Whenever I contemplate his death, loneliness creeps damply into my bones and sets up shop. Being without him will require the sort of courage I'm not entirely sure I have. Who else is there that will understand this?

But until the time comes, it is Daddy who is going to need me as never before. Now I clearly see that after losing Alenka, it was his Georgie Girl on whom he came to depend to keep himself going. From the morning we first set eyes on each other in the backyard, there was an ease between us, a reliance, a comforting sort of faith. Somehow, I'm going to have to summon up these strengths to help him through his last journey.

Along with these realizations, I'm buffeted with guilt. What Dr. Giovanni said is the absolute truth. There is a need for Daddy to square things. Which really means squaring things with his son, no matter what my personal feelings are in that regard. Except I've torn up the information needed for my father to set things straight.

I reel back into Daddy's bedroom. Peer into the wastebasket. Tip the contents on the floor. On my knees, I start trying to patch the pieces of paper together again, but George swoops in and takes charge. *Forget about it. You are in control. Do what you want.*

I scoop the trash back in the basket.

Before I crawl into my bed, bury my head in the pillow, and cry myself to sleep.

Chapter Thirty-One

WITH MATRON'S PERMISSION, I'm allowed to enter the ward early. The stitches prickle my lips when I lean over to kiss Daddy's forehead.

"Georgie Girl?" His eyes flicker open.

"Good morning. How are you feeling?"

"Bit coggly." He reaches for his eyebrow. "What is . . ."

I grasp his hand quickly. "Don't touch. You had a couple of stitches, that's all. Nothing to worry about."

Daddy closes his eyes again. For a long while, he doesn't move at all. I sit beside the bed to wait.

"Thought maybe my damned heart might've misbehaved again," he says eventually.

"It did. You had another heart attack yesterday. You're in hospital. The specialist examined you last evening. Do you remember?"

"S-sorry, darling."

"Don't be silly."

"Too much strudel." He tries to smile, but it doesn't work quite right.

"And the hot chocolate, I suspect. But Dr. Giovanni wants to keep you here for a few days. Run more blood tests, adjust your tablets."

"Stuck in Trieste a bit longer then," he murmurs.

"Nowhere I would rather be than here with you."

"Does Paul know what has happened?"

"Not yet."

I'm dreading the conversation. He will point out that he was right, that I was wrong to bring Daddy on this trip. That he would be better off in an English hospital. That I can't blame anyone but myself if things go from bad to worse.

"Lou and Annie?"

"Home safe and sound. Up at Wind Lake with the family."

Daddy manages to nod. "Georgina, I need to say . . . in case time runs out . . . I did love your mother."

I open my mouth to reply, but the effort seems to have exhausted him. Closing his eyes, he falls back into a fitful sleep.

And I do believe they loved each other in their convoluted ways. Despite the betrayal in Trieste—despite the betrayal in Newcastle—despite Daddy *not* confessing he had had a lover — despite Mummy *not* revealing he had a son—both were convinced they were protecting the other.

What of Paul and me? Did we love each other? We lived happily for a time. But it wasn't enough of the time. Compromise is at the heart of any marriage, I understand that. But early on, almost as soon as we relocated to Minnesota, it began to feel awfully lopsided, which was not helped by the green goblin George's propensity for intervention. Paul's family always seemed to come first. I know my inability to come to terms with all his relatives disappointed Paul. And I suspect that marriage, with its promise of constant love and physical intimacy, disappointed him too. Disappointed us both. A friend once described her own long marriage as akin to wearing a pair of comfortable old slippers. When she told me this, I thought of my old M&S mules, scuffed and down at heel, discarded under the bed. Slopping around in a pair of old slippers forever did not seem to me a heck of a lot to look forward to.

But Daddy is awake again. Fretful and fidgety. "Fetch him."

Beep, beep go the machines beside his bed. Drip, drip goes the saline into his veins. And cold grows my heart, until it feels as if a bloody great lump of granite has got lodged inside me. There is no need to ask who he is referring to.

What have I done? Nothing except wallow in my own self-centeredness. More precisely, what have I *not* done? How could I not have picked up the phone yesterday and called Janez Marusic? How could I have torn the letter to pieces? Yet undeterred, George chirrups away in my ear, protecting territory, raising objections, exerting his authority.

"Daddy, the situation is completely changed now. You've had another heart attack. It's probably wiser if I make arrangements to get you back home to England as soon as possible."

"No!" He gasps for breath. "Janez first." There is a big pause. "Then we see."

He tries to move his arm, straining the various attachments. "Need you, Georgie girl. More than ever."

He does need me. I have to pull myself together. The words I imagined Michael uttering in regard to Janez Marusic beat my goblin to the punch: —*put yourself in the poor man's shoes,* —*to never know his letter was received,* —*to never know his father has traveled to meet him*—"You're absolutely sure?" I ask.

"Sure as can be. Counting on you."

He is, of course. Just as he did in those years after the war when, in the dark of night, he would pluck me out of bed and sit me down to keep him company. Guilt grates on my conscience like grains of sand. I can't be so cruel as to keep this other child out of reach.

"All right, Daddy. Of course I will."

Chapter Thirty-Two

As soon as I enter our suite, it's clear the maid has already been. The beds are made, the bathrooms sparkle—and, to my horror, the wastepaper basket is empty. Finally, I am galvanized into action, running the entire length of the corridor, searching in vain for a cleaning cart. There is no one and nothing to be seen. Too impatient to wait for the lift, I tear down the five flights of stairs, looking, I imagine, like the wrath of God.

"I need the manager!" I shout in the middle of the lobby.

"Certainly, señora." The porter eyes me oddly. "Follow me."

"Signora Drummond, I was so sorry to learn of the collapse of your papa yesterday," says the manager as I sink into the chair in his office. He's a compact, middle-aged little man, with sleek, black hair atop a sympathetic face and a neat little moustache.

"I have a favor to ask," I gasp.

"Anything, signora. Anything at all."

"Where do the contents of your wastebaskets go?"

"*Perdonare?*" The poor man turns a bit green. He probably thinks he's being held hostage by a madwoman.

"The basket," I shriek. "From out of our suite."

"Si . . ."

"In it was a letter from Ljubljana, Slovenia. I threw it away by mistake."

"Si, si, now I understand. Come, Signora Drummond. Follow me."

He escorts me to a bank of employee lifts, and we descend into a basement area: part laundry, part storage, and thank God, part dry waste products. What the hell am I going to do if I don't find the letter?

It's as if the manager can read my mind. "You have name of the person?" he asks.

I nod. My tongue seems to have stuck to the lid of my mouth, and it's difficult to speak.

"*Bueno*. I have contact in Ljubljana Police. If we do not find your letter, they will be able to help you trace the individual, I am quite sure."

I collapse on the floor, and we methodically go through all the waste from the fifth floor.

He's oblivious to the bits of fluff and lint that cling to his elegant, gray suit. Miraculously, I spot a scrap of blue paper and pounce, like an animal after prey. I hold it up triumphantly between thumb and forefinger.

"Mamma mia!" His eyes bulge in disbelief. "*This is what the lunatic is after*," I can see him thinking, "*the remnants of a shredded letter.*"

Surely, I think, he will have me committed any minute—but trooper that he is, we continue to crawl through the debris together, gathering up the pieces, hoping against hope we can find most of the letter which I destroyed.

I could weep with relief when we eventually manage to collect a small heap of blue paper. The manager claps his hands. It is as if we are re-enacting a trite Italian opera in the basement of the hotel. I could kiss him, I really could. He helps me up, and I stagger back to the suite.

As soon as I have caught my breath, I sit at the desk and lay out the fragments. I did a good job of demolishing the letter, but slowly and surely, I piece enough of it back together to find and decipher the telephone number.

I get up to fetch myself a glass of water. The inside of my mouth feels like dry toast. I force myself back to the desk and sit down hard on the chair, staring at the number.

I remind myself that once I place this call, my life as I know it will never be the same. Going forward, I will have to accept the fact of a brother. A perfect stranger. And one I don't particularly want thrust into my life, especially now that Daddy is seriously ill. How will I manage to cope with this man, Janez, under such changed circumstances? A sob lodges in my throat.

I pick up the receiver. Drop it back in its cradle. *It isn't as if I don't have enough problems to deal with*, a voice inside me whispers. *A dying father, a husband who bores me to tears, contrary daughters whom I adore, a mother-in-law whose very existence makes Mrs. Danvers positively loveable, and last but not least, a broken heart in London* . . . Before George can raise his ugly green head, I grasp the telephone in both hands and ask the hotel operator to place the call to Slovenia. Now there is nothing for it but to sit back and wait. I smoke a cigarette on the balcony, waiting for the call to come through, and soon enough, it does. The phone rings, echoing through our suite like a warning—of what, I do not know. Do I answer it? My heart thuds hard. What if nobody on the end of the line speaks English?

But a man responds, as we do in the United Kingdom, by repeating his phone number—in Slovene, of course.

"Can I speak to Janez Marusic, please?" I hate the way my voice is wobbling.

"I am Janez Marusic."

My heart is thudding double time now—maybe I'm having a heart attack too—for there is a timbre to his voice identical to that of my father. I gulp back the sob, hardly able to believe it. I pull back my shoulders and continue on.

"I'm Captain Drummond's daughter. We are in Trieste. Staying at the Savoia Excelsior Palace. Can you visit us?"

"I will be there by early evening," he says. And the line goes dead.

The deed is done. What do I do now? The afternoon stretches out before me. I am far too nervous to try to nap. Or read. I am still feeling thoroughly adrift when the manager sends up half a bottle of wine and a small bowl of risotto with a vegetable salad, compliments of the hotel. Tucked into the linen napkin is a roll of sticky tape. What a dear, thoughtful man. When I finish my meal, I reconstruct the rest of the letter as best I can, and stick it all together, hoping that Daddy never, ever asks to see it again. Then I will have some explaining to do.

In the late afternoon, I take a hot shower, wondering what one wears to meet a sibling for the first time? Never in my wildest dreams have I anticipated such a dilemma, with all its hallmarks of a daytime soap opera. But I don't have time to consult Ann Landers.

So, I select a navy-blue linen pantsuit, hoping, I suppose, that it will lend me some sort of gravitas. My hair I wrap up in a modified chignon. The last thing I do is collect the photograph of Józef from Daddy's room, hoping that light can finally be shed on the mysterious child.

Then I wait nervously for a call that my visitor has arrived.

Chapter Thirty-Three

WHEN I STEP out of the lift, he is waiting beside the front desk.

"Signora Drummond? It is you, yes?"

The man takes a tentative step toward me. He is not especially tall, but broad shouldered, with thick black hair, prominent cheek bones, and a clear complexion. When he gets closer, I'm staring directly into Daddy's vibrant blue eyes. I reel into the nearest chair.

"I am sorry. I do not want to upset you. I am Janez Marusic."

"Yes, I can quite see that you are."

He sits down opposite to me and offers his hand.

I shake it. "Georgina Drummond. Gina for short."

"You are American?" I suppose he detects a slight accent. Michael used to say I sounded stuck halfway across the Atlantic, betwixt and between my birth home and my adopted home.

"No. My husband is American. We live in Minnesota. But I'm still a British citizen."

Janez Marusic gazes around expectantly. "I drove straight from Ljubljana. Where is the captain, please?" He hesitates, as if I may not understand. "Your father."

This is awful. The poor fellow has been anticipating a far different first encounter. How do I tell him? I summon all the courage I can and plunge ahead. "I did not want to give you this news over the phone. But I'm afraid Daddy collapsed yesterday. He is in the Maggiore Hospital."

An array of emotions gallop across the face of this man who is undoubtedly my brother.

Shock. Dismay. Disappointment.

"But I must go there immediately."

I gather myself up from the chair, taking full advantage of my height. "You cannot. Not yet. I'm sorry. He has had a heart attack." I put my hand on his shoulder and let the magnitude of this news sink in. "And he must have some forewarning before you meet for the first time."

Janez peers up at me. "It is just that I have waited—"

"Of course you have," I interrupt. "I understand. But don't you think we have a lot to talk about first? Why don't we have dinner together? Try to get acquainted a little?"

"Yes. That is sensible." Janez rises from the chair. "And I should inform you, I took the liberty to book a room. I was not sure what was to happen . . . our first meeting . . . how long . . . but I did not imagine the news of a hospital admission."

Following him into the dining room, I think that never in a million years would we be taken for siblings. I am Grandmother Drummond's clone. Tall, skinny, blonde, even if the hair is helped along these days. Janez is shorter, dark-haired, with high Slavic cheekbones and the blue eyes inherited from my father. Alenka's soldier lover.

The maître d' ushers us to a table beside the window. Without being asked, he brings a bottle of the local red wine he knew I had enjoyed on our first evening at the hotel, pours two glasses, and places the menu on the table between us.

"Captain Drummond must receive my letter, yes?" Janez asks, glancing at the menu without truly seeing it.

"He did. Only very recently—it was redirected many times.

Daddy asked me to bring him to Trieste. He was, in fact, writing to you when he collapsed."

"Thank you for telephoning me." Janez swallows a mouthful of wine. "It was kind."

Oh, no, it wasn't. You have no idea how hard I tried to be very unkind. I think of the mangled, taped-together missive on the desk upstairs. But I keep my mouth shut. He does not need to know. Not now. Not ever.

"It means much to me. To be able to meet my father at last. But so sorry he is ailing."

"Janez, he had a first attack about eighteen months ago. I was in the States when it happened. It took me a couple of days to get a flight, but the care he received was good. No surgical intervention. For which I was grateful." I savor my wine. "I am not sure he would have survived open heart surgery."

"In America, I understand they are scalpel happy," Janez says.

"That is how the specialist here put it to me yesterday. Daddy was in hospital for several weeks. Medicine and rest."

"That is exactly what I would have recommended."

I must look surprised because he leans toward me. "I too am doctor. Which is why I agree with the treatment he received in England."

I'm momentarily nonplussed. But what was I expecting? Just because he comes from a country that until recently was part of communist Yugoslavia, was I expecting a peasant? I blush with shame. "I didn't know that."

"Much we need to learn of each other." Janez smiles for the first time. And it is Daddy's smile. Blue eyes, now this. Suddenly, I have the urge to crawl under the table and bawl like a baby. How close I came to denying myself the chance to meet this man, to see for myself the traits he inherited from my father. And all because on too many occasions, I allow green goblin George to hold sway.

"There is something else you should know," I continue. "Before you wrote your letter, Daddy had absolutely no idea that you existed."

"No surprise there. My mati was too proud for her own good. She would not have interrupted your family with such news of me. Of that, I am positive."

"Oh, but she did!" The words burst out of my mouth before I quite realize what I've said.

His brow furrows. "What are you saying, please?"

Oh, good grief. What am I saying, indeed? Janez leans his elbows on the table, sensing some truth has inadvertently been disclosed. I've no choice but to try to explain.

"When I was a young child, my mother read a letter addressed to her husband. Read it. Burned it. I realized, just the other day, that it could only have come from your mother."

"Are you being sure?" His English slips in his distress as he slumps back in his chair.

"It was a blue airmail envelope. Very unusual in those days. My family knew of no one overseas. Who else could it have been from but your mother? I was young, but I understood enough to know it was news she did not want Daddy to receive." I let all this sink in. "It is no wonder your mother forbade you to try to find your father, Janez. When she did not hear from him, she must have believed he had utterly abandoned her."

Poor Janez. How cold and callous all this sounds. But I can't think of a less devastating way in which to impart the news. It is such a lot to take in. For both of us.

"I didn't understand what I saw and heard that day. And quite honestly, I had forgotten all about it till Daddy insisted I read your letter. Then it all came flooding back to me. But I didn't tell him any of it. My mother is dead. And I don't want him to think any the less of her now she is gone."

Janez inclines his head, but I don't know how to interpret the gesture. I have no idea if he is agreeing there is no reason to tell Daddy, or if he is going to decide otherwise.

I am suddenly famished, having eaten nothing since the risotto and salad. Seems a lifetime ago. I order an antipasto platter, as well as another bottle of wine for us both. While we wait, I pull sledge boy out of my pocket.

"I'm hoping you can shed some light on this." I slide the snap across the table. "All I know is the boy's name is Józef. I am guessing you named your son after him?"

Janez pulls out a pair of spectacles and studies the photograph. "Where did you get this?" he asks, clearly astonished.

"Daddy had it hidden in an old suitcase, until a few days before we came on this trip."

"This picture was taken beside the old well in Opatje Selo. Mati lived there many years ago."

"Why would Daddy have kept it?"

"A souvenir of sorts, I suppose. No, not right word." Janez looks sadly at the picture again.

"Not so long ago we buried Mati beside her son in the village cemetery."

"Her son? But you are her son."

"Of course. But before war, Mati was married. Her husband was murdered by the Nazis. Józef was their son. Mati's first son."

"Józef . . . the boy . . . this boy . . . is dead?"

Janez looks at me in growing bewilderment. I snatch the photograph back, feeling foolish. I hate not being cognizant of all the facts. Another failing of mine. "Why was Józef so important? Did Daddy even know the child?"

"You know nothing of what happen, do you?"

"I guess not," I say, slipping into American.

Janez suddenly tugs on the cuff of his jacket, and I am buffeted by emotions I barely understand. Any appetite I may have had is fast fading away.

"Captain Drummond oversaw mine clearing operations. That particular day, they were in an olive grove quite near to Mati's home. It was 1946."

A distant, explosive echo from another tragedy threatens to overwhelm me. One I do not care to ever talk about. I remind myself that the purpose of this journey is to discover all I can about this mysterious child.

"They used Italian POWs back then," Janez goes on.

"Real people?"

"They were Mussolini fascists to the bitter end. Laid mines for their German friends in first place. So why not?"

"Did they have mine detectors?"

"No. They lie down in long line, probe earth with special rods."

Good God, I think. Shouldn't that have been against the Geneva Convention?

"Somehow, Józef got into the grove. Your father . . . our father . . . shouted for him to stop. He did not. Józef step on mine. Was blown to pieces. Your father . . . our father . . . was the officer in charge. So, he must arrange for the body to be carried to my mati."

My head feels so light, I think I might pass out. I take deep breaths and concentrate on what Janez is telling me. At last, it all makes a terrible kind of sense. It explains Daddy's nightmares. Why, after coming home, he was plagued by night terrors. Why, on so many nights, he rescued me from unnamed dangers. Because he had been unable to save his lover's child.

All around us there are guests dining, but they are busily involved in their own conversations. For all intents and purposes, we might as well be alone.

I inhale deeply, and meet his gaze with my own. "Tomorrow, Janez, you will meet your father. It is time."

Then my tears flow. For a lost boy. For lost Michael. For my soon-to-be-lost father. For the sheer, numbing waste of it all.

Chapter Thirty-Four

I T IS AS if I've been hurtling up and down on a roller coaster. My back aches. My shoulders ache. My neck aches. The result of two very stressful days. I'd like nothing more than to collapse into sleep, but I can't avoid telephoning Paul much longer. I shed my linen pantsuit, slip into one of the hotel's terry robes, and lie flat on the bed. It doesn't help the aches much, but I place a call to the States anyway. It's afternoon at the lake. They will be outside tossing balls, sailing the boat, preparing to barbecue, whatever. Ellen answers.

"Well, well, well, this is a surprise. We're certainly missing you, Georgina. Louisa was saying just yesterday she hoped you would be home soon."

"Can I speak to Paul, please?"

"Don't you think it's time you got yourself back to your family, dear? I always think it's important we spend these holidays together."

"Ellen, this is urgent. Please try to—"

"Well, let me see. Where can he have got to?" She drops the receiver, which hits the telephone table with a dissonant clank. "Paul, honey, your wife is calling," I hear her shouting. "Paul. Paul. Paul . . ."

Minutes tick by. I wish I'd reversed the charges. That would serve her right!

"Here he is, Georgina. I found him for you. Your husband was having such fun with old friends of ours." Good grief. He's not eight years old anymore, you old harridan.

"What's up, Gina," Paul pants into the phone.

A scene of Whartons en masse flashes before my eyes: boisterous, sweaty, slapping one another on the back, like a "togetherness" advertisement for Folgers coffee.

"Actually, more than you will believe," I answer, blinking away the Wharton tribe image.

"Try me."

"Daddy had another heart attack early yesterday." I wait for the I-told-you-so's, but for once my husband holds his tongue. "He's in hospital."

"Honey, I am sorry." There is a catch in Paul's voice that's sincere. He has always admired my father. "How soon will you be able to fly him back to England?"

"It's a bit more complicated than that. Not for a few days, at least. Ultimately, I will leave it up to him."

"You've got to be kidding."

"You see, I managed to locate his son—"

"What the hell, Gina."

"Janez and I had dinner together. He doesn't look anything like Daddy—"

"What did I tell you—"

"*Except* for his sparkling blue eyes," I shout down the phone. "*And* his smile. It's uncanny."

"Isn't it though!" I swear he's laughing at me, and I'm so filled with disgust I want to slap him. "Paul, *listen* to me for once."

"For God's sake, Gina, half the men in Europe have blue eyes!"

"You don't understand how hard this is for me."

"No, I really don't. But I bet this means there's no chance of seeing you in the foreseeable future? Mom's already going on and on about the amount of traveling you do."

"Give me a break!" I scream into the mouthpiece. "Tomorrow I take Janez to meet his father, who is dying. *My* father, who is dying. How can you be so callous?"

"Because just listen to yourself! It all sounds like a cheap Harlequin romance. Wartime infidelity, out-of-wedlock child, return to the scene of the crime."

"Paul, this isn't helping me one bit."

There's a lull in the conversation. I shift this way and that on the mattress to ease my aches, but nothing works. I can't get comfortable.

"Do you want me to fly out?" Paul finally asks, somewhat reluctantly. "Help you make all the arrangements. You can't trust that son of a bitch from lord knows where. Don't let him interfere. I'll get your dad on a flight back to England. He'll probably need a nurse along, so . . ."

All the time in the background, his mother is hurling questions at him, instructions, even a reminder that it's time he was mixing cocktails for everyone.

"It's kind of you, Paul," I interrupt, my words dropping into the phone like ice cubes. "But it's one day at a time for now. Let's wait and see how Daddy does first."

"Have it your way."

"Paul, I'm sorry."

Although I'm uncertain what I am apologizing for. Not coming back when I said I would? Sympathy for how his mother organizes him, bosses him, speaks of him as if he is still a child? Or perhaps simply the sad state of our marriage.

"Call me again when you know more."

"I will. Bye."

I can't be sure anymore when my feelings for Paul started coming undone. Possibly as early as his discharge from the navy, when he insisted we move back to his hometown. After which, in no time at all, there were three of us in the marriage. Paul, and me, and Ellen.

I get off the bed, groaning like an old lady, and rummage through my cosmetic bag for some aspirin to ease the pains. Then I remove my makeup, brush my teeth, and drift back to bed, exhausted. But my mind is in overdrive, as it usually is after talking to Paul. I find myself back in the Minneapolis/St. Paul airport many years ago.

On our arrival from San Diego, my mother-in-law greeted us at the baggage claim, the entire Wharton tribe in tow. Balloons, welcome-home signs, whistles—it was more reminiscent of a political rally than a simple airport pick-up. Paul disappeared into a melee of siblings, nephews, and nieces, and there I stood, wondering, for the first time, exactly what I had got myself into.

Ellen wasted no time explaining why I was fortunate to have become a member of the family. True, no other Wharton had married a foreigner, but as I spoke English like a BBC news reader, the infraction would be overlooked. She explained how the entire family vacationed together, celebrated holidays together, and attended sporting events together.

Wharton women, she went on, were expected to be educated, but not work outside the home, except to do volunteer work. Thus making it crystal clear we were going to be at loggerheads. I disliked professional sports. I was not educated in the traditional sense of the word. I did plan to continue my career as a writer. By that time, I was selling stories and articles to children's magazines in both America and the United Kingdom, and although my picture-book manuscripts still languished in the slush piles of various publishing houses, I was determined to be successful one day. All this information Ellen imparted to me before we had even sat down for the first family dinner!

I remember having a genuine sympathy for how Jackie Kennedy must have felt when she was thrown into her clan. Both of us were outsiders who didn't care to sweat, and preferred books to touch football. The only difference was, she had married a philanderer—I had married Paul Wharton, steadfast and true, and with whom, at that time, I was still in love.

Chapter Thirty-Five

AS JANEZ AND I walk over to the hospital together, he informs me that he has already spoken with Dr. Giovanni to discuss our father's progress. I'm miffed. He is perfectly within his rights, of course, but I have already discussed my father's health with the good doctor. Male professionals taking charge. Well, I won't be taking a backseat, they can be sure of that!

"*Way to go,*" George hums in my ear.

We agree that Janez will wait outside the ward while I attempt to prepare Daddy for their first encounter. How will it be, I wonder? What do they expect of each other? I do hope Paul isn't right. When viewed his way, it does sound like a cheap, garish bodice-ripper.

Sunshine is pouring in through the big glass windows, giving the ward a cheerful air. Today, Daddy is propped up slightly, drinking a purple concoction. One of the machines has disappeared. He spots me and smiles weakly.

"Bet you wish that was wine," I manage to joke.

"Matron said it's grape juice." His face falls into a grimace of disgust.

"Never mind. I have a surprise for you."

"Really?" There's a catch in his voice, and his lips quiver slightly.

"Janez drove here from Ljubljana yesterday."

"Already?" He attempts to put his drink on the side table, but succeeds only in dripping sticky purple juice on the sheet.

"It's going to be just fine," I assure him, removing the glass. "We spent last evening together. He's very nice. A doctor."

"Fancy that. A doctor."

I sit in the chair beside his bed. "Daddy, he explained about Józef. What happened. Who he was." I take hold of one of Daddy's hands, and the old familiar twist of comfort passes between us.

"Larkins, my batman, said it was the worst bit of our war." Pulling away from my grip, Daddy splices his hands in the air, shifting in the bed; a bead of sweat forms on his brow. "His own son was killed early in the war, so Józef was special."

"Don't get upset, Daddy. Such a long time ago. And just think, today, you're going to meet Alenka's second son. Your son." I run my hand over his cheeks. "Would you like me to shave you first?"

"Please." I find the battery-powered razor in his toilet bag and start to run it gently over his face. "Handsome is as handsome does."

There is a swish-swoosh behind us, and when I swivel round, Janez is striding down the ward. He must have watched through the window in the double doors and determined this was as good a moment as any. As for Daddy, there is not a shred of doubt on his face as to who it is marching toward him. When Janez reaches the bedside, Daddy reaches for his hand and holds it firmly. It's clear he isn't going to let go until Matron chases us out of the hospital.

"I can hardly believe this is true." My father is beaming, his face radiant with pleasure. "My child before me. Why did your mother not tell me?"

My newly minted brother glances at me, but I shake my head. I'm coming to terms with what *my* mother did to *his* mother's letter. It was the act of a ferocious mother lion, protecting her cub, no matter the cost, including to her marriage.

Michael was the only person with whom I ever shared my

ambivalence regarding Mum. Everything changed after Daddy came home. Slowly but surely, she began to push me away.

As Michael saw it: "*Your mother probably felt discarded by you when she witnessed your immediate bond with your dad. In her eyes, it was a repudiation of all the years she had cared for you alone, and the only way to cope with her jealousy was to reject you.*" Of course, neither of us knew then about the missing puzzle piece, her devastating discovery of her husband's betrayal. Poor woman. My heart aches for her. In protecting me so fiercely, she lost me, in a very real sense.

I am at a loss what to do next, but Matron bustles over to save the day. Rather than admonish us for ignoring her visiting hours, she produces a chair for Janez and more or less commands him to sit. I love this woman. Queen of her domain. If she is already aware he's a doctor, it matters not one jot to her. "I hope this to-getherness is not going to be too much for Captain Drummond," she says, pouring him a glass of water and ordering him to keep sipping, otherwise she will put him back on the drip. When Matron has restored order and we are all firmly on our bottoms, she whispers to me that there is a private room available. If I wish, she will move my father later today. I do wish. I hug her. I am so grateful.

Daddy is still clutching his son's hand. "I had no idea about your existence." His voice is scratchy with emotion. "When we parted . . ."

"Mati did not know, either."

I recall the blood-spattered beginnings of Daddy's letter to Janez . . . *loved your mother heart and soul . . . if I had known . . .* For a moment, I wish he would tell us both what he would have done if he *had* known Alenka bore him a son. But only for a moment. Depending on his answer, my entire relationship with him might have been fundamentally different. All the years of my life from the time he came home, most especially the ability we have always had to bring a sense of calm and peace to one another, would not exist. Instead, it would be his son Janez with all the memories.

What might have happened, didn't happen. I've got to find a way to not let it be important anymore. The reality is now, and how the three of us are going to handle ourselves going forward. Put right what we can, and let the rest go.

"It was a long time ago, Daddy. We are both here now. Your daughter, *and* your son."

Chapter Thirty-Six

TRUE TO HIS word, Dr. Giovanni keeps Daddy in hospital for two more weeks.

Janez and I have a routine of sorts. He spends the mornings with his father, and has bought a small transistor radio so Daddy can listen to music, now he has a room to himself. I am well aware that Janez huddles with the good doctor whenever he gets the chance, which irritates me. But I keep quiet, and struggle to appreciate and understand the emotional situation Janez finds himself in. Of course, he wants to do anything he can for his father during the limited time we have left. But despite my determination to put right what we can and let the rest go, it remains a daily battle to keep George tamped down and under control.

I stay busy organizing schedules and deadlines. Penny, a true friend, very kindly arranged for someone at Moonbeam Mountain to pick up the car at Heathrow and drive it back to Cheltenham for me, and she has shipped out a box of books. For me, the complete works of Jane Austen. And for Daddy, Sir Francis Chichester's memoir, describing his magical circumnavigation of the globe single-handed, *Gipsy Moth Circles the World*. I've talked often enough about my father's love of sailing, and how he kept a small ketch at our holiday home, so Penny's choice of book for him is perfect.

When I was a child, Daddy soon stopped inviting me to sail with him because the slightest swell made me queasy, and he spent more time mopping me up than enjoying his time on board. Now,

I'm certain he was relieved to be alone. Being alone on the water would have given him opportunities to unpack and relive his time in Trieste with Alenka in peace, undisturbed.

This morning, I'm exploring. Tucked into one of the numerous alleys off the Piazza dell'Unita, I spot a junk shop. In the dusty window, perched on a pile of yellowed magazines, is a miniature oil painting of Castello di Miramare. It really is charming, something I might like to take home with me. When I step inside the dim, dusty shop, filled with an assortment of trinkets, I'm immediately transported back to a lazy Saturday morning in Wapping. Michael and I were lounging in bed with the newspaper and a pot of coffee.

"Lazy bones," he'd teased. "Last one dressed buys lunch."

Our habit of showering together slowed us down considerably, so by the time we decided who was *last ready*, the sky was darkening. It was low tide, however, so we pulled on wellies, thick jumpers, and parkas, and decided to walk along the shore to the pub. The sand was silty and heavy, and a line of shingle crackled under our feet. I wanted to stop to hunt for washed-up artifacts, but almost immediately thunder rumbled over the river. In no time, rainclouds draped the freighters in a thick gray shroud. Minutes after that, torrents of rain burst from the heavens. We clumped clumsily along in our wellies, making for Wapping Stairs. The rain sluiced down the steps, slick with seaweed. I slipped twice before we made it to the top and took shelter under a narrow foot bridge.

Michael pointed out a shabby little storefront, seemingly gouged out of the mold-stained wall. A weathered sign, *The Merry Mudlark*, creaked eerily, like a scene out of Dickens.

"Let's have a look inside," I suggested.

"Why not? I want to buy you something anyway, darling."

"Me too. Twenty quid limit!"

"You're on!"

A rusty bell clanked dejectedly, and we marched right in. An old man sidled out from behind a moth-eaten velvet curtain. He wore an old-fashioned, long black duster coat draped over a shiny suit. A set of rimless spectacles rested atop a red-veined, bulbous nose. Nothing about him seemed very "merry." It began to feel more and more as if we had stumbled back in time.

"Morning." His voice rasped, as if he hadn't used it for a while. "I have a veritable trove of treasures."

Actually, what he had on offer was a real mishmash of wares. Michael pored over a rickety table that almost completely filled the tiny shop. It was piled with books, papers, and rolled-up maps, and beneath it were boxes filled with who-knows-what, festooned in sticky cobwebs. I explored a muddle of medals and badges, buttons, ornaments, even a rusty dagger, all heaped on the windowsill. I wanted to find something unique, something Michael would get a kick out of, and I had almost run out of hope when I pulled a large, genuinely old paintbrush from under a picture frame.

When I turned to show it to Michael, he was holding a gorgeous purple amethyst glass inkwell with a brass-hinged lid in the palm of his hand. Clearly vintage.

"Oh, Michael, I love it."

"Belonged to Charles Dickens," the old man told us.

I burst out laughing. "I bet it did!"

But when I peeped out of the window, down the stairs to the river, and watched the tide creeping higher, I was inclined to believe the old man. I heard a pen nib scratching out the beginning of a masterpiece. *"In these times of ours . . . a boat of dirty and disreputable appearance, with two figures in it, floated on the Thames . . . as an autumn evening was closing in."*

Michael handed me the inkwell; I held it up to the light, such as it was, and knew immediately I would always believe it held the ink Mr. Dickens used when he wrote *Our Mutual Friend.*

"What do you have for me, Georgina?" asked Michael.

Surprise lit up his face when he saw the paintbrush.

"What a beauty!" He examined it carefully. "Definitely nineteenth century. Definitely horsehair bristles. Look at the dings on the wood handle, Gina. And look at the paint spatter patterns, too. I'll get them analyzed. Who do you claim used this brush, sir?"

But the old man shrugged, losing interest, no longer wanting to spin us a tale. We paid for our finds, and he wrapped them up for us in brown paper and string.

Gradually the memories dim, fading into the past. I'm in Trieste again, in this other cluttered shop of relics, feeling disoriented. I never want to forget those precious days with Michael, but they evoke deep sadness whenever they spring back to life.

I step quickly outside into the sunshine, forsaking the small oil painting, fearing a similar sort of fate could befall it, as befell our gifts to one another that day. When I went into Michael's flat a second time after the tragedy to collect what mementos I could, his estranged brother Liam had cleared the place out. I'd not even been aware of Liam's existence until he showed up like the proverbial bad penny and put Michael's flat on the market. But he'd done a thorough job. All that lingered in the bare, brick-walled rooms was the faint but seductive aroma of long-ago spices.

I fortify myself with coffee and a pastry on the Piazza before making my way to the hospital. Daddy has rallied enough to be able to sit in a rocking chair for part of each day. His private room is bright and cheery, and I'm reading him a chapter from *Gipsy Moth* when Janez shows up. He pulls out a chair and waits somewhat impatiently.

"Sorry to interrupt," he says, running out of patience before I've finished, "but I want to discuss a proposal I have for when Papa is discharged."

"*Probably kidnap him,*" George whispers in my ear. Daddy, however, beams, no such callous sentiments running through his head.

"Dr. Giovanni is firmly against you making any attempt to return to England."

"We know this," I snap. "He spoke to us both earlier in the week."

"And I do not think you will wish to live in the hotel again," replies Janez, ignoring me.

"Actually, I have begun looking at flats to rent in Trieste for us both," I inform him, slapping *Gipsy Moth* on the floor. A couple of pages curl up, and I blush with shame.

"You have?" Daddy looks at me, astonished.

"Gina. Papa. Listen to me," Janez says, as though my outburst has not occurred. "Mati's home in Opatje Selo belongs to me. Ava and I use as a holiday home, a getaway, I think you say." He turns to Daddy. "As you had your seaside cottage, yes, Bamburgh?"

My goodness, what a lot of ground you two have covered in just two weeks.

"But it's on the Karst," I complain. "I've been there. It's isolated. Primitive. There probably isn't even telephone service in the village."

Janez grins. "Believe it or not, there is telephone in our home. And over the years, Mati and me, we update the house. Running water, modern kitchen, central heating, comfortable beds. I would be truly honored to offer it to you both, for as long as you wish."

What he really means is until Daddy comes to the end of his life. "It's too far from the hospital. From Dr. Giovanni. What if—"

"Gina, I will visit most often to monitor Papa's health. Refill his medicines."

"Daddy, what do you think?" I ask, longing for him to agree with me.

But there is no chance of that. He looks like a schoolboy receiving a first-place ribbon on Sports Day. "I can't imagine a more satisfactory plan. Not in my wildest dreams—" Then he frowns. "But only if you can stay with me, Gina. What will Paul have to say? He may not agree to you staying on. You've been away so long already."

Indeed, I have, darling Daddy. And for all that time Paul has undermined me. Sown doubts about your son. Bullied me to fly you home. Even begun complaining about the girls, insisting they don't seem to take much notice of him.

But I must do what is right for my father. And what is right for me. The rest I will leave to the angels, or devils, or whoever the hell is in charge of the world. If I truly want a future that will make me happy, I must accept that I can't change the past. Including a half-brother.

I reach over and give Daddy a big hug.

"Then we will make your wildest dream come true, and as soon as possible implement the most satisfactory of plans. All that matters now is that you are able to be in a place that will make you happy."

Chapter Thirty-Seven

A WEEK LATER, the arrangements are complete, the discharge papers prepared. We will drive both our cars. However, I've no intention of being trapped on the Karst should anything at all go wrong today or later. I must admit to having had second thoughts about this venture, despite knowing how much it has given Daddy something to look forward to. The sky is overcast after a heavy rain, and I worry that it is too damp and chilly. But Janez is a doctor, and so his word carries more weight than mine around the Maggiore Hospital!

He already has Daddy dressed and sitting in a wheelchair. Inwardly, I simmer with indignation that Janez so easily takes over so many aspects of my father's care. Then I stop myself. Daddy is Janez's father too. I would have been a very resentful child if I'd had to grow up with a brother or sister, but I do have to admit my conflicted feelings provide a better insight into my daughters, as well as their seeming inability to abide one another much of the time.

Only recently, Louisa phoned to report that her sister had been stopped for speeding. Didn't I think she should be forbidden to drive my car anymore? Shortly afterward, Annabel called to let me know her sister had omitted the part where the officer let her off with a warning. A few minutes after that, Louisa called again to inform me her sister was now dressing like a slut, and only got off because she was wearing a miniskirt. At this point I instructed the hotel desk to hold any further calls from the United States that came in after ten o'clock at night.

I stride over to my brother and my father, a smile slicked on my face. "Good morning, Daddy. Are you absolutely sure you are up for this?"

"He is, Gina," replies Janez. "And I already conferred further with Dr. Giovanni."

I bet you have. Just because you are a doctor shouldn't mean you can steamroll my opinions willy-nilly. "Fetch your car around then, Janez. We'll meet you at the front entrance. I'm already parked there."

When Janez disappears, we bid a fond farewell to Matron. "Good luck, Captain Drummond," she says, bundling a thick blanket around his knees. "My prayers go with you."

I grasp the wheelchair handles and push Daddy slowly down a long corridor. "Are you positive you can manage the car ride? Positive this is what you want to do?"

"The doctor tells me it is the very best medicine in the world."

"Which one?" I snap, before I can stop myself.

"Darling, don't," he whispers, glancing over his shoulder.

I stop pushing and kneel in front of him. "Sorry. But I worry that going back to Alenka's home, never mind actually staying in it, will be too hard for you to bear. Have you really thought this through?"

Daddy touches my cheek. "When I asked you to bring me back to Trieste, I never dreamed this could really happen. Georgie Girl, it means so much to me. It is something I really, really want to do."

It's all very well, but what will the reality be like, I wonder, living in the house of his lover? When I stepped back into *my* lover's home right after our relationship was shattered, it was unbearable. I opened the door, and along with the lapping of the river, I was confronted with the beginnings of an oil painting on Michael's easel. Of me. Leaning against a door frame, our unmade bed behind me. I wore washed-out blue jeans and a crisp, white shirt. One knee was slightly raised; the sole of my bare foot was flat against the door itself. I was in shadow, my expression enigmatic. As if Michael was anticipating waste, loss, endings, even then. I fled in despair, not thinking to take it with me. Never imagining that the estranged brother would appear and presumably cast it out onto a rubbish heap.

Now, all I want to do is weep. But instead, I pull myself together and try to sound as cheerful as possible. "Then Opatje Selo, here we come."

Despite my brave words, it was with reluctance that I checked out of the hotel earlier today. The kindly and sympathetic manager kissed my hand and assured me I am welcome to return at any time, should it become necessary.

"How are the family doing?" Daddy asks when I start pushing the wheelchair again.

"I checked with Paul just last night. Let him know where I would be as of today. Everyone is very concerned, of course. Send their love. But Paul completely disagrees with what we are doing."

"I expect he's trying to do his best."

I pat Daddy's shoulder. "I know. I know. And now he and the girls are home from Wind Lake, the Tribe Wharton are keeping them well occupied."

"That's good." Daddy chortles. "I know how difficult it has always been for you to cope with your vast, extended family. But I love you anyway, Georgie Girl, warts and all!"

Janez pulls up, and we settle Daddy in the front seat of his car, where there is a little more room than in my rental. He grasps

Janez's arm. "When we get to the village, I want to go first to the cemetery."

"Certainly, Papa. We can do that."

Driving along behind father and son, it occurs to me that I don't even know how Daddy and Alenka met. The circumstances must have been odd. Territorial bickering. Political wrangles. Antagonistic armies. Was the attraction between them immediate? Did they make love in this house we are barreling towards?

The autumn colors are in full majesty, and despite low-hanging clouds, the drive is far prettier than when I first ventured up here, searching for this very same village. Best I forget that particular day.

Twenty or so miles later, I follow Janez down a sloping country lane to the cemetery. He parks outside the gate. We have the wheelchair in the boot of my car, but Daddy insists on walking with a cane, as if he cannot bear for the ghost of Alenka to see him defeated now by age and illness. We follow a winding path through the graves. Daddy knows exactly where to go. "I attended Józef's funeral," he explains.

Another piece of his life. It seems to me a brave thing to have done, given that his role was occupation-officer-in-charge at the time of the child's appalling death. He can't have been a popular figure in the village. Were he and Alenka lovers by then? If they weren't, how did they ever come together afterward? And if they were already lovers, how in God's name did the disaster affect their relationship? A pang of self-pity pricks my heart. But I remind myself Michael's and my great misfortune was cut from very different cloth—and our affair had no chance of survival for vastly different reasons.

We reach the farthest wall, where generation after generation of Marusics are huddled together, stones and markers tipping and leaning into one another. For some reason, I find it comforting. Far different from the dignified Garden of Remembrance, where we scattered Mum's ashes five years ago. This small corner feels more real, somehow, although for the life of me, I can't conjure up the words to explain why.

Daddy struggles to kneel beside the grave. He is breathing heavily. Janez steadies him. It is such a personal moment, I step away to give him privacy, but not before I hear Daddy whisper, "My Boadicea."

Boadicea? How curious. Paul likened his father-in-law's improbable story to a cheap romance novel, but that audience would not know "Boadicea" from a posh dish on a posh menu in a posh restaurant, never mind how to pronounce or spell it. The very idea makes me smile.

After several minutes, Daddy rifles around in the breast pocket of his blazer. Out comes the felt star he has had stashed away forever and a day. He holds it up to his lips, then places it tenderly on top of the mounded earth, beneath which lie the bodies of his lover and her child.

"Papa?"

"Your mother made sure Józef's little-boy Titovka cap was resting on top of his coffin and buried with him. Józef was so proud of it. Always wore it. Even . . . the day . . . he was killed." Daddy rubs his eyes. "Only seems right to bring Alenka's own star home now. Everything together in one place."

The sun breaks through the heavy clouds, and silvery streaks of light shimmer on a stand of trees beyond the wall. Janez and I heave Daddy to his feet, but as we turn to leave, he stops abruptly. Out of nowhere, his face blazes hot as a burning ember. He stabs with his cane at another, different name—DARKO—on the gravestone.

"No! Not right," he shouts. "I *know* where that body is." Just as suddenly his voice trails off, rattling like a breeze through dry grass. "Frightful mistake. Cannot be."

"What are you talking about, Daddy? How would you know such a thing?"

He lurches in my direction, hushing me. Clutches my arm. A minute passes. "Never mind. Better not to speak of it, I suppose."

"No, Papa," Janez says. "We will speak of Darko, father of Józef. You will be amazed at the news I can tell you of the Basovizza Foiba."

Dear God. That name. Basovizza. The village still firm in its allegiance to the doctrine of Tito—the village where I was accosted. At the very mention of that town, all I want to do is bundle Daddy up and return to our suite at the hotel. But then I observe Janez taking his pulse on the pretext of helping him into the front seat of his car, and remind myself how thankful I must be for small mercies.

"First, we drive to house," says Janez. "We will sit and gather ourselves. Come with us, Gina. I will fetch your car later."

When we turn onto one of several lanes leading off the village square, Daddy knows exactly where he is going: a two-story stone house, its façade glinting in a watery sun that has pushed through the clouds. The front door is painted bright blue, as vivid as the Adriatic on a clear day. A small iron balcony juts out from the second floor. A potpourri of emotions scatter across my father's face from joy to sorrow. Another piece of his life unknown to me.

"Welcome home, Papa."

A hole opens up in my heart when Janez speaks these words. Not because my goblin George is rattled, but because they reinforce what we already know: Daddy will never again return to England. Home is here now.

Chapter Thirty-Eight

A S WE ENTER, I picture the two lovers, Alenka and James, taking this momentous step over the threshold, into what might have been a future for them. The sort of step I longed to take with Michael. Somewhere in the home a wood fire is burning, and the sweet smell of apple wood sweeps me back to a different November day in London, a rendezvous with Michael in the George Bar at Durrants Hotel.

A fire crackled in that grate too. The flames curled and flickered. The wall sconces glowed against the paneled walls. Snow drifted down outside the windows. And Michael was waiting for me. He had arranged with the concierge to store my luggage, and we settled down in our favorite banquette close to the fireplace.

"Back when we started," he said, hugging me close, "at first I didn't mind you coming and going because I could miss you with the sure knowledge of your return. But enough is enough. Now I'm thoroughly fed up of missing you." Michael dropped to his knees, almost in the hearth itself. "When can we get married?"

Hovering in the background was the barman, holding a bottle of champagne in an ice bucket and two glasses on a tray, grinning inanely, much like a bad actor in a third-rate farce.

"I propose, in accordance with our backwards love affair, we go upstairs for a short honeymoon, starting this afternoon. And next year, when it's all sorted with Paul, I will carry you over the threshold of my flat, into marital bliss."

When the bottle was popped and the bubbly poured, I

discovered an antique wedding ring in the bottom of my glass—a wide, soft-yellow gold band, embedded with rubies. That day, I thought I had everything I wanted in the whole world.

I'm leaning against the blue door at Alenka's house for support, my heart thudding as I try to shake the remembrance out of my head. I take the opportunity to gaze around at what will be our residence for the foreseeable future. Ahead of me is a staircase to the upper floor. Just as Janez promised, the kitchen has been thoroughly updated. There's a stove, a refrigerator, even a dishwasher and a small washing machine tucked under the cabinetry.

"Ava arranged for a neighbor to stock the refrigerator for you, Gina. And for a bed to be set up for Papa downstairs in our sitting room. Let me show you."

The living room leads off the kitchen, a nice size, with French doors opening onto a surprisingly large garden. It's in this room that a fireplace is crackling away.

"This is lovely, Janez."

Daddy nods agreement, but he's beginning to look completely worn out. And no wonder—the day has already been filled with so many recollections. "I'm tired, Georgie Girl. Must rest."

While Janez helps him into his pajamas and administers pills, I take the opportunity to explore upstairs, which in turn reminds me of when I explored Michael's place on the river for the first time. Massive open spaces full of light, ancient brick walls, pictures everywhere. His whole life laid out for me to see. This is the exact opposite—small, compact, but charming in its own way. The wood staircase is steep. To my delight, I find that a small lavatory and washbasin have obviously been added to the home, carved into the space beneath the stairs. Essential for our needs, and I'm grateful that Ava thought to make up a bedroom downstairs for Daddy.

Upstairs, there are just two rooms, so it must have been a bit of a squash when Janez brought Ava and their children for holidays. I assume Alenka accompanied them, at least on occasion. She would have wanted to spend time with her grandchildren. But perhaps the memories of the house were too raw, and a lost husband and lost lover kept her away.

It reminds me of our cottage at Bamburgh—Mummy, Granny, and I there all summer long. Daddy driving up to join us on Fridays after work. It seemed back then that I spent every day on the beach. Digging in rock pools. Clambering over half-buried tank traps, enormous concrete blocks, intended to stop a German invasion and left over after the war. But in my young mind, they had been dropped there purely for the enjoyment of Miss Georgina Drummond. Part of the fabric of my childhood.

I select the larger bedroom at the front of the house because it opens onto the small balcony; because of the sweep of emotions it conjured for Daddy; because of its romantic Romeo and Juliet quality.

"Papa is sleeping," Janez tells me when I return to the kitchen. "Over supper, I will explain the mystery name on grave of Mati. Our papa was correct. Darko was not there when Józef was laid to rest."

"I worry this is going to overwhelm him."

"You are correct to be concerned, but I have examined him. He is doing well."

"Driving up here, I couldn't understand how coming to a place with such memories could possibly be good for him. But now I've visited the cemetery, and now that I'm physically in your mother's home, I realize Daddy must have yearned for this to happen ever since he received your letter. He wants to die as close to Alenka as possible."

When Janez smiles, real gratitude radiates between us. "I think you have hit nail on the head. Is the saying? Yes?"

I giggle. Where does he pick up these idioms?

"I must inform you also, Gina, tomorrow I return to Ljubljana for a few days."

"So soon?"

"My colleagues have been kind to cover all this time. But, of course, I will come very often."

"My car is still parked at the cemetery," I remind him.

"I have separate garage nearby. Give me the keys. I will put it away now. Tomorrow I will show you where to find it."

Tomorrow. Despite leftover resentment for how this man has turned our lives upside down, I am nervous about having complete responsibility for Daddy. No Janez. No Matron. No Dr. Giovanni. All alone on the Karst, without a word of Slovene or Italian to help. Then I shake off my doubts with a shrug. I'm a big girl. Well able to take care of myself.

"As soon as I organize coverage for my surgeries at hospital, re-arrange patient appointments, I will return. But please telephone me at once if you have questions or concerns."

He sounds so like the doctor he is, gesturing to the phone on the kitchen wall, making sure I know exactly where it is as if I am a child. I'm suddenly so filled with gratitude, I manage to take a step forward and dip to peck his cheek. It's the first time we have done anything besides shake hands. I'm shocked at myself, but Janez just smiles his "Daddy" smile at me. It feels like a small gift. It *is* a small gift. In a silly way, a bit like the warm fuzzy feeling I get when Peanut fetches the newspaper for me off the front porch on freezing cold Minnesota mornings.

I check through the fridge and truly appreciate the thought put into its contents. While Daddy rests, I prepare a huge bowl of salad, which I will dress just before we begin our meal, and put together and bake a quiche Lorraine. Lastly, I set the table. The pottery bowls, plates, and mugs I discover in the cupboard are an intense Adriatic blue, intertwined with bold, mustard-yellow stripes and colorful, green vines. So cheerful, in fact, that I feel a vague contentment. Especially now I have grasped the fact that Daddy, consciously or otherwise, has chosen to end his days behind the blue door, close to his lover. I must admit, after all, my brother's suggestion to bring him here will work well.

Janez produces a couple of bottles of wine from his cellar.

"Is it okay for Daddy to have wine again?" I ask as we sit down at the table.

"Gina, what is important from this point forward is he relax, rest, and be happy." There is the slightest of tremors in Janez's voice. "A wine or two is not going to make difference."

While we are talking, Daddy joins us, looking much revived. More like my daddy of old. I pour us all glasses of wine, pretty sure he overheard our last few words.

"Papa, I will tell you now the story of Darko? Yes?"

"Please, son."

Daddy's use of this term gives me an eerie shiver, but it isn't green-goblin selfishness as much as a quiet relief that he has the opportunity to know his adult son. Had Janez not written, Daddy would have died completely ignorant of the fact that he and Alenka created a child together. Somehow, to die without knowledge of his second child's existence does not seem fair to me now. Not fair at all. And with that, I shove George Goblin, Esq., deep inside my being, where I hope he will stay for a good, long time to come.

Janez has begun his story. "Once DNA testing become available, officials in Italy and Yugoslavia both agree to excavate completely all foibe on the Karst."

"Excuse me, what is a foibe?" I ask.

"Crevasses in the limestone rock all over the Karst," says Daddy. "Put to murderous use during the war. First by the Nazis, and then, it has to be said, by Tito's forces, out of revenge." The latter he says with resignation. "Remember, darling, I told you how I had to investigate the Jug atrocities, but back then there was no time, will, or equipment to complete the job."

"When Basovizza pit was emptied, there were too many remains to count, but eventually Darko was found, and we were able to identify the bones using DNA," explains Janez.

"But if Józef was dead, how could you run a match?" I have a horrific image of someone digging up the child's grave.

"Mati manage to track down one distant cousin, still living."

"Who would have guessed such a thing possible, back when we made our inspections." Daddy shakes his head in disbelief. "But for Alenka to finally bring her husband home where he belonged makes me very, very happy for her."

He looks so serene this evening, as if all the pieces of his life are slotting into place. Perhaps I'll be able to get things sorted once and for all with Paul soon. Then my life too can finally slot into place. Reminiscing earlier about how I was presented with my ruby ring has made me realize how much I yearn to be able to wear it. Who knows? Stranger things have happened.

"To the memory of Alenka, Józef, and Darko," we toast in unison, gazing solemnly at one another as the words give poignancy to the occasion.

As I toss my salad and slice the quiche, an inexplicable tremor tingles through my body, urging me—to do what? To not overlook the other Marusic, here in this room, and very much alive. It's slowly but surely becoming apparent to me how much and how soon I will need his familiar mannerisms to help me through the loss of my father in all the years that lie ahead.

A long moment later, I stand and raise my glass again.

"And to the long and happy life of my brother, Janez," I declare.

OCTOBER –
NOVEMBER 1946

Chapter Thirty-Nine

THE ORDERS ARRIVED at Castello di Miramare at the end of September, just as Drummond knew they would. No amount of fooling himself that they might go astray, get rewritten, or otherwise vanish was going to make it so. Even from the far side of his office, he recognized the brown buff envelope lying on the blotter on his desk. He sank into the chair and lit a cigarette before slitting open the package.

He and Larkins were scheduled to depart on or about November 12, as soon as a troop ship became available. Upon arrival, they would report to the regiment in Newcastle, approximately mid-December. He would be home again for Christmas, just like last year.

He did a quick calculation in his head. At least another six weeks of his here-and-now life in Trieste with Alenka, before he must bid her farewell. Pop her back in a bottle like a mythical genie. And say hello to a make-do life, filled with remorse, compromise, and the tormenting memory of the dead child.

Below the window lay the brooding Adriatic. In his mind's eye, he saw Alenka rising out of the pool, twisting water from her sopping black hair. The sun dappling her golden skin through the leaves. He must let her know the orders had come. But not yet. He needed to think. Needed to be alone. Needed to make sense of his life. Though God only knew how.

By the time Larkins showed up with the daily schedule, Drummond was numb, convinced that if he stabbed himself with a knife, he would feel nothing. He swung around from the window and motioned his batman to rest at ease.

"Just arrived." He gestured to the desk. "Orders. We leave Trieste in the middle of November. By sea. Best start thinking about what's to be packed up. What we'll be taking home with us."

"Yes, sir."

"Expect you're pleased. Back to brown ale and fish and chips at last."

"Yes, sir."

"You mother will be relieved too."

"Yes, sir."

Drummond looked up. "You quite well, Larkins?"

"Bit of a gippy tummy just come on."

"Sorry about that." Larkins did look a bit green about the gills. Drummond wrote a quick note to Alenka, explaining he was tied up all day, and slipped it into an envelope. "Deliver this to my place in Trieste, if you would, please. Then take the rest of the day off."

"Sir, what . . . are you . . . what are we going to do . . . ?"

"Just get going, Larkins, there's a good chap."

Drummond knew he would go mad cooped up in the castle with the orders he hadn't wanted lying on his desk, as well as boots ricocheting off floors, clattery typewriters firing intermittently like scatter-shot, and teacups rattling in and out of saucers. He shut and locked the office, climbed the staircases to his room. Flung off his uniform and pulled on a pair of civilian slacks, a blue shirt, and a heavy jersey. What else? A bottle of whiskey, two packets of cigarettes. He would get himself a boat for the day. Somewhere to be alone. Somewhere to think.

A fifteen-foot wooden dinghy was good enough to get him out to sea. He raised the sail and tacked into the Gulf. The Karst, and then the city, receded quickly in a coastal mist. Blessedly soon, he had the solitude he sought, bobbing on the waves.

All day, he sucked steadily at the whiskey and challenged himself to see how many lines of poetry he could repeat from memory. He struggled to sort out his competing emotions. England. Home. Mary, his wife, whom he had betrayed. Mother of his beloved child. Over and over, he reminded himself of his wedding vows. Once married, choice was not supposed to be an option. He knew that. Honor and responsibility were paramount, lessons his mother and father had instilled in him as he grew up. And he had believed them, did believe them still.

But he loved Alenka. It wasn't only lust that drove his desire. He worshiped her ability to grasp what she wanted, when she wanted it, how she paid respect to her own needs. He admired her abundant, bursting faith in her country and the new system she had fought so hard for. He took strength from her utter belief in herself. Her fierce disposition. Her self-respect. *And her lips opened amorously, and said—I wist not what, saving one word—delight. And all her face was honey to his mouth—* He trimmed the sail and slumped in the dinghy, unable to remember the rest of the Swinburne poem. But he did remember to prod the rudder with his foot once in a while. When the bottle was empty, he tossed it overboard, sinking gratefully into a drunken stupor.

The dinghy drifted.

Drummond's mind drifted.

The sun drifted.

IT WAS DARK WHEN he woke, his skin whipped raw by the wind, his hair thick and matted with salt. He had no idea where he was. He lowered his throbbing head over the side of the boat and sloshed it around in the cold sea water, trying to clear his mind, pull himself together. Clouds obscured the moon, but he thought he could discern land. Probably the Istrian Peninsula. He reset the sail in that direction, but an eerie calm had settled over the sea. What a bloody fool he was to have come out here alone, without alerting anyone of his intentions.

Then he saw it. A sea mine, floating off his bow, the tell-tale, lethal black humps dotting its surface like malignant warts. He longed for a cigarette, but couldn't remember if that would place him in even more danger. Not a breath of wind whispered over the water to aid him in escape.

There wasn't even an oar in the dinghy. And he hadn't bothered to check? He was pathetic.

Clumsy with desperation, he scooped with his hands in an effort to steer away from the mine. Rationally, he knew the blasted things were tethered somehow, but he could have sworn this particular beauty was finding a perverse pleasure in stalking him. Had it somehow broken free?

His life unspooled before his eyes. He and Charlie, off on their bikes. His father dying in agony, his mother following of a botched operation shortly thereafter. The brothers orphaned together, in their home in Newcastle, not even out of their teens. His wife-to-be offering comfort and a sense of belonging in the bosom of her own family. Georgina, his child, cuddling her bunny. And Alenka. Always, Alenka.

He felt himself fading away, just as he had watched comrades die on the battlefield. But he didn't want to die. Not like this. Dear God in heaven, had he survived the whole hellish war, only to be blown into a thousand pieces in the Gulf of Trieste? He knew he was still very drunk, but one thing came clear. To never have the chance to bid goodbye to Alenka, or set eyes on his child again, was unacceptable. He *must* stay alive, somehow.

He sensed a black shape looming on the starboard side. Rubbing his eyes, he heaved himself onto his bottom and craned his neck in its direction. A fishing vessel.

"Danger," he shouted at the top of his voice. "Mine."

Should he try to stand up and point at the black orb jouncing up and down beside him? He wished he knew more about the damned things. Why hadn't he paid more attention to the navy chap's briefing earlier in the year?

A bright light beamed across the water, almost blinding him. "German?"

A hopeless terror gnawed at his gut. If they mistook him for a Jerry, he knew exactly what they would do. Slit his throat and hurl him to the fishes.

"British," he yelled. *Believe me. Please believe me.*

There was a babble of voices. Possibly Croatian. He was too terrified to think straight.

Then a line spun through the air. He caught hold of it and tied it round his waist, realizing at the same moment he would have to swim for the ship. Whoever these men were, they were not going to risk getting any closer to the mine. And who could blame them?

Please don't let there be any more mines between me and rescue. Gingerly, he eased into the frigid water and began paddling. Time slowed. His arms ached. His head ached worse. Water filled his lungs. When he was pretty sure he was done for, rough hands hauled him into the fishing boat. Wrapped him in a blanket. Gave him a cigarette. Poured a vile liquor down his throat.

The boat changed course and headed for Trieste. Within a few short minutes, the night air filled with an overwhelming smell of metal, and his dinghy exploded in a fireball.

Chapter Forty

TWO HOURS LATER, Drummond's saviors slapped him on the back and chucked him, numb with cold, onto the Molo Audace. He crawled along the pier as far as the seafront, collapsed against a bollard, and was violently sick. All around him, the unsettled city stumbled on through the night, under its military occupation. Occasional gunfire split the air, jeep tires squealed, and drunks hollered. When he felt able to stand, he slogged around the Piazza dell'Unita in his sodden clothes, keeping well into the shadows, desperate to avoid a curfew patrol. With no identification and half drowned, it would be difficult to explain who he was and what he was doing. Somehow, by sheer good luck, he found his alley, dragged himself up the stairs to their room, and scratched ineffectually on the door.

"What has happen to you?" Alenka cried when she found him. "Where have you been?"

She dragged him inside, close to the stove. Shook him hard. Peeled off his waterlogged clothes. Wrapped him in a quilt off their bed.

"Talk to me, James."

"I went sailing . . ."

"You fool. Silly fool." She slapped him hard. "Why?"

He sagged onto a kitchen chair. "I needed to think."

"About what . . . ?" Her voice trailed off.

"It's hard to explain." But the set of her body as she began to brew a pot of tea revealed grief as well as anger. He realized she must already be aware that his orders had arrived. "You know, don't you, Alenka?"

"Yes, I know. Larkins warn me this morning when he deliver your note." She slammed cups down on the table in front of him. "We knew this time coming. Didn't we? Knew you would have to go home sometime."

Gazing at her, he saw resignation in her gray eyes.

"James, still no reason to drown yourself in sea," she admonished, much as Mary had scolded Georgie Girl when she spilled a glass of milk.

He began to shake again. "I got lost. There was a mine. Fishermen rescued me just . . . before . . . the boat blew up."

"Why did you not come to me?" Alenka yelled, jumping to her feet. "Why do such stupid thing?" She slapped her hand flat on the table, making the cups rattle. "If you *not* saved, what mess you leave behind. Me. Mary. Little Georgina. And no one ever know what happen to you." A sob escaped her lips. "Because you all blown up!"

He tried to pick up the tea she had poured, but couldn't get his frozen, stiff fingers to work. She watched him, cheeks blazing, hair billowing down her back, muttering in Slovene. Several deep breaths later, she sat down again and held the cup to his lips so he could drink.

"Now you listen to me, Captain James Drummond of Allied Command, and listen good. Because I knew our time must come to end, I make a preparation weeks ago."

"Preparation?" Drummond didn't feel anchored to anything, a bit like the warty mine. As if he were bobbing alone in the black water, until he was blown to smithereens, like she said.

"*Ljubcek*, I must build life different from this. Life after Darko. Life after Józef. *And* life after you."

"Alenka, I wish . . ."

She cut him off with a firm shake of her head. "No wishing, James. Is done. I have nursing job in hospital in Slovenia."

"When do you leave?" His voice echoed in his ears, as if he were underwater, sinking ever deeper.

"Soon."

Drummond struggled up from the table, shaking so hard he almost tripped on the quilt she had wrapped him in. "How long? Tell me, please."

"One week more."

Not the weeks he had anticipated when he had opened the orders. Seven days, and she'd be gone. He clung to the back of the chair. His body jerked, his teeth clattering around in his mouth like castanets. Before he could stop it, he loosed howl after howl, much like a creature left to die in the wilderness. Suddenly gentle, she ran a hand over his shoulders, applying pressure to stop the spasms before pulling him to his feet. "Come, James."

Alenka added more wood to the stove and settled him on the rug. She piled every blanket she could find over him and slipped down beside him, cradling him in her arms to warm his shivering body. When he ceased trembling, she pulled his head down to her breasts and rocked him like a baby, crooning Józef's favorite lullaby—

> *Medvedek ni bolan* (teddy bear is not ill),
> *Medvedek je zaspan* (teddy bear is sleepy),
> *Ko pride temn noc* (when the dark night comes),
> *Medvedek lahko noc* (good night, teddy bear)*!*

—until James's breathing calmed, and he fell into a deep, exhausted sleep.

DAWN HAD BROKEN OVER the Karst, trickling down the hillsides and into the bay, when boots sounded heavily up the stairs and a fist banged frantically on the door.

"Let me in! Open up!" Larkins burst into the room. "Where the hell is he?"

Alenka uncurled herself from her lover and rose to her feet, rubbing her eyes.

"Crikey!" Larkins gawped at the mound of blankets on the floor beside the stove. "Captain Drummond?" He dropped to his knees and pulled aside the bedding. "Is he all right?" he asked.

"I think so," whispered Alenka. "But he almost killed last night by sea mine."

"Sea mine?" The freckles on Larkins's cheeks stood out like vivid question marks.

"Swept out to sea. Rescued by fisherman, he said."

"So, where's the boat?" demanded Larkins.

Alenka raised her arms in the air. "Pouf."

"How could he be such a crazy fool!" Larkins tore off his beret and raked his hands through his hair, creating a tangled mess.

The crazy fool stirred. Rolled over. Sat up, groaning. Caught sight of his batman, still on his knees beside him. "Oh, good Christ." He tried to wrap himself up in one of the blankets. "Oh, my God."

Larkins got to his feet, grabbed his cap, and snapped to attention.

"I will make coffee for us all," said Alenka. "James, you have clean uniform in wardrobe."

"Sir, would you like me to help—"

"No, Larkins, I'll dress later. Look, I'm sorry about this. Really I am."

"It was just, when I didn't find you in your room and nobody seemed to know your whereabouts, I thought I had better check around," explained Larkins.

"Quite right. Damned embarrassing, all the same. Sit down, man, that's an order."

Larkins shuffled uncomfortably. Sitting in the presence of an officer was an out-of-the-ordinary situation, but an order was an order. He perched uneasily at the table.

Alenka set three steaming cups of Nescafé down. "Sorry, no sugar today."

"How much trouble will I be in over the damned boat?" Drummond muttered morosely.

Larkins took several large gulps of coffee. "Well, I been thinking. If you agree, sir, we can just ignore the boat business. There's no record of you taking it. I already checked the marina. If it blew to pieces, it's not likely any bits will wash ashore."

It blew to pieces, all right, and there would have been nothing left of me either, if the fishing boat hadn't turned up in the nick of time and taken pity on me. Drummond heard the explosion, saw the brilliant orange and yellow of the flames against the black sky, listened to the incoherent jabbering of the fishermen—all over again. His hands started to tremble.

Larkins rummaged around in his trouser pockets for a box of cigarettes and matches and set them in front of the captain. "Thought you might have run out, sir." While Drummond fumbled several matches attempting to light up, Larkins gazed at the tossed-aside, soggy clothing, representing his violent reaction to the orders. "Look, sir. You've had more than one bout of malaria since Africa. So, what do you say I report you laid up? File a sick chit for a few days."

"Say yes," whispered Alenka. "Please say yes."

Drummond looked to Alenka and back at Larkins, then nodded

his assent. Each of them sighed with relief that it was settled, and finished up the coffee quickly.

"I'll leave the jeep then, should I, sir?"

"Much appreciated, Larkins. Thank you again for your help."

"I'll check with you regular, sir. Let you know if you're needed at the castle, like. Keep you on top of things."

When Alenka ushered Larkins out onto the small landing, she kissed his cheek. "Thank you, special friend of Józef."

Larkins blushed furiously.

"Always in my heart, I will not forget what you do for all children in our village. And how you love Józef—"

Before Alenka could say more, Larkins clattered down the stairs, tears coursing down his cheeks.

Chapter Forty-One

A WEEK LATER, Alenka unlocked the familiar blue door in Opatje Selo. Drummond noted the gouge made by his boot when he had kicked the door in such fury. Since that day, always itching away at the back of his mind, was the possibility that he may never have possessed Alenka if Józef had not died so tragically. It was not something he had ever dared to ask her. But he would today. Time was running out.

"James, I go to cemetery to visit Józef for little while."

Drummond understood. After all, she was leaving her son alone in his grave for the foreseeable future. But at the same time, he clung hopelessly to the belief that if they could only stay together, safe in their Trieste room, safe in the cocoon of love they'd created, he could keep her grief from overwhelming her.

He fumbled to light a cigarette. "Let me come with you?"

"No." Alenka held up her hands. "Now I start to be alone."

He recalled his own farewells. To men who had trudged through deserts, slogged up beaches, lain in mud, struggled through snow. All left dead on foreign soil. Gone. But not forgotten. Never forgotten. Lives lost, but traces lingered. Always.

"Cover the furniture for me while I gone?" Alenka was saying. "Sheets are in dresser."

He nodded. He knew where the sheets were kept. The recurring memory of shrouding her son's body was like a sore that had not healed. He knew it never would.

Inside, the house was cold. He wandered around, considering

whether to get a fire going. They would not be staying long, he decided. He couldn't be too far from Headquarters for very long, just in case Larkins needed to find him. Drummond sat down at the kitchen table, where he and Alenka had shared glasses of wine on all those spring Saturdays while Larkins and his pals entertained the village children. Here he had gradually got to know her better, and learned to love her even more. Alenka, as he'd come to know during those conversations, had grown up on a farm outside the small village of Bled. She'd met Darko at the University of Ljubljana, where they were soon drawn to the Communist party. This led to involvement with the Partisans, and her husband's eventual death.

Glancing downward, he spotted Alenka's Titovka cap, discarded on the floor. He scooped it up. Held it close. Breathed in the smell of her hair. Picked fretfully at the red star. When the stitches gave way, he slipped the star into his pocket.

He remembered, just in time, to cover the furniture before Alenka returned. She was quiet, lines around her eyes and mouth, her face puffed with strain, but she shrugged away his attempts to console her. Instead, she unearthed a shabby cardboard suitcase from beneath the staircase and carried it up to the room where they had made love for the first time.

Drummond tramped after her. Settled himself on the bed. Watched Alenka pack up her belongings. Each item of clothing she folded nudged him closer to her leaving; one step closer to goodbye; one step closer to the rest of his life without her.

He cleared his throat. "Alenka, I have to ask something."

"Anything," she said.

"Would you have taken me into this bed if Józef had not died his terrible death?"

As he spoke, he was dazed to realize she was holding the same blood-stained shirt he had been wearing that awful day. It came to him again how she had taken it from him, folded it gently, and spoken the name of her son, before taking him for her own.

She completed her tasks, crossed the room, and leaned over him. "James, I fell in love with you, very first time I see you."

He burst out laughing. "You were pointing a Luger at my chest!"

Her lips twitched. "*Was* that first time, James?"

He was acutely aware of the star in his pocket, almost as if it were coming to life. He recalled the piles of uniforms littering the bank of the pool—how, in the mottled light, all the red stars had resembled splotches of blood. Was it possible she had seen him that day? He pulled Alenka down beside him and nestled her head in the crook of his arm.

"When Józef die, I think I die too," she explained. "Then I wake and see you in room. This room. Not leaving me. I crave to feel something. Anything, to keep myself alive. And who I want to make me feel so, was you."

He buried his face in her hair. Breathed her dear, earthy scents.

"So, you see, my *ljubcek*, how much I need you then."

"And I you, my darling."

"Together we share what happen. You made it so I stay alive." Alenka smothered his hand with umpteen tiny kisses. "But maybe now is time for my heart to break in proper way, like when Darko die."

"Alenka, I want so much to shelter and protect you from what happened."

"No more time," she whispered. "Now I am prepared to go. And is time you make your preparations, James. Preparation for life in England."

"I know," he muffled, his face still buried in her hair.

"You will make good life. In own country. With own house. Own child. Own—"

"Shh." James placed his fingers on her lips. Kissed her deeply. Slipped his hand beneath her skirt and sought her; caressed her; entered her; loved her.

Chapter Forty-Two

BACK IN THEIR room in the city, they lay side by side in bed, wide awake. A foghorn wailed over the bay. It reminded Drummond of Newcastle. The foghorns on the River Tyne, and how he heard them when he worked in the bank. How bereft their sound would make him when he returned there. Alenka would leave in the morning for her nursing position in Ljubljana. And he would prepare, as she had said, for his life back in England.

He stared at the uniform slung over the wardrobe door, knowing what he had hidden inside the breast pocket. His nerves were raw; muscles knotted; legs twitching. His trigger finger bounced as if he were waiting for a coming fight—waiting for the shooting to start.

They dressed in silence. Drank coffee in silence. When Drummond turned the key in the lock of the door for the last time, it required all his strength not to smash his head against the wood and scream.

Larkins picked them up and drove them to the railway station. A full eighteen months after the supposed end of World War II, Trieste's station was crowded with defeated soldiers trying hard to appear nonchalant; men too old to have fought on any side; malnourished families bent double with bundles on their backs; women wearing too much makeup, pretending a purpose other than the obvious. Italians. Slovenes. Croats. Serbs. Coming and going, with no clear idea of where they might end up. What was

268

considered one country today might be entirely another tomorrow. The war had upended the entire world. His included.

Alenka had tied back her thick, black hair with a red ribbon. Underneath her short, cream-colored winter jacket was the simple black dress she had worn for Józef's funeral. By her feet rested the small cardboard suitcase. It was freezing cold. Wind whipped down the platform, hurling grit in grim, gray clouds. The captain searched for Alenka's hand and gripped it tight.

The train for Ljubljana was announced.

"You have my address?" he whispered.

Alenka nodded. Picked up the shabby case.

"If there is *anything* you need, want, you will let me know?" Drummond begged. "Promise me."

"I do not think that is good idea," murmured Alenka, a catch in her voice.

He wanted to tell her it was. He wanted to tell her he didn't know how he was going to live his life without her. But his throat was wedged shut.

"It is a very good idea," he finally managed to gulp. His voice was a deep, throaty whisper, but he continued on. "None of us know what the future might bring in this fragile world we all live in."

He held onto Alenka for dear life as the train drew closer and closer, louder and louder.

Steam engulfed the platform, brakes squealed. The engine lumbered to a stop. Somehow, he must hold himself together.

A porter ran down the platform, opening carriage doors. Alenka managed to wriggle free of Drummond's arms and clamber awkwardly up the high steps onto the train, dragging her bag behind her.

A blinding panic closed in around him. He grabbed her hand. "Wait!"

Alenka spun around. "What?"

He leapt onto the train beside her. "I can't let you go."

"James, we talk too much of this already."

He pulled a train ticket out of his pocket. Held it up in front of her face.

Alenka's eyes widened, gleaming with surprise and the beginnings of tears. "Are you mad, James? Why you do this now?"

"You said everything is fair and equal in your country. You said you liked to pretend we live together. Grow old together. So, why not?"

"Why not! First of all, you think Tommy in uniform get through border crossing?"

"Then don't go, Alenka," he begged with absolutely no hope at all. "Please don't go."

Alenka placed both her fists on his chest, and pushed him backward onto the platform. "Go home, James. To your child. *She* is alive. She waits for you."

Drummond considered the ticket, sweaty in his fist. He considered his warrior queen, majestic in the doorway of the train. He considered right and wrong. He considered honor and disgrace. He considered his Georgie Girl, waiting, just as Alenka said.

He tore the ticket to shreds. The wind twisted the pieces into an eddy and swept them along the platform, onto the railway line. Gone, gone, gone. The deed weighed him down, heavy and leaden, as if he were bolted to the ground forevermore.

Alenka leaned from her carriage window. Locked her eyes with his. Reached down to clasp his hand. The hand that had held the ticket. She raised it to her lips. Nibbled each finger. "Love of my life." The tears that had welled in her eyes spilled slowly onto her cheeks. "For me, James, be happy."

Long after the train had left the station, after the steam had dissipated and the rattle of the rails had ceased, he stood rooted to the platform, oblivious to the sea of humanity swirling around him. Until he could no longer feel her body in his arms, her teeth grazing his fingers, her lingering scent, he would not, could not, move. *Long, long shall I rue thee, too deeply to tell.*

Chapter Forty-Three

CAPTAIN DRUMMOND AND Corporal Larkins were both to be berthed on a frigate, going as far as Gibraltar; from there they would have to wait and see what ship became available. Drummond was grateful. A longer, more leisurely way home to England. Time to compose his heart and mind, if that were possible.

Trieste continued on as an occupied city, and would for the foreseeable future. Brimming with lorries, jeeps, tanks, and material. British and Commonwealth troops slowly starting to leave. And flowing in, a steady stream of United States soldiers.

Larkins pulled to a stop outside the Savoia Excelsior Palace for the last time. Drummond took the steps two at a time. Thank heaven, one last redistribution of Jerry plunder was enough to take care of his mess bill—in the space of one month it had become a bloody disaster again.

Freight trains running along the central waterfront, shunting, switching, shuffling, shifting, made his head ache. "*Be happy, James,*" they seemed to say, over and over. Alenka's words to him. But how? How was he going to do that?

Just last night he had read a few words of Byron which pretty much summed up how he felt. *Though long and mournful must it be, the thought that we no more may meet: yet I deserve the stern decree, and almost deem the sentence sweet.* That he would never hold Alenka again was indeed a stern decree, but one he probably deserved for behaving dishonorably toward his wife. And so, in a peculiar way, the sentence did feel sweet to him. Bittersweet, anyway.

The quays were jam-packed with ships flying every Allied flag imaginable. Down the coast, Castello di Miramare glistened in the cold winter sunshine. It already seemed preposterous that he had ever been billeted in such a place, now that the reality of postwar Britain beckoned. A bankrupt country of food shortages, fuel shortages, housing shortages. Shortages of just about anything that made life bearable.

He still hoped to find persuasive words to ease Mary into the idea of his accepting the permanent commission he'd been offered and staying on in the Regiment. So far, he had not had much luck. Mary had taken it as a rejection. "After so many years away, aren't you content to stay at home?"

It had disheartened him; he believed strongly that he could be an asset to the army. It was obvious that there was not going to be any real peace in his time. Sadly, the Empire would have to be dismantled, piece by piece. By and large, he thought it had been a good empire, and he looked upon it with a mix of pride and affection, yet he understood that the winds of change were blowing around the world. India was already halfway to breaking free. There was sure to be unrest in the African colonies. All this would require a heavy troop presence, and his alternative was a stultifying life at the bank, where he most certainly did not want to be.

It was mayhem on the quayside. Huge gray ships rocked in the swell, gushing water from the bilges. The bay smelled of oil and fish. And of course, the inevitable seagulls screamed overhead. Larkins was fumbling about, Drummond's trunk and kitbag on the ground, but half the luggage still heaped in the jeep.

"Chop, chop, Corporal!"

"Sir?"

"All of that goes on board. Before Christmas!" he shouted, shivering into his greatcoat as a frigid squall roiled the air.

"That's my gear," said Larkins.

"For Christ's sake. It all goes in the same hold."

"Sir—"

"All of it on the ship, now, Larkins." Drummond looked at his watch. "Come on, man."

But his gentle giant of a batman didn't move. Just stood there, jostled this way and that by sailors loading the holds. What was wrong with the fellow? His ginger brows were knitted together. Even his freckles looked bleached out.

"Sir, I can't come with you. Sorry."

"Don't be a fool, Larkins. Of course you're coming with me. What on earth has got into you?"

"I'm getting married."

As if a mortar had barreled into Drummond's chest, the wind was knocked out of him.

"Good God Almighty, Larkins." He could barely get the words out. "Don't tell me it's a woman from one of the dubious establishments you and your mates frequent."

"Course not, sir. A local lass. She lives in Tomai."

"Where?"

"On the Karst. Slovene side."

Drummond struggled to process this information, to spit out some sort of reply. "Get a hold of yourself, Larkins. You can't stay behind. It's called desertion. I can't possibly let you. And besides, what would you do here? How in God's name would you support this woman?"

He gazed around the docks, frantic. More and more officers and men were arriving, causing congestion everywhere. But Larkins was trying to explain.

"She's a widow, sir. With four little 'uns what need a dad."

As much as you need the kiddies. The liaison was beginning to make a crazy kind of sense.

He supposed it had come about during Larkins's various so-journs into the hills, negotiating the sale of plunder on behalf of his mess bills. And the more he thought about it, the more sense it made that Larkins had turned down the chance of leave last Christmas. Larkins must have been wooing the woman way back then.

"Her husband had this farm," continued Larkins, some of the color returning to his cheeks. "Twenty acres. Pigs, a cow, goats. Small orchard of soft fruits. Right now, her old dad is helping her keep it running."

"Good Christ, man, do you really think you would be happy tilling the earth like Old MacDonald for the rest of your life?" Then Drummond remembered how adept Larkins had proved to be, milking the nanny goat for Józef. His disbelief was threatening to cascade into anger. Was it this easy to do whatever fucking thing you wanted?

"I'm a hard worker." Larkins's neck grew red, and his shoulders twitched slightly.

"Of course, I know that, Larkins. Don't doubt it for a minute."

Larkins stiffened considerably, but he didn't say anything.

"I can't turn a blind eye," the captain went on. "You know that."

"Really, sir?" The words landed in the cold air like slaps.

Drummond was stunned by his batman's tone—positively sub-versive. And it was a question, not an acquiescence. Any other officer would have struck the man.

"Is that a threat?" he barked.

Was it? Was loyal, trustworthy Larkins actually inferring black-mail? Implying that what was good for the goose was good for the gander? He tried desperately to ignore the memory of his torn-up train ticket scattered over the railway lines.

"No, sir. It isn't. But I'm dead serious. My mind is made up."

Drummond looked over the crowded quay; over the Piazza dell' Unita, where the Union Jack proudly flew; up to the plateau, to the mountains beyond, already dressed in a coat of snow.

He understood that on foot, Larkins would easily avoid border guards and lose himself in no time flat. Should he have disappeared too, into Slovenia, far from Allied jurisdiction? But unlike Larkins, he had a loyal wife at home, completely unaware of his treachery. And his little girl. Just as Alenka had reminded him.

"And really, sir," Larkins rambled on, shrugging, "how important would one corporal gone missing be, all this time after the war is got over with?"

His captain stood for a moment in angry silence, wanting to argue, but knowing how hypocritical it would be not to let his batman go. "Damn you, Larkins," he said.

"Yes, sir."

"Any other officer would lock you up. You know that, don't you?"

"Yes, sir. But you aren't any other officer. You're my officer."

Drummond toyed with his swagger stick, almost dropping it in his embarrassment. Eventually he stuck it securely under his arm, pulled off his gloves, and held out his hand. "We have seen a lot together," he said. "You and I."

"That we have, sir," agreed Larkins, grasping the offered hand and grinning ear to ear. But after the solid shake, the batman's smile faded. "Must say something, sir. About the laddie?"

"Yes, Larkins?" Drummond said, looking into the honest, open face of the man he had come to rely on so completely.

Larkins bit his lip. His chin quivered. He closed his watering eyes.

"It was the worst bit of our war," he managed.

"It was, Larkins. Indeed, it was."

A fleeting recollection of Józef's mangled body almost felled the captain right there on the pier. He realized that this dear, brave man, who had loved Józef to pieces, had found himself a ready-made family, one that was going to help him heal. No doubt about it.

Well, so be it. Drummond could not bring himself to march his batman to the guard house. Not after the war they had been through together. If Larkins had found a way to be happy, then bloody good luck to him. Whether he could live with himself—knowing how close he had come to doing the very same thing—well, that was a different question altogether.

"I'll do my best for you, Larkins," he said at last. "Should be able to come up with a plausible reason for how I mislaid my batman, somewhere between Trieste and Newcastle."

"There's just one more request, sir. Mam lives in Seaton Sluice." Larkins pulled a scrap of paper from his trouser pocket. "Wrote my address down. But Mam should wait to write till the hue and cry dies down. Explain for me?"

"Don't worry. I'll go and see her."

"Right, sir. Thank you, sir." Relief was written all over Larkins's face. His freckles had returned to their normal brick-red color, and his grin was broad.

"And the jeep? Are you absconding with military property too?"

Larkins chuckled. "Course not, sir. Taking it back to the motor pool, aren't I? Got to pick up Lucky. Can't leave him behind. My kiddies will love him."

Good grief. He'd forgotten all about Józef's cat. Alenka had bequeathed him to Larkins when she had moved into Trieste. Lucky was in good hands.

"I'll get your gear stowed on board now, sir. You take a bit of a stroll, if you can get through the throng. Probably best we separate now. Lose me sooner, rather than later, eh?"

Drummond snatched hold of Larkins's shoulders. Gripped hard. "Appreciate your loyalty."

He held onto Larkins longer than was perhaps necessary, as a sudden wash of loneliness swept over him. For all these years, Larkins, as well as carrying out his duties faithfully both on and off the battlefield, had proven to be a loyal friend and comrade.

"You're a good man."

With that said, Captain James Drummond turned quickly away. Another farewell. In time, he must teach himself to pack his wartime memories away in a secret corner of his mind. Visit them once in a while, but not allow them to float to the surface of the rest of his life.

He watched the winter sun spangling off Castello di Miramare for the last time.

OCTOBER –
DECEMBER 1994

Chapter Forty-Four

Once settled in Alenka's home, we fall into an easy routine. In the mornings, I fetch fresh fruit and vegetables we need from the village. After a few false starts, I've learned how to operate the washing machine, so we won't run out of clean underwear. Autumn is firmly established, but wrapped in our new clothes, we are perfectly comfortable. Anticipating cold weather, Penny shopped for me at Marks and Spencer in London, sending out warm jumpers, jackets, scarves, and gloves for Daddy and me. After lunch, if the weather is fine, we roost like satisfied homing pigeons in the wicker armchairs placed permanently beneath the apple tree.

"How much time did you spend here?" I ask.

"Not a lot." Daddy looks up the garden to the house. "This village was firmly on the Yugoslav side of the Morgan Line, so strictly speaking it wasn't within Allied jurisdiction. But during the spring of '46, my batman Larkins would pick up the kiddies for Saturday cartoon shows in Trieste. When we drove them back here, he and his pals organized games while Alenka and I sat in the kitchen talking and enjoying a glass or two of wine."

"Did you ever wonder if the affair might have burned itself out if you had been stationed here longer?"

Daddy looks into the apple tree branches, as if the answer might be lurking in the dappled leaves. "I truly don't, darling. Though I always knew we only had an allotted amount of time. And from the moment it all began, Alenka understood we would have to part."

Is it easier to bear that way? Michael and I had no inkling we would be separated. No idea our affair was destined to end.

"And for you?" I ask.

"Harder to wrap my head around, I suppose." He plucks at the cuff of his new jersey.

"So, it must have been incredibly hard to adjust to family life back home? To us?"

My voice cracks, and I am momentarily infuriated with myself. I don't want this to become a maudlin what-about-me conversation.

"Regardless of the circumstances, darling, home could never have been the same, whether Alenka had been part of my life or not. You have to understand, we had years of fighting, killing, doing and seeing things that no amount of whiskey could numb. No one came back the same, Georgie Girl. No one."

I gaze into the tree branches too. It's strange, in a way, to think I have only ever known Daddy as a returned survivor of the war. Our relationship began when I was already five years old, with no way of knowing who he was before he had to go and fight.

Daddy goes on. "I had hoped for a brother or sister for you, but your mother wouldn't hear of it."

No, she wouldn't, Daddy. And I know the reason why.

"All's well that ends well." I laugh a bit ruefully. "Now I do have a brother."

Daddy's cheeks color slightly, but I pat his arm to indicate I understand.

"But what of you?" he asks after a minute or two. "How was it? After your relationship with Michael O'Hannery ended? You went home to America and made a life? A good life for you and Paul, and the girls?"

How was it for me? Well, let me see. Sheer, unmitigated hell was what it was.

"You seem miles away, darling." Daddy gives me a small shake. "I do sometimes wonder—now the girls are grown—if you might be ready to change your mind?"

"What do you mean?"

"I rather get the sense you're preparing to return to Michael."

His innocent question cascades into an avalanche of new sorrow. But why wouldn't he ask me such a thing? Daddy has no idea what happened. Utterly undone, I burst into wrenching sobs.

"What on earth is the matter? What have I said?"

"I can't."

"Can't what? Why?"

In between great gulps, I explain, "Michael was caught up in the 1983 Christmas bombing outside Harrods."

Through my tears, my father's expression is one of shattered disbelief. He puts his arm around my shoulders. "Oh, my dearest Georgie Girl. I'm so sorry. He was such a charming, talented man. A lovely man."

He was that. However cliched it might sound, Michael O'Hannery was the loveliest love of my life. The sun is still warm, but I shiver. Daddy pulls me closer, so I can rest my head on his chest.

"I had gone home that Christmas to ask Paul for a divorce," I tell him. "But before I had the chance to talk about any of it, I saw the news on television. All of it. People running; smoke billowing; flames raging; sirens screaming."

"Did he die, Georgina?"

"The blast killed three police officers and three civilians. Ninety people injured. And I knew instinctively, before Penny even called, he was one of those folks." The searing television pictures unspool in my head again. I take deep breaths. "Michael was thrown in the air by the blast. He broke his back. Shrapnel pierced his vocal cords. He's completely paralyzed."

"But alive?"

"Alive." I push out of his embrace. "I visit Michael whenever I can. He's in a pleasant enough nursing home in Hampstead. His room is on the ground floor; it overlooks gardens. Sometimes the staff manage to wheel his bed outside for a little while."

Daddy looks stricken, to an extent that surprises me—it's not as if he knew Michael well. "I don't know what to say."

"There's nothing *to* say." I wave my hands helplessly. "Accepting that Michael and I had no future—that it was snatched away by an IRA bomb—was unbelievably hard."

A small, brown bird flutters onto a branch above our heads and begins to sing a forlorn melody. I close my eyes and let the music wash over me for several minutes.

"But I'm beginning to realize something, Daddy. Being in this house is helping me appreciate the time Michael and I did share. His loving me so completely, no matter for how short a time, is a rare gift. How many of us are lucky enough to have had that?"

Nodding, he leans close to me once more. "What struck me, when I met Michael, was how he glanced at you throughout our meal as if to say, '*This is the woman I cherish, now and evermore.*' We've been lucky, the two of us, Georgie Girl. Remember that."

"I told Penny recently that I'll mind it less when my skin starts to wrinkle, my hearing fails, and my feet swell, all because I was lucky enough to be infected with the sting of love."

"The sting of love?" Daddy asks.

"The day we met, Michael took me to the Wallace Collection to show me a painting by Jean-Honoré Fragonard, known informally as *The Sting of Love.*"

284

Daddy's hands tremble slightly, and he clasps them together. Recalling the moment when he was stung by love, no doubt.

"Did you try to make things work with Paul?" he asks after a while.

"You know how 'not-very-good' I am at compromise. For example, Wharton 'doings' at this time of year include the mandatory grilling of hot dogs and swilling of beer in a grubby parking lot in Minneapolis, prior to mandatory attendance at Vikings home games. The bribe, fifty-yard line seats. I can still remember Paul trying to explain to me why that was a big deal."

Daddy laughs out loud.

"Paul and I are used to each other. But that's not the same thing as enjoying each other, is it? Take Sundays. The end of the weekend. Back from some 'Ellen' function or other, by which time we've run out of things to say to each other. Boredom sets in. Then it's bedtime. Then the obligatory, once-a-week lovemaking."

"Oh, dear me."

"I know it all sounds trite," I say, pulling a bunch of Kleenex from my pocket, "but it built up." I wipe my eyes and blow my nose. "When I lost Michael, when I *had* to accept that he and I could never have the life together we had dreamed of, my frustration with Ellen and the tribe grew. The distance between Paul and myself grew. The yearning for home grew. More and more, I want my own life. To do the things that I enjoy."

"You'll soon enough have a place of your own, Georgie Girl."

"I will?"

"When I am gone, darling. Cross Keys Court."

When he's gone. The sorrowful side of this time we have together. Not unlike his affair with Alenka—it has to end, but there's no way to know exactly when that will be.

"Daddy, I honestly hadn't given much thought to the flat being mine one day."

"And who else, pray, would want to be surrounded by our family furniture? All the books, music, artwork that I treasure? Other than yourself?"

I touched his hand, to direct my wordless gratitude in our time-honored fashion.

"Daddy, do you think it's wrong of me not to keep trying to make the marriage work?"

"I don't know what to tell you, darling. I really don't. Back in my day, marriage was considered sacred. Even when one had behaved dishonorably, divorce was rarely an option. I had wanted to stay in the army. I was offered a permanent commission, but your mother was adamant. Wouldn't hear of it. Time to stay home. I had been away long enough. So, in the end, I did what I thought was the right thing. It's all any of us can do."

I clasp his cheeks. Still round and smooth and soft, despite his seventy-seven years. "And look how things turned out. That brother you wanted for me finally arrived!"

Fixing me with one of his piercing blue stares, he asks, "And how do you *really* feel about that? Tell me the truth."

I feel a flush beginning to spread across my face. "I admit, George was around for quite a while."

"I noticed."

"After your heart attack, I didn't want to share you. Especially with a sibling I had never met. And it drove me mad that just because Janez is a doctor, he more or less took over your health care."

"And . . . ?"

"I like him, Daddy. I really do. We're on the same page a lot of the time."

"Such as . . . ?"

"Such as both of us understanding that this is where you wanted to be. Needed to be. Close to Alenka."

"And both of you making it happen." Daddy's eyes well with tears, but the smile on his face is as staunch and steadfast as the trunk of the tree behind him. "How lucky can a man be, I wonder."

"Janez will help me to be happy again. I'm sure of that. When I look into *his* eyes, there you will be." I lean over to kiss my father's cheek. "He's turning out to be just what the doctor ordered!"

Chapter Forty-Five

S EVERAL DAYS LATER, returning from the local shop laden with fresh cream, bread, cheese, and olive oil, I notice a farm truck, splattered with mud, parked outside what I already consider "our" house, I'm feeling so comfortable here. An elderly man steps out of the vehicle. His ginger-red hair is flecked with white, and he has the ruddy complexion of someone who spends most of his days outdoors.

"Can I help you?" I ask, which is rather silly, as he almost certainly won't speak English. Despite the state of his truck, I notice the man has made an attempt to dress up—slacks and an old tweed jacket, which look distinctly out of place in Opatje Selo.

"Signora, I came as quick as I could—Captain Drummond *is* here?" He gestures to the blue door.

"You're English?"

"Aye, a Geordie. How do you know?"

I laugh. "Because I was born on the banks of the River Tyne. Lived there all my growing-up years."

The man claps his hands. "Then I'm betting you are Miss Georgina?"

"I am, but—"

"Corporal Eric Larkins. I was—"

"Daddy's batman during the war! What on earth are you doing hundreds of miles from home?" I take his proffered hand and shake it hard.

"Slovenia *is* home. Never went back to England."

Clearly, Larkins must be one of the many soldiers who stayed on because of wartime liaisons.

"Daddy never told me that," I say, wondering how that must have made him feel, considering that he had been in a similar situation.

"Corporal, my father's heart is failing. He is quite unwell now."

"Aye, pet, I know. I've kept in touch with the little laddies in this village, what played with Józef. Grown now, of course—middle-aged, matter of fact—but they let me know as soon as they discovered who was staying in Józef's house. I had to come. Hope you don't mind. Your dad was a real gentleman. The best of the best."

My hand flies to my mouth. A deep shudder passes through me, and right here in the lane, I erupt in a flood of tears. Larkins doesn't hesitate. He plucks the basket off my arm and wraps his arms around me. "There, there, lassie, don't you fret."

He is solid and comforting, and for some reason I don't feel embarrassed in the least to find myself in the arms of a complete stranger. His jacket smells faintly of a farmyard, fresh milk, and just a hint of hay.

"Please come inside," I say at last. "What am I doing bawling outside in front of the whole village?"

We step into the kitchen, comfortingly still save for the hum of the refrigerator. While I put my shopping away, Larkins looks around at the wood staircase with its tuck-under lavatory, the large kitchen table with its six matching chairs, the modern electrical appliances.

"Changed some, the place has."

I sense the air around us shifting back to an earlier time.

Then I understand. Larkins would have been with Daddy that terrible day. With Józef.

"You were in the house? After the accident? With my father?"

"Aye. Carried the little nipper inside meself. Laid him on the table." Larkins's breath is coming hard and fast, and when he talks the words sound as if he's pulling them up from a deep pit.

"I'm so sorry."

"I loved that boy." Larkins glances at me, pauses for just a beat of time. "And your dad loved his mother so very much."

"I know."

Larkins relaxes a little. "He nearly got us shot the day of the little lad's funeral. Dithering around in the village square, 'Should we stay?', 'Should we go?', me revving the engine, cursing at him to get back in the jeep."

"Good Lord," I say, trying to imagine the scene for myself.

"Good Lord is right," Larkins chuckles. "Somehow your dad and I survived."

"Alenka had another child, later. Another son."

"She married again?"

I shake my head.

Larkins's face is puzzled for a moment; then realization washes over him, and he gapes. "Oh . . . I see . . . but . . ."

I take his elbow. "Come and say hello to your captain. Perhaps he will fill you in."

We step through the French doors, onto the patio in the back garden, catching the morning sun. I had left Daddy trussed up tight in his tweed jacket, reading an English language newspaper Janez had found for him in Ljubljana. It is clear he's been dozing, but he is roused by our footsteps.

"You have a visitor," I inform him.

Glancing upward, he takes a moment to register the sight before him; then he eyes snap wide. "Good God!" He blinks in disbelief. "Larkins! Is it really you? After all these years?"

"Sir!" His old batman stands to attention, but his legs, no doubt stiff with age, don't quite have the snap-to of old. He manages a salute, however, all the time with a grin pasted all over his weather-beaten face. "As I live and breathe."

"I can scarcely believe it. Sit, please."

"If that's allowed now!"

"We're not in the army now, dear chap."

Larkins pulls out the chair opposite his captain, and I leave them to it. In the kitchen, I brew coffee and set a tray with Ava's pottery and a plate of her walnut cookies. She has been sending baked treats for us whenever Janez can get away for a few hours, and she is coming herself very soon to spend the weekend.

On my return to the garden, the two old soldiers are huddled over the table, recalling the hellishly rough sea crossing from North Africa to Sicily. Larkins is teasing Daddy about how he had loaned his greatcoat to Count Jean d'Neau, a French liaison officer assigned to their regiment. The count had promptly vomited all over it, causing my father to curse him up and down in perfect French!

I pour coffee and offer Larkins cream and sugar. "Miss Georgina," he says, "I have to tell you, your dad here should have arrested me, slapped me in the guardhouse, when I told him I weren't going back with him to England. Instead, he looked the other way." His spoon clinks vigorously around the mug.

Daddy clears his throat, trying hard not to smile. "I reported you missing soon after we sailed for Gibraltar. Let the powers that be assume you had fallen off the ship."

I turn in surprise. "Did they buy that, Daddy?"

"Not entirely sure!" He looks at his old batman long and hard. "But I would not have had it any other way. Larkins here got me through a lot, especially the throbbing, freezing hell of Anzio."

"Right enough, sir. Trenches. Snipers. Rotting corpses. Rats big

291

as bloody rhinos. Pardon me, Miss Georgina, but I tell you, it were like being trapped in the middle of a World War I film that had got stuck and never bloody ended."

I sit back and listen to the two of them, together in the watery sunshine, talking so vividly about the battles of the past. It is pretty obvious that even when soldiers get to leave their wars, the wars don't ever leave the soldiers.

Larkins helps himself to the biscuits. "Kiffle. The wife makes this all the time." He munches away happily, brushing crumbs off his chest every few minutes. "You dad went to visit me mam. To put her in the know, so to speak. Explain my whereabouts. And how to get in touch."

Daddy reaches for my arm and gives it a big pat. "You came with me, Georgie Girl. We went to visit a very nice lady in Seaton Sluice, shortly after I was home for good. Can you remember?"

I loved riding with my father in his car. Not only was it a chance to spend time alone with him, but it was so very different from our middle-of-the-night get-togethers, when I knew not to talk very much, that he just needed me near. During the day, especially on car trips, he sang songs. Encouraged me to tell him stories.

"A semi-detached house, on a cliff above the sea? Piles of snow everywhere?" Then the penny drops. "That lady was your mother, Larkins?"

"Got it in one, lass."

Daddy grimaces. "Felt pretty nervous that day, I can tell you. Wasn't sure your mother wouldn't chuck the coal scuttle at my head for leaving you behind. But I was confident she would spare a little girl."

"Really! So, you took me along for protection?" I ask, laughing.

"Turns out we had a lovely visit," Daddy tells Larkins. "Your mother sat herself down by the fire and told me she knew exactly why I was there. She had already had a visit from a senior officer in the Regiment who had the unenviable job of letting her know you were missing. Presumed drowned at sea. She hadn't believed a word of it, she told me, and wasn't a bit surprised when I assured her you were alive and kicking, and still in Europe. She laughed and laughed. Said you must have met a lass, at last. When I gave her your address and explained you could not ever return to England, all she said was you deserved a bit of happiness."

Daddy pauses; his breath is getting labored. "Did you find it, Larkins?" he asks. His countenance darkens, like a shadow crossing the sun. "Happiness?"

I look at the two of them. Larkins deserted. Stayed on. Lived in a communist nation. Never able to return to England. Deep in his heart, does Daddy wish he had done the same?

"In spades, sir." Larkins is beaming. "Didn't ever have regrets. Me and the missus had four more kiddies together. Three girls and a boy. Naturally, named the lad Józef. And that made a total of eight in all!"

"I have a son. He lives in Ljubljana."

"Miss Georgina said. I'm right glad to hear it, sir."

"And a grandson. Name is Józef, too," Daddy tells him. "Our boy was never forgotten, Larkins. Not for a moment."

"A splendid name."

"The best."

The old soldiers sit in a contented silence, born out of all the years they spent side by side as tragedy, fear, and personal griefs grew more and more intertwined.

When the quiet has stretched out for several minutes, Daddy clears his throat. "I hope you saw your mother again, Larkins."

"Did indeed, sir," the former batman assures him. "More than once. Mam would fly to Italy, soon as travel got a bit easier. The wife and me met her at the airport and smuggled her over the border. Still communist then, of course. She loved the farm. Loved the kiddies."

"*And* she gave me a jar of homemade toffee," I blurt, as more of that long-ago day comes into focus. I remember a lady hugging me in her little passageway, snuggling my scarf tight around my neck before Daddy and I braved the cold and snow again.

"Aye, Mam was always one for the nippers."

"As were you, old man," Daddy says with a grin. "As were you."

Despite his cheer, I can see that his skin is ashen after such an emotional morning. "You should rest, Daddy."

"Oh!" Larkins cuts across me, suddenly rising. "Almost forgot, sir. I've got something belongs to you. Don't worry, Miss Georgina, I won't stay much longer, but I just have to see the captain's face when I fetch it from the truck."

I settle Daddy at the kitchen table, a shawl around his shoulders. When Larkins returns, he has a square wooden box in his arms, a pile of old records in brown paper sleeves resting on top.

"Well, blow me down with a feather!" Daddy gasps. "My gramophone! Thought it must have ended up at the bottom of the Adriatic."

"When I went back to Miramare, I did a last check of your room, sir, and there was the confounded contraption, still on the table under the window. What a racket you used to make. Drove the other officers batty with the din."

"Did I?"

"Aye. Your nickname was Captain Caruso."

"Oh, my goodness me. I never knew."

"Never mind, sir. They put up with you for the most part. Living in a fancy castle with a high-brow seemed to rub off on them. So, anyways, since it was my mistake, I packed it up careful as I could, along with the records. Heavy load, I can tell you." Larkins chuckles. "Took the lot up to the farm."

"And kept them for me all these years."

"Never gave up hope I'd see you again, sir."

I clutch the edge of the kitchen table, feeling a bit light-headed. If Lou had not raised the issue of guilt, and Janez had not written his letter, and I had not agreed to bring Daddy to Trieste, and Daddy had not had another heart attack—this reunion would not have taken place. It's a miracle of sorts.

Daddy clasps the hand of his old batman. "Thank you, Larkins. From the bottom of my heart. Taking the time to seek me out means the world."

Chapter Forty-Six

AVA VISITS THIS weekend. I'm as nervous as a cat, my track record with sisters-in-law being so bleak. I want her to like me. But more importantly, I want her to like her husband's long-lost father. All our lives are made up of bits and pieces, and each of us has a different understanding of how they fit together. This complicates matters, I think. For Ava, Alenka was variously mother-in-law, grandmother, and Yugoslav partisan who bore the child of a British soldier shortly after the end of World War II.

As it turns out, I had no need to worry. A clone of any of my hyperactive sisters-in-law, Ava is not. She's a lovely woman, quiet and unassuming, but clearly comfortable in her own skin. She is shorter than me, which isn't surprising, as most people are. Her skin is clear and devoid of makeup; she has short, styled brown hair and a trim figure. Only her hands give away her profession. Potter's clay, embedded around her nails and in the creases of her fingers. Hard calluses on the pads of her thumbs. After I found the glorious dishes in the kitchen cupboard, Janez shared that they were the work of his wife. As well as teaching art history at the University of Ljubljana, Ava crafts pottery that is marketed in major museum stores throughout Europe.

She arrives, laden with an enormous basket of food and a no-nonsense hug, after which she immediately begins bustling around her kitchen. Meanwhile, Janez, armed with his stethoscope and a couple more English-language newspapers, visits his papa, wrapped up warmly against the chill, in the garden.

In this country, lunch is the more substantial meal of the day, which suits us well. Ava has me chop a large onion, while she proceeds to brown pieces of beef in hot oil. When the meat is done, she adds my onion, a container of homemade broth, and copious amounts of paprika, salt, pepper. Into her large salad bowl goes a bag of dandelion shoots, three hardboiled eggs, and four cooked, sliced potatoes. Separately, she mixes garlic, oil, and red wine vinegar for tossing, just before we eat.

Daddy has been anxious about this meeting too, but when we gather around the kitchen table to begin Ava's sumptuous feast, I am glad to see he is completely relaxed. His beam is so bright, I want to believe we will be staying in this haven for months to come. *If wishes were horses, beggars would ride, and if and if and . . .* In keeping with local custom, serving utensils are unnecessary. We help ourselves from the salad bowl with our own forks and spoons. Janez stopped at the local winery on the drive down and produces several bottles of Refosco Teran, which he announces is a prized red wine.

I can clearly understand why. It is an extraordinarily deep cherry red, with dense flavors of blackcurrant and raspberry.

Janez raises his glass. "A toast to each of us gathered here. *All* dear and beloved."

I am moved to pieces. The stress of the morning slides away, a state I never quite manage to achieve around the raucous, always-in-motion Wharton tribe.

After we sample our wine, Janez adds, "I assure you, this wine is extremely medicinal."

Amidst our laughter, Ava produces course after course with seeming effortlessness. A creamy mushroom soup and bread, both homemade; goulash with noodles; tossed salad; bowls of olives of every imaginable hue; and a pudding of delicate pancakes, filled with nuts and jam, that in no way resembles the thick, heavy version I'm accustomed to in Minnesota.

But best of all, we spend leisurely time between these courses deep in conversation. Daddy enjoys the soup with gusto, and despite taking very small amounts of the other dishes, he listens intently to everyone around him, interjecting every once in a while.

"Was Alenka steadfast in her support of Tito to the end?" he asks.

"Mati never wavered. He was her hero," Janez replies. "So, when ethnic feuds flare all over Yugoslavia after his death, she was in despair."

"And when Slovenia broke away altogether, and gained its independence just like that, her heart was broken," adds Ava.

"So sad her dreams were crushed," Daddy mutters, frowning. "When she had fought so hard and sacrificed so much in her young life."

"It was difficult for her," says Ava. "In some ways we think it hasten her death."

Janez adds, "She did seem to give up a little bit."

"But please tell me she led a happy life," Daddy begs.

"She did, Papa. Mati always had way of making the best of things."

"Always she talk of Józef her first child," adds Ava.

"Yes, she would, of course." Daddy's lips pucker, his voice snags.

"But she speak of you, Papa. Especially when I was younger. Tell how much she treasured knowing you, loving you, how the time you had together was like a never-to-be-forgotten gift. And how she gained another son."

"Then why, in the name of heaven, did she not let me know?" Now Daddy's voice bubbles as if a flood is dammed up inside him. "I cannot understand it. I really can't."

Janez reaches across the crumb-strewn table for my hand. His blue eyes silently beg for permission to tell his papa the truth. But in my head, I hear my granny—"*Get rid of the letter now*"—and my mum's brittle voice—"*Very well.*" I shake my head. I want the truth of what happened to remain in the kitchen at Eskdale Terrace. Nothing is to be gained by breaking Daddy's heart all over again.

But my tongue flaps uselessly, and before I can force enough breath to form my thoughts into words, Janez is saying, "Papa, Gina and I—"

We are interrupted by a sudden, almighty crash, as Ava drops the plate that held the crepes on the tiled floor. She glares across the table at Janez, warnings for him to be quiet blazing from her eyes.

As soon as I get on my knees to clean up the mess, Ava crouches beside me and grabs both my hands. "All I could think of to do," she whispers in my ear. "Some secrets best kept with the dead."

Words fail me, but I could weep with relief that she took it upon herself to intervene.

"What were you saying, son?" Daddy is asking when Ava and I get to our feet, each of us clutching sticky pieces of the broken platter.

Janez clears his throat. Looks sheepishly at Ava and me. "Only that Gina and I think it is time you rest for an hour or two."

"Good idea. But what a feast, Ava. It was splendid, wasn't it, Georgie Girl?"

"It most certainly was." I give Ava a hug, knowing she understands that the hug is for far more than the meal itself. "I will clear away the dishes if you will make the coffee, Ava."

I set a tray with Ava's mugs, pour cream into the small jug, and fill the sugar bowl. When Janez has dispensed his papa's medicines and settled him for a rest, the three of us put on jackets and wander out onto the patio to enjoy the coffee.

Daylight is fading. Stars start popping out. Somewhere beyond the village, an owl hoots. Ava pours us all coffee, and I allow myself one cigarette. And Janez, the good doctor, holds his peace. I'm grateful.

"Thank you so very much for inviting us into your home," I tell them both. "This time is so precious to both my father and me."

"For us too. We are thankful you brought James to us," remarks Ava. "And next week, the children are one day free of school. I would like to bring them to meet their *dedek*. If you are agreeable?"

Dedek. I smile. What a delicious word. "Of course, I'm agreeable. It will mean so much to both of us."

"But tell us more about your children, Gina," Ava continues, stirring cream into her mug.

"I have two daughters, Louisa and Annabel. They fight like cat and dog, I probably don't understand them at all, but I love them dearly. Lou has a science degree, but no idea what to do with it. At the insistence of her grandmother, Annie lasted a year in college and hated it. Much to her father's chagrin, Annie is painting scenery at a local theater for the time being. In my opinion, it's exactly what she needs. To use her hands. Get down and dirty with them."

Ava roars with laughter. "On a potter's wheel, perhaps!"

"Why not?" adds Janez, laughing too. "Good exercise! And afterward, Ava can immerse her in all the arts."

Which is, of course, what she wanted to do before her grandma intervened. It suddenly sounds so simple. Especially if such an immersion could take place well away from any Wharton influence. Far away!

"Ava—"

"Yes!" Ava clasps my hands, much as she did under the table, grazing my palms with her rough, callused thumbs. She laughs again. "Send your Annabel to me!"

Chapter Forty-Seven

THE WEEKEND SPENT with Janez and Ava was delightful. The weather remained fair, and father and son were able to spend hours together in the back garden. Ava unwisely attempted to show me the intricacies of Slovenian baking, and it was eventually agreed she'll continue to send us boxes of treats with Janez whenever he drives from Ljubljana to visit his papa.

A couple of days after they have gone home, I'm woken from a deep sleep by the ringing of the phone in the kitchen. I'm tangled and sweaty. Damn, damn, damn. It will wake Daddy. Unwinding myself from the bedding, I pull on a warm jumper and thud down the steep, narrow stairs on my bare feet. I pick up the phone quickly.

"Yes? Who is it?"

"Paul, here."

"For Christ's sake, it's the middle of the night."

"How is it going?"

"How can you possibly not have figured out the time difference yet? Call me tomorrow."

"No can do. I'm over at Mom's."

"So?"

"She has something important to discuss with you."

"Not now, Paul. It will have to wait till I get home."

I can actually hear Ellen's excited breathing, so anxious is she to have a go at me.

"Just hear her out, honey."

I glance over at my father. He still seems to be sleeping soundly. But for how long? And if I whisper, the old bat won't be able to hear me.

"Georgina, my dear, I have wonderful news."

Good grief. For one ghastly minute I envision her marching the entire tribe through Opatje Selo for a visit! Surprise!

I hook a chair out from the table with my foot, and sit down hard.

"Now listen to me, carefully, Georgina. I was at one of my Red Cross volunteer meetings early today, and just happened to mention your father's problems. My dear friend, Kitty, you remember her, stopped our meeting right then and there, got on the phone to her son. He is a cardiologist at the Mayo—"

I clench my jaw tight. "Ellen, Daddy does not have any problems—"

"And he has booked your dad in for diagnosis and treatment one week from today."

I'm incensed. How dare she try to take over my father's care? Who the hell does she think she is? Trying really hard not to shout, I say as calmly as possible, "He has been diagnosed, and he is being treated."

As if I have not said a word, she is rattling on. "So, you'll need to get yourselves back to Venice, fast as possible. Gertie's husband is sending the company plane to pick you both up there. You'll recall, he's a high-up in the Target Corporation."

Ellen is making me dizzy. I drop my head between my knees for a minute. Is she just being kind, in her own way? Is it me that has a problem with accepting help? But I didn't ask for help. As if I would even contemplate wrenching Daddy away from Janez, Ava, and the children, spiriting him off to America in the middle of the night. And for what? The most intensive, invasive, and expensive treatments they can come up with, to prolong his life ever so briefly, in the most unpleasant of ways.

"Ellen, it's extremely kind of you, but it really is not necessary. My half brother is a doctor . . ."

But she keeps talking over me. "That's all well and good, but where you are sounds terribly primitive to me. Just tell this man, whoever he is, that you've been offered the best of the best, skilled care. All arranged by your real family in America."

"Once and for all, you listen to me," I yell down the phone. "My father is being well cared for, living in a place that is very important to him, with *his* real family. My brother and I will *not* move Daddy from this house!"

Ellen is still blathering on when I stand up to slam the phone into its wall cradle, wishing I had let rip with some of Annie's choice swears. In the moonlight, I can see that Daddy is stirring. He manages to get his legs over the side of the bed. "Need the loo."

I help him put on his dressing gown and hold his elbow tight as he shuffles to the bathroom. When we are back in the kitchen, he asks for a cup of tea.

While I wait for the kettle to boil, I breathe deeply through my mouth and tell myself there is no reason to put up with Ellen any longer. As far as I am concerned, her sell-by date has expired. I push a snarl of hair behind my ears, pour the hot water over the leaves in the pot, and sit beside Daddy while it steeps.

"Who were you talking to?" he asks sleepily. "Got a bit heated, by the sound of things."

"It did. That was my mother-in-law."

"Ahh, Ellen," he murmurs, pouring himself a cup of tea.

"She's impossible. Ignores the wishes of everyone but herself. Needs constant gratification. A shrink would have a field day figuring out her obsessive need for control. She took it upon herself to get you booked into the Mayo Clinic today."

"What!" His face turns gray as the ashes in the grate.

"And get this! She's organized a private plane to fly you there."

"Please, please, don't make me go," he begs, clinging to my wrist.

"Of course not, darling. I wouldn't dream of it." I kneel on the floor by his chair and hug him tight. "Ellen Wharton is not going to meddle in our lives, yours or mine, ever again."

"So, we stay in this house. Close by Alenka?"

"Absolutely."

Daddy soughs breathily. "With my children to care for me. I reckon I'm the luckiest man in the world."

"It's so good to hear you say that." I sit beside him again and pour us both more tea. "You know, I realized something tonight. As our irrepressible Annie likes to say, '*It's time to stop pissing about.*'"

"She has a mouth on her, that one," remarks my father. "But what have you realized, darling?"

"That the girls are grown now. For better or worse, they have to start living their own lives. That the plain truth is—I don't have to live with Paul anymore."

Chapter Forty-Eight

I SPEAK OFTEN with Louisa and Annabel, and I am honest with them that they will not see their grandpa again. That he is slipping quickly now. But I remind them: "Grandpa said his goodbyes in the garden at Cross Keys Court, before I drove you both to London." And I add for good measure: "He knew full well what he was doing that day. How little time he had left, how important the trip to Trieste was to him."

However, Paul unloaded his scorn about Janez on his daughters before I had an opportunity to explain the situation. Their reactions have been typical. Lou holds back, not saying much one way or the other about the sudden emergence of an uncle, or asking how the situation came about. Annie takes it in stride, and is far more interested in regaling me with behind-the-scenes stories of her work at the Guthrie Theater than dwelling on things that happened years ago.

With each passing day, Daddy grows gradually more introspective. He sleeps later and longer, which Janez assures me is to be expected. He has shown me how to administer liquid morphine when and if our father should feel in any way uncomfortable. But today he is wide awake—it is the much-anticipated visit of Mia and Józef, to meet their English *dedek*. When the children walk through the front door, it reminds me a bit of an old Charlie Chaplin picture show. They lurch into one another, tongue-tied and awkward. Mia's hair is braided into long plaits, much like those I wore as an eight-year-old, and she bears a strong resemblance to her mother. Józef, on the other hand, with his mop of flaxen hair, resembles no one, especially not Ava or Janez.

In anticipation of this day, I yet again consulted Penny, who shipped out a copy of my latest book, *Malcolm Mouse, Explorer*, together with two copies of the accompanying coloring book, and two sets of colored Lakeland pencils in their trademark tin boxes. She added to the parcel two Marks and Spencer jumpers for the children, knitted in a sharp, navy-blue wool—a Tower of London beefeater emblazoned across one chest, the Queen's coronation crown across the other. Last but not least, she added a large box of English toffees.

Daddy rises to the occasion, determined to put on a brave face for his grandchildren, no matter how weary he is. He beams at the pair of them, struck dumb in the doorway, and beckons them over to the kitchen table where I have arranged the gifts. He opens up one of the coloring books and holds up the first page. They can't resist, and soon three heads are bent over the table, coloring diligently and sucking noisily on toffees, Daddy explaining the story of *Malcolm* as they go.

"Mia loves to draw," Ava whispers to me.

I notice too that the child has edged close to her *dedek*, and is leaning comfortably against his knee. Józef is not quite so composed, but he's listening intently to all that his *dedek* has to say.

"James, do you feel up to a stroll into the village before lunch?" asks Ava, as she busies herself at the kitchen sink. "It is cold, but sunny, and we can use your wheelchair."

Daddy grits his teeth. The damned thing mortifies him, but when his grandson begs, "Please, *Dedek*," and flexes his muscles to indicate how capable he is of pushing the chair, a long-ago recollection bubbles across my father's face. "Young man, you are the spitting image of your Uncle Józef," he says quietly, rumpling the boy's blond head of hair. "All over again."

"I know," states Józef proudly. "*Babica* Alenka told me many times."

Daddy nods knowingly.

The children put on their new jumpers, and I muffle a thick scarf around Daddy's neck before letting Józef trundle him down the gravel lane to the village square. Mia hops along beside them, holding onto the arm of the chair, singing her heart out—*Medvedek ni bolan, Medvedek je zaspan, Ko pride temn noc, Medvedek lahko noc!*—much to the delight of her *dedek*. A slight smile plays about his mouth. Many of the neighbors open their doors to greet the children with cheery waves.

"This was good idea, yes?" asks Ava.

"It was." We link arms, bringing up the back of our little procession.

"Have you talked to Annabel yet about coming to us to get her hands dirty?"

"I've decided to wait till I get home, and talk to her in person. There will be issues with her dad and grandmother, I'm afraid. I want to be on hand to support Annie properly, if the idea has any appeal for her. Which I think it definitely will," I add.

Ava gives my arm a gentle squeeze.

I settle Daddy in his wheelchair against a stone wall, where he can catch the pale shafts of sunshine. Ava and I sit beside him on a convenient wooden bench. It's near the village well, and we watch the children amuse themselves climbing on top of the cover and jumping off. "The well is ornamental now," Ava explains. "Running water was brought to village several years back."

So, even if I had found Opatje Selo that awful day I went looking for a grown-up Józef, I would not have recognized it from the old photograph. But I keep that particular day to myself.

"Tell us a story, *Dedek*," Mia begs, when they tire of the game. "About long ago."

"A story?"

"About Uncle Józef," suggests his namesake.

"Well, when your uncle was a little boy, my corporal found a stray kitten. He insisted we drive all the way from Trieste. A present for Józef."

"What was the kitten called?" asks Mia.

Daddy doesn't hesitate. "Lucky. Because he was black, and where I come from, black cats are lucky. But I tell you, your grandmother was not best pleased to be given another mouth to feed. Even when I pointed out a nanny goat tied up. Right over there." He points to a scraggly patch of earth across the square. "My man, Larkins, showed Józef how to milk the goat so he could feed his kitten till it grew bigger."

"What happened to the cat, *Dedek*?" asks Mia, her eyes wide.

Daddy shuts his eyes. His chin sags. I worry he is trying to talk too much. It has been an active morning already. But soon enough, up pops his head again. "When the time came for me to return to England, and your grandmother to go to Ljubljana, Larkins took Lucky away to live on a farm—where, I feel fairly confident, that cat enjoyed nine lives."

"Our uncle was killed," says Józef, flatly.

"But *Babica* Alenka said he came back to us when you were born," Mia reminds him, poking her brother hard. "She *always* said that."

"Do *you* think so, *Dedek*?" asked Józef. "Do *you* think he came back?"

"Indeed, I do," agrees Daddy. The two of them grin like conspirators who have known each other much longer than a couple of hours. There is such an astonishing likeness between sledge-boy

Józef and this Józef, I'm fairly convinced a little boy can have nine lives too.

"Time for lunch," says Ava, and we trundle back to the house with the bright blue door.

Ava serves a large platter of cold sliced meats and sausage, with freshly cooked cheese dumplings so light and zesty, I could devour the entire bowl. For Daddy, she has brought a homemade beef bone broth, and he manages a few mouthfuls with obvious enjoyment.

"Aunt Georgina, you should write a story about Lucky," says Mia, her mouth full of dumpling. "And I will draw the pictures for you."

"What a very good idea, sweetheart." Who knows? Maybe one day I will find a way into the story. But now does not feel like the right time.

While Daddy lies down to rest, the sun disappears behind thick clouds, and a cold wind blows up from the sea. Ava ticks up the central heating. When the children discover their *dedek*'s old gramophone, they are greatly intrigued by the strange machine. I show them how to wind it up, and we play a couple of records. They are badly worn and the needle dull, but Mia and Józef don't seem to mind, probably assuming old shellac records are supposed to sound this way!

Later, we gather around Daddy's bed for cups of tea, accompanied today by Ava's medenjaki, cinnamon honey biscuits, which quite literally melt in the mouth. Only when Ava mentions a family photograph album she has brought with her do worry lines crease Daddy's forehead.

"No, no, my dear. I would rather not look at pictures."

"But *Dedek* . . ."

"Shush, *cildren*!"

"Because in my mind, your grandmother is forever the young

woman I loved," Daddy explains. His voice sounds parched, like a breeze through dry grass, and I urge him to sip some tea.

"So, tell us about *Babica* then instead," pleads Józef. "Please."

"That I can do." Daddy drinks his tea, then pats the bedspread, and Mia and Józef clamber up to better hang on his every word.

"The day I met your grandmother, she was dressed in her soldier uniform. And imagine this"—he pauses for greater effect—"she leveled a German gun—called a Luger—at my heart."

"Was she going to shoot you, *Dedek*?" gasps Mia.

"No silly, he said 'heart,'" says Józef. "She loved him. Papa said."

Daddy beams. "Well, whatever the reason, your *babica* certainly caught my attention. I called her Boadicea, after a famous warrior queen from olden days. She was my warrior queen, because she was such a brave woman." He touches their cheeks in turn. "And I loved her deeply."

It is growing dark, and my father is clearly worn out. I gather up our cups and saucers on the tray, and the children wash up for me.

"Now it is time we are getting home," says Ava.

Daddy is too exhausted to leave his bed, but he takes hold of Ava's hand. "To be with my grandchildren, however briefly, was such a blessing."

I watch Mia and Józef pack their gifts in one of Ava's baskets. I wonder if they realize they won't see *Dedek* again. So many lost years. But at least I got him back here in time to know his family a little bit. Better than nothing.

Ava hugs me close. "Janez will return in two days. If you need him before, just telephone. Be strong, Gina."

I know there is very little time left. And I know that Ava knows this too. Somehow, I must try to be as brave and strong a warrior as Alenka.

Chapter Forty-Nine

MY CALLS TO and from the United States are decidedly less than helpful.

From Paul—*If Annabel doesn't go back to college, she will never amount to anything. Is that what you want? For her to be a loser all her life. It's all your fault. I blame you.*

From Lou—*Annie spilled a pot of paint on her head at the theater. Did she have it removed professionally? No, she shaved her head! She looks grotesque.*

From Annie—*So, I-can-do-anything Smart-Ass Lou gets an internship from the Minnesota Zoo to work with the dolphin program. It's ridiculous, Mom. She doesn't even like beasties, ignores her laundry, and stinks of fish the whole time.*

The phone is ringing again. Before I pick it up, I know it's my husband again.

"Gina, I'm booking a ticket to come and see the old man," he announces with no preliminaries. "Besides, we need to talk."

Though I've been expecting this, I don't know what to say. And to make matters worse, it's hard to decipher what Paul is saying. The line is poor tonight. Every few minutes, he sounds as if he is underwater.

"That will make a change," I finally snark down the phone. "Most of the time, it's all the things you *don't* say that drive me mad."

"You're so distant now," he complains, as if he hasn't heard a word I've said.

I giggle hysterically. An image of us both, five thousand miles apart, waving furiously across mountains and sea spins through my head.

"This is not funny, Gina. It's not a joke, either."

"Sorry." I clamp my hand over my mouth.

"It was ridiculous not to take Mom up on her offer. The Mayo is just down the road, for God's sake. Or at least you should have taken your dad back home to England."

But how much better to be comfortable here, I assure myself, enjoying his remaining days in peace, wrapped up in warm memories.

"He *is* home, Paul. In Opatje Selo. With both his children."

"Oh, for mercy's sake, Gina," Paul growls over the miles. "Not that nonsense again."

"Listen to yourself, Paul. You have just announced you want to fly all the way to Slovenia to visit your father-in-law—who just happens to be staying in the holiday home of his son—who will also be in the house, by the way—and whom you will no doubt choose to ignore while you are here!"

Meanwhile, another derisive snort travels across the wires. "Gina, this was supposed to be a three-week long vacation in August, and I haven't seen you since. It's almost Thanksgiving, damn it." There are some long minutes of silence while the line bubbles and fizzles its way under the Atlantic. "So, can I come?"

My mouth is dry. I long for a glass of water. But I can't reach the tap without dropping the phone. "No, Paul. It's far too late now. Much too much for Daddy to handle."

"Gina . . . please . . . ?"

"He only has a few days left to live." My throat is closing up.

"Gina, I don't want you to leave me."

I grip the receiver, my fingers slick with sweat. Cross Keys

Court looms large, and Michael's shadow beats against my heart. What can I say? *I'm stuck between who I am now and who I want to be, Paul. It is not the life I wanted, anchored in the middle of America, trapped in the Wharton compound.*

"Why did you insist we elope to Mexico, Paul? Was it to be sure you had got me safely married before I met the family?"

"What? You're bringing that up now?"

"Because I really want to know."

There are more bubbles and fizzes over the line before I hear Paul's voice again, sounding suspiciously as if he is at the end of an explanation that I've missed.

". . . for the best. I didn't want to lose you, Gina. Not then. And I still don't want to lose you."

"I haven't said I'm leaving you."

"There's never been a divorce in the family," he shouts, indignant again.

"That's because your mother rules over you all like Queen Bloody Mary."

"Who?"

"Oh, never mind," I grouse, but not before an image rises in my mind of multiple married-into-the-Tribe Whartons like me, sizzling at the stake. I'm rather appalled at myself.

"Lou told me you discussed divorce with them in London."

"Annie asked me, Paul. They are both aware of how we circle one another these days, every word chosen with care, delivered with frigid politeness. And when I do try to talk to you about what's upsetting me, all I get are platitudes. 'Everything will be all right.' 'I thought we were getting on better now.' 'We could take a vacation by ourselves.'"

"Well, why not? We could go away somewhere. A sort of second honeymoon."

Honeymoon. Sorrow settles its great fist upon my heart. I'm reminded of an antique ruby ring at the bottom of a champagne glass—placed there lovingly by Michael—when we both believed we had the world on that proverbial string, sitting on a rainbow.

"Look, Paul, I will almost certainly be home before Christmas."

"But will you stay home this time?"

"Paul, sometimes I just want and need to be by myself."

The silence between us stretches over the Alps, under the Atlantic, all the way to our hallway in Minnesota.

"Please don't leave me, Gina."

As I put down the phone, I hear Peanut whining for some attention, as well as Paul's imploring voice: "Please, Gina, don't leave . . . "

Chapter Fifty

WINTER IS TRULY here. Wind lashes the house, rattling roof tiles and thrashing the ancient apple tree. Daddy doesn't leave his bed; we spend our days now in his room, in front of a comforting fire. Despite the efficient central heating, there is something cheering about the flames, the smell of burning applewood. I set a match to the crumpled paper, nestled beneath the pyramid of logs in the fireplace. Sleet stings the French windows. Daddy has been sleeping most of the day, so I fix a pot of tea and carry the tray over to his bedside.

"Mmm . . . tea," he murmurs.

"Sure you're warm enough?" I ask, plumping his pillow.

"Don't fuss, darling."

I pour two cups. There is no longer any point in tempting him with Ava's sweetmeats; he subsists now on one or two mouthfuls of fruit jelly, or sips of broth. The mighty bora blows over the Karst, bringing with it a salty smell of brine. Outside in the lane, voices rise and fall in jerky crescendos.

Daddy takes a tiny sip of tea. "It is time, Georgie Girl. Feel it in my bones." He tries to focus on my face, but he isn't succeeding very well. "Seventy-seven years—good innings."

"I know it's time, darling Daddy." I run my fingers across his brow.

The wood crackles in the grate. Outside, the wind howls. Shadows lick up the wall in strange, spectral shapes.

"Arrangements made." Daddy gathers strength to go on. "So, rest easy."

I shift uncomfortably. When Paul raised these issues, I ignored him, coward that I am.

"Death certificate." He closes his eyes, falls backward. "Cremation. All sorted."

Whatever strength my father has summoned thus far deserts him. I stroke his dear, familiar face. After a while, his blue eyes flicker open.

"Not cross?"

"Not at all. Just enormously grateful that Janez is here to help us both."

"So pleased *you* are here." His breath is ragged, but he is still lucid.

"I'm glad we came to Trieste, Daddy. It was well worth it, don't you agree?"

"All because of *you*." Leaning forward, Daddy manages one more sip of tea. "Last thing Boadicea said . . . be grateful for *you*. *You* were alive. *You* were waiting for me." He takes another raggedy, gasping breath. "She was right."

If this is his roundabout way of letting me know he would not have abandoned me, it is enough. More than enough. "Alenka sounds like a wise woman. Perhaps I would have loved her too."

Daddy puts a hand on his poor, worn-out heart. "Perhaps, Georgie Girl. Perhaps you would." Shortly thereafter, he sinks into the pillows, spent, and falls into deepening slumber. In the firelight, his skin stretches parchment thin over his cheeks. He is slowly disappearing from me.

When dusk falls, I stoke the fire and retreat to the kitchen to warm up some soup for my supper. A little while later, Daddy gasps. I pour some morphine into a tumbler, lift his head slightly, and hold it to his lips. As I moisten his brow with a damp cloth, I rest my hand lightly on his chest until the interval between each shuddering gasp subsides. He lies back, breathing easier.

I lie down beside my father and hold his hand. His breathing is so shallow I can barely hear it, but as the night draws in, he somehow manages to turn his head slightly toward the window. What does he see? Whom does he see? There is real gladness in his face. He utters a long, satisfied sigh, then closes his eyes for the last time. I wait for the next inhalation of breath, but it does not come. I must watch his dear, gentle face grow still.

I keep holding his hand for a long time, so hard is it to accept that his life is really over. My heart, soul, and mind are knotted with grief. I need some time before I must face a world without my father in it. Eventually, in an agony of sadness, I busy myself, straightening out the sheets. Smoothing the eiderdown with the palm of my hands. Folding his dressing gown neatly. When I bend over to kiss each cool cheek in turn, the forlorn hope of waking him hovers unbidden in the room.

I remember being eight years old, woken from a deep sleep, swept up in his arms and bounced down the stairs to the kitchen. Still holding me tight to his chest, Daddy was about to burst through the back door when he jerked awake and eased me into a kitchen chair instead. "Secure for now, darling," he whispered. "We'll just wait here quietly until it's safe to go."

Daddy poured himself a glass of whiskey. I crawled into his lap and put my arms around his neck. I loved the smell of malt on his breath, the cigarette smoke swirling around our heads. "Have you a new story for me, Georgie Girl?"

I told him I had.

"Let's hear it then, darling."

"*Once upon a time, three birds lived at the London Zoo: Tommy*

Toucan, Fleur Flamingo, and Lucy Lorikeet. They hated being stared at. They wanted to be free. One day Tommy told his friends they were going to escape. Lucy suggested they knock off the keeper's cap with their beaks when he fed them, and while he got over the shock, they would fly through the open door. The plan worked beautifully. They flew away over a dark sea . . ."

I imagine I rambled on and on—my stories then were invariably long and convoluted. Which, I suppose, is what helped Daddy to calm down.

". . . the next day the three friends landed on a desert island. The only animals on it were wild birds! No humans ever stared at them again. But best of all, they were free at last!"

Daddy hugged me close. "Clever girl."

With this faraway story echoing through my head, I whisper in his ear that he is free now. That his Georgie Girl was with him. That we waited quietly together, until it was safe for him to go. Wherever he is now on his journey, I hope he can hear me still.

A few minutes later, I wrap myself in a warm wool jacket and step outside. Blessedly, the bora has calmed, as if by magic. A light ground frost shimmers in the moonlight. I sense the garden alert and waiting—for what, I do not know. Sheltered under the apple tree, I pull a cigarette and lighter out of my pocket. Drawing hard, I let the nicotine hit my lungs with a comforting wallop.

The full, white moon scatters shards of light through the bare branches like silver pins, and a myriad of twinkling stars spatter across the sky. I smoke my cigarette, wishing I could believe in a heaven. Angels and cherubs. An idyllic afterlife. Daddy's lover lies in her grave, close by. Why can she not come and gather him up? So that they can wend their way to paradise together? Most of all, I wish it could be as before—a world away from the here and now—when they too were young.

In the midst of my reverie, I become aware that the French windows, closed tight against the cold, are now slightly ajar. A wisp of air funnels over the patio, skims the hoary grass, and spirals up the trunk of the apple tree. Clusters of dried leaves rustle briefly, before the sliver of breeze disappears into the night sky. All that remains is a faint scent of salt from the sea and woody pines.

"Godspeed," I whisper. "Godspeed."

Chapter Fifty-One

AFTER JANEZ HAS handled the medical and legal paperwork and we have held a private cremation for Daddy in Ljubljana, I return to Opatje Selo to pack up my belongings. On the kitchen table is the letter I wrote to Paul a few days ago. I read it again, then burn it in the fireplace. What I want to say can be better said face-to-face.

I have developed a real affinity for this house where my father loved Alenka, where he came to die. It is freezing cold, but I wander around the garden, pausing beneath the apple tree to marvel again at the very real sense I had of their souls uniting. When I told Janez, he just nodded and hugged me tight. He gives me strength. Janez is quite the most valuable thing that my father has bequeathed to me. Daddy will never quite be gone from me as long as I have my brother's blue eyes to look into and that familiar smile to draw solace from, as long as I can catch the odd, anxious tug of the sleeve. When I recall my original ambivalence over contacting Janez Marusic, my heart plummets like a stone into water. Sometimes I can be my own worst enemy.

Shortly thereafter, I pull the blue door closed behind me and load my bags into the boot of the car. It will be a good three-hour drive to Venice, where I will finally rid myself of the rental car. What a monster bill that will be! Paul will not be amused when it arrives in the mailbox.

As I negotiate the icy roads on the Karst, I visualize my father, the young soldier, breaking the rules over and over again, seeking out his lover on these very same roads. The images grow even clearer when I drive through Trieste. His once-upon-a-time officers' club, where he imbibed too much whiskey; his fairy castle, proud on its limestone promontory, where he played his classical records too loudly; the magnificent Piazza dell'Unita, where I now know the forty-day stand-off with the Yugoslav army played out. It's a strange comfort to have breathed the air and walked the ground my dear father trod all those years ago. "Farewell, Captain James Drummond," I whisper as I leave Trieste.

FROM VENICE, I FLY to Amsterdam, and from there directly to the Twin Cities. Without delays, I will be home by late afternoon. On the long, tedious journey, I mull over how torturous it will be to step back into the bosom of the Wharton tribe. Unavoidable, since Christmas is almost here. But temporary—I will explain myself first to Paul, then my girls, in the New Year. Then we can sort out how we can all best move forward.

At last, the plane lands in Minnesota, and I reel out of customs after enduring the usual interrogation over my British passport, my permanent alien green card, and the length of time I have been out of the country.

Annie is waiting for me. "Welcome home, Mom," she shouts over the crowd.

An inch of deep-golden hair protrudes from her scalp. She has somehow managed to spray it into spikes, and the effect reminds me of a field of stubble.

"Darling, it's wonderful to see you." I give her a huge hug. "Where's your dad?"

"Said he was tied up."

"What's going on?" Paul has never not met me at the airport.

But part of me is relieved. We haven't seen each other since last August, and hanging over us both are the last words he spoke over the phone. *Please, Gina, don't leave me.*

"Are you doing okay, Mom?" asks Annie, avoiding my question.

"As much as I can be. Taking your grandpa to Trieste and on to Opatje Selo was exactly the right thing to do. He died where he wanted to be. Calmly. Peacefully. Which makes me very happy. Of course, I miss him. I always will. I find myself starting to recount a thought, or memory, or some such, but he's not here anymore."

"He was a wonderful man, Mom. The best grandpa ever." Annie stops midway to the parking garage to hug me again, causing other bleary-eyed travelers to stumble around us, mumbling rude complaints.

"But what about this new uncle of mine?" she continues, locating my car, opening the boot, and heaving my luggage in. "Dad didn't explain things particularly well except for calling it a lot of baloney."

Of course he did. "Lots to tell, but let's wait till we've gotten home and settled a bit."

The freeways are slick. Mountains of snow have turned the side roads into virtual tunnels. The monstrous new Mall of America is lit up like there's no tomorrow. Which there isn't—it must be bursting with last-minute shoppers, this close to Christmas.

"Slow down a bit, darling. Please."

Annabel laughs. "Yup. Mom's back for sure!"

"Just as well," I retort, as we speed over the Minnesota River.

"Grandma's still going on and on about St. Olaf, Mom. It's horrible."

"As it happens, I just might have a way for you to escape her clutches if you're interested. I'll tell you all the details over dinner."

When I open the door, Peanut barrels into me as fast as an

arthritic old dog's legs will allow. "Hello, you. Miss me, huh?" His stub of a tail throbs with joy.

Lou is thrashing pots and pans around in the steam-filled kitchen. "Hello, sweetheart. I've missed you too." I kiss the back of her neck, my only option, since she's busy at the stove, prodding potatoes in a pan of boiling water, adding brussels sprouts to another.

"I'm trying to fix your favorite meal, Mom." She gulps back tears. "But the Yorkshire pudding came out all wrong, and the roast beef is dried out."

"That's fine, love, honestly. Just turn off all the burners for a few minutes. Then I'll come and help you."

"Dad's in the den," she mutters, turning back to the plethora of boiling vegetables before her.

I wander down the hallway and open the door. "I'm back."

Paul lowers the newspaper he has been reading. Stands up. "Hello, Gina." After a moment, he adds a somewhat sarcastic, "Welcome home."

"Paul." I try to give him a hug, but as soon as I touch him, his entire body stiffens. "How are you?"

"Good. How was your flight?"

"Long. It's been a difficult few days. The cremation. Slovene paperwork to be handled, of course. But Janez took care of everything. I couldn't have begun to cope without him."

"Well, you shouldn't have been there in the first place. Then there wouldn't have been those issues, would there?"

I back out of the room, a worn-out sadness seeping my spirit. "Paul, I can't do this. Not tonight." Paul doesn't follow.

Back in the kitchen, Lou is scraping a soggy mess of Yorkshire pudding into the garbage bin. The shriveled roast still sits on the counter. Annie is on the phone, ordering pizza. I pull Lou into a bear hug. "Darling, you tried. That is *all* that counts. And I am very, very touched that you did."

I take a bottle of wine off the rack and open it, pour glasses for Paul and myself, and return to the den to try again. Paul is back to reading his paper. "Here you go," I say, offering a glass.

"No, thanks."

That's me put in my place. I sit myself on the sofa without a word. Peanut struggles to clamber up beside me, no such contrariness on his part. Stroking his head, I take note of how his muzzle has grayed even more in my absence.

The girls are whispering elsewhere in the house. Actually, the noise more resembles a pair of cats hissing, but I can't make out what they are arguing about, which is probably just as well. When the pizza delivery boy rings the doorbell, Peanut barks; Paul heaves an audible sigh of relief; Annabel flirts shamelessly with the poor fellow; Louisa huffs her contempt.

Annie plonks the greasy box on the table, and we gather round. The smell makes my stomach roil. I sip my wine, straining to think of something to say to deflect some of the tension.

"I have news for Annabel," I finally blurt out. "An idea her Aunt Ava has come up with. She's a professor of art history at the University of Ljubljana."

From the head of the table, Paul snorts.

"Mom, I *told* you, I am *not* going back to college," Annabel says quickly.

"Hold on a minute," I say, holding up my hand. "I'm not suggesting you do. Ava is a potter. She sells her wares all over Europe. When I told her that all you seemed to want to do was get your hands dirty, she asked if you would like to work in her studio. You can stay with Uncle Janez and the family."

"Oh."

"She made these," I say, sweeping my hair behind my ears to reveal the slender, feather-shaped, blue-glazed earrings Ava gave me just before I left.

Just as I hoped, the earrings catch Annie's attention. "Mom, they're gorgeous. You mean I could learn to make jewelry like that?"

"I don't know," I reply with a chuckle. "But Ava is offering you the opportunity to find out. Not just jewelry. Dishes, vases, pitchers, all kinds of things. If you think you want to, that is."

Paul goes suddenly still, only his fingers making faint twitching movements. He is clearly livid. "You propose sending Annabel halfway around the world to play with clay?!"

"Dad!"

"She's not responsible enough at home, never mind going off to live in some god-forsaken country nobody has ever heard of!"

"Yes, she is, Paul. One way or another, Annabel has got to figure out what it is she wants. The only way for her is by doing. Admit it. Getting herself the job at the Guthrie was smart."

Disgusted, Paul throws down his napkin. "Why didn't you tell me about this before?"

"Because Ava only just thought of it." Not entirely true, but close enough.

In the middle of this absurd conversation, Lou sets down her can of pop, wipes her mouth very deliberately, and stands up. "Why did you even bother coming back?" she says straight to my face.

I feel as though I've been dealt a sharp slap. "Lou, what on earth do you mean?"

I look to Paul for support, but his expression is blank. He's content to let Lou ambush me, with her conviction that black is black and white is white.

"You've chosen complete strangers over us!" Lou rants. "We don't even know this supposed uncle or aunt. It's ridiculous!"

"Louisa, this is nonsense. You're overreacting."

"And why is *she* rewarded every time she acts out?" Louisa waves a long, elegant finger at her sister. "She refuses to go back to college. She's hanging out with real weirdos, channeling Sinéad O'Connor, and you're suggesting she gets to go on being a bum! Seriously?"

"Lou, this is really none of your business."

Louisa looks for all the world like a totem pole planted into the floor, so rigid is she with anger.

"Of course, it isn't my business. Excuse me. You're not asking me if I'd like to go to Slovenia. It's all about Annie. It's *always* all about Annie."

"Look, Lou, I'm sorry you feel like this. I was under the impression that you were thrilled with your work at the zoo, that you—"

"That's my point! I've always done exactly what I was told. I've always gotten perfect grades. So Annie, who's never obeyed a rule in her life, gets to swan off around the world, doing fuck-all but playing with clay, like Dad said!"

For a moment I can only breathe sharply through my nose. "Louisa," I finally manage, "please act your age. You're twenty-two years old."

"And another thing. How could Grandpa have fooled around . . . cheated . . . on Gran? It's absolutely disgusting!"

"Lou, your grandfather loved Alenka. It doesn't mean he didn't love your gran too. Sometimes, people find they love each other in different ways. It is still love—"

"Is it?" interrupts Paul. "Is it really?"

"You can go to hell." Louisa lifts the box of pizza off the table, turns her back on me, and deliberately drops it upside down on the kitchen floor before storming off.

Turning to look my husband in the eyes, I manage to stammer, "What the hell is going on here, Paul?"

He gazes at some point in the distance. "Like I said, Georgina, welcome home."

Chapter Fifty-Two

Last night was not quite the homecoming I had planned, fool that I am. Did I really imagine all the underlying friction between the girls, between Paul and me, could take a back seat while we played "happy families" over the Christmas holiday? After the debacle that was dinner, Paul and I lay in bed side by side, tense and stiff, not touching, till he moved into the guest room, ostensibly to let me get some sleep.

And sleep I do, all through the night and well into the following day. When I finally rise, the house is empty. Presumably Paul is at work, Louisa at the zoo, Annabel at the theater. No notes anywhere to confirm one way or another.

I brew myself a pot of tea, make toast, and curl up with Peanut in the living room. Dear Peanut. But too soon, it becomes painfully obvious that he overindulged himself last night with the hurled-to-the-floor pizza, a treat long eliminated from his diet. I banish him to the den.

It isn't till later, when I check the family calendar on the kitchen wall, that I'm reminded it is Ellen's annual wine, dessert, and gift exchange party this very evening. But I have definitely not forgotten that the name I drew as my gift buddy last year was my mother-in-law. So, I gird my loins—by the time Paul and the girls have arrived home, showered, and gotten ready for the party, I'm prepared for the evening.

Paul drives the four of us through the snowy streets. What conversation occurs in the car is selected with care. There is no mention of the appalling confrontation last night. It feels as if each of us is reading from a prepared script. I long for the holiday to be over so the four of us can sit down as a family and hash out our grievances. For hash out we must.

Ellen opens the front door. She is a striking woman still, despite her advancing age, very much fulfilling her role as Wharton matriarch. Her long, gray hair, which she refuses to cut, is pulled into an elegant bun. Her skin is remarkably smooth and unlined. She has begun walking with a cane—a variety of canes, in fact, matching her various ensembles. I have determined it is to lend a touch of class, rather than provide for any particular physical need.

"Greetings, Georgina," she remarks. "Home at last. We were beginning to think we'd lost 'our Brit' forever."

I bend slightly and peck her cheek.

"Very sorry indeed about your dad," she rambles on. "Of course, if you had brought him to the Mayo, as I proposed, he might still be with us."

Instead of the few precious weeks we spent in Opatje Selo. Consolation enough. No pressure. No interventions. Just shared, peaceful days. Meaningful conversations. But Ellen would not understand that. I fix my jaw and keep silent.

All the family are clustered around an enormous Christmas tree in the two-story-high entryway. When the southern suburbs began to expand and develop, Ellen insisted on moving into this mammoth house, large enough to accommodate the entire family if necessary. For one aging, widowed woman, it's simply ludicrous. I greet my in-laws, accept their condolences, and smile where appropriate, before wandering into Ellen's living room to pull myself together.

It runs the breadth of the house, with an ornate fireplace on each end, scattered sofas, and a massive, antiqued gold mirror hanging on the wall. Among the forest of family photographs on the grand piano, there is an addition I haven't seen before: a very much younger Paul, his arm around a pretty girl—a bit buxom, but a fine example of how I imagine a Minnesota Princess Kay of the Milky Way to look. Judging from the prominent placement of her left hand on Paul's shoulder, I realize she must be the fiancée who dumped Paul shortly before we met.

Ellen slips up behind me in a cloud of Chantilly dusting powder. "You remember our old neighbor, Connie?"

"Well, actually, no, Ellen. Before my time, I'm afraid."

Why has the cunning old biddy pulled this memento out now, I wonder? Is she hoping against hope that I will finally bolt the compound? Perhaps, in anticipation, she is already at work on replacing me as fast as she can.

"Didn't Paul mention? Connie's back in town. It's *so* nice to have her around again after so long."

Curiouser and curiouser! I'm beginning to feel like Alice in Wonderland, trapped in the over-the-top Wharton Looking Glass, sparkling in the firelight.

There is no time for further conversation, as everyone is beginning to crowd into the living room. "Ah, here we all are together, my dears," croons Ellen. "Time to open our gifts."

When we are all seated on the various couches around the fireplaces and more wine has been poured, the carefully wrapped boxes are presented, opened, and dutifully cooed over. I'm last. All eyes swivel toward me, wondering no doubt what I will have come up with. Ellen looks expectant. I cross the floor toward her. "Happy Christmas," I say, placing my package in her lap.

She pulls greedily at the paper, then pauses, momentarily lost for words. "Well, will you look at this, my dears," she gulps, holding aloft an exquisite bowl, recently designed and created by Ava in her studio. "*A gift for your American family,*" she had suggested. "*From Slovenia.*"

"Oh, my goodness," Ellen mutters. "How unusual. Foreign. The colors are rather gaudy, don't you think?"

I've a great urge to grab my coat and storm out of this house. My feet literally itch with the need to pull my snow boots on. My head pounds with a longing for my dear, sweet father—a longing to be sitting in his living room amid the old familiar trappings. And most of all, I long to turn around and shout, "*If I had given you the Crown Jewels, you'd have found a way to reject them, wouldn't you, Ellen?*"

But before I can do or say any of these things, Annie pitches right in. Plucking the bowl from her grandmother's hands, she parades slowly around the room, so that everyone can have a good look. In the flames from the fire, the vibrant swirls of purple, blue, gold, and green burst to life in a turbulent dance. "My Aunt Ava made this," Annabel boasts. "She's a famous potter, and she teaches art history at the University of Ljubljana. That's in Slovenia. And *I'm* going there to learn the trade."

The entire family remains seated in stunned silence. Ellen scowls so hard I almost expect to see daggers protruding from her forehead. Paul shrugs, then decides it's time to fetch more firewood from the garage and disappears. My relatives shuffle their bums and concentrate on draining their glasses. Even the younger cousins are briefly shocked, before they slouch off to play with their new presents downstairs in the basement playroom.

"Louisa, dear, perhaps you could bring in dessert for me?" Ellen finally asks.

"Yes, Grandma."

"I'll help," I add, anxious to get away from the crowd.

While Lou slices two enormous Yule log cakes, I start the coffee brewing; then we push a large trolley, filled with platefuls of desert, into the living room. Conversation has started up again, but when I try to talk about my time in Italy and Slovenia, everyone deftly changes the subject, anxious not to upset Ellen further. I sit back from the group and nibble on the cake, which is absolutely delicious. I know the bakery from which Ellen orders her logs, although she likes to pretend she still makes them herself, and of course everyone plays along!

For a while we sing carols around the piano, but eventually it's time to gather up our gifts, dispose of the wrapping paper, and start pulling on boots and overcoats. Before I can finish bundling up, however, Ellen pushes through the family throng to waylay me one more time.

"Oh, Gina dear, I almost forgot. You perhaps don't know yet, since you've been away from home for such a long time, but my gift to all the family this year is a week of skiing up in Lutsen. Our vacation begins on the 27th."

I stare around at the faceless mass of Whartons—for that is how I think of them at this point in my life—as they try to figure out how I will react to this latest bid for control by Ellen. How I ache to put my hands on my hips, polish up my accent, and announce, *"Guess what, folks, I'm filing for divorce—from Paul, from Ellen, from the whole damned lot of you."* But when I glance at Lou, wringing her hands, dreading that I am going to make a scene, I curb my rage. That would be cruel and unusual punishment for my girls and Paul. They don't need to hear me shrieking out my feelings so crudely. So, I go on with the charade one last time.

"What a lovely idea, Ellen. How kind of you. How thoughtful."

"Of course, Gina, I wasn't at all sure you would even get back here in time for the holidays. But since I've rented an entire lodge, there will be room to squeeze you in. And I'm sure we can sort out some gear for you if necessary."

"I will certainly let you know what I need," I reply.

On the snowy doorstep, I wave goodbye to the gathered family, ignore Ellen's proffered cheek, and, as best as my mammoth down coat and clumsy snow boots allow, saunter casually toward our car.

Chapter Fifty-Three

B UT BY THE time we are all piled into the car, I can't contain my fury any longer. "So, everyone at Grandma's tonight knew about the ski trip? *You* all knew about the ski trip? How humiliated I would be?"

"We didn't know how to tell you, Mom. You were tired after the long trip," says Annabel.

"We sort of thought Dad should be the one to explain Grandma's plans," adds Louisa.

"I agree, Lou. So, why didn't you, Paul?"

He's rubbing the windscreen repeatedly with his great woolen mittens, cursing under his breath. Apparently, I'm doing an irritatingly great job of fogging up his windows. "I wasn't sure when you would finally show up," he mumbles. "And frankly, if you didn't know Mom's plan, you would have less time to come up with one of your creative excuses not to come with us."

Angry as I am, it's hard to argue with Paul's reasoning. Last Labor Day holiday springs to mind; I was happy enough to use my father's needs as an excuse then. But nonetheless, I'm still seething when we pull into the garage. Still seething when we push and shove our way into the house, laden with packages. Still seething when dear old Peanut greets me with a slobbery kiss.

"Speaking of excuses, when were you going to mention Connie?" I ask Paul, my voice cool as the proverbial cucumber. "Why the hell does your mother have your old engagement picture displayed on the piano?" *Manipulative old bitch that you are, Ellen Wharton.*

"You two need to sort this one out on your own," snaps Lou, peeling off her winter layers—jacket, scarf, sweater, boots, and socks—and creating a trail of clothing throughout the hall. "I'm going to bed."

"Me too," echoes Annie. But like Houdini, she first produces Ava's bowl from a repurposed Christmas gift bag. "Grandma said, since I was going so far away and probably would *never* come back, I might as well return this to 'the potter' because she didn't want it."

"Oh, for the love of God." If it weren't so sad it would be laughable.

After this, both girls beat a hasty retreat. Not, however, before Louisa kisses me good night, which is a huge comfort. I had visions of her turning her back on me forever. It's so hard for her to get beyond her black-and-white view of life, to consider other points of view. Soon a thumping beat of drums and discordant twang of guitars throbs down the staircase from the girls' respective rooms.

Paul is in the kitchen, his shoulders set stiff as a frozen shirt on a winter clothesline.

"I'll give Peanut a last walk," I say, bundling up again.

Escaping outside, I light a cigarette as soon as I reach the end of the driveway. I've managed to go several days without succumbing, but tonight is just too much. I pull the nicotine into my lungs, calming myself, savoring the notion that I will never have to see Ellen again. As of this moment, a secret nobody else knows but me. After a slow slither and slide around the block, we get back to the warm house. When I set Ava's stunning bowl on the table, I'm struck by how out of place it looks in my kitchen. Funny. I feel exactly the same way. As I trace the various ribbons of color circling the dish, a deep sigh escapes me. This does not go unnoticed by Paul.

He pours two glasses of wine, and we sit opposite one another.

"So, have you seen much of Connie?" I ask.

"After Ken was killed, she never remarried. Her son is Lou's age. Just graduated from West Point."

"That's not what I asked."

Paul shifts uncomfortably. "She helped out while you were gone."

"What do you mean, helped out? Our daughters are perfectly capable of—"

"Mom hosted the family in Red Wing for Thanksgiving. At the St. James Hotel. She invited Connie and Greg to join us. The kids met each other. Got on well. It was kind of nice, actually."

Kind of nice! And Louisa and Annabel never mentioned a word of this! Paul is obviously trying to tell me something, and I can guess what it is. So, I help him along. "And you cheated with Connie?"

"Yes."

This from the man I had always believed couldn't be bothered to stray. But of course, I had not factored in Princess Kay of the Milky Way reappearing so conveniently. Giving Ellen the perfect opportunity to manipulate her son back to where she has always wanted him to be in the first place.

"Only once, Gina. I had too much to drink. I hardly even remember."

"That's almost worse. The not-remembering part, I mean."

"It's not a good excuse. I know that. But I was lonely. I don't like to be by myself so much of the time, like you do. Quite honestly, I've never understood that part of you."

I know that, Paul. And I have never been able to explain it to you. The difference between lonely and alone. "There's only one thing that puzzles me. A few short weeks ago, you begged me not to leave you. Was that before or after this unintentional 'one-off'?"

Paul's face lights up in neon, flashing—*guilt—shame—sin*—across the table.

"After." He fumbles the bottle of wine and refills his glass. "Connie was here . . . you weren't . . ."

"Paul, I understand." After all, it's perfectly true that I've been leaving my husband alone for long periods of time. Under the circumstances, I'm in no position to object to what he's done.

For the first time since I got home, Paul relaxes, flinging his arm around the back of the chair. "You *do* understand?" he says. "Is it possible that we can sort things out? Or at least, can we try? Please, Gina?"

"No, Paul, we can't. It's over now."

Do I owe him the truth? That I had planned to divorce him years ago until the Harrods Christmas bombing took my lover away from me?

"Why? Is it really too late?" he shouts, both arms on the table now. "After I cheated one time? Only once!" He balls both fists, the muscles in his neck jumping.

At this moment, I know he really wants to hit me. Something that he has never done before. My heart feels tight in my chest, and the blood in my veins runs icy cold.

"What about you, Gina? Did you ever cheat?" He pounds the table with the balled fists. "On all those extended visits to England? All those summers over there with the kids? I did wonder."

Time slows. A dish crashes. Ava's hands weigh on mine. She whispers, "*Some secrets best kept with the dead.*" Some secrets *are* best buried deep. Just as I didn't want to hurt Daddy with the truth of what my mother did, I don't want to hurt Paul unnecessarily now.

"Why are you asking, Paul?"

"Because even if you did—even if it were true—I would forgive you. It's still you I want most of all." He lets his tears fall, does nothing to stop the flow.

Relaxing his fists, he lets me hold one of his hands in mine. Doesn't pull away. "Paul," I murmur, "please believe me. I did love you. If we had been able to make a life away from your family, we would have had a better chance of making a go of it. Here, where you can't resist all the mandatory 'Wharton togetherness,' you found yourself hobbled with me, a woman who needs the exact opposite. Solitude, and the freedom it offers: to hear the birds sing, to watch the sun rise, to smell fresh-turned earth. Not all the time. But some of the time."

I caress the familiar hand, smudged now with brown age spots. Paul won't be on his own long. Connie and Ellen will see to that. I pull gently on his wedding band. It slips free, and I place it on the table between us.

"Sounds to me as if Connie is more than happy to participate in the life of your family. She has known them all her life. And she will give you the consistency you crave. No travel schedules, deadlines, book tours. Take her skiing. Your mother will be thrilled."

I slip my own wedding ring from my finger, and place it beside Paul's on the table.

"Do you remember where we bought these?" I ask.

"From the peddler on the beach with his tray of trinkets?" Paul fingers our rings, sliding them gently back and forth across the table.

"Yes. You realized if we were going to marry in Mexico, we needed rings!"

He manages a faint chuckle, and as his face moves I see moisture in his eyes. "He smelled like pot and cheap wine, but he made us laugh."

"He did. We laughed at a lot of things in those days." One last time, I clasp his hand in mine. "You still deserve to be happy, Paul. We both do."

LONG AFTER PAUL GOES to bed, Peanut snuffling along at his heels, I remain downstairs, wide awake. Shapes, shades, and shadows dance around the bowl in the winter moonlight, reminding me of the ebb and flow of my marriage. The giddy heights of first love. The battle for autonomy within the Wharton family. Motherhood. Michael, and the growing longing for space and place after his loss. And then my father's death. All culminate here, at this table, on this night. Before I step into my future. Alone.

DECEMBER 1995

Chapter Fifty-Four

S ITTING IN THE lounge at Cross Keys Court, warm and cozy, my feet on a pouf, I look back over my first full year in England. The rubies in my ring wink and dance in the flickering firelight. A concert plays on the radiogram. And the handsome dog fox lopes across the lawn, leaving a perfectly precise pattern of pawprints in the thin crust of snow. I suspect he will continue to remind me he is still around, until I write his story.

ONCE A MONTH, I ride up to London on the train to spend the day with Michael. When I entered his room in the nursing home in Hampstead last January, a brittle winter sun shone through his window. He lay motionless in bed, but his eyes lit up as they followed me across the room.

"So much to tell you, my darling," I said, settling in the chair beside his bed. I looked steadily into his eyes and recounted in detail all that had happened since I traveled to Italy last August. When I eventually got to Ellen's diabolical party and acted out the various roles, I knew from the changing expressions in Michael's eyes that he was relishing every moment.

The finale was to pull Ava's bowl from my leather satchel and set it on the table beside his bed, where I knew the sun would catch all its iridescent magic.

"For you, my dearest heart." The corners of his mouth softened into the ghost of a smile.

WHEN SPRINGTIME ARRIVED, I scattered a portion of Daddy's ashes with my mum in the Garden of Remembrance. The remainder, Janez has shared with Alenka. We both agree the decision would have pleased our father enormously. I told Mummy how I had come to understand more clearly how and why our relationship had grown strained. I thanked her for taking good care of me, for loving me. And I assured her that Daddy had loved her too.

ANNABEL HAS BEEN IN Slovenia nine months already. It turns out she has an ear for languages. Apparently, my daughter learned every foul word there is in Slovenian, Croatian, and Italian within a week of her arrival! She proved to have an aptitude on the potter's wheel, and is now developing a passion for three-dimensional art. Annabel thinks she *might* study art at the University of Ljubljana. In the meantime, she has pierced her left eyebrow! Tattooed her right ankle! And claims to be madly in love with a fisherman from the Istrian Peninsula.

MY DEAR LOUISA HAS not got what she wanted from either parent. She is furious with me for leaving Paul. Furious with Paul for marrying Connie. Furious she has to cope with the reality of a stepbrother. But on the bright side, she consented to spend two weeks with me this past summer.

"I could use your help redecorating the guest room," I said, soon after she arrived.

"Choose your favorite color, Lou." *I want you to come and stay often, dear girl.* "Why not have fun making it your own?"

After some reluctance, she got into the swing of it, and we spent a couple of days in Montpelier shopping for new bedding, towels, pillows, pictures, and rugs. She finally decided on a beach theme: blue and turquoise bedding, golden-sand pillows, and a large rug depicting a night sky full of stars. "Because it reminds me of Bamburgh," she said.

Without prompting, she also reminisced about the long summers spent with Gran and Grandpa in the cottage by the sea. How I had stacked her room with all the Enid Blyton books I had devoured as a child. And how she and Annie had loved making up "Five" games and fighting over which one would get to play Georgina on any given day.

"Next time I come, I'll bring my vase full of Bamburgh seashells," Lou whispered.

"And I will call it the Bamburgh Room." I gave her a big hug. *Good girl, you're starting to remember the good things about your grandparents.*

Buoyed by our bedroom shopping, I suggested the following week that we visit the picture gallery, with a view to framing the people in Daddy's life.

"So, what exactly are you talking about, Mom?"

On the coffee table, I'd laid out the picture of Józef on his sledge. An old wartime newspaper clipping of Alenka, her Titovka cap perched at a rakish angle. A photograph of Mummy and me with my bunny during the war. And lastly, a photograph of Janez and his family under the apple tree in Opatje Selo. Immediately, a veil dropped over Lou's face, shutting out any acknowledgement of these newfound relatives. When she began to turn away, I grabbed her hand.

"Don't be like this, Lou. None of us are perfect. Families are fallible. Like pieces on a chessboard. Always in motion, forming, growing, changing." I point to Janez in the photograph. "Now I have a brother that I never knew existed till last year, and I'm grateful. He's a constant reminder of my father who I loved so much."

"I suppose so, Mom, but it sounds like you're saying we can all do whatever we like."

"No, I'm trying to say we try to do what is best. Remember the evening of Grandpa's birthday dinner, when you caused a scene, berating Annabel for not feeling guilty about quitting college?"

She nodded.

I picked up the picture of Józef. "Well, that very night, your grandpa unearthed this picture."

"Why? Did I make him feel guilty about something?"

"Not exactly. But he did feel responsible for this little boy's death."

"What happened?"

"Józef stepped on a land mine. He was killed. Your grandfather was in charge of operations that day."

Lou's big brown eyes sparkled with unshed tears. "How terribly sad," she muttered, picking up the old brown picture and looking at it carefully.

"I'll tell you something else, Lou—that night my immediate reaction was to make assumptions, to automatically think the child was your grandfather's. But when all the details finally emerged, I was able to understand, and feel real love for everyone involved."

The next day, we carried the precious pictures into town, and Lou asked if she could choose the frames. Not all the seams of her angry heart were mended during her visit, but it was a good start.

TOMORROW, I FLY TO Ljubljana to spend Christmas with my brother, his family, and Annie. Packed carefully in my luggage are

Daddy's medals and swagger stick. In the fullness of time, Janez can pass these treasures on to his own son.

Night has long past closed in. I raise a glass of Barolo.

"Here's to us, Daddy. Happy days."

Author's Note

I BEGAN THIS novel shortly after the death of my father.

In the beginning, I only knew that I wanted to explore what life must have been like for military and civilian persons alike after years of separation, in the immediate aftermath of a world war. Because of my own bond with my father, I wanted to explore the special relationship that often occurs between a father and daughter.

As is typical of many soldiers thrust into the hell of war, my father never spoke of his experiences. I have the sense now, looking back, that all he wanted was a quiet and peaceful life, with as little conflict as possible. Which is why I suspect my mother got away with rather a lot. But that's another story.

I had nothing much to guide me in fashioning this book, other than a picture he had sent of Castello di Miramare sometime in 1946 that had somehow survived. And I definitely recalled a photograph of a boy on a sledge, glued into the family album. When I was sorting through the family home after my father's death, I found the old album, but that particular snapshot had mysteriously disappeared. Perhaps I asked once too often who the child was!

Apart from the above related facts, the character of James in the novel has little in common with my father, it is not based on a true story, and most certainly the book's plot is an invention. But it is inspired by my love for him, and would not exist without him.

Acknowledgments

S PECIAL THANKS TO Aleksandra Mulic, for sharing with me her grandmother's incredible story of life as a Slovene Partisan during World War II. As of this writing, Vida Jurman is ninety-six years old.

A multitude of thanks to my daughter Katherine, who made the weeks-long research trip to Slovenia and Trieste possible. To walk in the footprints of my novel was a truly magical time.

Thanks to my writers-group readers, Loretta Ellsworth, Maggie Moris, Eileen Beha, Pat Schafer, Mary Losure, Nolan Zavoral, Phyllis Root, and Jane St. Anthony, for their insights, observations, and encouragement.

Thanks to Mary Kole for her professional counsel and direction.

Thanks to Cole Nelson, Patrick Maloney, Graham Warnken, and Victoria Petelin of Wise Ink Creative Publishing, for their invaluable guidance and wisdom throughout the editing and publication process.

Books that guided me along the way:

Trieste, and the Meaning of Nowhere – Jan Morris, Da Capo Press.

Tito, and the Rise and Fall of Yugoslavia – Richard West, Carroll & Graf Publishers, Inc.,

A Paper House, the Ending of Yugoslavia – Mark Thompson, Vintage.

Flashpoint Trieste: The First Battle of the Cold War – Christian Jennings, ForeEdge.

Trieste – Dasa Drndic, Mariner Books, Houghton Mifflin Harcourt.